INTO SPRING

The Next Generation

INTO SPRING

The Next Generation

A Novel by

Larry Landgraf

To: Marjorie
You get one shot at life.
Make it a good one. Live
strong and thrive.
Larry Landgraf

Fresh Ink Group
Roanoke

Into Spring: The Next Generation

Fresh Ink Group
An Imprint of:
The Fresh Ink Group, LLC
PO Box 525
Roanoke, TX 76262
Email: info@FreshInkGroup.com
www.FreshInkGroup.com

Edition 1.0 2017

Book design by Ann Stewart / FIG

Cover design by Stephen Geez / FIG

BISAC Subject Headings:
FIC000000 **FICTION** / General
FIC055000 **FICTION** / Dystopian
FIC028070 **FICTION** / Science Fiction / Apocalyptic & Post-Apocalyptic

Library of Congress Control Number: 2017930009

Paper-cover ISBN-13: 978-1-936442-44-7
Hardcover ISBN-13: 978-1-936442-43-0
Ebook ISBN-13: 978-1-936442-45-4

Table of Contents

Introduction

Sean woke up from a dream, the same dream, screaming just as he had the previous three mornings. The vision of him strapped to a table and a doctor standing above him was still vivid in his mind. A bright light shone from above and everything was fuzzy. The doctor was masked and the scalpel glistened in his hand. Two masked nurses watched as the doctor made his first cut.

I've died and gone to hell, he thought. *I'm not dead, but I've certainly gone to hell.* The pain in his groin was not quite as bad this morning, but he still felt the lingering ache. He reached down and felt for the missing parts, and began to cry.

Why did they do this to me? What are they going to do with me next? Only questions. No answers. Then he began to remember. *The men. They took my guns. I asked a question and a sharp pain in the back of my head. Then darkness. Why?*

Sean got up and turned on the light. He went to wipe his brow but stopped short and looked at his hand. Blood. Not a lot, but too much. Sweat trickled down his cheek. He walked over to the sink to wash his hands and face.

A banging on his door. Sean looked over at the clock. Then he remembered Sonny, Marcia, and little Lola. Sonny had come to get him and take him to work. He felt tired, his groin ached, and he didn't want to go to work. The blood reminded him of his sister, Debra. *She was always so bitchy when she got her period.* He couldn't help but smile, but it was short lived.

He had to get dressed. Sonny was pissed yesterday and the day before because he took too long to come out. Besides, he would get no answers until he did. *Sonny wouldn't answer my questions. Will he answer them now? And what's with Marcia? Every time I speak to her, she just gives me a dirty look then turns away. What's the matter with these people? I'll get some answers today.*

Sean got dressed a little faster than he did yesterday. It was early, the same as the past few mornings. The clock said 4:20. He met Sonny outside and got into the back of their pickup truck. A sharp pain shot through his groin as he lifted his leg over the side. Marcia and Lola crawled into the passenger side. Sonny drove to the boat and cranked up the old diesel motor. While the engine warmed a bit, they loaded their gear onboard. Soon they were headed out to sea.

The shrimp boat slowly chugged along and exited the harbor. Sean sat on the railing around the rear deck. The gentle breeze rustled his hair and was cool on his face. The air was heavy with the smell of the bay. Sean liked the smells—the salty air, the sea water, the aroma of fish and sea grass. He focused his attention on the water quickly passing by the boat. The churning water stirred small jellyfish which glowed green when they were agitated. The luminescent creatures fascinated and mesmerized him. They took his mind off his pain.

Sean looked forward toward the cabin of the boat. He could see Sonny driving and Marcia talking to him. Sean could not hear them over the hum of the engine. He knew, however, the conversation had to be about him. Marcia would occasionally glance back at Sean. *Yes, they're definitely talking about me.*

Sean turned his attention back to the water. *Robbie and I came here to find wives. I can never have kids now. Can I have sex? If I can't, what do I need a wife for? I'll kill those bastards for what they did to me. But who are they? It wasn't Sonny and Marcia, but who? Sean felt the tears welling up in his eyes again. Maybe I should end it all right now. Just lean over the rail. One second and I'll be in the water. Let the fish and crabs have me. Take a deep breath of the salty water. I'll be out like a light. No more worries . . . no more pain . . . no more problems.*

A few miles away from the Bayfront, Sean's best friend, Robbie, lay in a bed, out cold for several days now. His breathing was slow and steady. His face was flushed and a cool damp washcloth was across his forehead. He had not moved a major muscle since he was ambushed and brought here. His eyes twitched from time to time as if he were dreaming, but that was all.

"Why won't he wake up, Mother?"

"I don't know. They must have hit him awful hard for him to stay out this long."

"Is he going to die?"

"He may very well if he doesn't wake up soon."

Chapter 1

Two weeks earlier in Peaceful Valley . . .

Robbie ate a big breakfast and then met Sean at his house. The boys told Sam and Sally goodbye. "We'll be back in a year," Sean said.

Sally was in tears. "You two are too young to be going off on your own," she said. "You've never been away from home. You can't take care of yourselves." But she knew this was far from the truth. The boys had been taking care of themselves for years. Their survival skills were second to none. Maybe she was just being a little selfish, but Sean was her baby. She would always be the overprotective mother. It was hard, but she did understand why they had to leave.

No one saw Sam's tears. He hated to see the boys leave too, but he knew they had no choice. There were no women for them in Peaceful Valley and men needed women. He wiped the tear from his cheek as he watched the boys fade out of sight.

There are three families living in Peaceful Valley. Samuel and Sally Lin live across the river from the Lindgren homestead. They are of oriental descent and moved to Peaceful Valley to carve a new life for themselves five years before Sean was born. Debra was born a couple years later. Sam raises hogs and goats, but otherwise they live off the land. Sean is nineteen now while Debra is seventeen.

The Lindgren family consists of Eileen Lindgren, Lars' widow; James Lindgren, Lars' son, his wife Melissa, Reggie and Emily Carston's daughter; and James and Melissa's twin sons, Ronnie and Robbie. Lars Lindgren, the patriarch of the family died suddenly when the twins were four years old.

Reggie and Emily Carston live a couple miles upstream from the Lindgren's. Reggie is an ex-army contractor with a wealth of knowledge of explosives and a treasure trove of weapons stored in his formidable bunker. Lars and Reggie were best friends.

Ronald and Sara Weston were the original inhabitants of Peaceful Valley and lived downstream along the river from the Lindgren's. They both were brutally murdered by intruders shortly after Eileen arrived when she fled San Antonio as the city descended into chaos.

After they left the Lins's, Sean and Robbie made the trek to the Carston homestead. Reggie led them into his bunker, Emily tagging along. He filled their backpacks with enough survival food to last for a week—if they killed nothing along the way, which was highly unlikely. Reggie gave each of them a bulletproof vest onto which he'd attached fragmentation grenades, light sticks, fire starter, and some spare ammunition.

Reggie stood back and looked at the boys. Robbie had his .357 magnum on one hip and his .22 revolver on the other. His grandmother's .30-caliber carbine slung over his shoulder completed his arsenal. Eileen began letting him use her carbine a couple years ago. He loved the open sights which allowed him to quickly get on target.

Sean also had a .357 magnum on his hip. His rifle of choice, however, was an AR-15. The scope and accuracy of the rifle was excellent for long-range shots.

"You need a pistol for small game," Reggie asserted.

"I've got my slingshot," Sean replied pulling it out of his rear pocket. "I am more comfortable with it than a pistol."

"All right, have it your way," Reggie said with a smile.

Reggie also packed numerous trinkets like tweezers, sewing needles and fingernail clippers into the side pockets of the boys' backpacks. "Take these energy bars. They'll give you plenty of pep to get you on your way." He and Emily then gave them a big hug and kiss.

"We're going to miss you," Emily said as her tears began to form.

"It won't be the same around here," Reggie added.

They watched the boys head into the woods and out of sight.

"What are they going to find out there?" Emily asked.

"Probably not much for a while, but in Corpus Christi, who knows? I lost contact with my ham radio buddies there ages ago. The last I heard the place was a slaughterhouse."

The boys' final stop was to tell Robbie's parents their intentions. Sean and Robbie showed up at the Lindgren place all geared up for war, it appeared, and Melissa and James knew immediately something was up.

"It's time for us to get out of here," Robbie said. "Sean and I have been discussing this for a long time. Now that Debra has chosen Ronnie, I have no choice."

Melissa immediately began to cry.

"You boys know what you're doing?" James asked.

"No, but there are no women here for us. You know we need to go," Robbie replied.

James took a good look at the boys and knew they were set to go, as Reggie made certain they had everything they needed, and then some.

"Stay the night and get an early start in the morning," Melissa said.

"We have plenty of time to put nine or ten miles behind us," Sean stated. "As long as we have no problems, we can get a good start this afternoon."

"I am so proud of you," Eileen said. "You boys have grown up strong and smart. Keep your wits about you and remember everything I've taught you."

"We will," Robbie assured her. "We're going to miss you."

Eileen smiled and took a good last look at the boys. She had never seen them better prepared for anything. They would be a force to be reckoned with. "Yes, you two will be just fine."

They gave the boys a final hug and kiss. James and Melissa knew Sean and Robbie needed to go, but this didn't make it any less painful. James and Melissa waited on the front porch as they made a short stop by the old sycamore tree where Robbie's grandfather Lars was buried. When Sean and Robbie made their way back to the house, James and Melissa followed the boys around to the back of the house and down to the pier. James and Melissa watched as they crossed the stream and headed south into the woods.

They sat on the pier with tears in their eyes as their baby and his best friend left. They continued to watch long after they disappeared into the forest. Finally, James looked over at Melissa. He grabbed her hand and gave it a gentle squeeze. "It's about time we head inside," he said.

"It's going to be a long year ahead," she told James.

Chapter 2

Sean and Robbie traveled meandering deer trails, which made the trek much easier than trying to keep to a straight line. They found a snake for dinner. This was all that crossed their path. They walked what had to be eight miles and never got out of the brush. The good thing was no one was likely to be in the brush to cause them harm, and they didn't see anyone.

Just before dark, they made camp, setting up their two-man tent and gathering wood for a fire. When it got dark, they started the fire and cooked dinner. Neither was all that hungry, having had two of Reggie's energy bars each. They ate half the snake and saved the remainder for breakfast. They laid in bed for an hour or so discussing their adventure. It was a little scary for the boys to be out on their own, but they were doing exactly what they needed to do. They would have no future otherwise.

Robbie was seventeen years old, while Sean was nineteen. They were no longer boys. They were men, on their own for the first time in their lives. They were excited, but they were also concerned. They had only themselves to depend on. No more comfort of their parents' home, no more fully stocked smokehouse and root cellar, and the constant uncertainty of what the next hour, day, or week would bring. No one, however, could be better prepared for what lay ahead. The boys worked their entire life for this day. They were strong of body and mind, thanks to their parents and Eileen. Thanks to Reggie, they had a few more tools they hadn't thought about to better provide for themselves, with a little comfort along the way. They had everything they needed to protect themselves better than most people could. Maybe they were ready for their new adventure, and maybe they weren't, but there was only one way to find out.

They didn't sleep well their first night, but were young and would be fine. Adrenalin would keep them going until they got used to being out on their own. They got up at daylight, ate breakfast and again headed on their way.

By midday, they came upon a highway. They walked along the brush line away from the pavement until they came upon a sign: *Corpus Christi 87 Miles.* Robbie took out his map and found this road went in the general direction they wanted to go—not in a straight line, but close enough. They decided to follow the highway, as it would keep them headed in the right direction, and if there were more road signs, they could keep track of their distance to their destination.

It wasn't long before the boys spotted a farmhouse, mostly concealed by trees and brush. As they crept closer, Sean noticed some movement near the back of the home. The boys hid behind a tree and sat for a while to watch the house.

Directly a man came out to get some firewood and carried it back into the house. He came out for a second load, went back inside, and shut the door. Someone was definitely living there, but they didn't know how many or how well armed they were. The boys decided to wait until dark and then move in closer to investigate.

When it got dark, the boys crept closer to the home. Light flickered through the windows as if candles or flames from a wood stove lit the home. They peered into a side window and through tattered curtains saw a man, maybe in his fifties, sitting in a chair. Robbie went around to the back of the house and looked into another window. He saw the same man but no one else. Robbie went back around to Sean and the two moved away from the house to discuss the situation. They decided Robbie would knock at the front door while Sean watched the man from the rear of the house, pistol ready should the man turn violent.

Robbie stepped upon the side of the front porch and tiptoed to the front door. He took a position low and to the side of the door and knocked hard three times. "Hello!" Robbie hollered. Sean watched the man get up from his chair, drawing his pistol and moving toward the front door.

"Hello? I mean you no harm," Robbie said.

"Go away or I'll shoot," the man replied through the closed door.

"I mean you no harm," Robbie repeated. "I just want to talk to you." There was silence and Robbie continued. "I'm a traveler and I just want to talk."

Robbie heard the lock release, then the door knob turned and the door opened. The man had stringy, mostly gray hair. He also had an odor of smoke and sweat about him.

"My name is Robbie," he said.

"My name is Charles."

Robbie told the man he wouldn't hurt him, that he only wanted to talk, and they both holstered their guns. Charles invited Robbie inside.

"If I wanted to hurt you," Robbie said, "you would be dead now, but I mean you no harm."

Charles saw how well armed Robbie was and agreed with him.

"My friend Sean is outside. Mind if he joins us?"

With a brief nod from Charles, Robbie yelled through the open back window and told Sean to come inside. Sean put his gun away, came around to the front porch, and Charles let him in.

"What are two whippersnappers doing way out here in the middle of nowhere?"

"We're headed for Corpus Christi," Sean replied.

"I haven't seen anyone in ages. It gets mighty lonely when there's no one to talk to," he said. "I killed a couple men years ago, but the past few years it has been quiet around here."

Charles told the boys he was just trying to survive. "Looks like that won't be for much longer," he said as he began to cough again.

"You okay, Charles?" Sean asked.

"Yeah, I smoked all my life, and I think it's getting the best of me now. I ran out of tobacco decades ago, and what I've smoked since hasn't been the same. Probably killing me as we speak. I would sure like to have another pack of real cigarettes before I die."

"Sorry," Robbie said, "we can't help you."

Robbie told Charles they came from the north. "We're looking for wives. There are no available women in our valley. My brother is going to marry Sean's sister. She is the only girl back home. When she decided she wanted to marry Ronnie, that left no one for me. Being Debra is Sean's sister, he never had a choice. So, here we are. We love our valley and hate to leave, but if we want women we don't have a choice. We figured Corpus Christi would be the best place to look. If we find wives, we'll take them back home with us."

"Well, I'm glad you decided to drop in. It sure is good to have someone to talk to for a spell. Will you stay the night?"

Not really knowing Charles, Robbie thought they would all sleep better if they stayed in the woods, and therefore declined Charles offer. They swapped a few more stories, and the boys said it was time to get on their way. Robbie gave Charles a few packets of the survival food entrees Reggie had given him, and he and Sean left.

He doesn't look so good, Robbie thought. *He won't last much longer. Maybe the survival food will give him a few more days.*

The boys got back onto the highway, and though it was dark and they couldn't see very well, it was relatively easy to stay on the pavement with what little light the stars provided. They walked a couple miles before they went into the brush and made camp. Robbie built a small fire to boil water for their survival food packets while Sean gathered more firewood. When that was done, the boys crawled into their bedrolls and talked a while as they ate and watched the fire.

"We probably should have bypassed Charles' place and gone on about our way," Sean said.

"We will need to meet people if we're going to find women," Robbie replied, "but you're probably right. We're not likely to find women out in the middle of nowhere. There will always be risks when we meet people, and we need to take some chances, but our risks should be where our greatest possibility of success will be—in Corpus Christi."

Sean agreed. As the fire dwindled, the boys snuggled down into their bedrolls to get some much needed sleep.

The boys were up bright and early the next morning. They followed the brush line along the highway for a few days and came upon a flowing stream; the first they'd seen in a while. Getting low on water, the boys decided to follow the creek a couple miles, then if they saw no one, work their way back a mile and set up camp.

A couple hours later, the boys backtracked and made camp. They gathered wood for a fire and hunted for some fresh meat. Robbie got a rabbit with his .22 pistol, remembering Eileen's words on the value of a small caliber gun. The gun didn't make a lot of noise and it was not likely anyone heard the shot. Just before dark, another rabbit showed up at their camp and Robbie killed it as well. They now had plenty of meat for a few days. After dark, they built a fire, cooked the rabbits and boiled some drinking water.

After they had eaten their fill, they rolled out their bedrolls and gathered a little more firewood. Robbie broke off a mesquite thorn to pick his teeth while Sean clipped his fingernails and toenails.

"I don't know about you, Sean, but my stench is beginning to get the best of me. I think I'll take advantage of the creek," Robbie said as he began peeling off his clothes.

"Not a bad idea," Sean replied. "I didn't want to say anything, but I thought you crapped your pants."

"Ha! Ha!" Robbie replied. "You can't smell any better. I just can't smell you over myself."

A short while later, the boys were as clean as they were going to get and warmed up and dried by the fire. "I wonder what's happening back home?" Robbie asked.

"I don't know, but I miss my soft bed," Sean replied.

"I miss mom and dad."

"Me too, Robbie. I guess we'd better get some sleep."

"Need some more rocks over there?" Robbie asked as he crawled into his bedroll.

"Nope! I've got plenty. Good night, Robbie."

"Good night."

Having plenty of food and water for a few days, the boys made good time and closed the distance between them and Corpus Christi. There were more farmhouses along the highway, but this time Sean and Robbie made a wide swing around the places and continued on their way. A few days later, the boys found another road sign. They had made it to within twenty miles of Corpus Christi.

They found another small creek and camped a mile off the highway. Sean managed to kill a javelina just before dark. They roasted the meat over the open fire, trimming off and eating as much as they could while the meat was cooking. When their bellies were full, they dried the remainder over the fire so it would keep over the next few days.

The next twenty miles, the houses were closer together and there was less brush. This slowed the boys' forward progress down considerably. Most of the houses looked run down and vacant. It took three more days to reach the edge of the city where they found an abandoned two-story building. The boys decided to try to get onto the roof of the structure so they could survey the surroundings.

There was a steel ladder mounted on the wall of the rear of the building, but it was above their reach. Robbie tossed a rope through the rungs of the ladder and was able to pull himself up to the bottom rung. He was then able to pull himself up the ladder and make it to the roof. Sean followed Robbie up. A three-foot parapet around the building gave the boys some cover. The boys kept low and looked over the terrain all the way around the property. They saw no one.

The boys stretched out on the roof and waited for it to get dark. When night fell, the boys were able to stand up without fear of being spotted and took a good look around the sprawling city. There was at least a couple dozen areas where there were concentrations of lights. Outside these areas, however, there was only darkness. They also noticed two vehicles on the roads. There were people in the city, but they had no idea how many or what kind of reception they would receive.

It had taken Sean and Robbie twelve days to make it to Corpus Christi. There was life in the city, but were people still killing each other in the streets? Were there gangs or vigilante groups who would attack them without provocation? How many people would they find? Though they had no idea what the coming days would bring, they were ready to take on their task. Soon their questions would be answered.

Sean and Robbie ate their fill of the wild pig and settled in for the night, choosing to sleep on the roof where they could remain undetected. At first light, they climbed down from the building, looked at each other and smiled. They were ready to make their way into the city to get some answers to their many questions.

Chapter 3

Back at the Lindgren homestead . . .

One morning, Reggie and Emily had just arrived at the Lindgren place. Reggie had promised James he would help him work on the tractor. Debra came running up to the house. "Come quickly!" she cried. "Mom has burned herself really bad!"

"What happened?" James asked.

"She burned herself with a skillet of grease. All over her leg," Debra told them. "Please hurry!"

Eileen was nursing a badly sprained ankle and didn't think she could make the long trek. Reggie volunteered to stay with Eileen while James, Emily and Melissa followed Debra back home.

They could hear Sally screaming long before they reached the house, and they picked up their pace. Sam had cleaned the leg the best he could with a cool water and soap solution by the time Debra returned with the neighbors.

"Oh my!" Emily exclaimed when she first saw Sally's leg. Third degree burns covered about half her leg.

"I'm sorry, Sally, but we've got to get all the grease off," Melissa told her.

"It hurts so much," Sally said, her eyes glassy and a terrified look on her face.

"I know," Melissa said.

While Melissa and Emily continued to clean the wound, Sam prepared a dressing made of crushed aloe vera he pulled from a plant on the side of the house, a bit of wine, and the liquid from boiled willow bark.

"I'm sorry," Melissa said repeatedly as she cleaned on Sally's leg while James held her feet and Emily laid across her chest to hold her still. "The dressing won't work if we don't get all the grease off."

Debra couldn't watch. She sat at the kitchen table with her hands over her ears, sobbing and trying to block out Sally's gut-wrenching screams.

"That should do it," Melissa said. "I'm glad this is over."

"Me too," Emily agreed.

They hated hurting Sally, but they did what needed to be done. They applied the dressing and wrapped the leg with clean bandages. The rest was up to Sally.

"Is she going to be all right?" Sam asked.

"I don't know," Melissa replied. "The leg is really bad."

"I've never seen a burn this bad," Emily stated.

Back at the Lindgren place, Eileen took her pot of coffee off the stove and grabbed a couple mugs out of the cabinet. Reggie was sitting at the table and when she poured his cup, he noticed the top two buttons were open on her blouse and she was not wearing a bra. Reggie got a good look at her breasts. His palms began to sweat and his eyes opened wide as he focused on her.

"How about a little milk?" Reggie asked.

"You don't take milk in your coffee," she said.

"Not normally," Reggie replied, "but I think I'd like to have a little of yours."

"I don't think so!" she exclaimed, now noticing Reggie was looking down her top.

Reggie got up and walked around the table. He grabbed Eileen from behind and held her tight. He kissed her on the neck as he grabbed one of her breasts and squeezed. She struggled a little at first, but she enjoyed the attention. He turned her around and gave her another kiss on the lips. She could feel herself melting into his arms. He slid his hand down her back onto her butt and squeezed as he pulled her into his hardness.

Suddenly she stiffened up and pushed him away, tears running down her cheeks. She retreated into the bathroom and closed the door. Eileen turned the water on and washed her face. *Why did he do this? I can't do this . . . can I?* She dried her face and looked in the mirror. The tears returned and she wiped her face again.

Eileen came back out a short time later. "I'm sorry," she said.

"You're sorry?" Reggie asked. "For what?"

"For not pushing you away before I did. For not slapping you."

"Then you liked what I did?"

She paused for a minute. "Well . . . yes." She began to cry again. *It has been so long since a man touched me. It feels good . . . but . . .*

Reggie walked over to Eileen and tried to grab her again, but she stopped him this time. "We can't," she said. "What about Emily?"

"I love Emily and would never leave her, but our intimacy has all but dried up. She's just not interested anymore," Reggie said.

"I can't!" Eileen pushed him away again and headed out the door toward Lars' grave.

Reggie followed a few minutes later and found Eileen kneeling by her husband's tombstone.

"I loved Lars too, Eileen, and there's not a day goes by that I don't miss him. I know I could never miss him as much as you, but the difference is minimal. Lars would never want you to go without sex."

Eileen sobbed, though she clearly heard every word Reggie said.

"We both have needs," Reggie said. "There is no one else in the valley and there never will be. Emily has no interest in taking care of me, and I am not willing to go without. It's not healthy. You wouldn't want Lars to go without if it had been you that died, would you?"

Reggie was quiet for a while to let Eileen think. A short while later, they headed back up to the house.

"No one will know," Reggie said as they went inside.

When James, Emily, and Melissa returned a short while later, it was Emily who noticed something was amiss.

"What's going on?" she asked, glaring at Eileen's red, swollen eyes.

Before Eileen could reply, Reggie quickly changed the subject.

"We just got back from Lars' grave," he said. "You know how that goes. Anyhow, how's Sally's leg?"

Debra spent most days at the Lindgren homestead with Ronnie, getting to know him better, though she had known him her entire life. She knew he would make a good husband. She knew she loved him, but would he be a good lover? They had never had sex.

Two weeks with Ronnie answered all of Debra's questions. She was certain they were made for each other. The final decision was now up to him.

"Come over in two days," Ronnie said. "I'll have a decision for you then."

Debra kissed Ronnie and headed home.

Ronnie recognized Debra's wolf howl when she showed up early on the second day and returned the signal to tell her it was okay to proceed. He could tell she was excited to see him again. He led her out for a walk and Debra held on to Ronnie's hand as they strolled along. She kept looking at him and smiling, waiting for his decision.

"I like you a lot," he told Debra. "I want to love you, but my feelings for you are no different than my feelings for Sean or Robbie. You are more like a sister to me, so I'm really sorry, but I can't marry you."

Debra stopped and just stared at Ronnie for a few seconds, her mouth open and her eyes bulging. Then she slapped him hard across the face. "I hate you!" she screamed. She then ran home in tears. Ronnie watched as she disappeared into the woods.

As Ronnie headed back toward the house, he heard Reggie's familiar wolf howl. Ronnie returned the howl and met Reggie and Emily at the front porch. Melissa, Eileen and James joined them.

"You guys ready to head over to the Lins?" James asked Reggie.

"Yes," Reggie replied. "Are you coming along, Eileen?"

"Yes, my ankle feels much better. I have to see Sally. I hope she's going to be all right."

Melissa realized Debra wasn't here and asked Ronnie about her.

"She went home," he said. "I told her I couldn't marry her. She started crying and ran away."

"Darn. I was looking forward to another wedding," Emily said.

"Me too," Melissa added.

"You okay?" James asked.

Ronnie nodded and filled the group in on his conversation with Debra. "I don't know what the hell I'm going to do now though."

"Things change," Eileen said. "Some changes are good and some are not, but life is always about change. You take and deal with whatever comes at you."

"I guess you're right, Eileen, change is inevitable," Melissa replied. "Now I miss Sean and Robbie."

"We all do," James added.

"I should have gone with them," Ronnie said with a sullen look on his face. *I'll never find a wife now!*

"If we're going to the Lins, we best get started," James said, grabbing a cloth tote filled with potatoes, and led the way.

When the troupe got to the Lins's house, Eileen, Melissa, and Emily removed the bandages from Sally's leg.

"What did you put on the burn last time?" Eileen asked.

"Aloe vera, wine and willow bark brew," Melissa replied.

"Let's try something different this time," Eileen said as she prepared a new concoction. "That's all I can do for now," she added getting up when she had finished.

"We'll check on her again tomorrow," Melissa told Sam as they left.

"Thanks for the bacon, Sam," James said giving his cloth tote a pat.

"And you for the spuds," Sam replied.

"Sally may die if we can't get the infection under control," Emily stated on the way home.

"Yes she may," Eileen agreed.

Chapter 4

Back in Corpus Christi . . .

Robbie and Sean threw shells into the chambers of their rifles and flicked the safeties on. With their fingers on the triggers and thumbs near the safeties, the boys headed in the direction of the tallest building they spotted near the center of the city from their rooftop observation tower. Robbie led the way, having more training thanks to his grandmother, Eileen, but in reality, neither had any experience. They were armed and dangerous, each and every sense on high alert. It was time to put their plan into action.

The plan was to secure a tall building, then observe for two days and two nights to find and map concentrations of people and to learn more about what was going on in the city.

Robbie led the way through brush and around dilapidated buildings, not always able to see their intended destination. The city had deteriorated and was grown up with trees and tall weeds over the past two decades, since the grid shut down.

Suddenly, the boys heard a rifle shot in the distance and stopped in their tracks. They looked and listened for a while before proceeding with caution. They were well concealed but could walk up on someone at any time. The boys walked down alleys and fence lines, but stopped frequently to listen for voices or other noises. The terrain was not much different than the brush they'd worked their way through when they first left home, except for concealed caved-in buildings.

A woman's voice perked up Robbie's ears. As he moved forward he heard, "I need more firewood."

There was a wooden plank fence between the boys and the voice. Robbie moved closer to the fence and looked through a knothole in one of the boards. He saw a woman and a young boy about twelve years old. She had a fire going in an outside barbecue pit and the boy was carrying one log at a time from a pile stacked next to her home. A man then came out of the house with a pistol strapped to his hip. As the kid brought over more firewood, the man stood and watched the woman as she worked on the fire. They did not seem to be a threat, and Sean and Robbie decided it was in their best interest to keep going.

The boys quietly backed away. The next hour, the boys saw no one and continued to work toward the tall building about a mile ahead now. The boys then came upon what appeared to be a fortress. There was a solid wall of cars stacked three high, the center horizontal row upside down to eliminate openings. Every so often, there were single cars placed on top, obviously for sentries. Robbie and Sean sat a while to watch and listen.

Suddenly, someone spoke behind them. "Lay down your guns, boys."

Sean and Robbie turned around with stunned looks on their faces to find six heavily armed men with their guns pointing at them. "I said, lay down your guns!" he repeated louder.

The boys did as they were told and raised back up to face the armed men. As they did, two of the men rushed over and took the rifles as well as their vests with grenades, their pistols, and the holsters from their hips.

"You can't—" Robbie said.

"We can do whatever we like. We're the law around here," the burly man said.

The big man was the same one who had told them to lay down their guns and who appeared to be the leader of the group.

"What are you going to do with us?" Sean asked.

"You don't ask the questions," the leader said as he moved closer to Sean and Robbie. "Looks like we have a couple mountain men here, boys." He reached up and flipped the tail on Robbie's coonskin hat with his finger. His men chuckled. Then he looked down at the frilly buckskin britches. "Cute! Leather leggings, moccasins and adorned with feathers…you boys are purrrdy." He nodded to the man standing behind Sean and watched as Sean's eyes rolled back in their sockets and his legs buckled.

"What the hell?" Robbie yelled.

The big man stood and smiled as Robbie too, collapsed onto the ground.

Robbie forced his eyes open and tried to focus. The room was dark, his clothes were wet, and there was a damp washcloth on his forehead. He heard voices but couldn't make out what was being said. *Have I been shot?* His body was sore and his head hurt.

"I didn't think he was hurt that bad," Robbie finally made out as his head began to clear a bit. "I didn't think Frank hit him that hard."

"He didn't," was the reply in a female voice. "He's got a fever. He's brought a disease with him."

Robbie couldn't hold his eyes open any longer, and his mind went blank as he passed back out.

"Florence, I want you out of here. You'll get sick too, and I can't have that," Richard said.

"I have to help take care of him," she replied. "Mom can't do everything around here. Besides, if what he has is contagious, I've already got it."

"Dammit! I don't like this," Richard replied. "We should have killed both those boys when we first spotted them."

"And why in Hell didn't you?" Louise asked.

"Sandra said she wanted him alive; that I'm the Chief of Police and he was my responsibility. She didn't give me a choice but to bring him home. Now the little bastard is going to make us all sick; maybe even kill us." Richard stormed out of the room. "Dammit, Sandra," he yelled on the way out.

Florence wiped Robbie's face with a cool, damp washcloth. She touched her hand to his forehead. He was burning up with fever, but there was nothing she could do but comfort him. He would have to come out of this himself.

The next morning, Florence quickly finished her breakfast and went in to check on her patient. Robbie was still out. Florence went back to the kitchen to fix herself a glass of tea.

"How's our guest?" Louise asked.

"Still the same, Mom," she replied.

Florence finished making her drink, grabbed up the book she was reading, and headed back toward Robbie's room.

"Where are you going?" Louise asked.

"I've got to keep an eye on our patient."

"Let me know if he wakes up."

"I will, Mom."

Florence sat down at the side of Robbie's bed with a small candle for light and opened her book. She glanced over at Robbie to find him dead to the world and returned her attention to her book. After about an hour, she heard him moan. She put the book down, wrung out the washcloth, and wiped his face. Robbie moaned a bit more, but his coma continued, as did his fever.

The next two mornings, Florence's routine was the same and her patient's condition remained unchanged. On the third day, Robbie's odor began to get the best of her, and she decided he needed a bath. She gathered up a wash pan, a bar of soap, and a fresh washcloth. She also got fresh sheets for the bed. Then she locked the door. *Mom and Dad will kill me if they catch me cleaning him.*

As Florence removed Robbie's clothes and cleaned his body with the warm soapy water, peeling the bottom sheet down as she went, she noticed how well-built Robbie was. His muscular frame excited her, but not nearly as much as it did when she reached his genital area. She smiled but went on with her duty, trying to force his body out of her mind.

When she finished cleaning, rinsing, and drying him, she rolled his body from side to side as she put the new sheets on underneath him. She slipped a pair of her dad's tighty-whities onto Robbie and covered him back up.

Florence took Robbie's clothes and the bedclothes to the laundry room, hand washed and rinsed them, and took them outside to hang on the clothesline. She then returned to Robbie and continued to read.

Noon the following day, as Florence read and watched Robbie, she couldn't get the picture of his body out of her head. She had stared at his face for hours and wiped his brow with the damp washcloth more times than she could count. She had imprinted her memory with every feature of his face, but with his beard she couldn't really tell what he looked like. *A shave is what he needs.* Suddenly she hopped up and retrieved another wash pan, soap and her dad's razor. When she was finished, she was amazed at what she saw. Then a tear ran down her cheek. *I hope he doesn't die.*

Robbie stirred a bit and Florence reached over and felt his forehead. It wasn't nearly as hot as it had been. She smiled and got up and searched out her mother.

"I think he's going to be okay," she informed her.

"That's great," Louise said. "I'll tell your father when he gets back."

Florence fixed herself a snack and returned to Robbie. As she wiped his forehead, he began to stir. Then he opened his eyes. He blinked a few times as he got used to the darkness and looked around. Then he noticed Florence. *My god she's beautiful.*

"Hi there, sleepyhead," she said.

"Where am I?"

"My house. You have nothing to worry about. You'll be okay now."

"How long have I been here?" he asked.

"A week," Florence replied.

Robbie blinked a few times as he tried to make sense of the situation.

"A week?"

Then his thoughts turned to Sean. "What happened to Sean?"

"The man you came here with?" she queried.

"Yes."

"I don't know. He was taken away to another compound."

"Another compound?"

"Yes, I don't know what happened to him."

As he struggled to sit up in the bed, Robbie was overcome by a terrible thirst. "Water," he said.

Florence poured a glass of water and handed it to Robbie. He downed the precious liquid quickly, spilling a little on his chest. He then noticed he wasn't wearing a shirt. He lifted the sheet and saw the tighty-whities—not his own.

Then the hunger pangs hit home. "I'm starved."

"I'll get you something to eat," and Florence got up and walked toward the door. As she turned the knob, she glanced back at Robbie and smiled an affectionate little smile. Damn he's good looking. I'm so glad he didn't die. But now what?

Florence returned a short while later with eggs, grits, and bacon.

Between mouthfuls, Robbie asked more questions. "Who undressed me?"

"I did," she replied.

"Did you shave me too?"

"Yes. So many questions and I don't even know your name," she said.

"I'm sorry. I'm Robbie," he replied. "And you?"

"I'm Florence. Florence Ingalls."

"Nice to meet you."

"Likewise, though I wish it could have been under better circumstances."

"Not Florence Nightingale?"

She smiled and blushed. "No!"

"Did you take care of me all by yourself?"

"Yes, I did."

When Robbie had finished his meal and had another drink of water, he closed his eyes and drifted off to sleep.

That's okay, Robbie. We'll have plenty of time to talk.

Florence read her book for several hours, taking regular glances at Robbie. Finally, he began to stir again and she put her book down.

The first thing he saw was Florence staring at him with a smile on her face.

"What?" Robbie exclaimed.

"Nothing," she said.

"I've got to pee," he said and started to get up, but fell back to the mattress. Florence helped him raise up on the bed again, pulled the bedclothes back, and helped him sit on the side of the bed.

"I don't think I can get up."

Florence handed Robbie an old but clean spittoon. She steadied him as he struggled to remain upright on the edge of the bed.

"Well?"

"Well what?" Florence asked.

"Can I have a little privacy?"

"Nothing I haven't seen before," she replied. "Okay, I'll turn my head." She held onto his shoulder to steady him.

The flush on Robbie's face slowly faded as he peed. It wasn't much, but necessary.

"You don't have to be embarrassed around me, Robbie. I gave you a bath yesterday."

Robbie could feel the flush returning to his face as he concealed himself.

Florence helped Robbie lie back down, tucked the sheet around him, and left with the spittoon.

When she returned, she sat down beside the bed. Robbie had dozed off again. She read a while and Robbie did not wake up. It was getting late and time for her to go to bed and get some sleep as well.

Louise and Florence worked on breakfast while Florence filled her parents in on the progress of their guest. "His name is Robbie, and he looks to be fine. He's weak, but I'll get him up and he'll be as good as new in no time."

"Good," said Richard. "I'll put him to work next week. We need another hand at the Farm. He looks like he's used to a lot of heavy work."

"He's weak, Daddy. It may take a couple weeks before he's in shape for work."

"A week and he'll be ready," Richard grumbled.

Florence looked away from her dad. She knew he wouldn't let their guest freeload a day past a week and he'd pay for all his trouble with plenty of hard work, even if it killed him.

Florence fixed a plate for Robbie, poured a glass of sweet tea, and headed for the door.

"And don't you be getting too friendly with Ronnie. He'll be out of here as soon as he can work."

"His name is Robbie."

"Whatever."

"Yes, Daddy."

Robbie was already sitting up in bed when Florence went in. "It's good to see you up and rested," she said.

As Robbie ate, Florence informed him that her father would be taking him to the Farm in a week to put him to work.

"I'm grateful for all your help, but I don't work for your father," he said.

"You do now," she informed him. "You need to learn our ways. You are an intruder to my dad and nothing more. I don't see it that way, but to him . . . You will do as he says, or you will die. It's as simple as that."

"But I have rights," Robbie said.

"Not here. You do as you're told."

"And what about you? Do you do as you're told?"

"Yes."

"And if you don't?"

"Then I'm punished. Daddy wouldn't kill me, but he will punish me, and harshly. That's a fact."

Robbie was silent for a while.

"Promise me you'll abide by the rules, Robbie," Florence begged. "Daddy will kill you and not think twice about it."

Florence could see the gears turning in Robbie's head, and she sat silent while he pondered his options. He no longer had a weapon. At the moment, he didn't even have clothes.

"And I don't have a choice?" Robbie finally asked.

"No, none at all."

"Okay, I'll do the best I can. Have you heard anything about Sean?"

"No, but I'll see if I can find out something."

"Thanks," Robbie said. "What else do I need to know?"

"There are six main compounds in the city. Each is run by a chief. My dad is the Chief of Police. Sandra Hawkins is mayor over all the compounds. A better title for her would be dictator. She stays at the Farm. If Daddy takes you there, you will meet her soon enough. Watch out for her spies."

"Spies?" he asked.

"Yes, don't trust anyone."

"Not even you?"

Florence smiled. "Each compound is well-fortified though the Farm and the Airport are too spread out for it to do much good. The Police guard the perimeter of the city and protect the compounds as best they can. The Airport only has a few personnel. I almost never see a plane and then only at a distance. I'm not sure what really goes on out there."

"Interesting," Robbie said.

"Oh, do you fly?"

"No, but I've read a lot about flying. I'd like to try it someday."

"You won't have much free time around here. The Farm is always a busy place. I've been there a few times, and there's always a lot of people, mostly women, out in the fields. It's where a much of our food comes from. The police also hunt to provide meat for all the compounds. There seems to be plenty of deer and wild cattle, as well as smaller game."

"Do you know how they spotted us?" Robbie interrupted. "We thought we were very careful not to be seen."

"I heard they saw you walking around on one of the buildings," she replied.

"But it was dark. We kept hidden during the day and only walked around at night."

"All the police have night scopes. They can see you better at night than during the day."

"Well, that explains that," he said, rather frustrated. "And the other compounds?"

"The Bayfront is where the fishermen live. They provide shrimp, fish, oysters, and clams. They also provide sea salt. The farmers not only grow our crops; they also process our flour and cornmeal and provide fruits and vegetables. Except for an occasional man to help with the heavier or dirtier tasks, they are all women. Don't underestimate them though. They are quite a group of ladies. Many are lesbians, I hear. That's Sandra's doing. Without men to satisfy their needs . . . well, you know. I think some even prefer it that way.

"The Contractor compound contains men mostly, with all sorts of trades. They fix things and build things, but they also run our limited fuel refinery. They are good mechanics and keep our vehicles running and scrounge around for whatever else we need. There is one more compound, but it consists of only one centrally located building. The Hospital provides medical needs but are mostly for the chiefs and their staff. That's why you didn't get the benefit of their expertise.

"They also perform one more service. Most of the men in the city are *neuts*. Sandra and my dad won the war and to maintain their control they fixed the men. Almost all the male born babies are castrated at birth too. This is how they control the population and keep the men in line."

"They didn't castrate me though," Robbie said.

"No. They must have a plan for you. My dad would have let you die, except he needed a new hand for the farmers. Sandra may have another plan for you. When he found out you were sick, it was all I could do to keep him from putting you out of your misery."

"Does anyone leave here?"

"Not unless my daddy wants them to leave. I don't recall this ever happening. A few are buried here and there, but to leave outright? I don't think so."

Robbie finished up the last of his breakfast and tea. "That was absolutely the best meal I've ever had."

"Thank you," Florence replied. "The fact that you haven't eaten much for a week probably had a little to do with it though."

"No, really, it was very good."

"Thank you. You think you're up to getting out of bed and getting your muscles to working again?"

"I think so."

Florence stood up, took Robbie's arm, and helped him get his feet to the floor. As he sat on the edge of the bed, she grabbed him under the arms and gave a tug, but his legs buckled at the attempt and he fell back onto the bed, dragging her along with him. As she struggled to get back up, she inadvertently rubbed her breasts onto his chest and her body against his manhood. Robbie could feel the blood pulsing through his genitals, though in his weakened condition it wouldn't do much good. *Florence didn't seem to notice but maybe she enjoyed the closeness as much as I did.*

She smiled and stood up and made another attempt at getting Robbie out of bed. With difficulty, he was able to stand but was quite wobbly and his head began to spin. Florence steadied him.

"Let's try a few steps," she insisted.

"Do you think I could get some pants?" he asked. "This is a little embarrassing."

"Not until you get a bath, and the bed clothes need to be changed again."

They made their way to the door and then back to the bed, but the walking was more of a shuffle than steps. Finally back at the bed, Robbie plopped down on the soft mattress, exhausted.

"Guess it's going to take a little work to get back into shape," he noted.

"You'll be back to normal in no time," she said. "You up for a bath?"

"Why not!"

Florence retrieved what she needed. She pulled Robbie upright again on the side of the bed and cleaned his face, ears and neck and every square inch of his chest and back. She then grabbed him under the arms and with his help, lifted him to his feet. She pulled the chair over so he could hold onto it. She slid his underwear off and diligently scrubbed everything down to his ankles. She then helped Robbie back onto the bed and worked on his feet until they were squeaky clean. She slipped underwear and pajamas over his legs then helped him stand up to pull the clothes up. Finally, Robbie could feel the embarrassment and flush from his face lessening. Robbie held onto the chair again while she changed the linens and helped him back onto the side of the bed.

"How old are you, Florence?"

"Nineteen. And you?"

"Eighteen. Actually, seventeen and a half." *I can't lie to her. I owe her my life. I think honesty is best if I expect the same from her.* "Does it really matter?"

"No, not really," she replied with a smile. "You are so big and strong, or will be again soon. I thought you were much older."

"Really?" he said with a grin.

She smiled and helped him back into bed.

"Thank you."

"You have a beautiful smile," she added.

Robbie could feel the flush returning to his face.

"I have chores to do," Florence stated. "I found a book for you to read if you're interested." She laid a copy of *War of the Worlds* on the nightstand by the bed. "I'll be back later to check on you." And with that, she was gone.

Chapter 5

Robbie looked around the dimly lit room. The walls and ceiling seemed to be freshly painted and the wood floor was clean with a colorful exotic rug. Heavy curtains concealed the only window in the room. The handcrafted chair, nightstand, and bed appeared to be nearly new and of good quality. *These people are not poor.*

Robbie's thoughts then turned to his predicament. *Am I a prisoner?* He suspected he was, but Florence never locked the door behind her. Then again, there could be an armed guard in the next room or outside on the porch. Robbie tried to get out of bed. He rolled over and slid his legs over the side onto his knees. He began to get lightheaded and just leaned over and laid on the bed for a minute. He then tried to get to his feet. He got halfway up and his knees buckled, sending him to the floor. It took all his energy to drag himself back onto the bed. Frustrated, he reached over and grabbed the book Florence had left on the nightstand. *Prisoner or not, I'm not going anywhere.*

Florence returned a couple hours later just as Robbie was finishing the third chapter of the book. She had a big smile on her face when she came through the door. She was nicely dressed in a white blouse and plaid pants. Her shoulder length auburn hair was wavy and lustrous, accented with rosy cheeks and a button nose. Her sparkling eyes told him she was in a cheery mood. Robbie couldn't help but smile the instant he saw her.

She pulled her chair up beside the bed. "How are you doing?"

"I'm okay, but I need to get out of bed," he replied.

"Okay then, let's get you up."

"You wearing perfume?" he asked.

"Yes, do you like it?"

"Yes," Robbie replied as he took another whiff of the fragrance.

It took a bit of work, but Florence finally got him to his feet and led him across the floor. His legs just didn't seem to want to work. Robbie insisted that they keep walking. "I need to get my strength back."

"You will," she said, "Just be patient."

Then his thoughts returned to his predicament. "Am I a prisoner here?"

"Yes and no," she answered and her smile faded. "You are free to meander around the place when you get your strength back, but if you try to leave you will be stopped. Some of daddy's men are hanging around and will keep an eye on you. They have orders to shoot you if you try to leave. They won't bother you while I'm with you, though."

Yep, I'm a prisoner, but such a nice prison.

The next morning after breakfast, Robbie felt much stronger as he and Florence made their stroll around the room. He insisted that they go take a look around the house.

Florence held onto Robbie's arm as she led him out of the bedroom and into the hallway. They made their way into the kitchen. The kitchen was spacious and well-stocked.

"How do you get electricity?" he asked.

"Each compound has two wind turbines. There is an electrical grid in and around each compound. We are on the Police grid. We have all the electricity we need for our conservative uses."

"So we are in the Police compound?"

"We're not actually in the enclosure. We are outside the Police compound. Most everyone lives outside but near the barricades so they can get electricity."

"And who are in the compounds?"

"The headquarters for the Police, Contractors, and Bayfront are just for the important people. The rest live outside the fortifications but nearby, again for the electricity. There are no barricades for the Airport and the Farm. The Hospital is a compound in itself.

"The Farm was the major stronghold for many years, but now that there is some law and order, the Police have their own compound. There is not a big need for such barricaded compounds now, but no one took the initiative to tear them down. Maybe because there was always the fear that chaos might break out again."

"Looks like you're doing better," Louise commented as she came into the kitchen from an adjoining room.

"Much better," Robbie replied.

Florence then led Robbie around the rest of the house and back to his room, as his legs were weakening under the strain of their stroll. "Maybe we'll go outside tomorrow," she said.

"I'd like that," Robbie replied.

The remainder of the afternoon and evening, Robbie stayed in his room with Florence. She helped him to the bathroom a couple times, as his system was finally beginning to function properly with the addition of food to his diet. Again, it was quite embarrassing that Florence had to endure his terrible odor to get him up. And though she was a bit of a mother hen, he couldn't help but be impressed by the way she took everything in stride.

"Do you have a boyfriend?" Robbie blurted out.

"No, Daddy doesn't allow me to see anyone for very long. As soon as I get to like someone, he carts them off to another compound and I never see them again. When I turn twenty-one, he'll have a husband picked out for me and I'll be married."

"And you're okay with that?"

"I don't have a choice. That's how it's done here."

"Why did he let you take care of me?"

"In your condition he didn't think he had anything to be concerned about. Besides, in a few days you'll go to the Farm to work, and I'll likely never see you again."

"But I'd like to see you again," Robbie said. "Is there any way you can come to the Farm to see me?"

"I go with Dad occasionally to the various compounds, but he always keeps a close eye on me. I don't think we could see each other even if I were to visit."

"Try, will you?" Robbie insisted.

"I'll see what I can do."

"Really?"

"I will," she promised.

By the end of the week, Robbie was getting around fairly well and, right on cue, Richard showed up. "Looks like you're ready to go to work. Now you can start to repay us for all the trouble you've been. Get dressed."

Florence went to get Robbie's freshly laundered clothes. Robbie dressed and Florence gave him a hug to tell him good-bye, which got a frown from Richard.

"They took Sean to the Bayfront to work," she whispered in his ear."

"Good-bye," Louise said to Robbie on their way out.

"Where are you taking me?" Robbie asked, though he already knew. He wanted to get a conversation going to try to get some information.

"To Sandra. You'll work on the Farm for a couple weeks. You know anything about farming?"

"Some."

Richard seemed to be in a better mood now that he was out of the house and away from his daughter. He still didn't say a lot, but when he did his tone sounded more hospitable.

On the trip over, Robbie heard a faint sound like a big engine revving up in the distance. He looked at Richard. "What's that?" he asked.

"Our transport plane," Richard replied.

"You have planes?"

"A few. You know anything about them?"

"A little. I was always fascinated by them growing up but have never seen one. I've read a lot about them in books though."

"You know anything about engines?"

"Dad and I were always working on grandpa's old truck and tractor back home. He taught me a lot about keeping them running. An engine is an engine, I guess."

"Maybe when Ms. Hawkins gets finished with you at the Farm, we'll put you to work at the Airport. They're always complaining about the lack of good help."

As they got close to the Farm, Richard's tone changed again. He gave Robbie a stern talking to. "You cross Sandra and you're gonna be in deep shit! You understand?"

"Yes, sir."

"You just keep saying 'yes sir' or 'yes ma'am' and you'll be okay around here. You cross anyone and you're in trouble. Troublemakers are no good to us," Richard said patting his pistol on his hip.

"Yes, sir!"

For the first time since he'd met him, Robbie detected a slight smile. It only lasted for an instant.

He'd probably love the opportunity to use that pistol on me.

Richard pulled his truck up in front of the main house. It was a massive ranch-style home. On one side was a sprawling bunkhouse and numerous outhouses, including one gigantic hangar-style barn and a dozen smaller barns of various sizes. There were six tractors he could see scattered around the place and farm implements of all kinds, most of which Robbie didn't recognize. His grandpa only had a relatively small tractor in comparison and a few basic attachments.

A big, busty gal dressed in ranch clothes stepped out the front door and met Richard and Robbie at the front gate. She looked to be in her fifties.

The yard was well kept, and there were a few ladies tending the flower gardens on either side of the house. The front fence was lined with rose bushes covered with flowers of all colors.

Sandra gave Richard a manly handshake. "This is Robbie," he said.

"That the best you could do?" she snarled at Robbie.

"You get what you get," Richard replied.

Robbie started to say something, but then thought it better to keep quiet.

"If he gives you any problems just let me know," Richard stated.

"He won't be a problem, will ya boy?"

It wasn't a question, Robbie deduced by the look on her face.

As Richard got back into his truck and drove away, Sandra led Robbie toward a nearby hanger.

"Linda!" Sandra yelled out.

"Yes, ma'am?" came a voice from behind a tractor.

Robbie followed Sandra over to the tractor.

"This is Robbie. He's your responsibility."

"Yes, ma'am."

"You give Linda any problems and I'll cut your gizzard out, ya hear?"

Again, not a question.

Linda Gomez was fortyish and on the short side with dark black hair. She was good-looking, but the serious look on her face made her seem older. She didn't smile much, especially with Sandra nearby.

Sandra left the two to get back to whatever work Linda had been doing. Before she got out of sight, she turned around and took another brief look at Robbie.

"Be respectful of her," Linda said, "or she really will cut your gizzard out. You know much about tractors?" she asked in almost the same breath.

"Some," Robbie replied.

A couple hours later they had the tractor repaired, and Robbie was driving it around the yard with Linda standing on the drawbar. "You're doing quite well. Let's park it in the shed," she said pointing to one of the outhouses. They then went back to the main barn and began working on a combine.

Shortly before dark, Linda showed Robbie to his bunk. One of the other ladies brought him a sandwich and a strawberry drink. Linda introduced Robbie to Harold Butts, the only other person in the bunkhouse. Harold made no secret that he was seventy-three but could outwork most of the younger men who came in at planting or harvest time. He really couldn't, but liked to think so. He had a high-pitched voice with a bit of a southern drawl. His red hair and freckles were prominent. His skin was tanned and wrinkled from years in the sun.

"Not much going on around here right now," Harold said. "Next month it'll get crowded in here. Corn will be coming in and we'll need all the help we can get. The only reason you're here now is because Linda kept complaining to Sandra that she needed a helper. Linda always needs another hand for some of the heavier chores. I don't do lifting. The gals take care of everything around here except during planting and harvest time. Then there's just too much to be done. Me, I'm a permanent fixture. Well, I've told you enough. You need to get cleaned up and get to bed. We get up early around here."

"Yes, sir," Robbie said.

"You don't need to call me sir, Robbie. I'm Harry. One more thing. I'm here to see you stay put. I'll be your friend amongst all these ladies, but I'll be your worst enemy if you cross me or try to leave. There are no mice in this bunkhouse for a reason. I can hear one tiptoeing all the way on the far side of this building. So you stay put. I may be seventy-three, but I can hear better than anyone on the Farm." With that said, Harry went to his room and left Robbie standing there.

Robbie found towels and soap laid out. A new pair of coveralls was hanging from a hook. There were also two pairs of new underwear and a razor. Robbie took his shower and lay in bed but couldn't sleep.

How the hell am I going to get out of this mess? If I just lay low and do what I'm told, maybe I can get out of here alive. Can I get hold of Sean? It'll be weeks before I get all my strength back. Can we get out of here on foot? We can get away from the men, but we can't get away from their dogs. Think dammit, Robbie!

Robbie awoke to Harry banging on the door. Could it possibly be morning already?

"Time to get up, kid," the old man said.

"Okay!"

Robbie rolled out of bed, washed his face, and shaved. He got dressed and went into the central area of the bunkhouse. Harry was waiting on a bench.

"You think you can sleep all day around here, think again," he growled. Then he headed for the door. "Well, come on!"

Robbie noticed the clock on the wall as he followed Harry out of the bunkhouse. It said 4:30. How accurate it was, he didn't know.

They headed up to the main house where two women were cooking, a dozen were eating at the oversize dining table with Sandra at the head of the table, and everyone was talking at once. It got really quiet, however, when Harry and Robbie walked in.

The women ranged in age from their teens to fifty-something. Everyone was dressed in work clothes. Three of the girls smiled at Robbie—the younger ones.

"Well, get in and eat so you can go to work," Sandra said.

Harry led Robbie over to the stove and they each fixed a plate, Harry first. One of the ladies who had smiled at Robbie scooted over so he could sit down. She introduced herself as Sally Beecher. Linda sat opposite Robbie.

Sandra sat at the head of the table. "Get back to breakfast ladies," she demanded in a stern voice.

After breakfast, Robbie went with Linda. The work was easy—changing oil, greasing joints, and replacing electrical parts on the tractors and combines. There was a pallet of heavy oil cans and another stacked with tractor parts that needed to be moved, which is why Linda needed him, but other than that everything was light work. Lunch was promptly at noon, but only consisted of a ham sandwich and a fruity soda brought out to them. Dinner was in the main house promptly at sundown.

The work changed, but the routine was always the same. Robbie shoveled manure, pruned trees, fed cows, and even milked a cow or two. Nothing really difficult, but work, work, work.

With good food and the work, Robbie felt he was nearly back to his old self after the first week. He'd thought long and hard about how he was going to get out of this place, but opportunity hadn't knocked. In fact, just the opposite was true. He noticed that someone was watching him constantly. If he wasn't at Linda's side, Harry, Sandra or Sally Beecher was keeping an eye on him. At times he wouldn't see anyone watching, but if he stood up and looked around for too long, someone would always make their presence known.

Robbie also noticed something else. Sally always sat at his side during breakfast and dinner. She seemed quite friendly, just a few years older than he, and pleasing to the eyes from head to toe. She had bright red hair, sparkling green eyes, and a sweet smile Robbie liked a lot. She did have a downside though. Her filthy mouth wasn't something Robbie was accustomed to.

One morning she was in a pissy mood and Robbie made the remark that his grandmother would wash her mouth out with soap. Sally stormed off and clammed up for two days. She wouldn't even look at him, but on the third day she had cooled down and was back at his side. The conversation resumed and Robbie didn't mention his grandmother or soap again.

At the end of his second week at the Farm, Richard returned. He and Sandra had a long talk after which he motioned for Robbie to get into his truck.

"Time we find a new home for you, Robbie." Richard didn't mention where they were headed. "Seems like you did good at the Farm," he finally said. "Let's see how you do at the Airport."

When they arrived and Robbie saw all the planes, he had a lot of questions. "How many do you have? Do they all fly? Where do you get fuel? How many pilots do you have?"

Richard stopped in front of a hangar, blew his horn, and slid out of the truck, ordering Robbie to follow him. A man appeared at the hangar door, and Richard made the necessary introductions.

"Robbie, this is Russell Jackson. Robbie got good marks at the Farm, Russ. Let's keep that good streak going."

"Not a problem," Russ replied.

"No freak accidents this time, Russ." Richard laughed and they all headed inside the hangar.

"That's not up to me," he replied with a smile. "I'll be right back." He headed inside the office while Robbie and Richard waited nearby.

"Freak accidents?" Robbie asked.

"We buried the last two new recruits. Don't worry, do what you're told and there won't be any accidents."

Robbie frowned.

Russ returned with some coveralls and a bar of soap and pointed toward a row of numbered doors, obviously leading to sleeping quarters, at the side of the hangar. "Pick an empty one. That will be your new home."

Richard left while Robbie was in his new room. Robbie was only in his room five minutes before Russ was banging at the door.

"Come on, we've got work to do, kid."

Robbie immediately began asking questions. "Do all these planes fly? How many pilots do you have?"

Russ stopped in his tracks. "Who do you think asks the questions around here?" he said.

"You do, sir," was the reply.

"Good answer!"

Russ headed on toward the back of the hangar. He introduced Robbie to Jorge Guzman. "Best mechanic I have. Listen and learn," followed by a stern look and a frown. "Don't aggravate my blood pressure." Then Russ headed back to his office.

"I haven't seen any planes flying around since I've been here," Robbie stated.

"Oh, we don't fly them," Jorge replied. "We just maintain the planes so that if one is ever needed, it will be ready to fly."

Much to Robbie's surprise, Jorge liked to talk. It was like he hadn't talked to anyone for a long time and had stored up months of conversation. Richard and Sandra were all business. Robbie had gotten a few words out of Harry, but for the most part, everyone kept pretty quiet. He had questions and Jorge had answers.

Chapter 6

A couple miles away at the Bayfront . . .

Sean sat on the seawall with Sonny and Marcia Nguyen and their thirteen-year-old daughter, Lola, taking in the early afternoon sun while they ate lunch. As he nibbled on his fish sandwich, Sean eyed the guards across the roadway. The two big men smoked their cigarettes with their rifles laying across their laps. They never took their eyes off Sean.

The steady sound of waves slapping at the seawall drowned out the sounds of the people working nearby. A desalinization plant just down the street was busy with a dozen or so workers outside. There were certainly more inside.

The ice plant was down the seawall in the opposite direction. There were five trucks parked in front of and near a large doorway. They looked to be the delivery trucks. Few people were out and about, but there was obviously a lot going on inside. A steady hum of machinery could be heard.

Other fishermen mingled around their boats working on their nets and rigging. It seemed this was a never-ending chore, and Sonny was constantly working on theirs as well.

They watched as a truck from the ice plant backed up to the insulated box on the dock at the rear of Sonny's boat. Two men got out and dumped a load of crushed ice into the box, put the lid back on, and drove away.

Nothing drowned out the sounds of the occasional laughing gulls fighting over a morsel of food.

"Don't feed the birds," Sonny said. "They'll poop on you every time."

"Yes, sir."

"Time to get back to work," Sonny ordered now that he had the ice he needed.

Sean followed Sonny back to the boat. Marcia and Lola tagged along. "You ready to answer some of my questions now?" Sean asked Sonny.

"Shhh, too many ears," he whispered.

The June brown shrimp season was in full swing, but their catch was meager that morning. Regardless, there was still much work to be done. They headed the shrimp, packed them in 16-ounce mesh bags, iced them down in plastic bushel boxes, and loaded them into the back of Sonny's Dodge pickup. They also packed an assortment of fish, squid, and the occasional octopus or turtle in ice and loaded these onto the truck as well. Crabs were always kept alive in wooden crates covered in the shade on the boat until they were ready to be off-loaded. Marcia helped

Lola into the pickup and they hauled the catch away to Sean knew not where.

Sonny and Sean then cleaned the boat from stem to stern, after which they hauled fuel to the boat five gallons at a time and transported the remainder of the crushed ice to the insulated box on the boat.

Now that the shrimp net had dried, Sonny lowered it onto the boat and stretched it out. He and Sean went over the entire surface of the net looking for holes. Sonny showed the kid how to patch holes and tears, which he did with great ease. It seemed so easy, but when Sean tried, it never turned out quite as neat as when the master made the repair.

"You'll get the hang of it before long," Sonny assured him.

As they worked, Sonny began to answer some of Sean's questions. "You'll work with me for a couple years. I'll teach you everything I know if you are willing to learn. Then you'll get your own boat, if one is available, a wife and her kid."

"Wife? Kid?"

"When you prove you're worthy and capable, you will get a family of your own. If you cause any problems, you will die. It's as simple as that. Work hard and stay out of trouble and it can be nice around here. Show everyone you want to stay and the guards will go away. You can live a good life and be relatively happy."

"But I've got to get out of here," Sean said.

"Not going to happen," Sonny stated. "Don't cause any problems. You're good inside; I can see that, but trying to escape will get you hurt. There are eyes and ears on you all the time. They will know and they will kill you without thinking twice."

"But, dammit, I don't belong here!"

Sonny didn't say a word as he looked over at the men across the street.

Sean grimaced and turned his attention to the guards. He knew they would not hesitate to shoot him if he tried to leave. This was made very clear to him when he first arrived at the Nguyen's.

"Is Lola your daughter?" Sean finally asked.

"Not by blood, but I love her very much."

"And Marcia?"

"She was given to be my wife five years ago. The first year was rough, but Marcia is sweet. I know she has mostly ignored you since you've been here, but she doesn't trust easily. Give her time. She works hard, and I have grown to love her."

"Where did she come from?"

"The Farm. Only the women at the Farm are allowed to make babies. If someone outside the Farm is found to be pregnant or with a new baby, the mother and baby are killed."

Sean's eyes got bigger as he stared at Sonny, but he kept quiet.

"Loop and knot. The same size loop and the same knot every time," Sonny said trying to show Sean how to patch the net. "First, left to right, and then right to left until you get to the bottom. At the bottom, catch the loop on the bottom and tie. Then tie on the top. Simple!"

"Maybe it's simple to you, but it's not to me," Robbie replied.

"You'll learn. Then it will be easy."

"Can you find out if my best friend, Robbie, is okay?"

"No. And no more questions now."

By the time their work was finished and Marcia had returned to pick the men up, Sean was already getting tired. There was more work to be done at his new quarters at the Nguyen's, however. Sonny was a workhorse and never let up. Sean was feeling the strain though he was in good shape. His groin pained him as well. He certainly was not used to getting up at 4:00 a.m. every day.

When they reached their meager dwelling, Marcia and Lola went inside to begin dinner while Sonny put Sean to work on some outside chores. Sean noticed that his guards had followed them to the house again. *Bastards! I guess they have nothing better to do than to watch me. Why don't you just kill me and put me out of my misery? They'd probably love to do just that. I'm not going to give them that pleasure. I could have ended it all on the boat. Why didn't I? Maybe I can find the ones who butchered me. Maybe I can do the same to them as they did to me. But how can I with guns always pointing at me? I guess there's always hope.*

Sean cut up some fish to feed the live crabs on the aerated tables where peeler crabs were kept until they shed their shells. There were five of these crab bins and only two had crabs. Sonny added crabs from the morning catch to a third table and started the aerator.

"When the crabs shed their shells," Sonny told him, "the soft crabs are cleaned and eaten whole—pincers, legs and all."

Sean had never eaten crabs, but Sonny assured him they were a delicacy and he would love them.

When they were finished with the crabs, Sean fed the chickens and hoed in their garden while Sonny picked tomatoes, cucumbers, and greens. He took them inside to Marcia. Sean kept glancing over at the guards. He chopped harder with each stroke, taking out his frustration on the weeds. *Come over here a little closer, you sons-a-bitches. I'll chop you up into tiny pieces.*

"That's enough for now," Sonny said when he came back out to find Sean chopping wildly at the plants. "Let's go get some dinner."

Marcia prepared a nice salad to go with their fish and shrimp meal.

"How do you like the dinner?" Sonny asked Sean.

"Okay," he replied with a weak smile. *What I'd really like is a gun and my balls back.*

Sonny frowned and took another bite.

After dinner, Sonny took Sean to his separate bunkhouse where the guards were waiting. Sean went inside and heard the clacking of the lock as one of the guards secured the door behind him. The guards could now go home, but they would be back early the next morning to make certain he made the trip to the boat. They would again be waiting when the boat arrived back at the harbor.

The bunkhouse was cramped but comfortable. The bed was much softer than he was accustomed to but better than sleeping on the ground. He had indoor plumbing and a cabinet top refrigerator stocked with drinks and fresh vegetables for snacks. There was a single dim light in the center of the ceiling. *What else could I ask for? Freedom, maybe!*

Sean showered, prepared his clothes for the following morning, and stretched out on his bed. There was less blood on his underwear today from his surgery. He was healing, at least on the outside, and the pain continued to subside. As he stared at the light on the ceiling, his mind drifted to his best friend. Where's Robbie? Is he alive? Could he find out? Sean's situation was aggravated by his castration but the living arrangement was not so bad, but he felt like a raccoon trapped in a cage. He need to get out of here. But how?

The next thing he knew, someone was knocking on his door. "Time to get to the boat," Sonny hollered.

"I'm up," Sean yelled out.

"Ten minutes," he heard back, along with the sound of the lock being released.

The boat ride out was smooth. Marcia bedded Lola down on the floor in a corner of the wheelhouse. There were two boats ahead of Sonny's and the rest of the fleet followed. It was still quite dark as Sonny's boat sliced through the glassy water. The sets of red, green, and white running lights on the trailing boats spread out over the waters. Some veered left, others right, while Sonny continued straight ahead. There was no wind this morning as Sonny steered the boat and Sean readied the net just as Sonny had shown him on the first day out.

After thirty minutes, Sonny slowed the boat and let down the try net, a small sampling net hanging from the boat's outrigger. The sun was just about to peek above the horizon. He pulled the try net for ten minutes, then raised it back up, emptied the net, and counted the shrimp. Thirty-five.

"Better than yesterday," he mumbled to Sean.

Sonny returned to the wheelhouse and pushed the gearshift forward. He then waved to Sean waiting on the back deck for his signal.

Sean tossed the sack of the net into the water. By the time he reached the winch, the force of the water had pulled all the net overboard and was trailing behind the boat. Sean lifted the trawl doors with the winch and slid them over the stern into the water. The net and doors settled to the bottom of the bay as 300 feet of cable spooled off the winch and Sean stopped and locked the winch.

Sonny maneuvered the boat back and forth, zigzagging near the area where he had dragged the try net. An hour and a half later it was time to go to work. They pulled the main net in and dumped the shrimp onto the deck. "Good catch," Sonny said.

Sonny steered the boat again while Sean lowered the main net into the water. For forty-five minutes, Sonny and Sean separated the shrimp, crabs, and fish they wanted to keep from the garbage. The garbage consisted of jellyfish, insignificant fish, crabs below the legal size and numerous other bycatch. Sean pushed the bycatch overboard through the scuppers in the railing and washed the deck. Marcia steered the boat while he and Sonny worked on the back deck. She seemed to know how to do this task as well as Sonny. Lola slept most of the morning.

They iced the catch down in the insulated box, except for the peeler crabs and large crabs which they kept alive in separate containers and placed in a shady spot and covered with a burlap sack. When they completed processing their first catch, they got a short break before the net was again raised and the haul dumped on the deck for separation.

After the third tow, they pulled the net in, cleaned fish and sea grass out of the webbing, and hoisted it high into the rigging to dry. Marcia drove in while Sonny and Sean separated the catch and iced it down. They added more peeler crabs and large crabs to the first two catches, nearly filling the containers.

Sonny took over the driving and expertly maneuvered the boat into the proper stall. Sean tied the boat up, and as before, they processed and iced down the catch into containers.

Sonny and Sean talked more after Marcia had left with the day's catch. This was the only time they could talk without ears listening in, as long as they spoke softly where the guards could not hear.

"Did they cut you?" Sean asked.

"Yes."

"But why?"

"Only a select few men are kept fertile to make babies. That's the way it is. The farmers are mostly women. They grow more than just food."

"And it didn't bother you?"

"Of course it did for a while, but I couldn't change what happened. Getting mad wasn't going to bring my nuts back. Nothing was."

"Don't you want to get out of here?"

"To where? I have no place to go."

"You can go with me to Peaceful Valley."

"And what's there for me?"

"Freedom! For you, Marcia, and Lola."

"Marcia's a farmer. She would never leave."

"Now she's a shrimper."

"But deep down, she will always be a farmer. She will never leave. She reports to Sandra every week."

"Sandra?"

"Sandra Hawkins is the mayor, the leader of the city. She also runs the Farm. Ruthless bitch! Marcia would never cross her."

"Why not?"

"Sandra would kill her own daughter if she crossed her."

"She's that cruel?"

"Yes. She's not so bad most of the time. But when someone crosses her, look out. All the women at the Farm are brainwashed from the time they are sixteen until they get placed with a family. Lola will go to the Farm in three years when she turns sixteen."

"Can you still see her?"

"Maybe occasionally, but not often. She'll work there for at least five years and then be placed with a husband if one is available. During those five years, Lola will be worked hard and taught Sandra's ways. If she conforms, she'll become another one of Sandra's ladies, just like Marcia."

"And if she doesn't conform?"

"She disappears."

"As in dead?"

"Yes."

Sean sat silent pondering Sonny's words.

Later, when all the boat work was completed and prepared for the following day, Marcia and Lola returned to take them home.

Chapter 7

Meanwhile back at Peaceful Valley . . .

Melissa and Eileen headed out early to the Lin homestead. This had become a daily routine as Sally's leg continued to ooze pus and blood. Ronnie hadn't seen Debra in a while and tagged along. Eileen changed the medications nearly every day trying to find something that would work. Nothing seemed to help.

"If we can't get the infection under control, it may get into her bloodstream," Eileen said. "It may already be in her blood."

Eileen searched deep into her experiences and Melissa did the same for a clue as to what might help. Finally, they decided to try a recommendation from Ronnie.

"We've tried everything else," Melissa said.

Eileen cleaned the wound and Melissa applied a thick layer of crushed charcoal and wrapped the leg to hold the powder in place. They repeated this procedure for three consecutive days. After the third day, Sally's wound had dried up considerably. The infection had not been eliminated, but the new medication was working. It took another week to get the infection under control, but once they did, she began to eat better and feel better.

"We weren't certain you would make it," Eileen said. "It's so nice to see you finally improving. You'll be much more careful with the hot grease from now on, won't you?"

Sally smiled.

Sally decided she wanted to get up for a while. Debra got her robe and crutch and they slowly found their way outside where Ronnie and Sam were tending to the pigs.

Ronnie had not seen Debra for quite a while, and they decided to take a stroll and have a talk. "I'm sorry I haven't visited. With my mother, it's been hard to get away. We do need to talk, though."

"Yes, we do," Ronnie said.

Debra kissed Ronnie on the cheek. "I still love you, Ronnie. That will never change."

"I love you too, Debra, but as I've told you before, that love is a sisterly love. I wish it were different, but it's not. I have thought about us a lot. I know there are no more men out here and you need a man."

"Yes, and you need a woman too, Ronnie."

"Can we still be friends?"

"Of course. It won't ever be the same, and I might have some flashbacks and get a little grumpy from time to time, but we can still be friends."

"I'm sorry I hurt you," he added.

"You can't help the way you feel. I'll get over it. The problem is, I don't know what we're going to do now that we can't be together."

"We'll figure something out," Ronnie added as they strolled back to the house.

Sam, Sally, Melissa and Eileen were chatting on the porch when Debra and Ronnie returned.

"We better get back home," Eileen suggested. "James will need your help in the garden, Ronnie. There's a lot of work to be done."

Ronnie winked at Debra and led the way home.

When Melissa, Eileen and Ronnie got back to their place, they noticed James was talking to a group of people. They were quite surprised, as they had not seen anyone around the place for years.

James introduced his family to John and Kathy Wimberley and their five grown kids, Brooke, Charlotte, Kira, Zack, and Lance.

"Seems John and Kathy need a place to stay," James said. "They came here from San Antonio."

Eileen's eyes lit up when she heard the name of her old town.

"What's left of San Antonio?" Eileen inquired.

"Not much," John said. "That's why we're here. The town is all but dead. The river is so polluted it's not safe to be around. The city never could get any law and order established. Just kill or be killed. The few who are left still can't get along. Maybe in a few years they will all be gone and the place will heal up."

"That's sad," Eileen noted with a frown.

"Yes, it is," Kathy agreed. "It seems every edible critter has been eradicated. We knew we had to leave if we wanted to eat."

Ronnie and the kids strolled into the garden as the parents continued to talk.

"It looks as though you have a nice place here," John stated. "We don't mean to intrude, and we'll understand if you want us to move on, but we are peaceful people. We mean you no harm. We just want to find a nice place to live. We are hard workers and will work for everything we get."

James and the rest listened attentively as John continued with his story.

"We are God-fearing people, and we have brought up our kids to work hard, live free, and be thankful to others for their help. We will be good neighbors. We will fight to the death for what is ours, but we take nothing that is not freely given."

James looked at Melissa and Eileen and back to John and Kathy. "I tell you what, there is an abandoned farmhouse about an hour downstream from here. Melissa and I stayed there a while after the Westons died. You're welcome to stay there for a couple days. I haven't been there in quite a while and don't know what kind of shape it's in, but you're welcome to it. It's at least a roof over your head for a few nights. We'll think about what you've said and whether or not we want you to stay around."

"We've been taking care of ourselves for a long time," Eileen said. "I just don't know whether or not we need or want anyone else around. We'll have to think about it."

"I understand," John replied. "Like I said, we don't want to intrude where we're not wanted, but we will be an asset to your little group if you will allow us to stay."

"That sounds good," Melissa said, "but we will need to talk to the rest of our neighbors as well. This is not a decision that we alone can make."

"Come on kids," John hollered in the direction of the garden.

James pointed out the direction to the Weston farm and he, Melissa, Eileen and Ronnie watched as the group trudged out of sight.

"Ronnie," James said, "run over to Reggie's and tell him we need to have a meeting in the morning. First thing."

Ronnie headed upstream while Eileen went inside to fix some mint tea. When she came back out, they sat on the porch and discussed their potential new neighbors.

"Ronnie sure seemed to like the girls," Melissa noted. "More kids will certainly solve a couple problems. Security should be at the top of the list, but I'm thinking grandkids."

"But do we really want to have more neighbors?" Eileen said. "We don't need them, but do we want them?"

"They seemed like good people," Melissa said.

"Yes, they do," Eileen added.

"Let's wait to see what the Lins think," James said. "I think I'll run over there now and have a little talk with Sam and Sally. Sam won't come over because of Sally. I don't know if Debra will come. I'll be back as soon as I can."

Chapter 8

Shortly after breakfast, James heard Reggie's familiar wolf howl. He walked to the porch to welcome Reggie and Emily. "Come on in, folks," he said.

"Seven more mouths to feed," was Reggie's first comment.

"We may need to help them a little at first," James stated, "but they seem to be good people. John said they all knew how to handle firearms. They are a little short on ammunition, but they all carry some powerful guns. With a little ammunition from you, Reggie, they will give us some added knockdown power. Over time, they may be a good asset. The two boys are big and strong. They don't look like strangers to hard work."

"Well," Reggie said, "when do we get to meet them?"

"How about right now," James replied.

James grabbed a canteen of water and he and Reggie headed out. Emily decided she would rather stay and chat with Melissa and Eileen. Ronnie was upset that James insisted he stay and work on his chores.

Ronnie took a little over three hours to finish his chores and was cooling off on the front porch when he heard his dad's wolf howl. Ronnie howled back and his dad and grandpa emerged from the woods.

Eileen, Emily and Melissa came out to the porch with a pitcher of tea knowing the guys would be thirsty. "You guys ready for the meeting?" Eileen asked.

"Yes," they replied.

"I filled Emily in a bit about the Wimberleys," Eileen stated.

"Good," James said.

"This valley has limited resources," Reggie said to start the meeting. "Can Peaceful Valley feed seven more people?"

"There have always been plenty of deer and feral hogs around," Melissa brought up.

"Yes," Eileen added, "and if they can get their garden going, I don't think they'll have a food problem."

"Growing kids sure can eat a lot," James reminded them.

"Yes, they can," Eileen said smiling as she glanced over at Ronnie. "We may need to help them with seeds. It's too late in the season to get much started now, but if they can get the old garden in shape over the next few months, they can get a fall garden started. We can all chip in until it starts producing, but after that they should be okay."

"They seem like good people," Melissa added.

"I like them," Ronnie stated.

"You thinking between your legs, boy?" James inquired with a smile.

"They're cute," Ronnie noted.

"Sam asked if they liked bacon," James added, laughing. "If so, he'd have a new market for his hogs. 'Everyone likes bacon,' I told him. Sam and Sally both agreed they would go along with whatever we decided. They trust our judgement. Debra certainly liked the prospect of some new kids. 'Even if they're ugly,' she made the point of bringing up."

Everyone laughed, but then it got quiet. Each pondered the prospect of new neighbors.

Ronnie was first to speak. "I vote they stay," he said with a smile.

"Let's sleep on it overnight," Reggie finally stated. "We'll be back over in the morning and let you know."

"Sounds good," Eileen replied.

"Okay, Daddy," Melissa said, "we'll see you in the morning."

"It would be lovely to have someone else to talk to around here," Melissa stated.

"You getting tired of talking to me?" James asked.

"No, never," Melissa said, planting a kiss on him. "I'm just saying we'd have something new to talk about for a while and it would be wonderful to have another woman around. Mom and Eileen are okay, but there are just some things I can't talk about with them."

"Or with me, I guess," James said.

"Not really. You don't understand, do you?"

"No!"

Melissa knew James wouldn't understand. Men never do! So she did the only thing she could do. She leaned over and kissed him. "Good night, honey."

Bright and early the next morning, Reggie and Emily showed up with good news. "I think it will be okay to have some new neighbors," Reggie announced.

"We'll make it work," Emily said.

"We have come to the same conclusion," Melissa said.

"Shall we go inform them of our decision?" James asked.

"I'll go," Ronnie said with a big grin and a mouthful of breakfast. "I'll go by and get Debra first. She needs to meet her new neighbors."

The rest looked at each other and agreed that would be okay.

"Don't tarry, boy," James said, "I still have chores for you to do this evening before it gets dark."

Ronnie gobbled up the rest of his breakfast and shot out the back door like his hair was on fire.

"Looks like Ronnie and Debra are going to have some new friends," Emily said.

"And we may get some new great-grandkids as well," Eileen noted.

"I always knew I would become a grandmother one day," Melissa added. "I don't feel old enough."

"You never do," Eileen said. "I don't feel old enough to have great-grandkids, but I haven't looked into the mirror lately."

"You look just fine," Reggie said.

"Yes, you do," Emily added.

Eileen got up and started carrying dishes to the sink. Emily and Melissa got up to help. Soon the conversation drowned out the clatter of dishes. Emily was excited over the prospect of weddings. Melissa, while she was unsure of the prospect of becoming a grandmother, welcomed the likelihood of newborns.

James and Reggie wandered out to the porch so they could have a conversation of their own and to have a cigar. James sat and stared at the garden as he puffed on the cigar. Toward the end of his smoke, he realized Ronnie would probably be gone all day.

"You want to help me with the potato harvest, old man?" James said.

"Who you callin' old man, sonny?" Reggie fired back.

"Come on, pops, let's get some spuds into the root cellar. And we'll fix you up a hefty bag to take home. How many do you think you can carry at your age?" James added with a grin.

"More than you think, smart-ass!"

Ronnie was out of breath when he reached the Lins'. Debra and her mom were sitting out on the porch. "It's good to see you up and about Mrs. Lin," Ronnie said.

"It's good to be out," she replied. "What's the hurry?"

"Mom, Dad, Grandpa Reggie and Grandma Emily decided we're going to let the new folks stay at the Weston farm. We're going to have some new neighbors. I came over to get Debra and take her to meet them."

"Are they city people?" Sally inquired.

"They seem great," he said. "Maybe a little city and country. I just know Debra will like them. And she'll have two men to pick from."

Debra blushed. "Shut up!"

"Just telling it like it is. Come on. Let's get over to the Weston place," Ronnie insisted.

"You going to be okay, Mom?" Debra asked.

"Yes, of course. You and Ronnie go on. If I need something, I'll yell at Sam.

Tell him you're leaving, will you?"

Ronnie let out a big wolf howl as they approached the Weston farm. John and Kathy stepped out the back door, and the rest of the kids appeared from different directions.

Ronnie did his best to remember all the names as he introduced Debra to the Wimberleys. He immediately informed them that they were welcome to stay at the old Weston homestead. John and Kathy invited them inside.

"It still smells a little gross in here," Kathy said. "There must have been something dead in here for a while."

"We'll get it aired out in no time," John noted.

Ronnie noticed the place was pretty run down and dusty, but fixable. "You've got your work ahead of you," Ronnie said.

"Yes," Kathy replied, "but we've got five strong and healthy kids to help us."

Ronnie smiled and looked over at the girls. "And if there is anything I can do, don't hesitate to ask."

"And me too," Debra said, looking at the boys with a big grin on her face.

John, Ronnie, Zack, and Lance went outside to look around while Debra stayed inside with the ladies, though she felt the urge to go with the men. John led Ronnie over to the garden.

"Looks like the fencing needs some work and the weeds need cleared," Ronnie noted. "We have seeds and can help you with a fall garden if you can get this mess cleaned up."

"We can certainly do that," John said.

"There are plenty of deer around here, but my grandpa taught us a long time ago that we only kill bucks and only what we need."

"Your grandpa sounds like a smart man."

"He was," Ronnie said. "Grandpa Lars died a long time ago, when I was a baby. I learned much of what I know about him from Grandma Eileen. You met her the other day. You met Grandpa Reggie yesterday too. He's great, but he's no woodsman like my other grandpa."

"Well, boys," John said to Zack and Lance, "since we're going to be staying here, there's no better time than the present to get started cleaning up the place. You boys may as well get started on cleaning up the garden."

Ronnie and John strolled back toward the house. John stopped at the steps to look back at his boys. The weeds were flying. John turned back and led the way into the house.

"How things going in here?" he asked.

"Good," Kathy replied.

The ladies had already begun cleaning up the place, Debra included. The Wimberleys had hardly touch the place in the short time they were there. The house needed a lot of cleaning, organizing, and repairs, though much of any supplies were damaged by intruders and needed throwing out.

Ronnie was getting in the way and distracting the girls, so Kathy asked him to go back outside with Zack and Lance. After a couple hours, he yelled to Debra that he needed to get her back home if he was to get home before dark himself.

Ronnie and Debra made a wide swing by the garden on the way home. "Looks good boys," Debra said with a big smile.

"Thanks, ma'am."

Debra giggled and she and Ronnie were on their way, Debra's hips in full swing.

James and Reggie got all the potatoes dug and all the larger ones into the root cellar. James did most of the work, but Reggie did all he could. At sixty-six he couldn't be considered young anymore by any standards. He wasn't ready for the grave though. With his hormones stirred by Eileen, he felt younger than ever. He still thought about Eileen often, but she avoided eye contact with him most of the time now. This didn't stop Reggie from staring at her often when they were together. He could see she was wrestling with a solution to the problem. He knew she liked him and didn't want to give up sex forever.

Reggie and Emily spent the rest of the afternoon at the Lindgrens—Reggie helping James, Melissa working in the kitchen and doing laundry, while Eileen and Emily spent most of the afternoon talking on the sofa. Eileen really liked Emily, but she never mentioned her predicament with Reggie. If Reggie made any more advances toward her, she and Emily would definitely need to have a long discussion. She hoped Reggie would give her the time she needed to think the situation through.

Ronnie dropped Debra off at her house and he arrived home just barely before dark. Reggie and Emily had gone home too and could just barely see where they were walking when they arrived. Reggie headed straight out to his bunker and tinkered for a while.

Emily fiddled around the house and when Reggie came in, they showered and went to bed. Reggie was sound asleep in seconds. That had been their routine for some time now. Emily seemed content with the routine, but Reggie on the other hand was not about to give up sex. He didn't know what he would do about it, but he thought of Eileen constantly.

Suddenly, James, Melissa and Eileen didn't see much of Ronnie anymore. He was up early most mornings and was off to the Wimberleys', delivering nails, potatoes, or something else they needed. He always reported back on their progress in getting the Weston homestead back into shape.

"They're smart people and they work hard. In a week, they nearly have the place in as good a shape as ours," he informed them after his latest trip.

"And how are the girls?" Eileen asked.

Ronnie blushed. "They're fine." He couldn't hide his smile, and Eileen smiled as well.

"Debra usually shows up not long after I get there," he added. "Seems she's liking Zack and Lance."

"Maybe it's time we have a get-together," James announced.

"I think so," Eileen said.

Melissa instructed Ronnie to run over to Reggie and Emily's in the morning. James volunteered to go over to the Lins. Sally was mostly healed up and getting around well. The trek to the Lindgren's wouldn't be an ordeal for her.

Chapter 9

James insisted Ronnie help him with the corn harvest, and they got that out of the way quickly with Ronnie's hard work. He worked twice as hard to make time to visit the Wimberleys. As soon as the harvest was stored, he headed downstream.

The following Saturday, everyone showed up at the Lindgren's about mid-morning. Ronnie and James showed John, Zack, and Lance around the place. Reggie tagged along. James, Reggie and John spent most of their time in the barn searching for hose clamps, roofing nails and a few other things John needed to repair his pier and roof.

"It seems like the house is structurally sound," John remarked, "but it also seems like everything needs at least some repairs."

"You need some help?" James asked.

"No, me and the boys can take care of pretty much anything. That is, if we have the repair materials. Ronnie has been a godsend."

Reggie raised an eyebrow and gave John a stare.

"We catch fish most days and Lance and Zack kill a squirrel or two in between, but we didn't have any vegetables. Thanks for the potatoes."

"I'll send a sack of corn back with you and a few more spuds," James said. "We're a little short on potatoes, but the corn harvest was pretty good. We'll share what we can spare until you can get the garden going. I'll send along a couple jars of pickled beets too."

"Thanks," John said.

Reggie looked over at James.

"Don't worry, Reggie, I have plenty of pickled beets for Emily. The only way I won't have enough beets for her is if they die in the field. I'll keep that tradition going."

John looked at Reggie and James with a puzzled look on his face.

"James' dad got Emily hooked on his pickled beets decades ago," Reggie informed John. "Lars was my best friend as well. He's buried over by the old sycamore tree," Reggie said pointing in the general direction of the tree.

"We got the garden ready for planting and the orchard is all cleaned up," John continued. "Critters ruined some of the fruit, but at least the trees are fine and will do good next year. I think we'll get some pears soon."

"You'll get things going in no time," James assured him.

"I think so," John replied. "What do you think about planting something now?"

"It's a little early for a fall garden, but you should be able to get some okra, melons, and beans going. You'll have to water a lot more, but it can be done. I'll send some seeds along for you too."

"Thanks," John said. "We really appreciate all that you're doing for us. If there is anything we can do in return, don't hesitate to ask."

"We won't," James assured him.

"Things were pretty rough around here for many years," Reggie added. "We all hung together and helped each other. If we hadn't, we wouldn't be here now. You work with us, and we'll work with you."

"That's what neighbors do, right?" John asked.

Ronnie, Zack and Lance fished a little but didn't catch anything. They just sat holding their rods and talked. They didn't have the interest and weren't overly concerned whether they caught anything or not. Ronnie had spent most of his time with the girls while at the Weston place and had not gotten to know the boys all that well. Now was his time to get to know them better and vice versa. Debra, on the other hand, knew the boys quite well and was getting to know the girls a little better now.

Zack and Lance both loved to fish. Neither cared a lot about hunting, but that didn't mean they didn't know how. Between them they only killed a dozen deer in their lives and knew how to dress them, but thought they were pretty animals to look at.

"There weren't a lot of deer in and around San Antonio," Zack stated. "We only found some to kill after we got well away from the city."

"How long did it take you to get here?" Ronnie asked.

"Nearly a month," Lance replied.

"Why so long?"

"We found deer and feral hogs when we traveled. When we killed one we stayed and ate it until it was almost gone and then moved along until we killed another," Zack said.

Inside the house, Debra was enjoying her time with the girls for a change. Since Zack got along better with Brooke than he did with his other two sisters, and Debra and Zack had more in common, it was only natural that Debra got along better with Brooke too. Brooke was the oldest and smartest of the girls. She was also the most beautiful. Not to say the others were bad-looking, but Brooke had really fine, blond hair and the perfect complexion. Charlotte was rather quiet, while Kira always had something to say about everything. Debra didn't like talking to them like she did with Brooke.

Kira never seemed to sit still. She was always getting into things and nothing escaped her attention. Kira stopped to browse through all the books in the bookshelves at the Lindgren place.

"I just love to read," she announced.

"Go pick out one you like and you can take it home," Eileen said. "Brooke, Charlotte, you two are welcome to a book as well."

Brooke already had a book and diary which she always carried and declined the offer. Charlotte walked over to the bookshelf and picked out a book. "I like this one," she said holding up a book of poetry.

"That was one of Ronnie's favorites," Melissa noted.

Kira picked out *Huckleberry Finn* by Mark Twain.

"It's time to go," John announced.

James ran out to the root cellar and grabbed a sack of corn and a few potatoes. Melissa got the two jars of beets out of the pantry he'd promised.

"We'll check in on you next week," James said, and the new neighbors headed back to the old Weston place.

"Looks like they'll make fine neighbors," Reggie commented.

"I think so," Melissa agreed.

"At least they seem eager enough to become part of the community," James remarked.

The Lins headed out back toward home. "Good to see you doing so well, Sally," Melissa said as they parted.

Reggie maybe hugged Eileen a little too long as they were leaving, but no one noticed but Eileen. She didn't say a word when he pinched her on the butt.

"Why so solemn?" James asked her later as they were having a drink on the porch and watching the evening sunset.

"Oh nothing," she said, "just missing Lars a bit. I think I'll go have a talk with him," and she strolled out in the direction of the sycamore tree.

She picked two flowers along the way and knelt at the foot of his grave next to Buster. *You were the best dog ever, old boy. I love you too.* She placed one flower on him and the other on Lars.

After all these years, I still miss you as much as I did the day you died. I still love you with all my heart. You know what it's like to be lonely. You were lonely when we met. I was too, but didn't realize it until I met you and you stole my heart. You scared the hell out of me at first, but it didn't take long to realize that you were just trying to protect your property.

Your best friend wants me to have sex with him. Reggie has made that quite clear to me. But I love Emily too. I would never hurt her. What would you think if I had sex with Reggie? I miss you so much, but I can feel the hormones stirring when Reggie is around. At the same time, I can't do anything that would hurt you and your memory. Help me, Lars!

Eileen got up and picked a few more flowers which were more plentiful near the woods to place on Lars' grave. She placed more on Buster's grave as well. *I miss you too, Buster.* She knelt down and sat there a few minutes staring at Lars' headstone.

"I've got to go, my love," Eileen said as she got up. "Sleep well." And she headed back to the house, tears streaming down her cheeks.

Eileen didn't sleep a wink that night. She kept tossing and turning, with hormones dragging her toward Reggie and her memory of Lars tearing her in the opposite direction.

Eileen got up early and had coffee ready in no time. While she worked in the kitchen, she decided it was time to have a talk with Emily. She heard James and Melissa stirring and began breakfast.

"I'm going to see Reggie and Emily," she announced when James and Melissa came in.

"And I'm going to the Wimberleys'," Ronnie said.

"Kira or Charlotte?" Melissa asked, smiling.

"Brooke," he blurted out without thinking and blushed. "Kira is too immature. Charlotte seems to think she's the smartest person on the planet. Everything has to be her way. Yes, Brooke I like."

After breakfast, Eileen headed over to the Carston's and Ronnie was out the back door, almost without giving Eileen her morning bear hug, a tradition he had kept up religiously over the years. "You remind me so much of your grandpa," she told Ronnie. "Thank you for keeping up the morning ritual. It means a lot to me."

Ronnie gave her another quick hug, but then was out the door in a flash.

Eileen strapped her pistol on her hip and kissed James and Melissa. "I'll be back before dark," she promised them.

Eileen took her time, taking nearly an hour and a half to walk over to Reggie and Emily's. She had no idea what she was going to say when she got there. She couldn't decide whether she should talk to them together, or just Emily. She wished she had brought a jar of beets. *Dammit Reggie, look what you have gotten me into!*

When she reached the edge of their meadow, she gave out a long wolf howl. When Reggie stepped out onto the porch, she gave another howl and headed on toward the house.

"To what do we owe the honor of your visit?" Reggie asked as he started to give her a hug, but Eileen pushed him away remembering his butt pinch on their last encounter.

"Just lucky, I guess," she replied.

"Well, come on in."

Emily was just getting started on breakfast. "How about a cup of coffee?" she asked.

"Yes, I'll take a cup."

"And how about some breakfast?" Reggie asked.

"No, thank you, I had an early breakfast," she replied. "Just coffee will do."

"It's good to see you, Eileen," Emily said.

"I wish I'd have brought you a jar of pickled beets, but I left before I thought about them."

"I think I still have a jar left from the batch I made. I'm going to have to watch you make them next time you whip up a batch. Mine never seem to taste quite like yours."

"Mine are made with Lars's love," Eileen said with a smile, "not just my love of him, but his love of you. Making the beets for you gave him a lot of pleasure."

Emily then noticed the tear trickle down her cheek. "You okay?"

"I'm fine," she said, then she looked over at Reggie. "Don't you have something you need to do outside?"

"No."

"Yes, you do," Emily said in a deeper voice and glaring at him.

"Of course I do." He got up and headed for his bunker.

"I'll call you when breakfast is ready," she added.

Reggie grumbled all the way out the door.

"Now, what's up?" Emily inquired, giving Eileen her undivided attention.

"It's a long story. And I don't know exactly how to tell you."

Emily poured more coffee and sat down directly across from Eileen at the kitchen table. "We're best friends. You can talk to me about anything."

"I know, but this is difficult," Eileen said.

They just stared at each other for a few minutes. Emily did not want to make Eileen uncomfortable by being forceful.

"I may as well just come out and tell you," Eileen finally said. "I know you and Reggie haven't been getting along as well in bed as maybe he'd like. And Reggie has been making advances toward me to have sex with him."

Eileen waited for Emily's reaction. It wasn't quite what she expected.

"I still love Reggie with all my heart, but . . ." She paused and a tear ran down her cheek. "I haven't been interested in having sex with Reggie for a long time."

She paused again.

"I figured it was just hormones, or lack thereof. I thought something might have been going on between you two, but I didn't know for certain."

Eileen was dumbfounded by how calm Emily seemed. She reached out and took Emily's hand and gave it a squeeze.

Emily looked down at their hands then back up at Eileen. "I have often thought that I'd much rather have sex with you than Reggie."

Eileen's mouth dropped open. She had no words.

"I love you as a friend, more than you can know, Eileen, but I have thought about what it might be like to be with you. I would have never said anything. You and Lars . . ."

Eileen got up and walked around the table to Emily. "I miss Lars so much, and I still love him with all my heart, but I don't think I'm ready to give up sex for the rest of my life."

Emily got up and embraced Eileen, and the tears began to flow.

Eileen gave Emily a little kiss on the lips. Emily squeezed her back and gave Eileen a long, wet kiss and they stood there locked in a tight embrace and savored each other's rekindled passion.

After a few minutes, they sat back down across from each other and held hands. Both just stared at each other for a while, tears streaming down their cheeks.

"I don't think Lars would want you to live out the rest of your life without love and passion," Emily finally said.

Eileen was relieved about what Emily said, but she still couldn't find words to say to her. Eileen always had the right words, but for once in her life was speechless. She felt as if her eyes were bulging and that Emily would say something, but she was apparently lost for words too.

"Shocked?" Emily finally asked.

"More than shocked," Eileen answered, "but also relieved."

Emily smiled and cocked her head. "Well?"

"I don't know; this is so sudden," Eileen replied. "What about Reggie?"

"Can you see yourself being sexual with Reggie?" Emily asked.

"I don't know," Eileen replied. "I know he wouldn't have a problem with me, but I'm not certain how..."

"You could think of me while he's doing you, or you could think of Lars."

"I think I'd rather think of you," Eileen answered. "If I think of Lars, I'd probably break down and screw it up for all of us."

"More coffee?" Emily asked.

"Do you have something a little stronger?"

"Before breakfast?"

"I've already had breakfast," Eileen reminded Emily with a laugh.

Emily went to the pantry and got a bottle of their best wine and a pair of wine glasses.

A short while later, Reggie came in. "What happened to calling me in for breakfast?" Then he noticed the wine. "What the hell?"

"The ham is ready. Cold, but ready. You'll have to fix your own eggs, if that's what you want. We're busy here." Emily chuckled.

Reggie frowned and went to the stove. "Something I should know about?"

"You'll find out soon enough," Emily replied.

Chapter 10

Back in Corpus Christi . . .

Florence Ingalls was washing dishes when she heard a loud car horn. She stepped to the door and peered out. Her best friend crawled out of the driver's seat and headed to the house. Florence met her halfway.

"Well, Beka Livingston! What do we have here?"

"My new car!"

"Where did that come from?"

"Mom got it for me yesterday. Yay, no more bicycle! It's not new, but it's new to me," she said, giggling.

"How in the world did you rate that?"

"I've been nagging mom for months. I overheard her talking to a neighbor one day. He repaired cars for the Police and fixed up the car for his wife for a birthday present, but then she didn't want it. She said she didn't have anywhere to go. Mom finally gave in. And I get a couple tanks of gas a month."

She couldn't tell her Sandra helped out a lot too. That she's been spying on her dad for Sandra ever since Marcia told her she was sneaking down to the Bay front to see her boyfriend, Charles. *I wish I knew why Charles is so important to Sandra. Why won't she tell me?"*

"Wow! Can we go for a spin?"

"Of course."

Florence turned to her mother standing in the doorway. "Mom, can I go for a ride with Beka? Please!"

"Okay. Don't be long."

Giggling, the girls hopped in the car.

"Where shall we go?" Beka asked.

"How about the Bayfront?"

"My thought, exactly."

"What color is this thing anyway? Chartreuse?"

"It's pea green for your information, but I wouldn't care if it was dog shit brown! A car is a car."

"Good point!"

The girls were always happy when they were together. But now, Beka was ecstatic to have her car. Florence was happy to just be out of the house. They caught up on each other's lives, laughed and giggled all the way to the Bayfront.

Beka drove along the seawall and out to one of the T-heads where the boats were parked. They stopped and got out.

"I just love the smell of the sea," Beka said as she took a deep breath.

"Yuk! It smells like dead fish," Florence remarked.

Beka walked over to one of the boats, a sailboat named *Moneypit.* "Ahoy!"

Shortly, a head appeared out of the doorway to below deck. "Ahoy right back at you, Beka."

"Permission to come aboard, sir?"

"Absolutely."

Charles climbed the steps to greet the girls. His blonde sun-bleached hair glistened in the sunlight. He wasn't wearing a shirt and his well-tanned muscles rippled as he moved. Florence smiled at his six-pack.

"Florence, this is Charles Masters. Charles, this is Florence Ingalls."

"Hi Charles. Nice to meet you."

"Likewise, I'm sure."

As Beka climbed onto the boat, Florence noticed a young man on a neighboring boat staring at her. She was certain she had never seen the man before, but somehow he looked familiar. Florence stared back, and finally he looked away and continued his work cleaning on the shrimp boat.

"I'll be right back," Florence said.

She strolled over to the shrimp boat and again the young man looked up. She was certain she knew him, but at the same time, she knew she had never before laid eyes on him. Then, something clicked in her brain.

"Is your name Sean?"

"Yes, it is. How did you know my name?"

"Your friend Robbie described you perfectly."

"Robbie? You know Robbie?"

"Yes. Well, sort of. My daddy brought him home a few weeks ago sick and hurt. I helped nurse him back to health."

"Is he okay?"

"Yes, he's fine."

"Where is he?"

"He's working at the Farm. He asked to give you a message if I saw you. Just that he's okay and he's working on a plan to get the two of you out of here."

"I don't think that's possible," Sean remarked.

"I don't either, but Robbie seems optimistic. I told him to do as he's told and he'll live a while."

"That seems to be the rule around here," Sean acknowledged with a sour look on his face.

"Tell Robbie I'm all right and I'm at the Bayfront, okay?"

"Will do."

Florence meandered back over to the sailboat where Beka and Charles were.

Charles helped Florence onto the boat and handed her a soda.

The girls sat and listened to a tall tale about Charles' encounter with pirates as they sipped their drinks. If he hadn't had the fastest boat in the south, he would surely have died. Charles did most of the talking and Beka giggled with every word. It wasn't long before Beka got bored with his stories and decided it was time to go. She kissed Charles and he helped the ladies onto the dock.

"See you next week," Beka said.

Charles winked, first to Beka and then at Florence. Florence could see his affection towards Beka, but the wink to her seemed more like a keep-your-mouth-shut sign.

"Nice wheels, by the way," Charles yelled as the ladies crawled into the green pea.

On the drive back, Beka had a lot of explaining to do, as did Florence.

"I met Charles last year before Daddy died, when he was working on one of the engines on a shrimp boat somewhere around here. Isn't he dreamy?" She rolled her eyes.

"Isn't he a neut?"

"Yes, but that doesn't mean he can't have sex. It only means he can't have babies. That's perfect for me. I don't want to have babies anyway. Now your turn. What's with that guy you were talking to?"

"He and his best friend, Robbie, showed up a few weeks ago. Robbie was injured and sick. I nursed him back to health and he was asking about Sean. Until today, I didn't have a clue about who Sean was or what had happened to him. I just knew this guy fit Robbie's description perfectly. I had to ask."

"Now, what about this Robbie?"

"He's gone now. Daddy took him off to the Farm to work."

Beka could see Florence's eyes light up at the mention of Robbie, but her words seemed sad.

"But you've fallen for him."

"What?"

"Don't try to hide anything from me, Florence. I've known you too long."

Florence looked out the window for a minute. *Damn!* She didn't want to talk about Robbie because he was gone now. But she did want to talk about him.

"Florence . . . I'm waiting!"

Florence turned her gaze back to Beka. Beka could see a trickle of tears down her cheek.

"You've really fallen for this guy, haven't you?"

Florence could not deny the truth in Beka's words. "I couldn't help myself. He was so helpless. I . . . I . . ."

"You got it bad, girl! What are you going to do?"

"I don't know."

"Let me know if I can help, Flo."

"You'd help?"

"What are best friends for? Just let me know what you need and it's yours. Is he a neut?"

"No."

"You certain?"

"Absolutely!"

"How can you be so sure?"

"I gave him a sponge bath."

Beka giggled.

"I have to get after the dishes," Florence exclaimed as Beka steered the car up to the front of the house. "I've got to make sure I don't get on anyone's bad side and lose my liberties, or even worse, give Daddy an excuse to take his frustrations out on me. Come see me soon, will ya, Beka?"

As Beka drove away, Florence ran to the house and headed to the kitchen. Her mother had already finished up all the work in there. She found her mom in a bedroom.

"Mom, I said I would finish up in the kitchen."

"I know, but your dad will be home soon and it had to be clean."

"I'm sorry we took so long. I'll fix dinner, okay?"

"I was just about to suggest that. Knock yourself out."

Florence headed to the kitchen and began to work on the best dinner she could make. *I have to keep everyone happy around here if I'm going to get to see Robbie again.*

Sonny climbed out of the hole of the boat where he was changing the oil and filters. "I couldn't help overhearing your conversation with that girl."

"And?" Sean said, not sure where this conversation was going.

"I'm happy your friend is okay."

"Thanks."

"Don't count on you two ever seeing each other again, okay?"

"And why is that?"

"They won't let you guys get back together. They'll think you two will try to escape," Sonny declared.

"And they'd be right."

"Don't even hint that you want to leave around Marcia," Sonny added.

"And why not?"

"She'll report it back to Sandra. Sandra won't be pleased, and no telling what might happen to you then."

Sean sat dejected, staring at Sonny for a minute.

"And what's back home for you anyway?" Sonny inquired.

"My mom and dad. Other than that, not much." He hadn't thought about it, but that is all there is back there. There were no women, as if he had that need anymore. Mom, dad and a life of hard work to survive was all he could come up with. "What's your point, Sonny?"

"I'm just saying, you have really caught onto this shrimping business. You learn real fast and you seem to like the water. Maybe there is a life for you here after all."

"I'll have to think on it a bit."

Not another word was said. Sean put his hands over his face and massaged his temples trying to force some answers to the surface.

At the end of his first week working at the Airport, Robbie was receiving good marks from Russ. He did exactly what he was told, but his mind was constantly on something else—freedom!

After they had finished breakfast and were standing outside Russ' office ready to go to work, Russ made an *X* across Friday on the calendar in the hangar. He put his marker away and looked toward the doorway when Sandra Hawkins pulled up in her Jeep. She got out and walked over to where the two of them were standing.

"He ready to go?" she said, looking first at Russ then at Robbie.

Robbie stood there perplexed.

"I hadn't told him," Russ replied.

"All righty then, I'll explain on the way to the Farm. Get into the Jeep, sweetie" she said to Robbie, who had a puzzled look on his face.

Robbie slowly walked toward the Jeep and overheard Sandra tell Russ she would see him tomorrow. Sandra followed Robbie and told him to get in. Sandra got in behind the steering wheel, cranked up the engine, and went through the gears as she crossed the tarmac headed toward the northeast.

Sandra glanced over at Robbie, who still had a puzzled look on his face. "Don't look so concerned," she said, smiling. "You're going to have more fun than you've probably had your whole life."

Robbie's face changed from a look of puzzlement to a frown. He didn't know what to say so he kept his mouth shut.

After a few minutes, Sandra began to explain what was going to happen. "Every Saturday you will come to the Farm." She paused for a second and looked back over to Robbie. "My you're damn handsome, kid. I look forward to getting to know you better."

Robbie's frown deepened.

"Like I was saying, every Saturday you'll come to the Farm. Lunch will be prepared by a couple of my ladies, followed by plenty of time to relax and get to know them better. Later, an early dinner will be prepared. The dinner will be a private affair with only me, you, and one of the ladies. After dinner, just you and the lady will relax in her room. When she is ready, you will plant your seeds in her. You know what I'm saying?"

"I think so, ma'am."

Sandra paused again. "You've never made love to a woman, have you?"

Robbie paused and swallowed hard. "No, ma'am."

"Well, that's going to change tonight, only tonight it will be just you and me. I've got to make certain you are worthy of my ladies." Sandra looked over at Robbie and smiled. Robbie swallowed hard again.

The Jeep pulled up in front of the farmhouse and Sandra climbed out. She went around the vehicle to where the hesitant Robbie still sat, trying to comprehend the situation. Sandra opened the door for Robbie and he got out. Sandra then escorted him inside the empty house.

"Just relax and make yourself at home. Something to drink?"

"No, I'm fine," Robbie assured her.

"Suit yourself. Okay, let's go outside. I'll show you around the Farm. You didn't see much outside the barns when you were here before."

Sandra led Robbie through the kitchen and out the back door. There was a nice porch with numerous potted plants as well as bougainvillea and Pride of Barbados, which Sandra explained were her pride and joy. She then led him out to the row crops. As far as he could see, there was stuff growing. Some of the rows were barren, and Sandra explained they had already harvested a few of the crops. Others will be harvested soon. She pointed out the peanuts, cotton, milo, and soy beans, and then they walked over to row after row of strawberries. She reached down and picked a couple and handed them to Robbie. She grabbed a couple for herself and they walked back toward the house.

"I can see that look on your face," she told him. "I can be the nicest gal in the world, but you cross me and I'll cut your balls off in a heartbeat." They walked inside in silence.

When they got back inside, Robbie noticed there were a couple ladies in the kitchen. They'd prepared hors d'oeuvres and iced tea, no doubt at Sandra's earlier request.

Robbie and Sandra went into the living room area and the ladies served the treats and tea. They also turned on some soft music and left the room.

Sandra ushered Robbie to the sofa where she sat close to him. "Just go with the flow, Robbie. I'll be really gentle with you tonight."

Robbie had been virtually speechless since he first learned of Sandra's plans for him. Finally, he had to ask some questions. The only question he could think of so far was "why?"

Sandra turned toward Robbie and took his hand. "Men built the world as we knew it before the grid shut down, and men destroyed it. Richard Ingalls was my husband when the government and society collapsed. With him, we took over what was left of Corpus Christi and vowed to create a better world, at least for ourselves. We made the tough choices no one would make before. Slowly but surely, we created what we have now.

"What Richard didn't know at the time was that I had a different plan. When I gained control, I divorced Richard. Men would never again be allowed to rule, at least in our little part of the world. Most men are castrated—the police force, the few here at the Farm, the fishermen, and the mechanics. Richard is fertile, however, but that helps keep him in line. He now has another wife, Louise, and his own kid, Florence, both of whom you already know, but he also has many of the women here. He has his cake and can eat it too, so to speak. He knows that if he crosses me, he will be castrated just like the rest. Don't repeat what I'm telling you, or he will kill you before you can bat an eye."

Robbie listened and took a sip of tea from time to time, but he remained speechless. He couldn't believe what he was hearing.

Sandra continued. "We have no homeless. We have no lazy people. We have zero population growth." Sandra paused to take a couple of the hors d'oeuvres and a sip of tea. "We have all the food we need, and we have a near zero crime rate. Corpus Christi is a stable city, and if someone is unhappy, they are at least content and not willing to rock the boat. I aim to keep it that way."

Finally, Sandra turned away from Robbie, let go of his hand, and leaned back on the sofa. Robbie sighed and did the same. Sandra smiled at him. He returned a half-smile. That was all he could muster. Sandra got up and told Robbie to relax. "I'll be back in a while."

Robbie nibbled on the hors d'oeuvres. *It may be your perfect world, Sandra, but everyone is a prisoner. Does everyone like being held captive? I know I certainly don't. The food is good, but I feel like a pet—love and attention, but still the cage. I have to get out of here. Can I?*

Sandra's absence turned out to be quite a while. Robbie dozed off and was startled when Sandra touched him on the shoulder. "Good boy. You'll be well rested and ready for tonight. Need anything?"

"A restroom," Robbie replied.

Sandra motioned toward the hallway. "Second door on your right."

Robbie found the restroom and closed the door behind him. *I just thought I was in deep shit before. What have I gotten myself into? Can I get out of this?* He had no clue how he was going to avoid sleeping with Sandra, but he knew he had to play along. *If I don't perform for Sandra, she may cut my balls off. She seems nice, not the ruthless bitch others claim her to be, but she may be good on her word.*

Robbie finished up in the bathroom and then joined Sandra in the living room.

"Ready for dinner?" she asked.

"Yes."

Robbie hadn't noticed the aroma before, but now the pleasant scents seemed to fill the room. She led him through the kitchen to the dining room and offered him a seat at the opposite end of the table.

The good china and silver service were in place and as soon as he was seated, the ladies began to serve. The salad was a mix of spinach and lettuce adorned with pecans, radish slivers, slices of boiled eggs, carrot sticks, grated cheese and topped with a tangy dressing. When the salads were finished, the ladies served baked chicken with potatoes and gravy. *How does she know what I like?*

Wine and water accompanied the meal. Robbie had never had wine but enjoyed it immensely. The meal was finished off with cake and ice cream. *Probably why she's so fat,* Robbie surmised. *Certainly better keep my mouth shut about that. She'll definitely cut my balls off—and with a dull butcher knife.*

As the ladies cleared the table, Sandra got up and indicated to Robbie it was time to go to her room. She followed him down the long hallway admiring his tight butt. Robbie stopped at the end of the hallway, and she grabbed his buttocks and squeezed. Robbie jumped a bit and Sandra directed him left down another hallway.

"Second door on the left," Sandra said. "Take a shower and get into the robe. I'll take a shower in the master bath and be in the room across the hallway when you get finished." She indicated each doorway with her hand so there would be no confusion.

Robbie turned the water on in the shower and began to undress. He then stepped in and adjusted the water temperature. As he lathered up, he began to think about what was about to happen across the hallway. It appeared there was no way he could get out of having sex with Sandra without getting neutered. *If she were only Florence. I wouldn't have a problem having sex with her. I can keep my eyes closed and imagine I'm having sex with Florence. That's it; I'll pretend Sandra is Florence.*

Robbie rinsed, grabbed a towel, and dried off. He slipped the robe on and looked into the mirror. He couldn't look more than a second. Then he shook his head in disgust for being placed into this awkward position.

Robbie pushed the door open into Sandra's bedroom. She was sitting on the side of the bed wearing a skimpy, red lace outfit. She stood as Robbie walked in.

Sandra smiled and Robbie couldn't help himself—he smiled back. As Sandra walked over, Robbie's eyes fixated on her breasts. *Damn! They're huge!*

"You like?" Sandra asked.

Robbie blushed and looked away. He couldn't help but smile again, but he didn't have the words to reply.

"Come on over to the bed."

Sandra sat down on the edge and pulled Robbie close. "I'll be gentle," she said and pulled his robe open.

As soon as she touched him, though it was only his chest, Robbie could feel his body tingle and his manhood began to respond.

Sandra pulled at her outfit, and it sprang away from her breasts. "I'm yours," she whispered. "Enjoy yourself."

He reached for one of her breasts. It was more than a handful. She leaned over and kissed his nipples. They responded just as hers had when Robbie touched her. Robbie closed his eyes. *Florence! Florence!*

Chapter 11

Robbie awoke to the chirps of a mockingbird outside his window. He rubbed his eyes and looked around. He was in Sandra's bed, but she was gone. He got up and all he could find to put on was the robe he'd had on last night. He walked across the hall and his clothes were no longer where he had left them in the bathroom. *What do I do now?*

He walked to the doorway and saw Sandra coming down the hallway. She had his clothes. They were freshly laundered and neatly folded. "Put these on and meet me in the kitchen," she instructed. Her voice was back to its normal stern tone.

Robbie went into the bathroom, peed, and got dressed.

Sandra was sitting at the kitchen table. *Much more informal today. Is she disappointed with me?*

"Have a seat," she said.

Robbie took a chair directly across from Sandra as she directed. For the first time this morning, he looked into her eyes. She smiled and finally he felt a little relief. *Maybe she's not upset with me after all.*

"Bacon, eggs, and fruit okay with you?" Sandra asked with an even bigger smile.

"That sounds good," he said taking a whiff of the aroma.

"You about done over there, Margaret?" Sandra inquired.

"Two minutes," was the reply and then she brought over two cups of coffee. "This will get you started," she added.

When they finished their breakfast, Sandra asked Robbie to join her in the living room. He followed and took a seat as directed next to her.

"I'll take you back to the Airport when we finish our talk." Sandra turned to him so she could look directly into his eyes. "I'm pleased with your performance last night. Much better than I expected."

Robbie let out a sigh of relief.

Then she said something which was quite unexpected. "Who is Florence?"

Instantly he knew he was in trouble.

"Well?" she asked again.

If I lie to her, I may get myself into more trouble. I better tell her the truth. "Florence Ingalls," he replied, almost choking on the words.

Sandra was quiet for a while and stared intently into Robbie's eyes. Robbie could feel the beads of sweat forming on his forehead. "It doesn't matter," she said. She paused for a second. "You did good, Robbie. Don't ever lie to me."

"Yes, ma'am."

"All right, let's get you back to the Airport."

They made the trip back to the Airport in complete silence. Robbie didn't dare say anything for fear she would bring up the subject of Florence again. Sandra didn't seem to have any more to say about the subject.

Sandra pulled the Jeep to a stop and Robbie opened the door and got out.

"Robbie?"

"Yes, ma'am?"

"I'll see you next Saturday." Then she winked and gave him a wicked little smile.

"Yes, ma'am." Robbie closed the door and she drove away.

Jorge Guzman met Robbie at the hangar door. "Guess you made a place for yourself in Sandra's ranks?"

"Why do you say that?" Robbie asked.

"Otherwise, Sandra would have stayed and had a talk with Russ." Jorge smirked. "Okay, we have work to do. Get into your coveralls."

Jorge and Robbie spent the remainder of the day working on a Cessna Skyhawk. The plane looked brand-new. "Jorge, how did you get a new plane?"

"It's not new. There have been no planes made for decades."

"But it looks new."

"That's because I take very good care of her," Jorge replied.

"Her?"

"Yes, this is my favorite among all the planes. I named her Betty."

"And why is it your favorite?"

"It's a well-built plane. It was used as a trainer back in the days. It's easy to fly, easy to land, and is comfortable," Jorge said with a smile.

"How often do you crank her up and run her?"

"Never," Jorge replied. "Our job is to maintain the planes and no more. The only one we crank up is that old C-23 Sherpa over there. One of the pilots flies it down to Brownsville twice a month."

"What for?"

"Trade," Jorge replied. "They have stuff we need, and we trade them food for a variety of things. Some of the city survived when the grid shut down, and they need things we produce just like we need some of the stuff they produce and bring up from farther down in Mexico."

"Back to the planes," Robbie said. "If someone tries to fly one, they'll likely crash."

"Why is that?"

"Because the key component of the plane, the engine, is never tested. Everyone knows that the worst thing for a vehicle is to not use it, right? It's not enough for it to look pretty. The C-23 runs good, right?"

"Yeah." Jorge scratched his head and gave Robbie a twisted look, not understanding what Robbie was getting at.

"Russ said you were his best mechanic. You've got to know everything about planes and engines."

"Have you seen any other mechanics around here?" was Jorge's reply.

Robbie looked about the hangar. He hadn't thought of it, but there only seemed to be one mechanic around. "You mean you're it?"

"Yep." He paused a second. "I've only been the mechanic for a year," he added.

"Really!" Robbie was surprised. "You seem so confident."

"Oh, I've tinkered with engines most of my life, and I've read a few manuals, but I'm no expert. I guess I had more experience than anyone when they needed a new mechanic last year. I heard the one they had died. I couldn't get anything out of Russ about what really happened. I'm sorry to disappoint you."

Robbie looked over and smiled. "No disappointment . . . just surprised."

Jorge stood and stared at Robbie.

"Well, how about we crank this baby up and take her—excuse me, Betty—out for a spin tomorrow?"

"I don't know," Jorge replied with a nervous look on his face. "I'll have to check with Russ first. And Sandra and Richard must also be notified and approve of the change."

"Well, let's ask Russ."

"Russ left right after Sandra left. You didn't see him?"

"No."

"He told me this morning he had some business with one of the contractors and that he wouldn't be back until in the morning. We'll ask him then."

"Works for me," Robbie said.

"Let's call it a day, Robbie. Get a shower and some sleep. We'll talk to Russ first thing in the morning."

"Good night, Jorge. I'll see you at first light."

Robbie got out of his coveralls and into the shower. He stood under the shower head and let the warm water hit the back of his head and run down his back. He closed his eyes and thought about Betty.

Robbie was tired but he couldn't get to sleep. His mind was churning with thoughts and questions. *Betty could be my way out of here. Can I fly? I've read about it. Jorge said she was easy to fly. With a little practice scooting around on the tarmac I think I can get the hang of it. I know the basics, the flaps and speed. What else is there to know?*

Russ, Sandra, and Richard would never let me take the plane out . . . unless they think I'm afraid to fly. I can tell them I'm afraid of heights. This just may work! Then his thoughts turned to Sean. He knew he couldn't return home without him.

And what about Florence? She got me through a night with Sandra. Could there be something there? I think I could really get to like her . . . a lot!

The next thing he knew, his alarm was buzzing. Robbie's eyes popped open and he slapped at the clock. He wanted to get up, but he felt so tired, even after a night's sleep.

Ten minutes later, Robbie was in the hanger near the front of Russ' office. He didn't want to seem over anxious, but he was. *Calm down. I have to be cool and convince Russ this is the logical thing to do.*

Shortly, Jorge came out and a few minutes later, Russ drove up. Jorge and Robbie were waiting at the door to his office when Russ walked up. They asked to have a meeting. Russ led them inside.

Thirty minutes later Robbie walked out of the office doing his best to control his emotions. But he couldn't contain the smile on his face. Sandra and Richard would be called over for a meeting tomorrow.

"Where is the manual on the Cessna?" Robbie asked Jorge.

"What for?"

"If I'm going to help you maintain these things, I may as well try to learn as much as I can about them. Since you like Betty so much, I thought I'd start with her."

"Look over there," Jorge said pointing to a cabinet next to the workbench.

Robbie opened the door and there was one stack of papers. He pulled them out onto the workbench and began looking through them. There were no manuals on the planes, but he found one sales brochure with Cessna Skyhawk across the top and a photo of the plane underneath and another on the Piper Cub. Some of the pages were torn out, so there wasn't much information. These were the only two on the planes. He set these aside. There were a couple *Playboy* magazines, one of which he added to the airplane brochures. Some papers on vending machines and old records on the jets contained no useful information about the jets; just old maintenance records. He stacked the papers he didn't need back into the cabinet and took the two brochures and the *Playboy* into his room.

He pulled out the *Playboy* first and looked through a few pages. When he found the centerfold, he opened the page and held it out at arm's length. He couldn't help but smile. *Damn! I don't have time for this!* He stuck the magazine under his pillow and grabbed the booklet on the Cessna and walked back into the hangar. He crawled into Betty and opened the booklet. The only thing he found useful was the photo of the dashboard with most of the gauges, knobs and levers labeled. There were some old grease smudges and many items were not readable, but the booklet was still helpful. *Payload . . . where is the payload? It's not here.* Then he noticed some papers between the seats. A preflight checklist. Helpful, but nothing about the payload.

Richard and Sandra showed up at noon. Russ, Jorge and Robbie were talking in Russ' office when Sandra opened the door and she and Richard walked in.

"What's going on, Russ?" Sandra asked.

Russ pointed toward Robbie.

Robbie asked Sandra and Richard to have a seat where he could face the entire group. Then he began. "A plane which just sits idle deteriorates much faster than a plane which is used regularly. The only motor that still runs back home is my grandpa's tractor. That is because it is used in the garden throughout the year. Everything else has cratered due to lack of use. The Cessna Skyhawk and the Piper Cub are cleaned and lubricated, but the main component, the engine, remains unused. All I'm saying is they need to be started up and taxied around on the tarmac a couple times a month."

Everyone listened attentively to Robbie's spiel without interruption. When he finished, there was only one objection. "What's to keep you from flying away?" Richard asked.

"I'm deathly afraid of heights," Robbie answered. "If I get more than a few feet off the ground, I get nauseous. I've tried to fight it, but I've passed out and gotten hurt several times working on roofs back home. I don't know what it is, but I've never been able to overcome it. If I try to fly a plane, I'll crash and most likely die."

Robbie was calm and cool. He never cracked a smile. He was dead serious and everyone felt it. No one moved. No one said a word. They all just sat and stared at Robbie for several minutes. He could tell they were giving his proposition serious consideration.

Sandra was the first to speak. "Okay, I'm convinced. If it's better for the planes, I think that's what we should do."

Richard, the perpetual pessimist was not totally convinced but agreed to go along with Sandra. "But I'll hold you personally responsible, Sandra."

"I'm good with that."

Russ was in no position to disagree with Richard or Sandra. Jorge never had a say in the matter.

Richard left and made his security rounds. He checked in with all the police sergeants and, satisfied there were no breaches, headed home.

As soon as Richard walked in the door, Louise knew he was in a bad mood. "Where the hell is dinner?"

"Dinner will be ready in an hour," his wife replied, "at the usual time." She poured a glass of tea and handed it to him. "What's got you in such a mood?"

Richard didn't say anything. He walked over to the kitchen table, pulled out a chair, and sat down. He chugged the tea and handed the glass to Louise.

"Another?"

"Yeah."

She refilled the glass and set it on the table beside him.

"I should have killed that boy when I had the chance . . . and his friend too."

"Robbie?"

"He's working at the Airport, and it looks like Sandra has taken him under her wing."

"So what's the problem?"

"I don't know. I can just feel it in my gut. That boy's going to be a problem."

Richard heard a noise, got up, and stepped over to the hallway. "Florence!"

Florence quickly ducked back into the bathroom, stuck a toothbrush in her mouth, and peeked out of the door toward the kitchen. "Yes, Daddy?"

"What are you doing?"

"Just brushing my teeth. I didn't know you were home, Daddy," she said with a straight face.

Richard turned around and walked back over to the table, picked up his tea and walked out the door. "Call me when dinner is ready," he said as the door slammed shut.

Florence took the toothbrush out of her mouth. She looked into the mirror. The corners of her lips curled up into a smile.

Robbie was up bright and early the next morning as was Jorge. Jorge moved the wagon used to tow the C-23, from in front of the Cessna and parked it to the side. They then pushed the Cessna to the hangar doors. Jorge hit a button on the wall, and the hangar doors began to open. Jorge helped Robbie roll the fuel cart over to fill the tank on the Cessna. They checked all the fluids and then climbed in.

"You take the pilot's seat," Jorge said.

"Really?" Robbie asked with a big smile.

"Sure, why not?" Jorge replied. "I couldn't live with myself if I hurt the old girl. I can kick your ass if you damage her."

Robbie grinned at Jorge. Jorge shot him a serious look. "Just be careful."

Robbie grabbed the preflight list and went through the items with Jorge. Robbie looked over all the knobs, levers, and gauges. Jorge pointed out Betty's main features and gave Robbie a quick course in the operation of the plane.

When Robbie asked about something Jorge didn't know, he would say, "You'll find out soon enough;" or "That's not important right now;" or "You'll remember better if you figure it out for yourself." Robbie knew he wasn't a bona fide airplane mechanic. Was he now going to find out Jorge didn't know squat about flying Betty?

The past year, Jorge had polished, greased, and lubricated every plane in the hangar. He assumed all that had to be done is to put fuel in the planes, crank them up, and they would fly. Whether or not this would be the case should one of the planes be needed to fly, Jorge was clueless.

"Turn that," Jorge said pointing his finger. "Now pull that. Push this." Suddenly, Betty roared to life. "Just like driving a car."

Russ walked to his office door and watched. Robbie glanced over toward him and waved with a big grin on his face, but the sour look of uncertainty on Russ's face dampened his mood.

Robbie turned his attention back to Betty. He eased the throttle up and Betty began to creep forward. Robbie gave her more throttle, and they were soon out of the hangar and up to walking speed. A little more throttle and they were moving along nicely. Robbie steered the plane across the tarmac and onto the taxiway. He and Jorge began checking all the gauges. Everything seemed to be normal.

Robbie weaved the plane back and forth a few times, then began checking to see what all the other controls did. One by one, he checked everything he could find. *It's going to take a while to remember all this stuff.*

When they reached the main runway, Robbie gave the plane more throttle. When the indicator read forty miles per hour it got a little scary, and Robbie slowed the plane back to twenty miles per hour. He looked at Jorge and smiled.

Richard relaxed a bit when he saw the plane slowing. When they made the turn back onto the taxiway, he put his AR-15 back into his truck. Richard sat tight until the plane rolled into the hangar. He got into his truck, cranked it up, and drove out of the brush at the end of the runway and onto the access road.

When Robbie killed the engine, Jorge hopped out and closed the hangar doors. Robbie sniffed the air. He detected a slight odor, but he couldn't see anything wrong. He decided it was some of the 'new' burning off the long-idle engine, got out and patted the side of the plane. "Good girl."

When he walked around to the front of Betty, he noticed a few drops of liquid on the floor underneath the plane. He reached down, touched the spots, and smelled his finger. *Smells like oil.* Then he ran his hand along the cowling and found more liquid. He grabbed a wrench and Jorge walked up.

"What's the matter?" Jorge inquired.

"Seems we have a leak."

Inside the engine compartment they found more oil. Jorge touched the liquid and put it up to his nose. "This is hydraulic fluid."

They traced the liquid to the hydraulic pump. "Looks like one of the seals is going out," Robbie said.

"Yep. You're pretty smart for a kid," Jorge joked.

Robbie smiled. "Stuff like this happens when the engine sits idle for a long time. Remember what I said about my grandpa's old truck and my dad's motorcycle. If we'd have tried to fly this plane today, we would have surely crashed somewhere."

Jorge agreed. "I'll go inform Russ."

Chapter 12

Saturday rolled around and so did Sandra. She got out and stepped through the open side door. "Hello!"

Robbie and Jorge emerged from the C-23 Sherpa. "Guess I'll be working alone the rest of the day. Don't do anything I wouldn't do," Jorge said with a smirk.

Robbie started peeling out of his coveralls and hung them on a nail beside the workbench along the wall of the hangar. He joined Sandra and they got in her Jeep.

Unlike the trip to the hangar last week, Sandra was quite talkative on the way back to the Farm. She had all kinds of questions about their excursion with Betty out to the runway.

"The Cessna runs good," Robbie said. "There was a hydraulic leak, but we got that fixed. A bad O-ring. Most problems develop slowly. If the planes are used regularly, you can catch them early and avoid a disaster."

"Well, I'm glad you got that taken care of," she replied.

"I didn't expect to get queasy, but just the thought of the thing getting off the ground made me a little uneasy." That was a lie, but Sandra bought it.

She didn't say anything, but Robbie did notice a slight smile out of the corner of his eye. *I must make absolutely certain that she thinks I'd never try to fly the Skyhawk.*

With that, Sandra changed the subject. "I have several ladies I'd like you to meet. I was very pleased with your performance last weekend. As much as I would love to have another round with you, that is not why I want to keep you around."

Robbie was surprised but kept quiet as Sandra laid everything on the table. "You seem to come from good stock, and we need to keep the gene pool rich. We need healthy people to work hard and make our community strong for generations to come. I believe you will be a great asset toward that goal."

Robbie became nervous. *Who does she think I am, the local whore? Am I only good around here for my sperm? Sounds like a damn cattle ranch and I'm the prize bull!*

Robbie was at a loss for words. Sandra, on the other hand, was not. Then she brought up the last thing Robbie wanted to hear—Florence Ingalls.

"Would Florence be an incentive for you to decide to settle here permanently?"

She looked over but didn't say anything else.

"I owe Florence a lot. She took good care of me. We got to know each other very well, and she's pleasing to the eyes."

"Yeah, she's a good-looking gal. And from good stock too. I think you two would make a fine couple. I'll make a deal with you. I'll get you two together, and you can see if you like each other. You, on the other hand, must give of your gene pool to all the ladies I choose for one year. If, after that year, you and Florence want to make a family, I'll make it so."

"You know I'll need to think about it," Robbie said.

"Of course," Sandra replied. "I wouldn't believe you if you made a snap decision. I'll give you a couple weeks. Think that's enough time?"

"I think so."

"Now about my ladies," she said. "I just want you to get to know a few of them this weekend. You don't have to perform unless you want to."

Robbie's heart and spirit rose tremendously with that statement. Sandra looked over and smiled and Robbie managed a weak smile in return.

"The ladies should have a nice lunch ready," Sandra said as they pulled up in front of the farmhouse.

Feeling a little better now that he was not going to be forced to perform this weekend, Robbie's demeanor improved significantly and he got out of the Jeep as soon as it stopped and walked around to Sandra's side. He was not quick enough to open the door for her, as was his intention, but when she noticed what he was trying to do, she acknowledged his attempt.

Monday morning, Robbie and Jorge were hard at work on the C-23 Sherpa getting it ready for a trip to Brownsville. The plane was on the tarmac, fueled up and ready to go. A pilot came by and started the engines and did his check. By late afternoon everything they needed to do was finished. Tuesday, trucks delivered cargo throughout the day. Wednesday morning the plane was ready and the pilots showed up on schedule. Jorge, Russ, Hank, the pilot, and Mark, the copilot, were in the office going over last minute details of the shipment and the items to be picked up.

Robbie was sitting on a stack of pallets waiting for further instructions when he noticed a car he had not seen before coming up the access road. The car pulled up near the fuel tanker behind the plane and stopped. Two girls got out and headed over to Robbie.

"Florence!" Robbie exclaimed.

"Yeah," she replied with a big grin.

Robbie was taken aback how quickly she managed to find him. The thought had crossed his mind that he may never see her again. "How did you find me?"

"I overheard my daddy talking about your move to the Airport. Thanks to my best friend, Beka Livingston, and her new car," she said turning to Beka, "we can go places on our own."

"Nice to meet you, Beka. Nice car too!"

"Don't say a damn word about the color," Beka demanded.

Robbie frowned as he glanced over to Florence.

"Around here," Florence said, "a car is a car. She just got it last week. We couldn't go far on our bicycles, but now we're mobile."

"So, Florence and Beka, why are you here?"

"I saw Sean down at the Bayfront last week," Florence replied. "I recognized him from your description. He's working on a shrimp boat. We talked for a while and I told him I'd get a message to you."

"What's the message?"

"Just that he's okay. He was concerned about you."

"Cool." Robbie let out a sigh of relief. "That's great. I've been worried about him too. I wasn't certain he was still alive. I've got to see him. Let me think."

Could he get out of here one day? What would happen if he got caught? Maybe that wouldn't matter so much if he really got on Sandra's good side. Maybe another night with her? Robbie smiled. He turned his back to Florence and Beka and strolled a short distance away, stopped and turned back around. *Desperate times call for desperate measures. Sandra wasn't that bad. In fact, she's the best I've ever had. She's all I've ever had!* He definitely needed to think about this a little more. Robbie walked back over to where Florence and Beka were standing.

"Can you come back next week?"

"Maybe," Beka replied.

"I've got to have some time to think this over. I've got to see Sean."

Florence looked at Beka. "We'll see what we can do," Beka said.

"How are you doing, Robbie?" Florence asked.

"I feel good. Keeping busy." *I can't tell her about Sandra's proposition. I have to think about that too.*

"It's certainly good to see you, Florence."

"You too, Robbie," she replied affectionately.

"We better go, Florence," Beka stated and turned toward the green machine.

"Yeah," she acknowledged.

"Nice to meet you, Beka," Robbie said.

"You too," she said over her shoulder as she strolled toward the car.

"Thank you for finding me, Florence."

She gave him a peck on the cheek and turned to follow Beka.

"See you next week?" Robbie asked.

"I hope so," Beka and Florence replied in unison.

They climbed into the car and sped away.

Robbie walked back over and sat down on the pallets. He certainly had a lot to think about.

Jorge, Russ, and the pilots walked out of the hangar and toward the C-23.

Russ watched as the door to the cockpit closed and he and Jorge walked over to where Robbie was sitting. Robbie got up.

"Keep your seat, kid," Russ said. He sat back down and Russ and Jorge sat down beside him.

Suddenly, the engines of the C-23 roared to life. "Sure is loud," Robbie noted.

"Ever see a plane take off, Robbie?" Jorge asked.

"No."

"Well, you will now," Russ added.

The engines slowly revved up and the plane began to inch forward. When the plane got away from the hangar, the engines screamed and Robbie felt for the first time the power of the engines as the blowback from the propellers swept across the men.

"Wow!" Robbie bellowed.

"You don't want to be behind one of those things when they get going," Jorge said.

"Don't want to be in front of them either," Russ added. "They'll suck you into the props and you'll be ground meat."

The men sat as the plane rolled down the taxiway and then to the downwind end of the main runway. The plane stopped momentarily and Robbie could hear the engines rev up and begin to whine loudly even from this distance. Robbie got up and walked farther out on the tarmac.

When the brakes were released, the C-23 lurched forward. Robbie smiled in amazement as he watched the plane gain speed and lunge into the air. While the plane climbed upward, it also banked slightly to the right. Just before it reached the scattered puffy clouds, it straightened up on a due south course headed for Brownsville. Within minutes it was above the clouds and out of sight.

Robbie walked back over to Russ and Jorge.

"What do you think, kid?" Russ asked.

"Cool!" was all he could say.

Chapter 13

The rest of the week Robbie tossed and turned every night. His thoughts occupied every waking hour and many hours when he should have been sleeping. He couldn't help himself. This was too important if he would ever have a chance to get out of here. He was anxious to see Sean. He hoped Florence and Beka would return and take him to the Bayfront.

Sandra would likely expect him to start producing babies. All the ladies he met and was expected to impregnate were good-looking and eager without exception. And Sandra . . . *Her breasts felt good, firm, yet soft. She kissed well. It felt so good to be inside her, warm . . . yes, wonderful! As long as I don't have to look at her, she can be anyone. Yes, even Florence. Yes, I can do her again! I must. One day when I think I can fly the Cessna Skyhawk, Sean and I, and maybe even Florence and her mother, will be out of here. Or we'll all die trying!*

One thing that weighed heavily on Robbie's mind was Jorge and Russ. In order to get out of here, they would both likely need to die. They would never let him get out of here alive. He thought he could kill Russ without a problem. He didn't know him. He was just an obstacle. But Jorge . . . it didn't take long, but he'd become a friend. Could he kill him? Maybe Sean could take him out. Maybe Jorge could come along. But if Florence comes, could the Cessna take the additional weight? No one knew the payload and that's critical. Jorge was not your average lightweight. He pushed 220 hard. Robbie had a lot to think about. *I'll get it all figured out . . . but when?*

Sandra showed up right on schedule. On the drive back to the Farm, it didn't take long for her to notice he was tired. "You seem bushed. You not sleeping?"

"You've given me a lot to think about. With Florence, your girls and your proposition," he said.

She had no idea how little that was, compared to everything else he had to think about, but it did answer her question and it seemed to satisfy her.

"You up to tonight then?" she asked.

"Yes, but I thought I'd like to have a little more practice with you before I take on one of your ladies."

Sandra was surprised. More than surprised, she was shocked. "Really now?"

"Yes."

There was a long silence. Sandra glanced over at Robbie and he was staring back with a big smile on his face. They rode the remainder of the way in silence.

When Sandra pulled up in front of the farmhouse, she didn't hurry to get out. She watched as Robbie got out and ran around to the driver's side and opened her door. She slid out and looked directly at Robbie. "Well, sir, looks like me it is. And thank you for opening the door."

"Yes ma'am."

She giggled and strolled toward the house. Robbie shut the door and followed.

Monday, Richard stopped by the Airport. Jorge didn't see him, but Robbie noticed Richard go into the office with Russ. Robbie frowned and turned back to his work. He had a bad feeling about this guy.

"How's the boy doing?" Richard asked Russ.

"Doing great. He seems to enjoy working on the planes, and he's quite helpful around here, always cleaning up. I don't have to say a word to him. He and Jorge get along well. A few more weeks and the whole place will be spotless."

"Good to hear, but keep an eye on him. I don't trust him," Richard stated.

"Aw, he's all right. I don't think you have a thing to worry about. He and Sandra get along well too. If I didn't know better, I'd think he's banging her rather than the other gals out there at the Farm. Sandy's as friendly as I've ever seen her. Definitely not her bitchy self. The kid is well-mannered and respectful. Maybe a little of him is rubbing off on Sandra."

"Well, I don't like him. There's something about him that rubs me the wrong way. You keep an eye on him and let me know if you see anything out of the ordinary."

"Speaking of out of the ordinary, Florence and a friend of hers were here the other day. I don't know what they were doing, but they talked to Robbie for a while and left."

"What?" Richard roared and jumped to his feet.

"Hey, it seemed innocent," Russ tried to explain.

"Dammit!" Richard was out the door before Russ could say another word.

Russ wasn't certain if he would try to take the meeting out on Robbie or Florence. His uncertainty was answered when Richard stopped momentarily in the hanger to look around and, not seeing anyone, headed for his truck. His tires squealed on the tarmac and he sped away.

When he got home, Richard got out and slammed the truck door. As soon as he stepped inside the house, he yelled, "Florence!"

Louise was at work in the kitchen cleaning up her mess. "Look at the peach cobbler I've made. I know you love peaches."

"Florence!" He yelled louder this time.

"What's up with Florence?" Louise asked.

"The tramp went out to the Airport to see that bastard, Ronnie."

"Robbie," she corrected.

"Whatever."

Florence stepped through the kitchen door. "Yes, Daddy?"

Richard walked over to where she was standing, reared back, and slapped her across the face. "You little bitch. You won't ever go to the Airport again when I'm through with you." She screamed and melted onto the floor. When he grabbed her by the arm and reared back again to hit her, Louise grabbed his arm.

"Please don't, Richard. Please!"

Richard shoved Louise hard toward the table. She caught the corner, sliding the table over, and the cobbler toppled to the floor. The glass container shattered. Louise fell across a chair and then to the floor, onto the cobbler and broken glass. She screamed as the shards cut into her arm and side.

"Don't, Daddy! Stop!

Richard then turned back to Florence. He yanked hard on her arm and backhanded her across the face again. Florence fell hard and lay silent, crumpled on the dusty floor.

In spite of her pain, Louise crawled over to Florence, screaming at Richard all the way and leaving a trail of blood across the floor. "Get out of here, you bastard! Get out!" Richard turned for the door. Outside he could hear "Bastard! You killed my baby!"

"Oh my baby!" Louise whimpered as she cradled Florence in her arms. She leaned in close, relieved when she felt her daughter's warm, feathery breath on her cheek. She lowered Florence to the floor and placed an oven mitt she saw nearby under her head.

Louise got up and went to the sink. She ran cold water onto a dish towel and went back over to Florence. She wiped her face with the cool rag and she began to moan. "Thank you, Lord!"

Relieved that Florence was alive, Louise couldn't ignore the pain in her side and arm any longer. And she looked at all the blood on the floor. She went back over to the sink. She had bled a lot, but the wounds were not all that deep. They did hurt badly, but she would heal. She opened a drawer and found some duct tape. She removed the shards of glass from her cuts, taped a paper towel over both wounds, and returned to her daughter. Louise cradled Florence's head in her lap again and continued to wipe her face with a cool rag.

About thirty minutes later, Florence finally opened her eyes. Louise could at last squeeze out a smile. Her baby was going to be okay now.

They both managed to get up and make it to the bathroom. As they undressed, Florence noticed her mother's bloody makeshift bandages for the first time. She began to cry again.

"It's all right. They'll heal."

Florence got into the shower first while Louise got the tweezers and made certain she had gotten all the glass out of her wounds. When Florence was finished, Louise showered taking extra care with the cuts. After Louise finished drying, Florence began to work on her mother's cuts. The duct tape and paper towels worked well again for bandages.

They dressed and went into the kitchen. Louise locked all the doors. *That won't keep him out if he really wants to get in, but it will at least tell him that we don't want him around.* When that was done, Louise got some ice for Florence's face and they worked together to clean up the mess on the floor. Then she went to the butcher's block and found the biggest carving knife she had.

"That son of a bitch won't bother us anymore," she told Florence.

"Dammit, Sandra!" Richard exclaimed. "That little bastard has got to go. If you don't get rid of him, I'll kill the little son-of-a-bitch myself."

"Lower your voice and sit down, or you'll be the one going, Richard."

"Now—"

"I said sit down and shut up!" Sandra demanded.

Richard complied, but he was still steaming.

"Robbie goes when I say he goes," Sandra continued, "and right now you are a lot closer to leaving than he is."

Richard opened his mouth to speak, but Sandra stopped him in a heartbeat.

"I'll tell you what I've been thinking," Sandra continued. "I think Robbie and Florence might make a good couple."

Richard hit the ceiling. "Over my dead body!"

"That can be arranged," Sandra said with an evil little smile. "A lot quicker and easier than you might think too. You don't make the rules around here; I do. I'd have thought you'd have learned that a long time ago."

That took the wind out of Richard's sails and he settled down a little. He knew Sandra had all the power. He knew Sandra had the support of most of the police force. He knew that if Sandra wanted him dead . . .

"I'll tell you what you're going to do. You are going home to be the best husband and father you can be to your family. You are going to stay as far away from Robbie as you possibly can. And should your paths cross, you are going to ignore him. Got it?"

Richard got up and headed to the front door. As he reached for the doorknob, he turned back to look at Sandra and started to speak. She waved her finger at him indicating he should keep his mouth shut and leave as she had instructed.

Richard opened the door and left without another word.

"Damn bitch!" he exclaimed as he got in his truck. *She can't talk to me like that. But she did, and I let her. It's my own fault, but I'll get her, dammit.*

Richard started the engine and drove toward home. But he couldn't go home. He couldn't stay with a friend or word would get back to Sandra that he didn't go home and she'd find out what he did to Louise and Florence. *I guess I'm sleeping in the truck for a day or so.*

Chapter 14

Beka showed up on Florence's doorstep a couple days later. "What the hell happened to you, girl?"

"Daddy found out I went to the Airport."

"Let me see that." Beka examined Florence closely. Her right eye was completely swollen shut. The whole side of her face was black and blue. "I can't say I've ever seen anyone look quite as bad as you . . . without being dead, that is."

"Thanks, Beka. Just what I wanted to hear."

"So, I guess we're not going back to the Airport then?" Beka asked.

"We're going all right, just not this week. Maybe next week, okay? I can't let Robbie see me like this."

"I've got news for you, girl. That's not going to clear up in a week. Probably not in two weeks."

"Well then, maybe we'll see Robbie in two weeks."

"How about the Bayfront then?" Beka asked. "It doesn't matter who sees you there."

"I don't want to leave Mama here by herself. Daddy hit her too. Not anything you can see, but she fell on some glass and cut herself badly."

"Is she okay?"

"Yeah, she'll be fine in a week or so. The cuts looked bad, but they weren't all that deep. Bled like bloody hell though," Florence told her. "Mom's sore, but she heals quickly."

Louise flushed the commode and walked toward the kitchen. "I thought I heard voices," Louise said as she walked in. "How are you, Beka?"

"I'm good, Mrs. Ingalls. Florence was telling me about your cuts. Are you all right?"

"Sore, but I'll be okay," she responded.

"Mr. Ingalls—"

"Mr. Ingalls won't hurt us anymore," she informed Beka. "No, he won't." She showed Beka the butcher knife she kept with her at all times now.

Beka gasped when she saw the knife. "Can you use that against Mr. Ingalls?"

"I hope I don't have to, but we're prepared for that bastard."

Beka turned toward the door and Florence followed her outside. "I don't think your mom can use that knife against your dad," Beka stated. "Your dad has a gun. Besides, she's not nearly as big as your dad. He'll just take it away from her and use the knife on the two of you."

"I know," Florence said.

"Do you still have the gun I gave you?"

"Yes, I hid it in the bottom drawer of my dresser."

"Get it out and keep it handy, will you, Florence?"

"Yeah," she replied in an exasperated voice.

Beka wasn't certain Florence could actually use the gun on her dad, but at least she would have a fighting chance. "I'm going to the Bayfront," Beka said. "I'll see you next week, okay?"

"I'll expect you," Florence replied.

"Take care of that face, you hear?"

A tear streamed down Beka's cheek as she walked back to the car. She wasn't certain Florence was strong enough to deal with her dad. Florence was the only friend she had. She couldn't afford to lose her, but there was nothing she could do but wait to see how this played out.

Robbie and Jorge walked out onto the tarmac. The C-23 was coming back loaded with supplies from Brownsville. The plane was very quiet coming in, in contrast to the take-off, Robbie noticed. Then, just before touchdown, the engines roared and the plane slowly descended until the wheels touched down with a big puff of smoke.

"What are they bringing back?" Robbie asked Jorge.

"Wait and see," he replied.

They strolled back to the hangar doors and Russ walked out as well. The plane stopped on Jorge's mark, and the engines puttered to a stop. One by one, several vans and pickups began to pull up beside the plane. Jorge, with Robbie following closely, walked over to the rear of the plane. Robbie heard the clank of the locking mechanism, then the hatch began to slowly open. The drivers of the vehicles gathered around the cargo door. Russ waited near the cockpit for the pilot to open up.

When the cargo door was fully open, Robbie followed Jorge inside. There were three pallets of supplies. Jorge worked on removing the netting from the rearmost pallet. Robbie jumped in to help. As they got the netting off, Russ made his way to the cargo area with a clipboard in hand.

Jorge pulled box after box off the pallet, naming off the contents to Russ who marked the items off his list. Each package was handed to Robbie who in turned handed the package to one of the men at Russ's direction. Grapefruit, oranges, lemons, coffee, mangos, sugar, vanilla, leather, cigarettes, fabric, pottery . . . and the list went on and on.

A couple hours later, the cargo was divided among all the drivers and they quickly departed. Russ went back to his office followed by the pilots.

"Well, now you know what we get on our shipments," Jorge said to Robbie.

"You can't get those things locally?"

"Some, but not in the quantity we need," Jorge replied. "For a while we had some citrus, but about ten years ago we had a terribly cold winter. It killed most of them. Coffee, vanilla, and some of the other things, we never produced. When our supplies ran out, we had to find a source. We found out about Brownsville through some scavengers who wandered up this way from down there. Sandra sent some men down to see if we could get some trade going. It was slow at first, but eventually we got a good exchange established. A little fresh citrus and coffee now and then are quite nice. Sugar is essential. Any more questions?"

"No, I guess not," Robbie said.

Richard pulled into the driveway, got out, and walked to the door. He pulled at the doorknob, but it was locked. He pounded on the door. Seconds later, he saw the curtain pull back and Louise's face.

"Open the door," he demanded.

"Not going to happen," Louise replied.

"Come on, baby, I'm not going to hurt you."

Hearing the ruckus, Florence went to the kitchen. "Don't do it, Mama," she pleaded.

"Please, baby," he said. "I love you. I'll make it up to you."

There was quiet, and Richard sat down on the porch steps. He put his head in his hands.

"He's crying," Louise said walking over to the stove to check on her pot of stew.

"Let him cry. He should cry. He deserves to cry . . . or worse."

"I've got to let him in, Florence."

"You can't, Mom. He'll hurt us again," Florence said.

"He could break in and hurt us if I don't."

"Then we'll die fighting, Mom."

"Maybe he's learned his lesson this time."

"Yeah, like he learned his lesson when he thought you were screwing the electrician last year, or when he hit me because of Beka's cousin before that. Men don't change. He hurt us bad this time. Next time he will kill us. Are you willing to take that chance?"

"I don't know."

"I don't want to die. I'm going to see Robbie again soon, and if Daddy finds out, which he will, he *will* kill me and you too. He'll think you let me see Robbie. He'll kill you for that."

Louise walked back over to the door and peered through the curtain. Richard was still sitting there with his face in his hands. *Florence is right. But can I tell him to leave? Will he go?*

"Tell him now, Mama. I'll help you stand up to him."

"Both of us are still in bad shape," Louise said. "We are no match for him in the condition we're in."

"You've got to tell him something now, or he won't leave."

"Maybe in a few days. Then we will have a fighting chance."

"Dammit, Mama."

"That's enough." She turned back to the door and pecked on the glass. Richard looked over his shoulder at Louise peering through the window. He got up and walked back to the door.

"Come back in a few days," she said. "Then I'll let you know what I've decided." She let the curtain drop and backed up for fear of what he might do.

There was a loud bang on the door, followed by silence. She could hear his footsteps, his truck door slam and the engine start. She let out a sigh of relief.

"You can't let him back into the house," Florence said again.

"Go to your room. I have to think about this."

Florence went to her room and shut the door. Mama's going to let him back in. I can feel it. If she does, then we're both dead.

Florence went to her dresser and pulled open the bottom drawer. She reached under some winter jeans and shirts and found the pistol. She walked over to her bed and sat down. The revolver was cold in her hand. *Can I shoot this thing? Can I shoot Daddy? What if I miss? If I miss, I'll be dead. If I don't shoot, I'll be dead. I've got to do this, and I can't miss. I have no choice.*

She opened the latch, pulled the hammer back part way to the catch, and one by one let the bullets drop onto the bed as she turned the cylinder. She picked up the bullets, looked at each one, and laid them back on the bed. Then she cocked the hammer and pointed the pistol at the door. She squeezed the trigger. She cocked the gun again, pointed and squeezed. Again and again she practiced shooting the gun. She felt confident she could shoot it. Then, one by one she reloaded the gun. She placed the pistol under her pillow. Then she stretched out on the bed and stared at the ceiling.

Chapter 15

Robbie and Jorge worked hard cleaning, lubricating, and otherwise preparing the C-23 for its next flight. Robbie also kept busy rearranging and organizing around the hangar. When Saturday rolled around, he was shaved and showered when Sandra drove up.

Robbie inquired more about the crops produced at the Farm and about the distribution of the goods that were flown in from Brownsville as they drove to the Farm. Sandra, however, wasn't interested in explaining.

"I've got some nice gals lined up for you to meet today," she informed him.

Robbie didn't say anything.

"Well, aren't you interested?"

"I guess so," Robbie replied.

When they reached the farmhouse, Robbie opened the door for Sandra. "You're going to spoil me," she said with a chuckle. "I'm getting to like this."

The lunch table was perfectly set, and a half dozen ladies were busy with the final preparation. Sandra introduced Robbie to each, but for the women, Robbie needed no introduction. "I'm sorry," Robbie said, "but I'm terrible with names. It'll take a while for me to remember."

The ladies just smiled. "That's not a problem," Jade said and grabbed Robbie. She planted a big wet kiss on his lips. "I'm Jade. I bet you don't forget my name so quickly. Then she grabbed him again and gave him another kiss. "Now Robbie, what's my name?"

"Jade."

"Yes, J. A. D. E. —Jade!"

Robbie blushed. *I guess I won't have any trouble remembering some of your names,* as he winced from the pain of insufficient room for his expanding organ. His first boner of the day, but maybe not the last. *These gals look gorgeous. All dressed up, and for me. Especially Jade.* He noticed her jet-black hair second. He then noticed her slender figure and he couldn't miss her full lips, but he noticed her breasts first. They were significant to get his attention. Not huge like Sandra's, but large and well-suited for her frame. And they felt good when she pressed them into his chest, not once, but twice when she laid the kisses on him.

Sandra sat at the head of the table, while Robbie took the opposite end. The ladies sat three to a side. Sandra kept quiet most of the meal, just watching the interaction between Robbie and the ladies.

They certainly had a lot of questions about where he came from, which led to more questions. They asked how he was liking Corpus Christi, how his work was going at the Airport, and especially wanted to know if he was going to stay in Corpus. Sandra watched Robbie intently while he thought for a second and answered their questions.

Robbie praised all their hard work, especially in preparing such a fine meal, but also for all their efforts in their outside chores at the Farm. Robbie then complimented each and every lady on their dresses, including Sandra, and finished by saying, "I think Corpus Christi might be an excellent place to settle down and make a home. After all, the reason I came to Corpus Christi was to find a nice lady. There are no ladies for me in Peaceful Valley."

Sandra was pleased with his answer and let out a big smile that Robbie didn't see as he was intent with his discussion with the ladies. Little did Sandra know that much of what he said was nothing but lies. He did like the ladies very much and enjoyed the conversation, but was he going to spend the rest of his days here? Not on your life!

For the next several hours, Robbie spent about an hour alone with each lady in the living room. The others worked in the kitchen and dining room, cleaning up and preparing a variety of desserts that they each took to Robbie when it was their turn to spend time with him.

Jade was the last to have her time with Robbie. She was the oldest of the ladies at twenty-three, and Sandra had already decided she would be the first to have her night with him.

Jade took Robbie a strawberry cream tart. She sat down beside him and leaned in close with one arm around his shoulder, her breast pressing against his arm, and fed him every bite of the strawberry delight.

Robbie squirmed a bit as Jade gave him his second boner of the day.

"Something the matter, Robbie?"

"I could use a bathroom," he replied.

She got up and led Robbie down the hallway past the bathroom he had showered in when he was with Sandra, and then down another hall which cut left. At the end of this corridor, Jade opened a door into a suite. She followed Robbie in and pointed to a bathroom. Robbie headed in that direction and Jade shut and locked the suite door.

When Robbie came out, Jade had removed her shoes and unbuttoned a couple buttons on her blouse. She walked over and put her arms around him. She squeezed her breasts against his chest and gave him a little kiss on his ear. When she did, she whispered, "Sandra said you would spend tonight with me . . . if you have no objections." Then she looked directly into his eyes.

"No objections whatsoever."

"Perfect," Jade said.

Jade sniffed Robbie's neck. "I think you need a shower." She then grabbed him by the shoulders and gently encouraged him back toward the bathroom. She followed and when in the center of the room, turned him to face the large mirror over the double vanities. Very slowly, she began to remove his clothes. Halfway through the process, Robbie slipped off his shoes and socks as Jade began to undress.

When Robbie raised back up, his task complete, Jade was down to her bra and panties. Robbie's only article of clothing remaining was his tighty-whities. Jade wrapped her arms around him and pressed her breasts against his back as they both stared at each other in the mirror. Jade could see he was nervous but that didn't affect the expanding bulge in his shorts.

Jade gently rubbed his chest and kissed him on the neck for a few moments. "How about that shower?" With that said, she reached down and pulled his briefs down, revealing his manhood fully at attention. Robbie blushed again as Jade grabbed him by the shoulders and pointed him in the direction of the large shower.

She followed and by the time they had reached the sliding glass door, Jade had her bra and panties off. She turned the water on, adjusted the temperature, and grabbed the bar of soap. She walked him through the water then out of the spray, and lathered Robbie up from head to toe. She could feel him relaxing as she worked her expertise. She then turned Robbie toward the water and rinsed him off. She noticed he had his eyes closed and took the opportunity to plant another juicy kiss on his lips. When he opened his eyes, Jade handed him the bar of soap.

"It's your turn."

Robbie took the soap and for the first time he got a good close-up look at her body. He rubbed the bar over her chest, paying special attention to her breasts and nipples. Her hair was jet-black, but in contrast her breasts were as white as the rain lilies which were so numerous back home after a spring rain and pointed directly at Robbie. Her nipples were as pink as a Texas evening primrose.

Robbie cleaned and then he cleaned some more. She giggled. He wasn't cleaning; he was playing, and she didn't mind one bit. Yes, he's playing. He had never seen such a beautiful sight.

"That's enough," she finally said. "I need a little cleaning further down."

Robbie grabbed the bar of soap again and lathered up his hands. He then got down on one knee and began to work there. Now he noticed that she was partly shaved. She had a little jet-black patch trimmed into the shape of a triangle pointing to the area that she likely intended him to find a little later when they made it to bed.

Jade helped him clean the area. She sensed his inexperience in cleaning a woman. "I'm sorry," he said.

"Not a problem. You'll get better in time."

Robbie finished by working his way down to her feet, after which they both rinsed off and dried. Jade handed Robbie a robe and then grabbed one for herself. Again, she pulled him close, gave him a kiss, and pushed him back so she could look into his eyes. "What's my name?" she asked.

"Jade," he said without hesitation.

She smiled.

"Let's go lie on the bed and talk for a while," Jade suggested.

Robbie followed her lead and noticed the mirror on the ceiling immediately upon entering the bedroom. They lay on their backs looking at each other in the mirror. Robbie no longer felt embarrassed being with Jade.

"I really like you, Robbie," she said.

"I like you too."

They both lay there staring at each other's reflection. Robbie couldn't take his eyes off Jade's face. *She has to be the most beautiful girl I've ever seen.*

"Whatcha thinking?" she asked.

"Nothing much," he replied.

Whatever it is, I bet I can get his mind off it. She reached down and slowly pulled her robe open, revealing everything. She didn't say a word.

Robbie didn't say anything either. He certainly liked what he was seeing and it wasn't long before there was a noticeable protrusion in his robe. Jade reached over and exposed Robbie. She then touched him and Robbie let out a gasp.

Jade turned and got on top of Robbie, laying her breasts on his chest and planting another kiss on his waiting lips. The kiss was long and juicy, just as juicy as she had become in anticipation of him. She backed into his awaiting hardness.

Jade played and toyed with Robbie, lavishing him with kisses and nibbling his ears, enjoying him as much as he seemed to enjoy her for nearly an hour. They didn't say a word; just intently savored the moment. He kissed back and constantly fondled her breasts. He seemed amazed by them and maintained his focus on them the entire time. Jade loved the attention.

Finally, Robbie grabbed her buttocks. He pulled her hard into his manhood, forcing her back and forth across his slippery body while thrusting upward. Jade pulled at him too, both more rigid and intense with every second. Jade began to moan, as did Robbie, and neither could hold back any longer. They exploded and pulled each other ever so tightly together. Jade gave out a long loud groan as Robbie filled her with every last drop of his love.

They melted into each other, a puddle of one, exhausted and spent. After a while, Jade slid off and lay beside him.

She opened her eyes, looked at Robbie in the mirror, and reached over and touched him. He slowly opened his eyes and looked back at her. She took his hand and gave it a squeeze. He smiled. She returned the smile. They didn't need words. Their expressions said it all.

Jade looked at and admired his body. He was young, strong, and she liked the way he looked. At the same time, Robbie was looking at and taking in every square inch of her body. Her long slender legs, accented at their junction with an arrow. His gaze was affixed there for some time. His gaze then worked upward toward her breasts. He smiled again.

Finally, he looked at her face and into her eyes. They were fixed on his. Yes, she was definitely a jewel to be admired.

"You like what you see?" she asked.

"Very much." He closed his eyes again, still totally exhausted.

"Me too."

Jade closed her eyes as well and they both drifted off to sleep.

Monday, Florence was taking her morning shower when she heard a banging on the door. She hurried out, dried, and slipped on her panties and robe. She then went into her room to finish dressing. She knew her mother was in the kitchen and it would take the both of them to deal with her dad.

Louise turned the stove off and walked over to the door. She pulled the curtain back.

"Let me in, baby," Richard said. "I won't hurt you. I love you and miss you, sweetheart."

A tear ran down Louise's cheek.

"I could have busted the door in the other day. I don't want to hurt you. I love you."

Click.

Richard turned the knob and pushed the door inward. It swung open and hit the doorstop. "That's better, darling," he said as he stepped in, grinning.

"I love you too, Richard."

The instant he stepped in, however, his tone changed. He reached back and slammed the door. "You stupid bitch!" he said as he backhanded her across the face.

Florence had just removed her robe when she heard her mother scream. She quickly reached under the pillow, grabbed the pistol, and hurried to the kitchen in only her panties. She stopped at the entryway with her hands behind her, concealing the pistol.

Richard looked in her direction, and an evil smile appeared on his face. He just stood there looking at his daughter. He had not seen her naked since she was a child.

"Well, what do we have here?" he muttered.

"Damn you, Daddy!"

He laughed.

Florence brought her arms around and leveled the pistol at Richard's chest. She glanced at her mother on the floor. Then her eyes focused on Richard.

"And what are you going to do, shoot your loving daddy?"

"I will!"

"No, you won't," he replied. "You won't shoot your daddy." He took a couple steps toward her.

Florence cocked the pistol, steadied the gun with her other hand, and aimed at the center of his chest.

Richard stopped and just stared at her. "You've grown into a beautiful woman, Florence," he said with a wicked laugh. "Maybe I'll just fuck you before I kill you."

Florence squeezed the trigger.

Richard's eyes got as big as golf balls. He grabbed his chest and looked down at the blood on his hands. His mouth gaped open as if he was trying to say something when his legs buckled, and he fell to the floor.

Florence lowered the gun and stood staring at the body. Then she began to cry.

Louise pulled herself up and into a chair. Florence slowly walked over to the kitchen table and sat down beside her mother, not taking her eyes off her dad. They both sat and stared. He was not breathing. He was dead.

"That bastard won't hurt us anymore," Florence told her mother.

"You shouldn't have killed your daddy, Florence," Louise said, sobbing.

"The son-of-a-bitch was going to kill us!"

"No, Florence."

"Yes, goddammit! He was going to kill me, and then he was going to kill you. He was probably going to make you watch him rape me first."

They hugged then both just sat there sobbing.

Richard had been the source of a lot of pain for Louise and Florence. Louise loved him, but she hated him as well. Finally, she realized this.

"You're probably right," Louise said.

"You damn right I'm right!"

Louise looked back over toward Richard. *We've got to get rid of the body,* Louise thought. *What will Sandra do when she finds out we've killed Richard? She can't find out. But she will . . . eventually. What will we do with the body?*

Louise got up and locked the door. She pulled the curtain back and took a peek outside. *No one likely heard the shot. No close neighbors. No one outside.* "The body . . . think dammit, Louise." She turned to Florence. "Go get dressed."

Florence still had the gun in her hand. She returned a short while later, dressed and without the pistol. Her mother was sitting at the kitchen table with the butcher knife she had kept close since Richard left.

"What are you doing, Mommy?"

"Thinking about how to get rid of your daddy."

"And?"

"Cut him up into small pieces and bury him in the backyard," she replied.

"Gross!" Florence said with a disturbed look on her face. "Really?"

"Yes, really. Your dad said there is clay down about two feet. The clay is hard, so we can't make a whole deep enough to put the whole body in. It'll have to be done a piece at a time. There's a shovel out back. The dirt is sandy on top and will be easy to dig. No one will see you back there for the trees. That will work."

"Me digging?"

"Yes, unless you want to cut him up."

"Never mind. I'll make all the holes you need."

"And go all the way to the clay. And when we cover them up, we need to put something on top so no one will know what we did."

"What about that stack of paving stones Daddy was going to use to make a patio out back?" Florence suggested.

"Perfect! Why don't we just build a patio?"

"Okay, we have a plan. You go get started on the holes where the patio is going to be."

Florence went outside and started on the holes. Louise got some plastic garbage bags and walked over to the body. She looked at him, then walked back over to the sink and grabbed a hand towel. She went back to the body and laid the towel over his face.

Where to start?

An arm in one hand and the butcher knife in the other—*just like cutting up a chicken . . . a big goddamn chicken!*—she made the first cut at the elbow. The hand jerked and she screamed. She began hacking at the body with the point of the knife. There was no further movement and she breathed a sigh of relief. *Just residual muscle movement.*

The knife was sharp and easily cut through his clothes to the meat and then the tendons. It didn't take long and she had the forearm off and into the bag. She put a twist tie on the bag and took it to the back door.

Florence had the first hole dug. Louise tossed the bag into the hole, and Florence quickly covered it up and packed it down.

Louise repeated the procedure with the upper arm and then with the other arm and legs. When they were finished, she sat there for a minute and looked at the tiny appendage where she cut the legs off. She hadn't seen it for years, but she hated it with a passion. *How many bitches have you been in?* She began hacking at the thing until it was a bloody mess and unrecognizable.

Finally, she began working on the head. She left it covered, but as she cut she imagined that he would open his eyes, say something or maybe bite at her. It didn't happen, but she was glad when the task was over. She carried it out and placed it in a hole. "Goodbye, you sorry bastard!"

"Good riddance," Florence said as she covered the bag with dirt.

"The body won't fit into a bag. I'll have to wrap it up in a sheet, and you'll need to help me get it out here. Dig the last hole bigger and as deep as you can."

"Okay, Mama."

When Florence finished the hole, she went inside to help her mother carry the final package to the patio.

"Where's the gun, Florence?"

"I hid it in my drawer."

"We've got to get rid of the gun too. Go get it."

Florence returned and dropped the pistol into the hole. She then covered the last of Richard's remains with sand and packed it with her feet.

"Start covering the area with the pavers and I'll get started cleaning up the blood inside," Louise instructed.

"Yes, Mama."

When Louise finished up inside, she went outside to help Florence finish laying the pavers, but she had already finished. "Looks good, Florence."

"Thank you."

Florence wheeled the barbecue onto the patio while Louise dragged a couple chairs over.

"Thank you, Daddy," Florence said. "You make a beautiful patio."

Out of nowhere, Louise started laughing. Florence looked at her and smiled.

"Let's go get a shower," Louise suggested.

Florence removed her clothes and got into the shower first while her mother got undressed and carefully removed her bandages. The bleeding had stopped but removing the bandages caused them to open up slightly. She got into the shower when Florence finished and cleaned every molecule of Richard's blood off her body. Her wounds continued to drain. She patted the cuts dry and applied new bandages.

They dressed and put all the soiled clothes in the washing machine. Florence then helped her mother get started on a late lunch.

They were both relatively quiet as they prepared the meal and even quieter as they sat at the kitchen table and nibbled at their food. Noticing that Florence was not eating much, Louise was the first to speak. "I can't eat."

"Me neither. This food is making me sick."

"Maybe we should talk."

They both pushed their plates away.

"Let's go into the living room," Louise suggested, getting up.

Florence followed and they sat on the couch. "Where did you get that gun, Florence?"

"I've had it for a while. Beka gave it to me last year when Daddy hit me in front of her. She said he was a mean son-of-a-bitch and that I'd need it one day. It's the same gun she used to kill her daddy. He was a mean son-of-a-bitch too."

"I didn't know."

"Nobody knew. Just me and Beka. I don't think her mama even knew. Maybe she suspected, but Beka never told her. He raped her twice. Third time's a charm, they say. His body is in a vacant house down near the Bayfront. She showed it to me once."

"When did this happen?"

"Early last year. That's when we became best friends. She needed someone to talk to, and I took a blood oath that I'd never tell. You've got to promise not to tell too. Not even Beka. If you do, she won't trust me anymore."

"I won't," Louise promised. "But Beka will find out about what happened here, won't she?"

"I don't think I can help that. Beka will be here in a day or so. She's going to know something happened. I have to tell her."

"I understand, but that is as far as it can go."

"Beka can keep a secret better than anyone."

"Good."

They paused and stared at each other, tears running down their cheeks.

"We need to get our story straight. Richard will be missed and questions will be asked."

"He won't be missed around here," Florence said with a chuckle.

"I know, but I don't think anyone else will see things the same way we see them. That's why we need a good story."

"Like what?" Florence asked.

"Like he came back today and we wouldn't let him in. He went to leave and his truck wouldn't start, so he left on foot. We never saw him again and don't know where he went. It's simple and we won't make a mistake as we might if we try to make up an elaborate story."

"And if they ask questions we can't answer?"

"He hurt us the other day and he left," Louise added. "He left this time just like he did the last time. If someone asks anything else, just play dumb. We don't know anything. If they do find out, I killed him, not you," Louise said.

"No, Mama."

"Yes!"

Louise gave her daughter a big hug. "We'll get through this, sweetheart. Just keep to our simple story."

Chapter 16

Beka showed up on Wednesday. Immediately she knew something was askew. "Why is your dad's truck in the driveway? Where is he?" Questions! Questions! It didn't take Beka more than five minutes to get the whole story out of Florence and her mom.

Beka knew she would be getting a lot of questions from Sandra. Beka and Florence after all, were best friends. Spying on Richard was one thing, but she couldn't tell Sandra that Florence killed her dad. Flo could tell Sandra that she killed her daddy as well. If Sandra found that out, she'd be dead meat too.

"So, do you want to go to the Airport?" Beka asked.

"I can't now," Florence replied.

"How about the Bayfront?"

"I can't leave Mom alone."

"She can go too. What do you say, Mrs. Ingalls, want to go to the Bayfront?"

"Come on, Mama. It'll do you good to get out of the house."

"Okay," Louise said hesitantly. "Maybe if I get out of the house for a while I can get some sleep tonight."

"Come on Mrs. Ingalls, you can ride in front."

Florence hopped in back and leaned forward between the split front seats.

"What color is this car anyway?" Louise asked.

"Why is everyone so damned concerned with the color of my car?" Beka growled.

"Sorry, Beka," Louise said apologetically. "I didn't know it was a touchy subject."

"A car is a car," she replied without further explanation.

The remainder of the trip, Louise sat watching out the window.

"Not much to look at is it, Mrs. Ingalls?" Beka said.

Junk was scattered everywhere. Corpus Christi had always been known as the Sparkling City by the Sea. Trees and brush covered up some of the trash, but most of the city was and probably would always remain a junkyard.

When they reached the harbor, Beka didn't see Charles's sailboat. "Let's go down Ocean Drive," she announced.

She turned around and headed back to the street along the seawall and took a left. It wasn't long before she spotted Charles's sailboat out in the bay. He was headed back toward the harbor, but it would be at least an hour before he got docked. Beka drove on down Ocean Drive, taking in the salty smell of the sea. The sun was out, and there was a gentle breeze out of the southeast. Only a few cotton balls dotted the sky. "What a beautiful day for sailing and for a drive," Beka said.

"Wonderful," Louise remarked. "It's cleaner here too."

"The drive is great, but I still think it stinks around here," Florence said.

A couple miles down, Beka pulled into a short road to nowhere. It ended where the shoreline had eroded into the pavement and had crumbled into the sea.

"Look at the shrimp boats," Beka said pointing east. "I wonder what it's like to work on a fishing boat."

"A lot of work, I bet," Louise replied.

"Too much work," Florence added. "But I sure do like shrimp; more than anything. I wish we could have them more often."

"We get what we get," Louise reminded her.

"I wish I could sail away from here with Charles," Beka said, changing the subject. The talk about food was beginning to make her hungry. "I'd never come back."

Beka let out a sigh. Obviously her mind was far away. *The boat gently bouncing with the waves and the water splashing against the side of the boat. The gulls gliding high overhead. Charles with his shirt off and bronze skin and sun-bleached hair glistening in the sunlight. Sipping a piña colada and watching the endless expanse of the ocean, headed to Martinique or Turks and Caicos.*

Suddenly she snapped out of her daydream. She reached down and turned the key, and the engine roared to life. She turned around and headed back to the harbor. A couple shrimp boats were waiting for the sailboat to get out of the way so they could get to their stalls. Charles eased his sailboat into his spot as Beka pulled up near the boat slip and killed the engine.

She got out and ran over to the *Moneypit.* Charles put the last rope on the piling and turned to greet Beka. She flung her arms around him and gave him a big kiss. "I've missed you," she said.

Florence and Louise stood beside the car.

"I think I'll take a stroll around," Louise told Florence. "I need some time to think."

Florence heard the roar of a boat engine and turned to see Sean standing on the back of the shrimp boat with a rope in hand as the captain was parking in his slip. The engine hummed again and Sean tossed the rope onto a piling and tied it up. He grabbed a second rope and did the same.

He looked over and saw Florence. He waved and Florence walked over. "Hi, Sean."

"Hi, right back," he said.

Marcia had hold of Lola's hand and was the first out of the cabin of the boat. She stepped onto the dock and gave Florence a frown and squinted at her, taking a really good look so she would not forget the face. Then she got into their pickup and backed it up to the boat.

Sonny stood in the doorway of the cabin, noting what was going on. "You've got work to do, boy," he said.

"Yes, sir," Sean said, returning his attention to his chores.

Florence strolled back over to Beka and Charles. Charles offered Florence a soda.

"No, thanks," she replied. "I'm fine."

Sonny, Marcia, and Sean unloaded their catch into the back of the pickup just as they had so many times over the past few weeks. It wasn't long before their task was complete and the truck ready to roll. Marcia took one more look at Florence before she crawled into the truck with Lola and drove off.

Florence gazed around to see where her mother had gotten off to. She was some distance away, meandering around some of the empty boats. Florence then turned to see Sean cleaning on the boat. Sonny had gone back inside the cabin, so she decided to go back over.

"Hi again, Sean."

"Hi. I'm sorry, but I forgot your name."

"Florence. I told Robbie you were here. Beka and I will try to bring him down here next week."

"Thanks, Florence. I gotta get back to work."

"Okay."

Sean got busy cleaning up the boat, and Florence wandered back to the *Moneypit.*

"I couldn't help but hear you two," Sonny said from the cabin doorway. "You be careful. You'll get yourself into a passel of trouble."

"I'll be careful, but I've got to see Robbie."

Louise was making her way back toward the *Moneypit.* Florence joined Charles and Beka.

"I'll take that soda now," Florence said.

Robbie's eyes popped open. It's daylight. *The damn alarm didn't go off again.* He jumped out of bed and got dressed then splashed some water on his face. He dried, quickly brushed his teeth, and went into the hangar.

"About time you got up, sleepyhead," Jorge said from behind the Cessna.

Robbie walked over. "Why didn't you wake me?"

"No need. Not much on the agenda today. Besides, Sandra will be here a little later."

Yes, she would be here today, Robbie thought. *I wonder what she has in store for me this time. I wonder what happened to Florence. I've got to find a way to get to Sean. Florence said she would be here this week. I wonder if Jorge will help me. Does he have a car? He hasn't tried to go anywhere since I've been here. Russ has a truck, but he'll never let me use it, especially if he knows what I'm going to do.*

"Do you have a car?" Robbie asked nonchalantly.

"No. There's no place I want to go," Jorge replied. "If I need to go somewhere, it's usually an errand for Russ, and he lets me use his truck."

So as not to arouse any suspicion, Robbie changed the subject. "Why don't we ever work on those two jet planes over there?"

"I don't know anything about jets," Jorge replied. "A couple of the pilots wanted to fly them, but I told them I didn't know how to work on jets. 'You guys can fly them, but don't blame me if you crash,' I told them."

"What kind are they?"

"The one on the right is an F-15 Eagle. The other is an F-22 Raptor. Fighter jets."

"Wouldn't they be good for defense around here?"

"Yes, those are some really badass jets. That's why the pilots wanted to fly them. We can make jet fuel and we have rockets and ammunition for the machine guns over in a warehouse, but if I can't maintain them, the guys can't fly them. It's as simple as that."

"My friend Sean knows a lot about jets," Robbie said.

"Yeah?" Jorge eyed Robbie with a surprised look on his face.

Robbie nodded. He then changed the subject again. *Now if only he will tell Russ or one of the pilots. I wonder how bad they want to fly the jets.*

"I think I'll go get ready to go to the Farm," Robbie said. "Sandra will be here any minute."

Jorge nodded.

Robbie went to his room. He decided to brush his teeth a little better and put on some deodorant. When he went back into the hangar, he expected to see Sandra waiting. She wasn't there yet so he walked back over to where Jorge was fiddling with the Piper.

"We going to take this one out for a spin when I get back?" Robbie asked.

"It's next on our new rotation schedule," Jorge replied.

Robbie smiled. He liked taking the planes out. Everything else around here was just work. This was the exciting part.

Sandra was about two hours later than usual.

"See you tomorrow," Robbie said and joined Sandra at the hangar door.

"Later!" Jorge replied.

"Sorry I'm late," Sandra said.

"No problem," he replied.

"I'll be right back," Sandra said. "Wait here."

Sandra went into the office to see Russ. A few minutes later she came back out and had a few words with Jorge. She then joined Robbie and told him to get into the Jeep. They drove off and Sandra was quiet for a long time. Robbie noticed she seemed to have something on her mind. *I wonder what she was talking about with Jorge and Russ.*

"Richard is missing," she said out of the blue.

"Richard Ingalls?"

"Yes. That's why I'm late. I went to his house. Seems there was a domestic squabble and now he's missing."

I wonder if this has anything to do with Florence not showing up last week.

"Do you know what happened?" Robbie asked.

"Only that there was an argument and Mrs. Ingalls told Richard to leave. His truck wouldn't start, so he left on foot. No one's seen him since."

The rest of the trip to the Farm was quiet. Sandra obviously had a lot on her mind. Robbie's head began churning too. Not just about the Ingalls, but about what was in store for him at the Farm now that they were getting close.

Sandra led Robbie up to the house. She then opened the door and let him in first. There were only two ladies waiting for him this time. Brenda and Joy greeted him as soon as he walked in the door.

"Have fun," Sandra said. She pulled the door closed behind Robbie and headed back to the Jeep. Brenda and Joy immediately pulled him toward the dining room where lunch was ready.

The gals ushered Robbie to the seat of distinction at the head of the table and served him like he was king and they were his maids.

He was not king, though. A king is not a prisoner. A king takes all the time he needs or wants to eat. Brenda and Joy only allowed him fifteen minutes and they literally drug him to one of the back suites. Not the one he was in last weekend with Jade, or the one with Sandra, but in the same general area. The gals giggled constantly, nipping at his ears and lavishing him with little kisses. It was as if they were virgins and couldn't wait for their first time.

They sat Robbie down on the bed, turned on some soft music and began dancing for him in the middle of the room. As they danced, they slung articles of clothing here and there across the room. Their bras and panties they slung at him.

Robbie adjusted himself, relieving the strain in his britches. He gawked at the young, smooth bodies standing before him. *Their breasts are not quite as large as Jade's, but they are just as beautiful in their own way.* His eyes followed their flat stomachs downward. They were clean shaven, and Robbie began to drool.

The two women didn't stand there long. They hurried over and grabbed Robbie's arms and pulled him upright. Thanks to the ladies, his clothes didn't stay on long. Brenda pushed Robbie back onto the bed, and they both pounced on him. They did things to Robbie he couldn't have thought of or dreamed about.

Two hours later, the gals took him to the shower where they cleaned every inch of his body. They dried him and then took him back to the bed. Joy pulled out a deck of cards and showed him how to play spades in the nude. In an hour, the women became bored with the game and pounced on Robbie again.

Robbie awoke alone the next morning. He had fallen asleep shortly after the ladies ravaged his body for the second time. He didn't know whether they had stayed with him or had gotten up early without waking him.

He heard a knock at the door, and Sandra peeked in.

"Breakfast is ready."

On the drive back to the airport, Sandra asked how Robbie liked Joy and Brenda.

"I like them a lot," he replied. "I've been trying to think of a word to describe them."

"Rapacious?"

"I don't know that word," Robbie replied.

Sandra defined the word.

"Yes, rapacious fits."

They smiled at each other.

"Am I a prisoner here?" Robbie asked.

Sandra was surprised by the question, "Yes and no. Why do you ask?"

"I was just wondering. I've only seen the Airport, Farm, and the Ingalls' place and in between. I just thought I'd like to see more of your city. I've never seen the ocean."

"It's not the ocean, only the bay."

"I know, but I've never seen it."

"Are you going to try to escape?"

"I don't have any place to escape to," he replied.

"You could try to go home."

"But my mission is not finished here."

"And what mission is that?"

"To find a wife."

"What were Florence and Beka doing at the Airport the other day?"

"You know about that?"

"I know everything that goes on around here. Except what happened to Richard. But I'll find that out too, sooner or later."

"Florence just wanted to say hi. I think she likes me."

"And do you like her?"

"Yeah. She's sweet. And I owe her, at least partially, for saving my life."

"Have you thought about my proposition?"

"About you fixing me up with Florence?"

"Yes."

"Yes, I have."

"And have you come to a conclusion?"

"Yes. I'll take care of your girls for the next year. And you'll still set me up with Florence?"

"Yes. Deal then?"

"And I won't be a prisoner here?"

"No."

"Then it's a deal."

Sandra was still smiling when she pulled up in front of the hangar. "Yeah, have a look around if you want. Be careful. I don't want one of Richard's men shooting you."

"I'll be careful. Thanks."

"See you next weekend?"

"Absolutely."

Sandra smiled. Her woman's intuition was telling her he was being honest with her. *Even if he isn't, Beka will keep an eye on him.* "I'll have a talk with Russ."

Sandra went into Russ's office while Robbie joined Jorge. A short while later, Sandra gave Robbie a thumbs up on the way out. Robbie smiled.

"What was that about?" Jorge asked.

"Sandra's going to let me take a look around town."

"Really?"

"Yes."

"And why would you want to do that?"

"I've never seen the ocean."

"I've never seen it either," Jorge said.

"Really? You've lived here all your life and have never been to the Bayfront?"

"That's right."

"Sandra said it's only the bay. Still, if you can't see land on the other side, it'll be like an ocean to me. Maybe we can go see it together."

"I'd like that."

Suddenly, Russ appeared in the doorway and motioned for Robbie to join him in his office.

"Yes, sir?" Robbie asked.

"Jorge told me that your friend Sean knows a lot about jets," Russ replied.

"Yes, sir. My Grandpa Reggie was an army contractor. He was fascinated with jets too. He had several magazines and manuals about them, which he let Sean have. Sean didn't have the interest I had in Shakespeare and Thoreau."

"Do you know where Sean's at?"

"No, sir."

"Sandra told me he's down on the Bayfront. He's supposed to be on a shrimp boat somewhere down at the harbor. I asked her if it would be all right if I brought him here for a week or so to see what he knows about those jets out there."

Robbie just stood and listened intently. It was all he could do to maintain his composure and keep from smiling.

"I'll get down there in a few days and bring him back here," Russ added. "Or maybe it would be better if you went down there to find him. Besides, you know what he looks like. At your convenience, of course."

"Yes, sir."

"Sandra also said it would be all right if you had a look around town a bit."

Robbie nodded.

"That's all, Robbie."

"Yes, sir."

Robbie walked back into the hangar. Once he had gotten away from the office and out of Russ's line of sight, he could not contain his smile any longer. He could also feel the goose bumps on his arms. *Yes! I'm going to see Sean.*

Chapter 17

On Wednesday afternoon, Robbie was surprised to see a green car pull up to the hangar. He walked over and Florence and Beka got out. Both had big smiles on their faces.

Robbie immediately noticed Florence's black eye. "What happened to you?" he asked.

"Daddy hit me."

"Can we go for a drive?" Robbie asked.

"Really?" Beka inquired with a surprised look on her face.

"I think so," he said. "Let me go ask Russ. Sandra said I could get out of here some, but I have to check with Russ, the Airport commander."

"Cool!" Florence said.

Robbie trotted inside the office. A few minutes later he was back with a big smile on his face. "He wasn't overly happy because he had a lot of work scheduled for today, but since Sandra had already approved of me going out, he didn't put up a big fight. We've got two hours. Now tell me about your black eye, Florence."

The girls looked at each other.

"Sandra said your daddy is missing. You know anything about that?"

Still not a word from Beka or Florence. Robbie leaned forward between the seats and noticed a tear streaming down Florence's cheek.

"I can't talk about it now," Florence said and began to bawl.

"Okay, Florence. I won't push."

Robbie leaned back to give Florence a little space. "Where we going, Beka?"

"The Bayfront."

"Good, just where I wanted to go."

Robbie stared out the window as they passed one dilapidated building after another. Brush had grown up around most. There were old commercial buildings as well as areas where there were mostly residences. Most were in really bad shape. When they reached the Bayfront, the buildings looked a little better. There were a few businesses that were open and people mingling about. There was one apartment building that looked like people were living in it. Other than that, the place was desolate.

"Not much to see around here," Robbie noted.

"Nope," Beka replied.

"Where are all the people?"

"It's too hot now. Most will be home. Not that many around anyway," she said. "There are usually more down the way, around the salt and ice plants. Some stay on the boats or nearby."

Robbie sat quiet for a while. Beka pulled up behind the *Moneypit* and hopped out.

Florence turned to Robbie. "Your friend Sean works on that shrimp boat over there," she said, pointing.

"Where would he be now?"

"I don't know. I just know they come in around noon, and he's usually here a couple hours. Then he goes home, wherever that is."

"Russ said maybe I can come here and pick Sean up in a day or two and take him to the Airport. I told Russ he could work on jet engines."

"Can he?"

"No, but that's what I told Russ. It seems they'd like to be able to fly their jets."

Robbie watched as Beka ran to the sailboat and kissed the man onboard. "What's that about?"

"Beka's boyfriend," Florence replied. "That's how I found Sean. I recognized him from your description. Beka comes here almost every week to see Charles. Let's get out. I'll introduce you two, and then we can go for a walk."

Florence led Robbie to the *Moneypit,* made the introduction, and told Beka their intentions. As they walked along, Florence grabbed Robbie's hand. She looked at him to see if it was all right. Robbie smiled. "I never liked the smell of the Bayfront," she said. "It doesn't seem so bad today."

"I think it smells good," Robbie said. "I've never smelled the ocean. Well, most of the time it smells good," he added, pointing to a rotting fish in the harbor.

Florence smiled.

"It's cooler here," Robbie said. "It gets mighty hot at the Airport, especially in the hangar during the heat of the day. The sea breeze feels good."

Florence kept squeezing Robbie's hand and finally he noticed. "Something the matter?" he asked.

"Can I trust you?"

"You saved my life, Florence. I owe you a lot. I would never hurt you."

With that, tears began to run down her cheek again. Robbie stopped and pulled Florence to face him. "You can trust me."

"I killed Daddy," she blurted out.

Robbie's mouth dropped open. "What?"

"I killed Daddy. He didn't give me any choice. He was going to kill me and Mama."

"How?"

"Beka gave me a pistol a long time ago. She said she knew Daddy was bad. That one day I would need the gun just like she needed it with her daddy."

Robbie could not believe what he was hearing, but he also knew Florence was telling the truth. Robbie could feel her trembling as he held onto her hands. He pulled her close and gave her a big hug. Florence looked up at Robbie and gave him a salty kiss. Robbie squeezed her tighter and kissed her back. He could feel a tingle he had not felt before. He was not feeling an erection, like he did when Jade, Brenda, or Joy kissed him. This was different.

"Look, Charles," Beka said, pointing at Robbie and Florence down the line of boats. "Looks like we're not the only lovebirds down here anymore."

Russ came to the hangar door when he heard the door slam. Robbie waved good-bye to the girls and walked over to Russ. He looked at his watch.

"Sorry," Robbie said.

"I'll give you the twenty minutes this time..."

"Yes, sir. Thank you, sir."

"All right, come on into my office."

Russ pointed to a chair and Robbie sat down. "Where did you go?" he asked.

"Down to the Bayfront. I've never smelled the ocean."

"Did you see Sean?"

"No, sir. The boat was there, but Sean had already left by the time we arrived."

"But you at least know how to get there now?"

"Yes, sir."

"Do you think you can drive my truck to the Bayfront and bring Sean back here?"

"Yes, sir."

"The boats usually come in around noon. This late in the season, they may stay out a little longer to make sure they finish up the season on a high note. You can leave here around 11 o'clock. You may have to wait around a while, but you won't miss him."

"Yes, sir."

"That's enough 'yes sirs' for one day. Go help Jorge the rest of the afternoon."

"Yes, sir."

Russ smirked.

Robbie checked with Jorge and he'd finished all the chores that Robbie should have done. "I owe you, Jorge."

Robbie went to his room and showered. He then stretched out on his bed. *I'm going to get to see Sean tomorrow. Not only that, I'm going to be seeing him every day, for a while at least.*

Promptly at 11:00, Russ walked to the office door. Robbie and Jorge were busy at the rear of one of the planes. He whistled and held up the keys.

Robbie walked over to Russ and took the keys. "Can Jorge come along too?" he asked. "He's never seen the ocean."

"Why the hell not?" Russ growled. "That will just about round out my day."

Robbie whistled. "Come on, Jorge. We're going to the Bayfront."

Jorge dropped what he was doing and joined Robbie.

"Have you driven a truck before?" Russ asked.

"No, but it can't be any harder than driving a plane."

Russ couldn't dispute his logic.

After Robbie pulled away from the hangar, he tried to get more of the answers he desperately needed. "Jorge, if you could go anywhere you wanted, where would you go?"

"I'm happy where I'm at," he replied.

"I know the world is pretty messed up, but wouldn't you want to be out on your own somewhere?"

"No. I don't work all that hard. I have a nice place to sleep every night. I get plenty to eat. Why would I want to leave that for the unknown?"

"Good point."

If I ask too much he might get suspicious. If I mention Peaceful Valley, he might say something to Russ. I can't tell him life may be shorter than he might think. I guess I best let it go.

The boat Florence had indicated Sean was on, wasn't in the stall. At least it was gone, so he knew sooner or later Sean would show up.

Robbie and Jorge got out and looked around. Jorge walked along the bulkhead, looking at all the boats while Robbie walked down the roadway toward the bay.

When Robbie made his way to the end of the T-head lined with boat slips, he could see two shrimp boats coming in. They both had a huge flock of seagulls following. From a distance all the boats seemed to look alike. He could only hope Sean was on one of them. He had waited long enough, but he would wait as long as it took.

As the boats rounded the jetty protecting the harbor, Robbie recognized one of the boats. He could see Sean, too, his head down, hard at work at whatever he was doing.

Robbie strolled back toward the stall where the boat would park. They had just finished tying the boat to the pilings when he walked up. Sean looked up and saw Robbie for the first time. His mouth dropped open, and he gave Robbie a wave and a smile.

Marcia and Lola were the first off the boat, and Marcia gave Robbie a suspicious eye on her way to her truck. Robbie moved onto the ramp alongside the boat. Sean jumped onto the ramp and gave him a quick hug. "Good to see you, Robbie."

"You too, Sean. You okay?"

"Better now. Don't say anything you don't want Sandra to find out about in front of Marcia," he whispered, shifting his eyes toward her.

"Sandra? Mayor, Sandra? You know her?"

"I know *of* her. Marcia is one of Sandra's spies."

Splat! Robbie looked down at his arm. White slime was running down his forearm. "Hazard of the Bayfront. Seagull shit won't hurt you," Sean said, laughing.

"Maybe not, but it's nasty." Robbie noticed numerous spots on Sean's shirt.

"Seagulls do three things—squawk, eat, and shit! They do keep the place cleaner and smelling better than it would be without them," Sean informed him.

Sonny appeared at the cabin door and yelled at Sean. "You've got work to do."

"Yes, sir," Sean replied and jumped back onto the boat.

Sonny turned his attention to Robbie. "And who are you?"

"I'm Robbie," he said, reaching into his pocket to pull out a note Russ had written. "I have something for you," he said, extending his arm.

Sonny walked over to the boat railing and grabbed the note. He unfolded the paper and began to read. Then he looked straight at Robbie. "Sean works for me now," he proclaimed.

"Not anymore," Robbie replied politely.

Sonny grumbled and walked back inside the boat cabin. Sean finished packing up their catch, and Sonny came back to help him carry the boxes to the truck.

When Marcia drove away and Sean had finished hosing down the deck, he turned to Sonny. "Captain!" Sonny looked up at Sean. "Permission to leave the boat, sir?"

"Go on. Looks like I don't have a choice." Sonny growled.

"Here's our ride," Robbie said, pointing to the truck.

Sean smiled. "How did you rate a truck?"

"Long story."

"That guy's probably keeping an eye on you, Robbie."

"You think?"

"I know Marcia watches me. I don't think they'd let you come down here without someone keeping tabs on you."

They got in and waited for Jorge to return.

Sean's got a point there. Something else to think about, I guess.

"Nice tan," Robbie said. "And you look good too. I guess the sun and sea agrees with you."

"You look good too . . . minus the tan," Sean said. "What have you been doing?"

"Working at the Airport mostly. I'm sure glad I found you. I've been working on a plan to get us out of here."

Robbie knew Sean had heard him, but to the excited Robbie, he didn't seem nearly as happy. "What's the matter, Sean?"

"Long story too."

"Well, we'll have time for some long stories. You will be working at the Airport for a while. And with a little luck, we'll be out of here before you know it."

Sean was silent. Robbie gave him a curious look.

"Everyone at the hangar thinks you're a great jet airplane mechanic."

"And how did they get that idea?"

"I told them."

"But I don't know the first thing about jets. Well, I do know some from what I've read, but not nearly enough to pass as a mechanic."

"Well, starting today you are a jet mechanic. You'll just have to fake it. I'll help you. Just dig around and grunt and groan about the workings of the engine. They don't know how to work on them either. They'll never know the difference."

"But I can't fix an engine where it'll fly," Sean said, exasperated.

"They don't have to fly. You just have to fake it for a while, and in the end you can inform them that they've sat too long and can't be fixed. I don't think they really expect you to get them going. I think they only hope you can. Think you can do that?"

"I'll do my best."

Jorge finally made his way back to the truck. Sean was sitting in the front, so he got in the back seat.

"So this is the new jet mechanic?" Jorge asked.

"Yes, sir," Robbie replied. "This is Sean."

"Yeah, right!"

They stopped by Sonny and Marcia's place so Sean could pick up what few belongings he had. They then headed to the Airport.

"Well, Jorge, what do you think of the ocean?" Robbie asked.

"Stinks! Pretty and cooler down there, but it still stinks."

They made the rest of the trip in dead silence except for the hum of the engine. They pulled up to the hanger, and Robbie pulled the truck in the spot Russ always parked. Inside, Robbie introduced Sean to Russ, returned the truck keys to the nail on the wall where Russ always kept them, and then took Sean to the far side of the hanger to see the jets.

"Thanks for taking me to the Bayfront," Jorge said then went about his own business.

"Voila!" Robbie said, pointing at the two jets. "The one with the vertical tail-fins is an F-15 Eagle. The other is an F-22 Raptor. Fighter jets."

"Got it."

Robbie then showed Sean to his room. When Sean had put away what little stuff he brought with him, they walked back into the hangar. Robbie pointed to a stack of coveralls. "See if you can find one that will fit you." It didn't take long.

When Robbie and Sean found Jorge, he was in the cockpit of the C-23 Sherpa. "Let's go take a look at the jets," he said, as he walked out through the cargo door. He didn't know they had already taken a quick look at the planes.

"F-15 Eagle, right?" Sean asked.

"Why, yes," Jorge replied.

"And that one looks like an F-22 Raptor."

"Well, looks like you know your planes, Sean," Jorge responded. *Maybe I've underestimated this kid.*

Jorge and Robbie watched as Sean walked around and grabbed the flaps and everything else he could see to wiggle. He kicked the tires and ran his hands over the fuselage. "The tires need a little air," he said. He hit the underside of the wings with his fist and listened for anything unusual. "No fuel in these things, right?"

"I don't know," Jorge replied.

"If there is, it'll have to be drained and inspected for fuel degradation. You have a ladder so I can get into the cockpits?"

"Around here somewhere," Jorge replied.

"How about I do that in the morning? I've been up since 4:00 a.m. and I'm beat."

"Yeah, you and Robbie take the rest of the afternoon off," Jorge suggested. "You two probably have a lot to talk about. I'll go tell Russ."

"Let's grab a soda and we'll go to my room and relax," Robbie said.

Jorge wandered over toward the office.

When the boys got to Robbie's room and had the door shut, Robbie informed Sean that the big transport plane was a C-23 Sherpa. "The yellow one is a Cessna Skyhawk, and the blue one is a Piper Cub. Just so you know, in case anyone asks. The old green helicopter at the back isn't maintained. I overheard Russ say that it didn't fly when it was brought in here. Besides, there are no replacement parts to fix anything if it did fly."

Sean sat and listened, but he seemed to be in a faraway place. "Something troubling you, Sean?"

Sean hung his head. "Remember that long story?"

"We've got time. I'm listening."

He paused for a moment. "I think I'm going to stay here."

"What?"

"You heard me. Up until a few days ago, there were a couple goons with guns watching me every day. They watched every move I made. Then they disappeared. I felt free. I felt like I was no longer a prisoner. I have gotten to know Sonny and Marcia, and they are good people. Marcia is a little strange, but she's . . . well, she's Marcia. I think something happened in her past and she is slow to trust, but I'm beginning to feel at home here. At least on the Bayfront. I like being out on the shrimp boat and the smell of the salty air. The work is hard, but it's rewarding."

Robbie didn't know what to say. Then he noticed his tears. Sean wiped his cheek with his arm.

"I can't have a family."

"Sure you can," Robbie said. "That's what we came here for—to find wives and go home to raise a family."

"You don't understand, Robbie. They castrated me. I can never have a family of my own."

Robbie's mouth dropped open. "They didn't!"

"They did. I hated them at first, but I don't know who they are. It wasn't Sonny or Marcia, but whoever they were, I think they butchered the job. It was very painful at first, but I healed.

"Sonny and I talked about it. He was castrated too. But they gave him a family and he's happy. He's not so interested in sex, but he cares for Lola and Marcia. Most of all, he cares for the shrimping business. That's where he gets most of his pleasure.

"I can't go home like this. There are no women there. And even if there were, they wouldn't have me. I could never have a family back home. At least here I can have one, but mostly I can find happiness in shrimping. I never cared for helping Dad raise hogs or working in the garden with Mom. There is nothing at home that I really cared about doing except playing with you, Ronnie, and Debra.

"The last couple weeks I have thought a lot about home, but I've thought about shrimping and fishing more. It gets into your blood. It seemed like a boring routine at first, but the longer I was there, I realized that it's different every day. You never know what you are going to pull up. Sometimes it's an old tire or log, but most of the time it's more kinds of fish, crabs, jellyfish, and other creatures I have never seen. And shrimp! Brown shrimp mostly and a few seabobs, mantis shrimp, and rock shrimp. Sonny said in the fall there would be white shrimp. 'Green tails' he called them. Big shrimp. Big enough you can put them on a barbecue. Sonny loves his shrimp on the barbie."

"I don't know what to say," Robbie said glumly.

"I'm tired."

"Well, let's get a good night's sleep and we'll talk some more tomorrow,"

Robbie said with a yawn.

Robbie showered and went to bed. He was tired, but his brain was working overtime. *This is certainly going to put a kink in my escape plans. Can I do it without Sean? What am I going to tell his mom and dad? Shit!*

Chapter 18

Back in Peaceful Valley…

Melissa sat looking into her cup of coffee.

"You hardly touched your breakfast," James noted. "What's the matter?"

"Robbie has been gone for weeks. I miss him."

"And he and Sean are going to be gone for months. You can't sit around here all the time worrying about them."

"I know. But they could be hurt or dead for all we know," she said.

"Knowing those two, they have probably already found a couple sweet gals and are having the time of their lives."

"I know, but I just worry about them."

"Come on, finish your breakfast. We've got work to do." He got up and headed for the back door.

"Check the water first, honey," she said. "It was running a little slow this morning."

"Will do."

James met Ronnie coming around the house with a few squirrels he'd bagged on his early morning hunt. He held them up to show his dad and then headed down to the pier to clean them.

"Eileen will certainly be happy to see those fellas," he said to Ronnie.

Ronnie smiled.

Melissa heard Eileen stirring in the bedroom and began to fix a plate for her. She came out a short time later dressed for her day. "Water's running a little slow this morning," she announced.

"Yeah, James is working on it," Melissa replied. "Slept in a bit this morning didn't you?"

"Yeah, I had trouble getting to sleep last night. I had a bad feeling about Sean and Robbie."

"I've been worried about them ever since I got up," Melissa said. "I hope nothing bad has happened to them."

"Me too. Seems a little strange for both of us to suddenly have some bad thoughts about the boys."

"Yes, it does."

"What time did the neighbors say they were going to be over?" Eileen asked.

"About noon. Sleeping late and now memory problems, Eileen?"

"I guess I'm getting a little old, but I got up didn't I?" she replied with a smile.

James checked the cistern and then chopped wood for a couple hours before it got too hot. Afterward, he put his trunks on and took a dip in the river. He then went in to change and get ready for their noon meeting.

Melissa and Eileen made plenty of tea along with a big pot of stew and some snacks for the meeting.

"What did the new neighbors want to meet about?" Eileen asked James.

"I don't know, Eileen. They only said that after harvest, they had something to discuss with us."

"Well, I think it's damn strange," Eileen added.

"We'll find out soon enough," Melissa said.

A short while later, it sounded like they were surrounded by wolves with all the people converging on the place. Samuel and Sally Lin came up from the back. Reggie and Emily Carston came in from upstream, and the new neighbors came in from downstream.

James went to the front door and returned their wolf howls, while Melissa did the same at the rear door. Soon they were all gathered inside.

"I don't think there have ever been this many people in this house," Eileen remarked.

"You kids fix yourselves a bowl of stew and go out on the porch to eat," Eileen said. "There's not enough room in here for all of us."

"Yes, ma'am," some of the youngsters replied.

Everybody filled their bowls and once they were seated, John offered up a prayer for the food.

"Our cistern is getting low on water," James informed Eileen and Melissa. "That's why the water pressure is low."

"Ours is pretty low too," John remarked.

"Yeah, this is the dry time of the year," Eileen reminded them.

"We'll get some rain soon," Melissa added. "In the meantime, we'll just have to make due with well water."

"At least it was dry during harvest," James added.

"Thank God for that," Kathy said.

"Amen," John added.

"I remember when I first moved here, Lars was struggling to make a decent crop. James's irrigation system changed everything."

"Mighty fine stew," Kathy said as she emptied her bowl.

Everyone agreed.

"All right. Get out of here, guys," Melissa said when everyone had finished eating. "We'll clean up the dishes."

The men went out to the pier and James pulled out three cigars and offered one each to Reggie and John. He knew Sam wouldn't want one.

"I don't approve of smoking," John added.

"Well, we don't mind an occasional smoke," Reggie said with a sneer.

"That's enough, Reggie," James said. "Different strokes . . ."

A half-hour later, James suggested they go back inside. "The ladies should have things cleaned up by now."

As they gathered around the kitchen table, John stepped over to the front door and informed the kids the meeting was starting.

"We would rather stay out here and talk," Brooke said.

"Suit yourselves," he replied.

John shut the door and walked back to one end of the table, but he didn't sit. "I'll be blunt. I wanted this meeting because we need to build a church. We need a place to worship God."

"And which god is that?" Reggie spurted.

John was taken aback a bit, but never missed a beat. "Our lord and savior, Jesus Christ."

"I don't think I know that one," Reggie said. He did; he was just being an ass, and Emily swatted him for it.

"I don't know if we really have a need for a church," James joined in. "I think it would be a waste of our time and materials. We have so much work around here. It seems like I never get caught up on chores. I don't think we can spare the time."

"But we need a place to worship," John reiterated, "and it's not a waste of materials to build a church for our maker. As far as time, we must make the effort."

"I think what James is saying," Eileen explained, "is that we can better worship the god of our choice privately, whenever and wherever we happen to be when the need arises. For me that might be at Lars's grave. For Melissa that might be in the house. For James that might be in the garden or the fishing pier. What he's saying is that we don't need a special place to pray."

"Besides, if we built a church," Reggie spouted off again, "if I were to walk inside, it would likely ignite spontaneously and burn to the ground."

Emily swatted him again, though he might be right.

"I don't know if I can live here without a church to worship in," John added. "If we are going to build a bigger and better community, there must be a church."

"I agree," Kathy spoke up. "Our kids need to grow up with God."

"I say we take a vote," Reggie announced abruptly. "I vote no."

"I vote no too," James said quickly.

Emily and Eileen both frowned at the guys. Neither could understand why guys had to be so quick and decisive.

“Have some compassion dammit, Reggie,” Emily said. “While one day, if our community grows large enough, there may be a need for a church, I don’t think now is the time.”

“I agree,” Eileen said. “So, for now, I’ll have to say no.”

“I think a church would be nice,” Sally said.

“But we have too much work. We don’t have the time to spare to build a church,” Samuel pointed out.

“I know,” Sally said. “Even though a church would be appealing to me, I’m sorry, Sam is right; we don’t have the time.”

“I’ll have to agree with James,” Melissa added. “I vote no as well.”

“There! You have it,” Reggie said in the smart-ass tone he’d had all afternoon. “Looks like there’ll be no church.” As Reggie’s lips curled into a smile, Emily shot him a disapproving look, removing the smile immediately.

“This isn’t the last of it,” John declared loudly. “Come on, Kathy.” With Kathy on his heels, John stormed from the house, rounded up the kids, and headed back to the old Weston place.

John Wimberley steamed all the way home, not saying a word. Kathy could hear him grumbling to himself and kept quiet. The kids knew what happened and also that they would be working extra hard for a few days until their dad cooled down. They chatted amongst themselves, hanging a hundred feet back. From time to time, John would look back with a grim expression on his face to make certain they were still following.

Ronnie and Debra walked inside with confused looks on their faces.

“What’s going on?” Ronnie asked.

“I never expected that,” James said, ignoring Ronnie.

“What?” Debra asked loudly.

“That they’d want to build a church . . . and that they’d be so insistent about it.”

“A church?” Debra exclaimed.

“Yes, a church,” Eileen told her.

“Of all things,” Reggie said. “Don’t they know how hard we work around here to just live?”

“Devout religious people always need a church,” Sally said. “I think it would be okay, but I don’t know when I’d have the time to attend. There is always so much to do.”

“I don’t have anything against churches,” James admitted, “but we don’t have the time to waste to build one.”

Eileen and Emily didn’t say a word. Neither was overly concerned with John’s proposal now that it had been squashed. They were more concerned with keeping their secret. If the Wimberleys found out . . . what a ruckus that would cause, knowing now how religious they were.

"We've overstayed our welcome," Samuel said.

"Nonsense!" Eileen said. "You and Sally are welcome here anytime and for as long as you want. That's the way it has always been, and it's not going to change."

"Thank you, but we'd better get home. We have a lot of chores to finish before it gets dark."

"Thank you, all of you, for your hospitality," Sally added, "but we really should go."

"It's getting late," Emily stated. "We need to go too. If we don't leave soon, we're not going to get much done before it gets dark on us."

"Love you guys," Reggie added. "It's been a hoot!"

Hugs and kisses were shared all around and Sam and Sally headed for the back door. Debra followed.

"Bye, Debra," Ronnie said.

"Bye."

"See you tomorrow, Eileen?" Emily whispered in her ear as they hugged good-bye.

"Yes, about mid-morning?"

"Yes."

When they arrived at the Westin homestead, John opened the front door. Kathy and the kids followed him inside.

"I think we need to have a discussion," he announced.

"What's up, Daddy?" Brooke, the eldest, asked.

"You didn't hear what was going on in the meeting? We were certainly talking loud enough."

"No, Daddy. You guys were so noisy; we went down to the river. What's up?"

"It seems like the neighbors don't believe in God," he said. "I asked them if we could build a church, and they were against it."

"Why?" Lance asked.

"They don't have time for God," Kathy answered.

"They won't make time for God," John said, correcting her. "They said they won't make time to build a church, and they won't waste materials. I don't think they believe in their creator. They owe everything they have and everything they are to God, yet they say they don't have the time."

"John."

"Waste materials!" he repeated even louder. "If that's the case, then they are all a bunch of savages!"

"Calm down, John," Kathy said.

"They are all a bunch of savages!" he repeated loudly.

Chapter 19

Eileen showered and dressed before Melissa had breakfast ready. "Smells good," she said as she walked into the kitchen.

"Going somewhere?" Melissa said.

"I thought I'd visit Emily and Reggie today. We didn't get to talk much yesterday with the meeting and all. I miss Emily and unless you have something else for me to do . . ."

"No, not at all. You go and have fun. Take all day if you need to."

"I'll be back well before dark. It gets a little scary out at dusk."

James and Ronnie came in and they all had breakfast together. Ronnie wanted to join Eileen on the trip to the Carston's, but James vetoed that to Eileen's relief. "I've got a lot of work lined up for you today, young man."

Eileen strapped on her holster and checked the pistol. "See you later."

"Bye, Grandma."

Eileen smiled. *I love that boy so much. And I love being called Grandma.*

Eileen blew a kiss toward Lars's grave on the way out. *I love you, honey. Maybe you should take a long nap today.*

Halfway to Reggie and Emily's, Eileen sat down on a log. She had plenty of time. Besides, she needed to think. She grabbed a bottle of water out of her backpack and took a sip as she watched the sun coming up behind the trees. The sky was clear and the wind calm. She took a deep breath. *It's so peaceful out here.* A Great Kiskadee cried out in the distance. Its mate, no doubt, answered back nearby. A red squirrel scampered along the ground and up a tree. Then it chattered at Eileen as if to say, "You're not supposed to be here. This is my territory."

Eileen loved the valley and everything in it, but it looked as if things were about to change, thanks to the Wimberleys. If they built a church in Peaceful Valley, she'd have to attend . . . and that meant going to confession. She couldn't let that happen. She couldn't let John and the others find out about her sins.

Eileen got up and it wasn't long before she made it to the edge of the clearing. She gave out her wolf howl, and Reggie opened the front door and returned her signal. She gave Reggie a kiss on the cheek and they went inside.

Emily had prepared mint tea. Eileen handed her a jar of pickled beets, for which Emily gave her a big smile and 'thank you'.

They sat at the kitchen table. No one said a word. They all knew what was going to happen. This was not their first date. Reggie's hair was all slicked back. Obviously he had already taken his shower. Emily finished her tea quickly and got up to take her shower.

Eileen finished her tea as well, and went into the bathroom with Emily. She began taking off her clothes and neatly folded and stacked them on the vanity while Emily finished up in the shower. When she turned off the water, Eileen was waiting with a towel and dried her off from head to toe. She gave her little kisses on her breasts on the way down. She just loved Emily's full and relatively firm breasts.

When Emily was dry, they went into the bedroom. Reggie was lying in the middle of the bed, naked as a newborn baby. Eileen and Emily looked at each other and back at Reggie. The sight of the two ladies threw him into a full erection. The ladies giggled.

Debra stopped by the Lindgrens and picked up Ronnie and they headed over to the Wimberley's. Ronnie let out a wolf howl, and it was immediately returned by Lance. Ronnie and Debra made their way to the house.

"Is Zack around?" Debra asked.

Lance looked around and not seeing his brother, yelled his name. Ronnie didn't see Brooke and followed Lance's remedy. Brooke and Zack came out, but so did Charlotte and Kira.

"What's up?" Charlotte asked.

"We thought we'd go for a swim," Ronnie said.

"And I've brought a slab of bacon," Debra added. "Daddy butchered a hog last week. My daddy makes the best smoked bacon in the valley." She smiled proudly and handed the package to Charlotte.

Charlotte took the bundle to her dad who had come to the doorway. "They brought bacon, and we're going swimming."

"Thanks for the meat, but you're not going swimming," he yelled out. "You two little heathens get home."

"They're not heathens, and we're going swimming," Brooke yelled back.

"The hell you are!"

"Now John, let them go." Kathy said as she walked up behind him.

"They're not going!" he repeated loud enough for all to hear.

"John! John!" He turned around the second time she said his name. "Let them go. If you don't, you're going to drive a wedge between yourself and your kids that you'll never repair."

"But—"

"Don't but me," she said. "Let them go, John, then we'll talk."

John turned back to the kids. "Okay, get out of here. Go."

"We'll be right back," said Brooke and the girls ran to the clothesline to get their swimsuits.

John and Kathy watched as they disappeared into the woods.

John backed away from the doorway and closed the door. "Now what do you want to tell me?"

"You drive your kids away and you'll regret it the rest of your life," Kathy said. "Listen, I hated my dad. He was strict and ruled with an iron fist. I hated him for it. Do you want your kids to hate you?"

"No."

"They're grown up now. They have to learn things on their own. They will make mistakes, but they will learn from them. And they will come to you, to us, when they need guidance. They won't do something crazy like I did when I was younger." A tear ran down her cheek. "Something which could ruin their lives forever." Kathy paused for a second. "I guess we need to have a talk. Go over to the sofa, John, and I'll get us some tea."

Kathy made a couple cool glasses of wild berry tea and joined her husband. Her hand was shaky when she handed John his glass.

"Now, what do you have to tell me?"

"Something I should have told you a long time ago. I'm sorry, but I was just too embarrassed for a long time. Then, after a while, it just didn't seem important to tell you."

"What?" he asked.

She paused and took a deep breath. "Daddy was so strict that I felt like I was in prison." Kathy began to cry again.

"Go on. I'm listening."

"You're going to hate me too," she whimpered.

"No, I won't. I love you. I'll always love you."

Kathy took another deep breath.

"Daddy wouldn't let me have friends. I couldn't go out on weekends to meet with classmates from school. I couldn't have friends over. The only time I got to see anyone was in school. They asked me to join them and Daddy always refused to let me go. After a while my friends stopped asking. I curled up in my little shell at home.

"I studied and I read books. Wonderful books about shining knights and handsome princes who would come and rescue the fair maidens and take them away to live happily ever after. I prayed for my handsome prince to come carry me away. I prayed and I prayed, but he never came.

"Then, one day I ran away from home. I stole all the money I could find in the house and I left. I went as far as the money would take me. I took a bus to San Antonio. I told you I had lived all my life in San Antonio, but I came from Phoenix. I lived in San Antonio five years before we met. Most of those five years were a bloody hell!"

John sat there with his mouth open. His eyes were bulging and sweat beaded up on his forehead.

Kathy took a deep breath and continued. "I got off the bus hungry and broke. No one would hire me. I was dirty and probably stank to high heaven. I found a guy, who was about as dirty and as smelly as I was, and would give me enough money for a meal if I had sex with him. I did."

John gasped. He was speechless.

"The next day I had sex with him again and a third time a couple days later, when he ran out of money. But I got enough money to stay in a cheap hotel one night to take a shower and get a good night's sleep."

John began to wheeze as he gasped for air.

"You all right?" she asked.

"I think so," he replied.

"I cleaned my clothes and myself the best I could. I walked the streets and sold my body to anyone who wanted it. I was good-looking. More so than most I met doing the same thing I was. I made enough money to get a regular room at a little bit better motel. I now had a room I could take the guys to, instead of doing it in the back seats of their cars. Some liked doing it in their cars . . . a quickie . . . but they always wanted a discount.

"After the first year, business picked up significantly. I made a lot of money. I picked up a lot of regular clients, and they paid good money for me. Too much money. Many hurt me and my body took a beating. I suffered mentally as well. To ease my pain, I started taking drugs. All the girls on the streets took drugs, and I joined the club. I'm sure there were a thousand stories out there just like mine in every city.

"I got busted so many times I can't remember. I spent dozens of nights in jail, detox, and then back to the streets. Other prostitutes, some I recognized, were in adjoining cells. I listened to them screaming night after sleepless night. I'm sure I did my share of screaming too.

"Finally, one night a new guy wasn't satisfied with my services and beat the crap out of me. He shoved me out of the car at a hospital and left me on the concrete near the emergency entrance. I crawled over to the glass doors and when they opened in the middle of the night, someone noticed me.

"That guy . . . I don't even know his name . . . he broke my nose and jaw. I had two black eyes. I had a broken finger and scrapes probably from the concrete at the hospital. I felt like I had fallen off a ten-story building.

"I spent three days in the hospital, and then I went to jail and detox for the umpteenth time. I stayed in lockup for nearly a month.

"When they finished with me, they took me to a church rehabilitation center for prostitutes. They locked me up too. They convinced me that I could get better with God's help. That I could get off the street and live a normal life. I guess I showed them I was willing and they took me in. I spent a year there and think I was mostly rehabilitated. That's when you caught my eye. You were a newly ordained minister sitting in for the regular pastor who was ill. You were young, but you delivered a powerful sermon which I remember to this day."

John smiled.

"I knew you were destined for great things."

"I remember you too, sitting there in the third pew," he responded. "You smiled when I pounded my fist on the dais."

"Yes. And you said 'Yea, though I walk through the valley of the shadow of death, I will fear no evil . . .' with heart and conviction."

"Yes. Psalms 23:4."

"I'm sorry I didn't tell you a long time ago, John. Do you hate me?"

"No, I don't hate you. But this is a shock. I need some time to process it. I can't believe you've kept this from me for so many years."

"I'm sorry. I wanted to tell you for a long time. I was afraid you'd hate me. I'm still afraid you'll hate me. Then after the first year or so, I wanted to tell you but just never seemed to find the right moment. How do you tell your husband that you were a prostitute?"

They just sat there staring at each other for a few moments.

"So why are you telling me all this now?"

"We've had no normalcy in our lives since the grid shut down. You have been bossy and overprotective since that dreadful day. I know you were just trying to protect us, so we lived with it. I lived with it. But we are not in San Antonio anymore. Things are different here, and we have a chance at a normal life. It may be tough here, but we don't have to be worried for our lives day in and day out like we were in the city."

"But there are still dangers, Kathy."

"Yes, there are, but our new neighbors are not the enemy. You can't rule our kids with an iron fist anymore. You can't force stuff down their throats, and you can't force stuff down our neighbor's throats like you did with the church. Please don't drive a wedge between you and the kids, and don't do the same with our neighbors. You were mad because you didn't get your way and you took it out on our kids.

"Our neighbors are not bad people. They have been trying to survive just like we have. There is no church here because there is no preacher. Now we have a preacher but no church. I know you want a place to worship God, but these people have not had a formal religion in their lives for many years. People don't change so easily. Maybe, with a little time and gentle urging, they will come around to your ways. And they may not, but you can't force them. I like this place and we can have a normal life with our kids if you'll just let it happen. Please, John!"

She leaned over and gave him a little kiss.

"I've got a lot to think about," he replied.

"And I have dinner to make," she said as she headed into the kitchen. "How about some breakfast for dinner? Shall we try out some of this fresh bacon?"

"I'd like that," he replied.

Kathy awoke tired. She hadn't slept well at all last night. John, on the other hand, slept like a log. She knew because he snored most of the night.

When she was done in the bathroom, John had just finished getting dressed. She walked over and wrapped her arms around his neck and pressed her lips to his cheek. "I love you," she said.

"I love you too," he replied and went into the bathroom.

He said the words, but she could already tell things were going to be different between the two of them. Maybe he didn't hate her, but he seemed a little cold this morning. She felt her eyes tearing up as she walked into the kitchen to get started on breakfast.

Kathy took the second batch of bacon out of the skillet and started the eggs as one by one the kids filed in.

"How was your swim yesterday?" she asked.

"Good," Brooke replied.

"Is Daddy okay?" Charlotte whispered.

"Yes, he's fine," Kathy replied. "He was a little upset because the neighbors didn't want to build a church. We had a long talk while you were swimming. He'll be fine now I think."

"Good!" Kira said with a smirk.

After breakfast, John put the boys to work as did Kathy with the girls. After they got the place cleaned up and settled in, it didn't take them long to realize that there would always be an endless list of chores that needed to be done every day.

Due to the lack of rain, John put the boys to work hauling well water and dumping it into the cistern. John got busy patching some roof leaks while it was dry. After the kitchen was cleaned up, Charlotte and Kira worked in the house while Kathy and Brooke worked in the garden cleaning up the weeds and vines the boys had missed and preparing new beds for the fall garden.

Chapter 20

Meanwhile back in Corpus Christi . . .

Sean was up much earlier than Robbie. Getting up at 6:00 a.m. was easy after getting up at 4:00 every morning to go shrimping. Sean looked around the hangar until Robbie showed up. He was looking the F-15 over when Robbie made his way into the hangar.

"What do you think?" Robbie asked.

"About what?"

"The F-15, what else?"

"I bet this thing would be a killer plane to fly. Like a screaming eagle," Sean said. "I found the ladder too. Help me drag the thing over here, and I'll take a look in the cockpit."

Sean pulled the tarp off the already open canopy and crawled into the front seat.

"Nothing works," he said. "Is there a battery in these things?"

"I don't know," Robbie said. "You're the expert."

They both laughed.

"We better find out," Sean said. "And soon, too, before what's-his-name shows up."

"Jorge?"

"Yes."

Sean looked around to see if he could find a battery compartment. He then climbed out. "We've got to find the battery, Robbie. If there is one."

They looked inside the landing gear compartments and for hatches where the internal workings might be hidden. Jorge walked up behind them.

"How's it going?"

Sean grumbled something inaudible. Robbie stepped over next to Jorge. "He's checking everything from top to bottom."

"What's it look like in the cockpit?" Jorge asked Sean.

Sean grumbled again so that neither Robbie nor Jorge could make out what he was saying. That was intentional on Sean's part.

"Need some help?" Jorge asked.

Sean ignored him for a moment. *What do I say? Maybe I should be short with him. I hope he doesn't get too mad and hit me or something.* Sean got out from under the plane and walked about halfway over to where Jorge was standing.

"There are a million things I need to check on this aircraft," Sean said arrogantly. "If you two will just leave me alone for a while, maybe I can figure something out in a month or two." Then he just stared at Jorge with his eyebrows raised, hands on his hips, and his head cocked a bit.

Jorge took a deep breath and stared at Sean for a second. Sean didn't bat an eye.

"Okay! Excuse me for butting in."

Sean turned back to the aircraft, while Robbie and Jorge went about some other business across the hangar.

Later that evening, Sean joined Robbie in his room again for another soda.

"Do you get these things all the time?" Sean asked, holding up the soda.

"Yeah, don't you?"

"Hell no. Mostly all I got was water. Marcia made a weird tasting tea from time to time, and Sonny had a stash of what he called whiskey, but mostly just water. The tea tasted a little better than water, but the whiskey tasted like fermented seagull shit."

"You figure anything out about the bird?" Robbie asked.

"Hell no! I did find a couple wrenches to open up a compartment or two," Sean replied. "I think you need some special tools to work on those things. Keep Jorge away as much as you can, and maybe he won't find out how stupid I am about these jets."

"I'll do what I can, but I don't think you have to worry about him after what you said this morning. He was pissed for a little while but got over it pretty quickly. He just chalked it up to you being wound a little too tight . . . like all jet mechanics are wound tight."

"Can I talk to you a little more about you staying here in Corpus Christi?" Robbie asked.

"Sure," Sean replied, "but you're not going to change my mind if that's what you're after."

That was exactly what Robbie had in mind, but he could see the resolve in his eyes. He knew that once Sean put his mind to something, nothing would deter him.

"I love being out on the water," Sean said. "Sonny was showing me how to drive the boat and maintain the thing. The waves splashing against the hull, the calm cool mornings . . . once it got daylight, you could see forever. There are no trees to get in the way. Of course, the bird shit is a pain in the ass, but that washes off.

"Another thing . . . there are vacant buildings everywhere. Any size I want to move into. They'd just take some cleaning up. I could have a castle if I wanted."

Robbie listened to Sean's reasons for staying. He now seemed at peace here. Nothing he could say would change his mind.

"Sure going to mess up my escape plans though," Robbie said.

"I'm sorry. Maybe I can still help if you tell me what you want me to do."

"I may do that, Sean. It's going to take all I can do to get out of here without getting killed."

"At least you don't have some goons watching your every move like I did until just a few days ago. I wondered why they left."

"It could be because their chief disappeared," Robbie said. "They could be out trying to find him."

"Do you know what happened to him?"

"No," he replied. That was a lie, but he couldn't tell anyone Florence had killed her dad, not even Sean. If Sean were to see her again, which was highly likely should he stay here at the Airport for a while, and he said something about Richard, Florence would never trust him again. *Yes, a little lie is better. If Sean does find out, I'll tell him that I lied to protect Florence.*

The next morning, Sandra showed up on schedule. Robbie didn't tell Sean that he was her whore. They had talked mostly about Sean and never got around to his long story.

"I'm taking care of some stuff for Sandra over at the Farm," he said on his way out. "You take care of those jets, and I'll see you tomorrow."

He left Sean scratching his head in the middle of the hangar.

Sandra saw Robbie coming her way, so she waited in the Jeep with the engine running.

"Did you find Richard?" Robbie asked when he got in.

"No," Sandra replied. "I can't figure out what happened to him. I've had men out scouring the country for him. Nothing!"

"Maybe he just left town," Robbie suggested. "Florence said he and her mom had a fight and she ran him off. Maybe he decided to leave the city."

"I don't think so, but it's a possibility."

"What are you going to do for a new chief in the meantime?"

"People like him are a dime a dozen. I've already replaced him. Richard has been rubbing me the wrong way ever since you two boys showed up."

"Was it something I did?"

"No, actually it was something I did," Sandra said. "I didn't let him kill you."

"Thank you, Sandra."

"My pleasure," she said with a smile.

Robbie hadn't seen Sandra in such a good mood up to now, despite the fact Richard was missing. It was almost like she was in love with him. *Damn! She is,* he thought. *But I can use this.* Sandra was thirty plus years older than Robbie, but she was getting downright giddy.

When they got to the Farm, Barbara and Kim had lunch ready when Sandra and Robbie walked in the door. They were all smiles. They were surprised, as was Robbie, when Sandra joined him at the table. Even more surprising to Robbie was that she sat next to him rather than on the opposite end. The girl's smiles disappeared as soon as Sandra sat down.

"You may serve us now, ladies," Sandra instructed.

As soon as lunch was finished, Sandra told the girls they could go to their rooms. Robbie noticed they appeared confused, but they left promptly, willingly and without discussion. Sandra wrinkled her brow and gave them a bit of an evil look, which she made certain Robbie didn't see, and the girls followed Sandra's instructions.

"Go have a seat on the sofa," Sandra said. "I'll refresh our glasses and we'll chat a bit."

Sandra returned and joined Robbie. "Did Sean get a chance to look at the jets?"

"A little."

"And?"

"It's too early to tell. Maybe next weekend I'll have something for you."

"Do you mind entertaining me tonight?" Sandra asked with a sly grin.

"No, not at all."

Perfect answer, whether he means it or not.

When Robbie returned to the Airport, Sean was full of questions. Jorge was nearby most of the day, so the long version of the story would have to wait until they were alone later that evening.

"I did manage to get into the electrical systems," Sean informed Robbie. "I put a charger on them yesterday."

"Great," Robbie said.

"Let's see if we can get some things going." Sean climbed up the ladder to the cockpit of the Raptor. Robbie climbed up behind him and squatted on the outside while Sean tried to figure out the knobs, switches, and buttons.

Sean flipped a switch and the dashboard lit up. He grinned at Robbie. "I wonder if this thing is loaded."

"I don't know."

Robbie yelled out to Jorge.

"How should I know? You guys are the experts."

"You still pissed off about the other day?" Robbie asked.

"I'm sorry I pissed you off, Jorge," Sean said. "There are just so many things to check on these planes and I needed some space."

"That's all right," Jorge said. "There are rockets underneath the wings. I think I'd assume the guns are loaded too, but you might check. Be careful which buttons you push." I'll stay well away from the front of your plane until you get it figured out."

Sean smiled and went back to work. "Well, at least the guns are labeled," he told Robbie. "And the rockets too. Maybe I won't accidentally shoot one of these things off. The gauges show there is fuel in this thing too. We need to drain a little and test it. If that stuff has been sitting in the tanks for years, it may ruin the engines."

"Sean?"

"What?"

"I've got an idea. The guns are pointed at the wall. There is nothing out back to hurt, and a few holes in the wall aren't going to matter. Try firing off a couple rounds."

"In here? Jorge will kill us."

"It'll keep him away from the plane and out of your hair," Robbie said and chuckled.

Sean looked down and turned on the power to the guns. There was a whine on the wing. He pushed the button. Sean jumped at the *rat-a-tat-tat-tat-tat* and yanked his finger from the button. Robbie almost fell off the ladder. Sean quickly cut the power off to the guns.

"Well, we know for certain they're loaded now," Sean said with a laugh.

"I didn't think they'd be that loud!"

Russ came running out of his office. "Son-of-a-bitch!" he screamed.

Jorge was face down on the concrete. He got up once he heard Russ screaming.

Russ cautiously walked up to the Raptor. "What the hell is going on out here?" he demanded.

"Sorry, sir. It was an accident," Sean explained.

"At least it wasn't a rocket, sir," Robbie stated.

"Jorge!"

"Yes, sir."

"Make certain those boys take all the armaments off those two jets before they do anything else," Russ demanded. He then grumbled all the way back to his office.

"Well, boys," Jorge said. "You heard the man."

"Yes, sir."

Jorge walked off shaking his head and grumbling, "damn those boys!"

Sean and Robbie spent nearly a week removing all the armaments from the two planes. Not because it was that hard a job, but they just didn't know how to do it. Plus, the rockets were extremely heavy. Good thing there were only four on the F-15 and two on the Raptor.

When the planes were disarmed, Robbie set a ladder against the wall next to the hole they made. He didn't know how many rounds were fired, but they made a ragged hole almost big enough he could stick his head through the opening. He smeared roofing cement Jorge gave him around the opening and screwed a piece of sheet metal over the hole.

"Good enough!"

He and Sean never got around to Robbie's long story because of the gun incident and all the time and effort they put into disarming the planes. When Saturday rolled around, Sean remembered and reminded Robbie they needed to have a long talk when he got back.

Barbara and Kim made lunch for Robbie once again. Sandra didn't attend this time, to the delight of the girls. The talk had gotten around about Robbie, and they couldn't wait to get their hands on the hot young stud, especially having had to wait an extra week to get their turn. They weren't disappointed.

Louise was preparing breakfast when she heard dogs barking outside. She turned off the stove and slumped into a chair at the kitchen table, wiping away a stray tear as she heard Florence scurrying down the hall.

"What's all that racket outside?" Florence asked.

"I think they found your daddy." Louise leaned over, her face buried in her hands.

"What are we going to do?"

"I don't think there's anything we can do. Remember, I killed your daddy, not you."

Florence and Louise jumped when they heard a banging at the door. Louise began to bawl. She knew what was going to happen next.

Again, there was banging on the door. "Open it, Florence."

Florence opened the door to find two guns pointed at her face. She began to cry as the men rushed in and grabbed her and her mother. One of the men pushed Florence against the wall, pulled her arms behind her, and handcuffed her. The other man yanked Louise up and did the same to her.

"Don't hurt my baby!" Louise yelled.

The men dragged Florence and Louise through the house and out the back door. Louise saw the plastic bags. One of the dogs growled at her. One bag was torn and a hand sticking out. The torso, still wrapped in bedclothes, lay exposed as well. Another plastic bag containing Richard's decomposed but still recognizable head was exposed for all the world to see. Several unopened bags were scattered about.

"I'm Mathew Helms," one of the men stated, looking directly at Louise. "Care to explain?" He held up a revolver on the end of a stick.

"Richard beat us and I killed him," Louise stated, bursting into tears again.

"No, I killed him," Florence blurted out.

"Shut up, Florence," her mother demanded.

"It doesn't matter which of you did it for now, but we'll get to the bottom of this," he stated.

Suddenly, three other men appeared on the scene and were instructed to search the house for more weapons. Finding nothing, Mathew ordered them to uncuff the women and take them back inside.

"For now, the two of you are under house arrest. There will be guards stationed outside. Try to leave the house, and you'll be shot on sight. No questions asked. Understand?"

"Yes," Louise replied.

"Cover the body back up," Mathew ordered. He took another look at the remains, shook his head, and left.

Chapter 21

Sean and Robbie finally got around to their talk.

Sean listened intently as Robbie described his exploits with Sandra and the girls. He tried hard not to let his disappointment show, but it didn't work.

"I'm sorry, Sean. I forgot you were . . . that you can't—"

"It's okay. Sonny was castrated, and he has sex with Marcia. Though he can't have kids, he does enjoy sex with the proper motivation. Maybe with some extra motivation, I can too . . . if I get the chance."

"I'm sure you will."

"There don't seem to be many opportunities out there. Looks like all the unattached women are at the Farm."

"Maybe so, but there have to be other girls somewhere," Robbie assured him as he reached under his pillow and pulled out the *Playboy* and handed it to Sean.

Sean grinned.

"The Farm may have most of the girls, but I'm beginning to resent Sandra and the way she runs things. Don't get me wrong, the girls are great, but the fact that I don't have a choice rubs me the wrong way."

"Don't let it get to you," Sean said, flipping through the magazine. "I'd change places with you in a flash."

"Maybe you'll get one of my kids one day . . . and its mother," Robbie said.

"Are the girls good-looking?"

"All of them so far."

"These sodas sure are good," Sean commented. "I like the strawberry flavor too. I'm going to miss them when I get back to the Bayfront. I don't feel like a prisoner here. I guess I'll be an inmate again when I get back down there, and detainees don't get much. Marcia will feed me good and I like her seafood, but I guess I'll have to get used to drinking mostly water. I guess that's about all a prisoner can ask for."

"Maybe we can sneak some back with you," Robbie said. "They keep us pretty well supplied around here. I don't think they'll miss a few."

"That would be great. I guess we better get some sleep," Sean said, handing the magazine back to Robbie. "This thing certainly won't help my cause."

"See you in the morning," Robbie replied.

Sean pulled the blanket up to his chin. Listening to Robbie talk about the girls had excited him. He let his hand wander to his groin, hopeful, but found the talk had caused no reaction. He squeezed his eyes shut, fighting the tears welling there, and soon fell asleep.

The next morning, Robbie watched as a man he didn't recognize pulled up at the Airport and headed straight for Russ's office. A short time later, Russ stuck his head out of the door and called Robbie over.

"Robbie," Russ said, "this is Mathew Helms. He is the new Chief of Police around here."

"Mr. Helms," Robbie said politely, extending his hand.

When Mathew didn't return the gesture, Robbie stuffed his hands in his pockets, fighting the urge to wipe away the sweat he knew was beading on his forehead. He braced himself for what was coming.

"Robbie, I have some questions for you."

"Yes, sir."

"Have a seat," he instructed.

Robbie got comfortable and politely answered all Mathew's questions about the Ingalls. The questions were simple at first, but became increasingly more difficult to answer.

"Do you know what happened to Mr. Ingalls?"

"Only that he disappeared."

Robbie tried not to fidget under Mathew's intense gaze.

"Have you been to the Ingalls's home?"

"Not since I was brought here."

"Not even once?"

"No, sir."

"Have you seen Louise Ingalls or Florence Ingalls?"

"Not her mother, but Florence has been here a couple times."

"And did she seem upset?"

"No, sir."

Chief Helms paused again, and the next question knocked Robbie's socks off.

"Do you think Florence is capable of murder?"

Robbie's jaw dropped. "What?"

"Murder. Do you think Florence could kill her father?"

"No, sir." Robbie swatted away the trickle of sweat that now made its way down the side of his face. "No, sir," he repeated. "Florence is the nicest girl I've ever met. She is warm and caring. I wouldn't be here today if she hadn't nursed me back to health. She wouldn't harm anyone or anything."

Mathew put a finger to his chin and waited.

"Did . . . did something happen to Mr. Ingalls?"

"Some of my men found him buried behind the Ingalls's home."

Robbie opened his mouth to speak, but nothing came out.

"So you don't know anything about this?"

"No, sir," Robbie lied again, his mind swirling with questions he couldn't ask. He stuck to his story.

"Where's Florence? Can I see her?"

"No. Absolutely not!"

"What have you done with her?"

"If it's any of your business, Florence and her mother are under house arrest. Some of my men are posted front and back."

"What's going to happen to them?"

"There will be a trial."

"A trial?"

"Yes, just as soon as Sandra can get it set up."

"Is Sandra a judge?"

"She will be for this case. Anything else you can tell me?"

"I don't think so, sir."

"Now don't lie to me. If you know anything, you best let it be said now. If something comes out in the trial that you haven't told me, Sandra will be all over you like ugly on a monkey."

Mathew concluded his interrogation and Robbie walked back into the hangar to resume his work.

The remainder of the week passed quickly as Robbie and Sean finished up their work on the F-15 and concentrated their efforts on the Raptor. When Sandra arrived to pick him up on Saturday, Robbie's heart nearly pounded out of his chest—and not for the usual reasons. He needed information that Sandra could no doubt supply.

"Good morning, Robbie. You ready?" she asked.

He swallowed hard, willing his heart to stop pounding so he could focus. He had to remain calm or Sandra would know something was up.

"Yep, I'm ready. It's great to see you."

Robbie watched the scenery fly by as they headed for the Farm. It was nothing he hadn't seen before, but at least it was a distraction.

"So, I guess you've heard we found Richard Ingalls buried behind his house?"

"Yes." *Short answers. Say as little as possible.*

"It looks like Louise Ingalls killed him. He beat her and Florence, and she killed him. I don't know where she got the gun, but she shot him in the chest." She paused a few seconds. "The only problem is that Florence has confessed to the murder too." Sandra paused again, looking over at Robbie. Do you think

Florence could kill her dad?"

"I don't think so," he said, forcing himself to maintain eye contact with Sandra.

"I don't either. But it does present a dilemma. The other was at least an accomplice, but which one of them killed Richard?"

"What will happen to the person who killed him when you figure it out?"

"Firing squad."

"Even if it turns out Florence did the killing?"

"Yes."

"But Richard beat them. I saw Florence's black eyes. Maybe it was self-defense. Would that make a difference?"

"There is still the issue of the gun. Where did that come from? They are not supposed to have a gun."

"Why not?"

"The only people who are allowed to have guns are the police and me. No one else. That's the law."

Then how are people supposed to protect themselves? he wondered, though he knew he couldn't ask. "So just having a gun can get you executed?"

"It could if that gun is used to kill someone. We'll get at the truth on Wednesday," she said.

"Wednesday?"

"Yes, the trial will start on Wednesday. Russ will bring you here to testify."

"Me? But I don't know anything."

"But you saw Florence at the Airport. You will be asked questions, as will Russ."

"What about Sean and Jorge?"

"No, Russ already informed me that they don't know anything. Sean didn't get to the Airport until after you saw Florence. And Jorge told Russ he didn't know anything."

"And who else will be there?"

"I've already told you more than I should. You'll find out the rest beginning on Wednesday."

The remainder of the trip was quiet and uneventful. Robbie was polite and opened the doors for Sandra as usual.

"Who am I seeing today?" he asked as they headed inside.

"Jade. By special request from her. Seems she's taking a liking to you."

Chapter 22

Sandra pounded her gavel on the desk. The room became quiet. It wasn't your usual courthouse, just one of the many barns at the Farm. Chairs had been brought in and arranged to resemble a courtroom. A large desk for Sandra, a chair alongside, and desks for the defense and prosecutor. The floor looked clean, but it still smelled of oil and fuel. It had the appearance of a courtroom, but Sandra knew otherwise. She wanted it to appear that there was some justice in her little world, though she knew that in the end the only justice there would be was hers.

One by one, people were marched in to answer questions, all loyal Sandra followers, until a dozen had been chosen for the jury. Then witnesses were brought in to be examined then cross-examined by Sandra's handpicked attorneys.

Robbie and the other witnesses were scattered around outside the makeshift courthouse, far enough away to prevent seeing or hearing what was going on inside. Each had their own personal guard, and they were not allowed to associate with each other.

Sandra assigned Robert to guard Robbie.

"So, do you do this often?" Robbie asked.

Robert grunted, spit tobacco juice, and wiped his mouth with his sleeve.

"Nice day we're having," Robbie stated.

Robert snorted. "You trying to get me in trouble for killing a witness, boy?"

Robbie shut up. An hour went by and some of the ladies brought sodas out to the witnesses and their guards. It was three hours before Robbie was called in to testify.

Robbie saw Florence and her mother for the first time in a long time, sitting alongside the defense attorney. Florence was wearing a plain dark dress and her hair was put up on top of her head. She cracked a smile when she saw him. He tried not to smile back so as not to adversely influence the jury. He wasn't certain it had worked.

After nearly an hour, everyone had finished asking him questions, satisfied he told them the truth, the whole truth, and nothing but the truth. Yes, he had lied on several occasions, but had they believed him? He wasn't sure, but he did the best he could. Afterward, Robert escorted him back outside with the rest of the witnesses. *Nothing to do now but wait and see.*

Sandra put on a good show as judge. The attorneys weren't nearly as competent, primarily taking their cues from Sandra. Maybe that was the best she could do. Maybe that's the best she wanted to do. The outcome probably wouldn't be any different one way or the other. Florence looked attractive. So did her mother. That probably won't help them though. *I better expect the worst.*

Florence and Louise were the last to testify.

"Richard beat me and he beat my baby," Louise stated. "Every time he was having a bad day, whether we were the source of his irritation or not, he took it out on us. He threatened to rape and kill his own daughter in front of me before he killed me. I killed him in self-defense. If I had not killed him, Florence and I would be dead now."

"And where did you get the gun?" the prosecutor asked.

"Richard had it. It was his. I found it one day when I was doing laundry."

"I'm told that Florence actually had the gun and that she killed Richard."

"No! Absolutely not. I killed him. Florence was on the floor after Richard hit her. I killed him!"

When Louise was asked to step down, Florence took her turn in the witness chair. As soon as she sat down, she fell to pieces, bawling uncontrollably and couldn't answer the questions posed to her. Finally, she gained a little composure and the prosecutor asked one question: "Who killed Richard?"

Florence looked at her mother through teary eyes, but she could see well enough to notice Louise's nod with a stern look on her face. She pointed at her mother. Louise smiled and breathed a sigh of relief.

When the trial ended, Robbie asked Sandra if she would drive him back to the Airport. Russ could have driven him, but Robbie wanted to talk to her. The mere hour he spent in the courtroom, he was clueless about what the outcome might be.

"How are you going to feel if Louise and Florence are convicted of murder and accessory to murder?"

"Is that what's going to happen?"

"Looks like it."

"But they were defending themselves!"

Sandra didn't respond. He imagined Sandra knew it was self-defense, but he couldn't tell her anything else. She would know he was more involved and she'd know he lied under oath. He could be an accessory, and just maybe he'd get the firing squad too. *But they killed him in self-defense, dammit!*

"I like Florence a lot. And her mother was good to me as well. Will you really kill them?"

"That's the law."

"Can't you do something?"

"If I don't carry out the law, *my* law, then I'll seem weak. I can't let that happen. The whole city will crumble."

"When will you know whether they're found guilty or not?"

"The jury usually doesn't take very long. I may know this evening when I get back to the Farm."

"Will you let me know?"

"Yes I will, Robbie."

"If they are executed, can I be there?"

"Yes, it's a public affair. All the members of the jury, the witnesses, and all the heads of the various departments will be there. Anyone else is free to attend as well. Are you sure you want to go?"

"Yes."

What am I thinking? Do I really want to go see someone I care about and her mother shot to death? Can I stop it if it comes to an execution?

Sandra showed up at the Airport at mid-morning. Robbie watched as she went inside Russ's office and shut the door. Ten minutes later, she came out and walked toward Robbie and Sean at the Raptor. She wasn't smiling.

"The verdict is in," she announced to Robbie.

Sean was in the cockpit of the Raptor. Robbie sat down on one of the steps of the ladder. He didn't say anything; he just stared at Sandra.

"The jury found Louise guilty of murder," she said. "She will be executed tomorrow at noon."

Robbie blinked trying to ward off the tears.

"And Florence?"

"The jury found her guilty of being an accessory after the fact."

"And the punishment?"

"Lashes and hard labor at the Farm. She will be confined for a year. She will work in the fields, and when she's not working, she will be locked up."

At least Florence will live. Can't do anything about her mother. If I try, Florence will die in her stead. Or with her mother. Damn!

"You can ride with Russ to the Farm tomorrow."

"Okay," Robbie replied glumly.

Sandra left without another word. Jorge had been working behind one of the other planes and heard the conversation. He walked over to the Raptor.

"Really sucks doesn't it, boys?"

"Can't something be done?" Robbie asked.

"Sandra is a cruel bitch," he replied. "What's done is done, and there is nothing you can do about it. Just be glad for Florence."

"But she's getting lashes!"

"Yes, but she will live."

"Still sucks."

"Sandra is especially good to you Robbie, but don't think for a minute that she won't turn on you if you cross her. I've been around here for a long time. I saw what she and Richard did to gain control of Corpus Christi.

"Richard was a real badass," Jorge continued. "He had a lot of friends. Hoodlums, all of them. They killed a lot of people who didn't suit them or, rather, who didn't suit Sandra. She was the brains behind the takeover, but she killed a few too. Or so I heard. Any way you look at it, the blood is on her hands as well. And I'm talking thousands—men, women, and children.

"Once she had control, she double-crossed Richard. He was powerless to stop her. His hoodlums weren't really his thugs like he thought. Though they took orders from Richard, Sandra had some of her men in the group who brought the rest onto her side without Richard's knowledge. He never was all that smart. Sandra married him before the grid shut down, used him to gain control of the city when the chaos began, and then threw him away like a dirty dishrag when she was finished with him. She couldn't get rid of him totally though. He had one redeeming quality that Sandra needed. He was a ruthless bastard who could still take care of much of her dirty work. So she gave him a new wife, and shortly thereafter he and Louise had Florence."

Robbie understood Sandra a little more now. Deep-down, she only cared about herself. A person's worth was decided only by what they could do for her. Louise had no real worth. Florence, on the other hand, could be used against him.

"Well, that's enough about Sandra, boys. Maybe you two should get back to work," Jorge said.

"Jorge," Sean said before he could leave.

"What?"

"Can I go to the execution too?"

"And why would you want to do that?"

"I've never seen anyone executed."

"I don't think it's something you want to see, but I'll ask Russ."

Jorge walked over to Russ's office. A few minutes later, he stuck his head out of the door. "You can go," echoed throughout the hangar.

Russ made Robbie and Sean ride in the bed of the truck. Luckily it had a headache rack for the boys to hold on to, and Russ was old enough that he didn't drive too fast. At the far side of the Airport, Robbie pointed to a doe and her yearling grazing along the tree line. Russ's truck was too loud to have a conversation and the wind whistling by their ears didn't help, so the remainder of the trip they pointed at what interested them.

When they arrived at the Farm, it was abuzz with people. Robbie followed Russ, but gave him a little space, while Sean lagged further behind. Russ went straight to Sandra, who was sitting in a large padded chair that was obviously brought out just for her. There were people sitting in a line of chairs extending out on both sides. Most of the spectators were instructed to stand behind those seated.

Robbie stopped when Russ patted Sandra on the shoulder. Sandra got up and shook Russ's hand. Sandra's gaze turned toward Robbie and he nodded when their eyes met. Robbie's attention then turned to all the people who had gathered.

Robbie noticed many of the men wore pistols on their hips and carried rifles. *I guess they're the police force.* Many of the other men wore various types of uniforms but carried no guns. Robbie guessed they were contractors. Most had patches on their shirts, but he never got close enough to read any of them.

The majority of the people were women. Most wore plain casual dresses. Robbie assumed some were the contractor's wives. He recognized Jade and Joy. Jade gave him a smile and a wink. Robbie caught Joy's attention as well and she waved. Robbie smiled back.

Sandra clapped her hands and everyone got quiet. She took her seat of honor. Mathew, the new Chief of Police, took a seat at her side. The jurors sat down, leaving two chairs next to Sandra. Others filled the empty spaces with their wives, obviously guests of distinction, but Robbie didn't know how. He hadn't noticed these people before, but remembered some of them from the trial.

Jade, Brenda, Joy, Kim, and Barbara took seats next to Mathew, as did five more ladies Robbie hadn't seen before.

Robbie felt a push from the people behind him. He and Sean moved forward as did everyone else until they were behind the row of chairs. Robbie was directly behind Sandra. Sean stood behind Mathew.

There were two empty seats remaining. Then Robbie heard a scream and looked toward the barn where the trial had been held. He couldn't see anything over the people until Florence and two immense men in comparison with pistols on their hips came around the crowd and escorted her in. Her hands were cuffed in front of her. Her hair was mussed and she looked a fright. He wanted to say something, but he dared not.

The men brought Florence in front of Sandra, and she locked eyes with Robbie. She settled down at the sight of Robbie. One of the guards turned her around and forced her down onto the chair next to Sandra. He sat next to Florence while the other left.

Robbie looked at the cross erected no more than fifty feet in front of them. A rope hung down from each end of the crosspiece. He then heard a ruckus toward the barn again. The guard who had escorted Florence to her seat and another guard of equal stature held onto Louise's arms as they walked her toward the cross. Eight men with rifles followed in single file.

The eight men lined up about halfway between Sandra and the cross while the two burly men took Louise to the cross and secured her hands to the ropes. She was unusually complacent and responsive for someone who was about to die. Why doesn't she fight back? But he knew that would be futile. And what's she saying? He could see her lips moving. She was saying something, but not loud enough for him to hear.

When they had secured her hands, they blindfolded Louise. Her lips never stopped moving. She was talking to herself. "I saved my baby. I did the right thing. I saved my baby. I did the right thing."

"Shut up," one of the guards said, which Robbie did hear.

Whatever she was saying obviously irritated him, though Robbie couldn't make out her words. The two guards walked over to the eight men with rifles, got their guns, and took their places alongside them.

Mathew Helms got up from his seat and walked over to the end of the line of shooters. He took a position out of Sandra's line of sight to Louise and waited for her signal. Robbie looked down to see Sandra's head nod. Mathew then raised his arm and the line of rifles zeroed in on Louise's chest. When he dropped his arm, all ten rifles fired in unity.

Everyone was quiet. You could have heard a pin drop if not for the sobs from Florence.

Robbie's knees nearly buckled as he stared at Louise's body. He had no clue why she was dressed in white, but it definitely accentuated the crimson ribbons of blood that appeared from head to toe. It was almost as if these people enjoyed what they were seeing. Were they that bloodthirsty? *There's something seriously wrong here,* he thought.

Two men took Florence away. She couldn't have seen Robbie again through her teary eyes if she had tried. *She'll probably cry all night. Maybe I'll cry a little myself. The wrong woman was executed, but I know why. Her baby lives. I think I'd have done the same thing if I were in her place. She did the right thing.*

Chapter 23

Sandra didn't show up at the regular time on Saturday. Robbie figured the trial and execution interfered with those plans. He didn't sleep well for several nights. He couldn't get the image of Louise's bloody body out of his head.

Sean didn't seem to have any trouble sleeping. Or at least he didn't mention a problem. He and Sean still worked on the jets, trying to figure out if they would ever fly, but both knowing they never would. They would make certain they didn't. This was only an excuse for them to stay together. Betty was the only plane they wanted to make certain would fly. They did well faking their inspection of the planes, and Jorge never figured out they didn't know what they were doing.

"What did you think of the execution?" Robbie asked Sean. "Was it what you expected?"

"Not really," he replied. "Everyone else seemed to enjoy it. Or at least they didn't appear to be bothered by it. I don't think I needed to see another person killed. I expected it to be exciting. It wasn't though. It was sad."

"That was my thought," Robbie replied. "I knew Louise. I hated to see her die, but I know why it happened. She shouldn't have died. She was protecting herself. It was self-defense. No, it was wrong."

Robbie looked over at Sean to see if he had picked up on his mistake. *I can't say that I know why it happened. I can't tell Sean I know Florence killed her dad. Apparently Sean didn't notice. I've got to be careful what I say.*

Though Robbie was quite fatigued, he continued to work hard while engrossed in thought much of the day. He had a lot more to think about now.

Sean didn't want to leave. Louise was dead, and now he'd have to bust Florence out of her prison to take her with him. He still had to practice driving the Cessna, then hope he could fly it when he got it off the ground, if he could get it into the air.

What is he going to do about Russ and Jorge? Would he have to kill them? What if one or two of the pilots show up unannounced? Can he get Florence out of jail? What will Sandra do? Could he get out of here before she finds out what's happening?

The next day, Sandra showed up at Beka's house. She tooted the horn, got out, and walked to the porch.

Beka pulled back the curtain as she was walking up the steps. "What the hell does she want?" she said under her breath and opened the door.

"Can I see you alone?" Sandra asked.

"Yes, ma'am." Beka followed Sandra out to her Jeep. When she turned around to face Beka, the look on Sandra's face scared her.

"I don't think you're keeping me informed about things," Sandra said. "If you ever want to see that damn sailor again, you'd better keep me updated. I'll take your car away too, and that's the very least I'll do. I know you knew more about Richard, Louise, and Florence than you were telling me. That's settled, but you damn well better tell me the instant you find something out about Robbie or Sean. I've given Robbie a few liberties because he's been on good behavior, but I don't trust him."

"I'm doing the best I can," Beka replied.

"Well, your best better be just a little bit better. If I find out you're not telling me something again, you'll find yourself in a passel of trouble. Do you understand?"

"Yes, ma'am," Beka replied with a fearful look on her face. She knew exactly what she meant.

Sandra got back in her Jeep and drove off, slinging gravel toward Beka. *God-damn bitch!* Beka thought.

Beka showed up at the Airport a couple days later. Robbie didn't expect to see her. They went around the outside of the hangar where they could have some privacy. Sean continued to fiddle with the jets.

"What are you doing here, Beka?" Robbie asked.

"I heard the rumors. I had to see if they were true. You were the only one I could think of who might be able to give me the answers." These were lies, but she certainly couldn't tell him she was checking up on him for Sandra.

"They executed Louise. Sean and I were there. They locked Florence up. They never found out that she really killed Richard, but she is going to be locked up at night and doing hard labor during the day. And she's going to get lashes. She'll be at the Farm for a year if I can't get her out of there. But at least she'll be alive."

"What do you mean, if you can't get her out?"

"I'm going to get out of here. I don't know when yet, but I'm going to try to take Florence with me. Sean wants to stay here."

"Why in the world would he want to do that?"

"He likes the Bayfront and shrimping," he replied. "Florence getting locked up, and all the way over to the Farm, has seriously altered my scheme. I was hoping to get out in a few weeks. Now it may be months before I can get things figured out and a foolproof plan in place."

Then Beka dropped another bombshell on him. If Robbie and Florence were to actually get out of here and Beka didn't inform Sandra about the plan, she was surely dead. Sandra would think she helped them whether she did or not. She'd at least think she knew about the plan. Either way, she would be in trouble.

"Think you might have room for one more passenger?"

"And who's that?"

"Me."

"You really want to go?"

"I'm not positive, but Mom and I don't get along. We never have. Florence was—is—my best friend, after all. Yeah, I just may want to come along if you have room for me."

"Well, so far it would be just you, me, and Florence. The plane will certainly handle the weight easily. Maybe you can help me bust Florence out and get her back here. Your car would certainly help. At least you'd have no trouble getting here."

"No problem. Mom doesn't pay any attention to what I do. My car runs good too. We can escape in it."

"I'm sure the car would hide well in the weeds, but they will follow us. Our best chance is by air."

"What? I thought we were driving out of here."

"No, I believe it will be best if we fly out. It will be faster, and it'll make sure they can't follow. And we will be in the safety of Peaceful Valley in a matter of hours," he said.

"And you're a good pilot?"

"I've never flown a plane," he informed her.

"Shit! No, double shit! Are you serious? You've never flown a plane, but you're going to fly us safely out of here?"

"I never said it would be safe," he said. "I've been practicing driving the Cessna on the tarmac and runway. I'm learning the controls. There are not that many on the little planes. The flying should not be all that hard. I've read about flying. Speed and flaps. The plane should basically fly itself."

"But you've never actually flown before!"

"And you'd never driven a car before your mom gave you one. Did you have any trouble driving?"

"Well, no, but if the engine were to conk out, I'd be stuck on the side of the road. If the engine dies on the plane, we'll fall. It's not the same as pulling over to the side of the road."

"I'll make sure it doesn't fall."

She frowned and stood up. "Well, I've got to go," Beka said.

"Thanks for stopping by."

Beka gave Robbie another hug and they both walked back to her car. She got in and Robbie watched her drive away.

She couldn't help but smile as she looked into the rearview mirror and saw him standing on the tarmac. "Damn, he's hot!"

Jorge helped Robbie fill the fuel tank on the Piper Cub, and they pulled it out onto the tarmac. Sean asked if he could go for a ride this time. He'd never been in a moving plane.

"It only has two seats," Robbie said. "You'll have to ask Jorge. He usually insists on going."

Sean ran around to the other side of the plane. "Jorge, can I go with Robbie this time?" he asked like a kid in a candy store.

Jorge scratched the back of his head. "Yeah, I guess it will be okay."

Sean returned to where Robbie was standing. "Okay, Sean, climb in," he said.

Robbie climbed in the cockpit and looked at the controls. Within seconds the engine was humming. He let it warm a minute as he worked the flaps and checked the gauges. Everything seemed good and he eased the throttle up.

"This is great," Sean said.

Robbie turned to look at the excitement on his face as they rolled across the tarmac. Sean had a big grin and was intently staring out of the windows. Robbie couldn't help but smile.

Robbie turned the corner toward the main runway. He wiggled the plane back and forth across the center stripe. He then brought the plane up to thirty miles per hour.

"Yeeehaa!" Sean hollered as he jumped up and down in his seat as much as he could, straining against the seat belt.

Robbie could feel the plane jumping as they sped down the runway. This light plane, he could feel every bump on the runway, every joint in the concrete and now Sean bouncing in his seat. Robbie realized just how light this plane was and how sensitive it was to anything which might affect it. If it were windy, how would this affect the handling of the plane?

Sean was still jumping up and down as they pulled up to the hangar. Robbie shut off the engine, and he and Sean got out.

Jorge walked over to help Robbie and Sean push the plane into the hangar. Jorge glanced out toward the end of the runway. When he saw the pickup driving away, he turned back to the plane not wanting to alert Robbie or Sean to the runway guard. "The light Cub is easily pushed around," Sean noted.

"She ran great," Robbie said.

"Good to hear," Jorge replied. "Now let's get the cowling opened up and check it out, top to bottom."

Sean went back to the jets while Jorge and Robbie worked on the Cub.

Sandra showed up at the regular time on the following Saturday. There were again five young ladies preparing lunch and setting the table. They were not the same ones as before. Sandra had chosen new girls for Robbie to meet. Robbie recognized them from the execution.

They were all beautiful and in the same age range as the previous five. And they were anxious to meet Robbie and get better acquainted with him. Different girls; same routine, but when they made their way to the bedroom, the routine changed. Each gal proved she was different from the others. Robbie never knew what to expect. He was pleasantly surprised each and every time.

The next morning when Sandra was ready to take him back to the Airport, Robbie asked if he could see Florence. Sandra hesitated a moment. She decided if it would keep him happy and breeding her girls, it wouldn't hurt. "I guess so," she said.

Robbie and Sandra walked to the back of the same large barn where the trial was held. Down a short corridor there were five cells. Florence was in the last cell. The others were empty. Florence smiled when she saw Robbie.

"Can I go inside?" he asked.

Hanging on nails on the wall opposite the cells were metal rings, each with a single key. Robbie watched closely as Sandra grabbed the key to Florence's cell, inserted it into the lock and turned. She then slid the locking bar over and pushed the door open. Robbie walked inside.

The cubicle was small and had a musty odor. Florence seemed reasonably clean, as was her new residence.

Robbie could immediately see the tears welling up in her eyes.

"Can we have some privacy, Sandra?"

"Yes, but I'll have to lock you inside. You've got thirty minutes."

Robbie waited for Sandra to leave and put his arms around Florence. She jerked away when he touched her back. "I'm sorry," he said, having forgotten about the lashes she'd received.

Sandra went straight to the bunkhouse and found Sally Beecher. "Every time Robbie comes to the Farm, you stay close," she said. "I'm going to let him see Florence. When he talks to her, you will listen in on their conversations and report back to me. Don't tell anyone, and damn sure don't get caught."

"Yes, ma'am."

"They're in there now. Get to work."

Back in Florence's cell, Robbie stepped up on the bunk bed and looked out of the small, barred window. There was no one outside, but someone could easily listen in if they chose to do so. *I've got to be careful what we say.* He sat on the bed and held Florence's hands.

"How are they treating you?" he asked.

"Now that the lashes are over, good. They feed me well, and I get a shower every few days. It just gets so lonely in here. They don't have much work for me to do until my back heals, so mostly I sit in here and think. That's the hard part."

"I miss you, Florence."

"I miss you too."

They sat and stared at each other for a while. Florence wiped her tears.

"I think I love you," Robbie whispered.

He could see the tears welling up in her eyes. He gave her a hug as best he could without touching her back. He could feel her trembling.

"I've loved you since we met," she whispered.

"I'm going to get you out of here, Florence. It will take a while, maybe a month or two, but I'm working on a plan."

Her tears began to flow uncontrollably and she gave him a salty kiss.

"Do they have guards? I didn't see any when we came in."

"Sometimes, but not usually. I don't think I could get out of here if I had to. I think they know that."

"Good. That will make it a little easier."

"How are you going to get me out?"

"I don't know yet. I have a lot of thinking to do. I'll let you know as soon as I can. I don't want you to have to stay in here any longer than necessary."

"Do you really love me, Robbie?"

"I think so. I know I want to be near you, and I think of you constantly."

She squeezed him tight. "I'll be here for you when you decide."

Robbie heard a noise and scooted away from Florence. Seconds later, Sandra appeared.

"Keep your chin up, Florence," he said as Sandra opened the cell door. "Maybe with good behavior they'll let you out of here early."

He winked at her and she smiled.

"It's good to see you don't treat your prisoners badly, Sandra."

"As long as they behave themselves," she replied, giving Florence a hard glare.

Sandra locked the door and she and Robbie headed out to the Jeep. The drive back to the Airport was relatively quiet.

"Thank you for letting me see Florence," he said as they arrived at the hangar.

Sandra didn't say anything. She didn't even acknowledge that she heard him. Robbie knew she had.

When Sandra got back to the Farm, she immediately searched Sally Beecher out. "I couldn't hear anything from where I was at," Sally explained. "There was too much outside noise to hear what was being said inside."

"We have to do something about that," Sandra stated. "I need to know what they are talking about."

That night at the Airport, Robbie lay in bed tossing and turning until the wee hours of the morning. *How the hell am I going to get Florence out of her cell and off the Farm without being seen? Can it be done? Jorge and Russ must be taken out first, then I'll have to go to the Farm and get her. Beka has to be here by the time we get ready to leave. Can Beka help me get Florence out? It may be too much to ask for her to be here in the middle of the night. Early maybe, but not early enough to go get Florence. Her mother would know something's not right.*

The Cessna needs to be near the hangar door and ready. It will take time to get it into the air. And can I fly the thing? I think I can, but I won't know for sure until I'm doing it. If Sean goes back to the Bayfront, I'll have to take care of Russ and Jorge. He'll certainly go back to the Bayfront as soon as we can't keep up our charade about getting the planes going. Can I take care of Russ and Jorge myself? If Sean is going to stay here, he can't really be mixed up in my scheme. That will get him killed after I leave. And what about the pilots? I never know when they are going to be here. What if someone else shows up? Mr. Asshole Sheriff or one of his goons. They can show up at any time. So much can go wrong. So many details to plan. And how the hell am I going to get Florence away from the Farm? That is the big problem. If she were still at home, Beka could just drive her over here. But that's not an option anymore. Dammit Robbie, think!

Robbie sat straight up in bed. He'd managed to oversleep and knew Jorge would be mad. He hurried out of bed, threw on his clothes, and made a mad dash for the hangar. Sean was just coming out of his door. *Well, maybe it's not that late.*

"We've got to get the C-23 ready for another flight to Brownsville," Jorge announced as Robbie and Sean approached. He hooked up the pull cart while Robbie went to the fuel tanker. Once the plane was on the tarmac, Sean helped Robbie with the fuel hose. Sean checked the tires and landing gear and gave the plane a sharp eye over. Soon, the cargo door was open and the plane ready for flight.

But where is the cargo? Robbie thought.

A few minutes later, a truck arrived from the salt plant, followed by one from the hospital. They parked and waited for instructions. Russ came out and the men loaded one pallet from the salt plant and a small box from the hospital and the trucks left. *This can't be all,* Robbie thought.

Russ stood for a minute looking at the horizon. He scratched his butt and went back inside. Jorge seemed confused as well.

An hour later, the trucks from the Farm began coming in. Sandra was also with them. *Mighty unusual,* Robbie thought. Sandra went straight in to see Russ while the trucks parked near the plane. Directly, Sandra came back out, hopped in her Jeep and drove off. She gave Robbie a look, but didn't say a word.

Russ came out with his clipboard and monitored the loading. He checked the items off his list one by one. Corn. Check. Milo. Check. Potatoes. Check. When Russ had finished his list, he told Jorge the plane would go out first thing in the morning.

"Sir!" Robbie yelled out as Russ headed back inside.

Russ stopped.

"Sir, what's going on?" he asked.

"None of your damn business, boy," Russ replied and walked away.

Something's up. Sandra had to have said something. He hasn't been like this since I first got here. Does it have anything to do with Florence? It has to be something about me. Did she find out about my escape plan? Was someone listening outside the window after all? No, if they had, Sandra would have been all over me yesterday. But what?

Robbie worried about Sandra's visit all week. He noticed Jorge was more aloof and Russ seemed to have a renewed interest in what was going on in the hangar. He peeked out of his door often and sometimes would just stand and look around. He never said anything though. Just stood and watched Robbie and Sean.

By the end of the week, Sean informed Robbie there was nothing else to check on the jets. The batteries were charged and additive added to the fuel. Robbie followed Sean and watched him climb into the front seat of the Raptor. Sean turned the power on to the Jet Fuel Starter (JFS) and pressed a button. The plane began to hum, and exhaust from the JFS blew out through the open hangar doors. Sean checked to make certain the brakes were on and hit the Engine One button. The hum soon turned into a whine. He hit the Engine Two button and momentarily the plane was screaming.

Russ came out of his office and walked over to Jorge. "You think he knows what he's doing?" Russ asked.

"I certainly hope so," Jorge replied. "If he doesn't, he's going to make an awful mess in here."

Robbie strolled over to where Russ and Jorge were standing and attentively watching Sean.

"Robbie . . . he know what he's doing?" Jorge asked.

"Oh, hell yes."

Sean eased the throttle forward and the engines grew louder and the blast of exhaust out of the hangar doors increased. Suddenly, the plane began to roll forward. Sean immediately throttled the engines down. The Raptor stopped about three inches from hitting the F-15. "Whew!" He turned everything off and smiled.

Sean climbed out of the cockpit and walked toward the others. Robbie ran to him, grabbed him by the waist, and jerked him into the air. "You did it!" he yelled with joy.

"Congratulations, son," Russ said. "Is it ready to fly?"

"I'm sorry to say, no, sir."

"But you got it going," Jorge said.

"Maybe so. It may fly, but there are so many little problems. You saw the brakes didn't hold. Some of the gauges don't work. It's just sat idle for too long. How many years?"

"But you ran it!" Robbie exclaimed.

"Maybe so, but it's a death trap. You do what you want, but you'll kill your pilots. And the F-15 is dead. It won't even start."

The hopeful mood suddenly turned sour. Russ, dejected, headed back to his office.

Chapter 24

Right after breakfast, Sandra got wind of an argument between Jade and some of the other girls. She hurried out to the bunkhouse. "What the hell is going on out here?" she yelled.

Then she saw Rachel on the floor in a puddle of blood and Jade holding a knife. Several of the girls began to speak at once.

"Shut up," Sandra demanded. "Who saw what happened?" Beatrice and Charlene were the only ones who held up their hands. "The rest of you get out of here," she demanded.

Sandra waited for the rest of the girls to leave. "What's going on, Jade?" Sandra asked.

"I don't know," she replied with a sullen look on her face. "She just started screaming at me and pulled the knife out. Some shit about you and Robbie. I think she wanted her turn with him; as if it were my fault. I don't know why she wanted to stab me. She fell on the knife as we scuffled on the floor. I didn't mean to kill her. Shit happens when you play with knives."

"Is that how it happened?" she asked, turning to Beatrice and Charlene.

"Yes, ma'am," they replied.

"Dammit!" Sandra exclaimed pausing to think for a minute. *Two witnesses. There's nothing I can do.* "Okay, take her out and bury her."

"Yes, ma'am," they all replied.

Likely goddam story! Dammit! Jade and her two best friends!

Sandra paused a second. "Beatrice, you and Charlene still want your turn with Robbie this evening?"

"Yes, ma'am," Beatrice replied.

"Of course," Charlene added, smiling.

Sandra headed back to the house to find Kim and Amy working in the kitchen. Kim was Sandra's most trusted lady. She could always depend on Kim. Sandra nodded to her and headed toward the hallway. Kim followed a few seconds later and they stepped into the bathroom and closed the door. "Do you know what's going on?" Sandra asked.

"I don't know for sure, but Jade's not happy. She and a bunch of the other girls are planning something big, I think. She saw you and Robbie going to see Florence. She likes Robbie and I think she's jealous of Florence. That's all I know."

"Yeah, I already know that. But that can't be all of it. Keep your ears open, will you?"

"Of course."

Back outside, Jade got the backhoe and she, Charlene, and Beatrice took Rachel's body to the cemetery. "Thanks for backing me up," Jade said.

"I thought Rachel was on our side," Charlene stated.

"Me too," Beatrice agreed.

"No one can find out," Jade told the girls. "We've got to be especially careful around Sandra now." *Dammit Rachel, why couldn't you keep your damn mouth shut?*

Sandra showed up at the Airport late-morning. She went into Russ's office and a few minutes later, Russ called for Jorge, Robbie, and Sean to join them.

"Sean was able to get the Raptor started," Russ said, "but apparently there are a lot of other problems that won't allow us to fly and use it. Also, he says the F-15 won't even start."

"Too bad," Sandra said.

"What do you want to do with Sean?" he asked Sandra.

"You don't need him anymore?"

"No, ma'am."

"Then take him back to the Bayfront. I'm sure Sonny will be happy to have him back. The summer season is winding down, but he'll have a lot to do to get ready for the fall season."

"If you're not in a big hurry to get back to the Farm, I'd like to take him to the Bayfront, if you don't mind," Robbie said. "I probably won't see him for a while, and I'd like to say good-bye."

"I guess that will be okay," Sandra said. "Take my Jeep . . . and hurry back."

The boys went to get Sean's belongings, and Robbie grabbed a few cans of soda to stick in his bag. They got into the Jeep and headed out.

"I don't know when I'll be able to see you again, Sean. I'll get down when I can."

"I'll look forward to it. Maybe you can go out on the boat one day."

"I'd like that."

"I'll talk to Sonny and Marcia to see if that's okay."

Sonny and Marcia were just pulling into their stall when Robbie drove up. "Let me give you a hand with those ropes," Sean said.

Sonny smiled and tossed Sean a rope.

"See ya, Sean."

Sean turned and waved.

Robbie picked Sandra up at the Airport. She let him drive for a change. Robbie didn't say anything for a long time. He was hoping Sandra would, but she kept watching the road ahead.

"You showed up unexpectedly on Monday," Robbie finally said, looking over at Sandra.

She didn't say anything and kept looking forward, but Robbie could tell she was thinking.

"Seems we have a conspiracy," she said directly.

Shit! So someone was listening outside the window.

"And it concerns you."

"Me?" Robbie asked, acting surprised.

"Yes, you and Florence."

Robbie could feel the hair standing up on the back of his neck.

"It seems that Jade saw you and me going in to see Florence."

"And?"

"I'm not sure. I think maybe she's jealous of Florence. I know she likes you. Maybe she thinks Florence should have died along with her mother. Jade is not like the rest of the girls. She has a mean streak running through her. I'm not sure I know what she wants. I've kept her around because she's smart and a damn good organizer and worker. She gets more work out of the girls than I ever have. And when the men come in to work, she can certainly keep them in line."

Robbie breathed a sigh of relief.

"I think she thinks she can run the Farm better than I can. She may even be conspiring to take over. I can't get a thing out of the other girls. All I get are a few rumors. I need something I can act on."

"What are you going to do?"

"I don't know. I need information. Will you help me?"

"Of course," he replied. "What can I do to help?"

"You will be with Charlene and Beatrice tonight. See if you can find out anything about Jade and what she's up to. Don't let Charlene and Beatrice know you're snooping for me. They are friends with Jade and may tell her if you pry too hard."

"I'll have to ask a favor in return though," Robbie said.

"And what's that?"

"Just that I can continue to see Florence. I'm concerned about her and she gets depressed easily. I just want to help keep her spirits up. Is that too much to ask?"

"No, not at all," she replied.

Robbie pulled up in front of the Farm house and Sandra introduced him to Charlene and Beatrice.

Charlene and Beatrice were very chatty. Robbie had things to think about, but the girls made certain his mind was on them and nothing else.

After a four-hour romp in the bed followed by another hour for their shower, Robbie finally was able to stretch out on the bed, relax, and think a bit with Charlene lying on his left arm and Beatrice on his right.

What am I going to tell Sandra tomorrow? I didn't ask a single question. I can make something up, but it's got to be believable. At least she doesn't know about my plan.

Would she believe Jade is planning on killing her? If Jade has thoughts of taking over this Farm, she would have to kill Sandra first. Maybe I can make Sandra think she is. Wow! What if Jade really is? Maybe I should confront Jade. If it's true, maybe I could join forces with her. She apparently likes me. Wouldn't that be a twist? Maybe I can trade the Farm for my freedom—and Florence's. Then I wouldn't have to kill Russ and Jorge. I could just fly out of here. Now that's an idea. But would that work? If Jade really does like me, she could double cross me and kill Florence. She could make me stay here whether I want to or not. More choices. More questions. So complicated... Robbie soon dozed off.

Robbie heard a rooster crowing. Then he felt someone fondling him. He opened his eyes and looked down. It was not Charlene or Beatrice. He didn't know where they were, only that they were gone. Her head was between his legs. He recognized the big butt sticking up and the hair. It was Sandra. He lay back and enjoyed the sensation.

Sandra then crawled up beside him and smiled. "I just thought I'd add a bonus for you snooping for me."

"I'm sorry I can't be a little more responsive."

"That's no problem. I'm sure you were maxed out last night with the girls."

"Yes, I was."

They both smiled and Sandra rested her head on Robbie's arm.

"Are you about ready to head back to the Airport? We can talk on the way back."

"Can I see Florence first?"

"Sure. Thirty minutes. Be careful and try not to let Jade see you. I'll wait for you in the Jeep."

"Okay."

Robbie got dressed and made his way out to the barn. After his visit with Florence, Robbie met Sandra outside at the Jeep and he crawled in beside her. The rear wheels spun a little in the gravel as they pulled out of the driveway.

"How's Florence?" Sandra asked.

"She's doing well, but you already know that."

"Yes, I do. I wanted to make certain you knew. She's confined, but otherwise taken good care of. Now, about Jade . . ."

"It's hard to tell. There's definitely something going on, but Charlene and Beatrice were tight-lipped. You said not to pry too hard."

"Yes, I did. Maybe I'll set you up with them again. That okay with you?"

"Fine. I'll be sure to be well-rested next time. They are a handful. A couple handfuls!"

"Have you seen Beka Livingston lately?" Sandra asked.

"Yes," he replied. "Right after Louise—"

"What did she want?"

"She was wondering if the rumors she'd heard were true. Why do you ask?"

"Just curious. Russ tells me stuff. Checking his accuracy. He's getting old and a little senile. I never know if he's on the level or not."

"Yeah," Robbie said. "I guess we all get there sooner or later."

"Yes, we do," she replied. "Some of us sooner than later."

Who does she think she's fooling? I'm smarter than that. She's checking up on me.

They looked at each other and smiled. When they arrived at the Airport, Sandra headed for the office while Robbie went to his room to change clothes.

"Anything out of the ordinary going on with Robbie?" Sandra asked Russ.

"Not that I can tell," he replied.

"There was an incident at the Farm with Jade. Something is definitely going on, but I can't put my finger on it. I think Jade is planning something. I don't know whether Robbie is involved or not. I think I'll send a few men out here to keep an eye on the planes to be on the safe side. You keep your eyes and ears open too."

"Yes, ma'am," he replied.

Jorge was working hard polishing the Piper Cub when Robbie walked up.

"You know these things used to be all yellow?" he asked.

"No," Robbie replied.

"Yes, every last one of them."

"Then why is this one blue?"

"I can't answer that. Someone must not have liked yellow or didn't like his plane looking like every other Piper Cub in the country. Who knows? Just thought I'd share that with you."

"Well, thanks for sharing, Jorge."

Robbie gave Jorge a quizzical look. He wasn't sure why Jorge was telling him this strange story. *Jorge and I haven't had a good talk recently. Maybe he feels like I've been neglecting him. I've certainly had a lot on my mind.*

"Anytime. Not much for you to do this afternoon, Robbie. Why don't you take the afternoon off? Go have a soda."

"Thanks!"

Robbie got his drink, walked out of the hanger, and found a comfortable spot in the shade. *I've got to get Florence out several hours before daylight. They don't have dogs at the Farm so that's not a problem. If I only had a night-vision scope. I'll use Russ's truck, but he and Jorge must be taken out first. I can't be caught on the road in the truck. I can't park too close to the Farm. Someone could be on guard at night. I'll just have to take a chance there are no guards, or if there are, I can get around them. One guard with a night-vision scope and I'm screwed.*

If I help Jade overthrow Sandra . . . No! No! No! That's a bad idea from the start. It doesn't even sound good. I don't know Jade at all. Sandra seems to think she's a little nuts. Can't trust Jade. Can't help Jade. That's asking for trouble. Okay, it's settled. I go with Sandra. Sorry, Jorge. Sorry, Russ.

Robbie got up to go inside when he noticed two trucks coming his way. He sat back down and waited. They drove right up to the hangar and six men got out. They all had guns.

Robbie stood up and two of the men pointed their rifles at him. He threw his arms into the air.

One of the men went into the office. He came back out with Russ. "He's okay," Russ said to the men pointing the guns at Robbie and they lowered them.

"What's going on, Russ?" Robbie asked.

"Seems like there was an incident at the Farm. These men are here to guard the Airport."

"Six of them to guard three of us?"

"They're not here to guard us," Russ replied, "they're here to guard the planes. In particular, the C-23 Sherpa."

"What kind of incident?" Robbie asked.

"We're not at liberty to say," the apparent leader of the group said, the same guy who'd gone in to see Russ. Three of the men took up posts around the Airport. They had night scopes, Robbie noticed. Russ took the leader and the two remaining men inside and showed them a place to bunk. Robbie followed, but went to his room and laid down.

Back at the Farm, Sandra finally got to bed at 10:00 after a busy day. She slid her pistol under her pillow and closed her eyes. Thoughts of Jade, the Airport, and Robbie floated around in her head for a while, but she finally got to sleep.

Down the hall, Terry read in her room for a while until she was sure everyone in the house was asleep. Just before midnight, she tiptoed to the kitchen, turned on the light, and put on a pot of coffee. Suddenly, she noticed someone on the back porch. She thought it was Jade and opened the door. She was surprised to see one of Sandra's guards. "What are you doing here?" she whispered.

"Sandra asked me to keep an eye on the place for a few nights," he replied.

"How about a cup of coffee?"

"I would like that," he said with a smile.

Terry pulled the door shut and walked back over to the stove. *Jade will be here soon. He's going to screw up the plan.* Terry poured a cup of coffee, grabbed a butcher knife, and walked back to the door. She concealed the knife as she pulled the door back open and stepped out onto the porch. "Here's your coffee," she said and handed him the cup.

"Thank you, ma'am," he said, and took a sip.

When he put the cup to his lips, she shoved the knife into his gut just under the ribcage, thrusting upward.

Across the way, in her room at the far end of the bunkhouse, Jade lay on her bed fully dressed, going over the plan in her head. A tap at the door and Charlene and Joy came in. A short time later, one by one, more girls showed up. By 12:30 everyone was there—a dozen of Jade's most loyal supporters armed with knives and machetes. Jade gave them additional instructions and then headed for the main house.

Joy and Annie went to the barn where Florence was held. Jade and the rest advanced toward the back porch to meet up with Terry. Jade saw the guard and looked over at Terry. Terry nodded. Jade knew Terry had single-handedly saved their scheme and likely all their lives. Jade wasn't surprised though. She knew how deadly Terry was with a knife.

Joy went inside the barn and headed back to Florence's cell. Annie followed. Joy didn't expect there'd be a guard, but she quickly improvised. "Sandra asked us to check in on Florence," she said as she peeked through the little opening on Florence's door. "Everything all right?"

"She's fine," the guard replied. Then Joy watched his eyes pop wide open as he gasped when Annie came up from behind him and shoved her knife into his ribs. Joy opened the door and rushed over to Florence who was sitting up on the bed by now. She hit Florence before she could get up and forced her back onto the bed. To Joy's surprise, Florence fought back, screaming and swinging her fists.

"You damn little whore," Joy yelled and hit her again in the face.

Annie came over with her knife and Joy managed to get another good blow in on Florence and held her down.

"Now you're going to die, bitch," Joy said. Then she heard the cracking skull as the guard who was hiding in the adjoining cell came in and hit Annie with his rifle.

"You're the one who's going to die," he said, staring into Joy's surprised face. He squeezed the trigger and Joy fell on top of Florence.

Back inside the main house, the shot woke Sandra, and she slid her hand under the pillow for her pistol. Just as she did, her door opened. Sandra reached for the light on the nightstand and flipped it on. As she turned her attention back to the door, Charlene lunged at Sandra with her knife, but Sandra was ready and fired. Jade was right behind Charlene and jumped on Sandra before she could get another shot off. Sandra was a big gal, and Jade was no match for her. They scuffled over the gun, but Jade could not get it away from Sandra. Sandra hit Jade repeatedly with her fist and the pistol until Jade fell to the floor. Jade was out cold, but Sandra hit her again for good measure.

Sandra rushed out of her bedroom and down the hallway. Screams and obscenities were flying from all directions. Sandra turned lights on as she made her way down the hall to the other bedrooms and fired at everyone she knew was not supposed to be in the house. When she ran out of bullets, she ran back to her room, reloaded the revolver, and headed upstairs. By the time she had finished there, her gun was empty again.

Sandra went back to her room to check on Jade. As she was reloading her gun again, Jade moaned. Before she could recover, Sandra rolled her over and tied her hands behind her back and yelled for Kim. "Keep an eye on Jade," Sandra said then hurried out to the barn.

The remaining guard had secured Florence in her cell and dragged all the dead bodies to the front of the barn when Sandra came in. Sandra looked at Joy, Annie and the dead guard and shook her head.

"Come with me," Sandra told him.

Sandra and the guard returned to the house, and Sandra instructed the man to take Jade to a cell. Sandra and Kim then checked on the rest of the women in the house. In all, she'd lost six of her gals including two of her best cooks, but all of Jade's supporters were dead.

"It's going to be a long night," Sandra said turning to Kim. "I want all these bodies in the barn and the house spotless by daylight."

"Yes, ma'am," Kim replied.

Kim turned to the other women who had gathered around her and Sandra. "You heard her," she said.

It was well after sunrise before everything was under control, and Sandra headed to the Airport. Robbie saw her pull up in front of the hangar and watched from the workbench as she got out and went straight into the office. The leader of the armed men followed. The two of them and Russ were in there over an hour.

"What do you think is going on, Jorge?" Robbie asked.

"I don't know," he replied. "They don't always let me in the loop. It must be serious though."

"I gathered that."

Finally, Sandra was the first out of the office. Robbie looked over and she motioned for him to come over.

"Change clothes and come with me," she said.

Robbie changed and got into the Jeep and they hurried off, Sandra grinding the gears as they flew across the tarmac. The guards Sandra had stationed at the Airport followed in their trucks.

"What's going on?" Robbie asked.

"You'll find out soon enough."

That was the last thing she said. It was obvious to Robbie she had a lot on her mind. The remainder of the trip Robbie stared out of the window.

When they arrived at the Farm, there were armed men everywhere. Instead of pulling up in front of the main house, she pulled up in front of the barn where the trial was held and Florence was confined in a tiny cell in the back.

Sandra got out and Robbie followed. He kept his mouth shut, but looking here and there at all the activity going on. Sandra led him toward the barn. She went on inside, but Robbie stopped in his tracks just after entering, a guard bumping into him trying to get around him.

Robbie looked at the bodies lined up on the floor. There was more than a dozen, maybe two dozen. He didn't count. They were mostly women, all covered with blood and lifeless.

A single body lay across a table, arms and legs outstretched and tied to the table legs. It was a woman, but this one wasn't dead. She was only wearing panties, quite alive and screaming in pain. *She looks familiar.* He walked a bit closer. *Jade!*

Robbie thought they were trying to save her life, but then he knew better. Sandra walked up, and with a clenched fist, hit her in the face.

"Shut up, bitch!" she screamed. Everyone in the room got quiet. Jade got quiet as well.

Robbie watched as men came in pairs to remove the lifeless bodies from the room. Shortly, two different men came in and gathered up another body. He assumed they were taking them out for burial. *How many more were taken out before I arrived?*

Sandra talked to Linda, Harry and some of her guards and the chatter grew louder. Sandra then walked over to Kim and some of the housekeepers and talked to them as well. Several conversations were going on at once, and Robbie couldn't make out much of any of it.

Robbie walked over to the dead bodies and took a closer look. *Charlene! Beatrice! Joy! Terry!* He recognized some of the others, but either didn't know or remember their names. He then distanced himself from the bodies. Besides, he was in the way. More men came in to retrieve bodies and take them outside.

Sandra walked back over to Robbie. She grabbed him by the arm and led him toward the back of the barn. "What's going on?" he asked.

"All in good time," she replied. "Florence has been asking for you."

"Is she all right?"

"Scared, but okay."

Florence's face lit up when she saw Robbie.

"I'll be back in a little while," Sandra said as she locked the two in the cell.

"What happened?" Robbie asked.

It was obvious she had been crying—a lot.

"She hit me and called me terrible names . . . then she tried to kill me," she replied, sobbing continuously.

"Who? Who tried to kill you?"

"I don't know . . . one of Sandra's girls."

"But why?"

"I don't . . . don't know. Sh-she just tried to kill me. She grabbed me around the throat. I couldn't breathe. Then there was a loud noise, a gunshot, and she fell on me."

Robbie pulled her close and held on tight. She wasn't just trembling now. She was jerking with every sob. Robbie squeezed her a little tighter. She couldn't talk for her crying.

When Sandra returned and opened the door, Robbie pried Florence off. She lay down and curled up into a fetal position. "Please don't go...please," she said, not able to stop crying.

"I'll be back tomorrow," he said, looking at Sandra.

She nodded.

"Tomorrow, Florence," he repeated.

Robbie followed Sandra back to where Jade lay on the table. A couple ladies took her ropes off and put a blouse on her limp body. She is still out cold from Sandra's blow, but apparently not dead. Otherwise, someone would have taken her out for burial. Two women tied her hands while a third lady tied her feet together. I guess she's going into a cell. All the bodies that were on the floor were now gone.

Sandra looked around then headed for the door. Robbie followed her out of the barn and up toward the house.

"You hungry?" she asked.

"Not really."

Inside, Sandra asked Brenda and Kim to prepare some sandwiches and snacks. Brenda and Kim were best friends and behind Kim, Brenda was Sandra's second most trusted lady. They were the only two of Sandra's girls she wanted in the house.

Sandra and Robbie sat on the sofa. "Jade tried to kill me during the night," Sandra told him.

"So you were right. Jade really did want to take over?" he asked.

"Yes. Fortunately, I'm a light sleeper. I heard a shot and woke up. When the door open I grabbed my pistol. Jade and Charlene were surprised when I flipped on the light. I shot Charlene and captured Jade."

"I'm glad you're all right."

"Jade had a group of women backing her. They tried to take out my primary supporters."

"Florence said one of your girls tried to kill her," Robbie said.

"Yes, Joy. I had two guards keeping an eye on Florence. Joy killed the first guard, but I had a second guard hidden in the cell next to Florence. Joy didn't know about him.

"Usually we don't keep but one or two guards around here," she continued. "I called in a few extras with night scopes to keep an eye on the place. Jade didn't know about them. I didn't know what they were up to. I thought they might just be trying to get out of here. That's why I put the guards on the Airport. Jade's a decent pilot, I hear, so I thought they might just try to leave. I think her dad was one of the pilots at the Airport years back. I don't know if she's ever flown a plane by herself, but I've been told she's read all my books about flying and knows how. We can't afford to lose the transport plane. We need supplies from Brownsville."

"What are you going to do with Jade?" he asked.

"I'm going to get some answers out of her first. Then she'll be executed."

"Another trial?"

"No trial this time," she replied. "I caught her red-handed."

Brenda and Kim brought in a tray of sandwiches and snacks along with a couple sodas. Sandra grabbed a ham sandwich, took a bite, and looked over at Robbie.

"I guess I'm a little hungry after all," he said.

They chatted about the events while they ate, and then Sandra took him to her bedroom.

"I've been up all night. I'm going to take a short nap," she said. "Will you join me?"

"I'm not sleepy," he replied.

"Suit yourself."

"I'd like to see Florence again if I may, if you're going to sleep."

"I guess that will be all right. Don't let me sleep more than a couple hours, okay?"

"I'll be back in two hours to get you up," he replied.

Robbie grabbed a couple more sandwiches from the tray in the living room and went outside to the barn. There were three guards to get through to get to Florence. The last guard secured the door behind him. Florence was excited to see him again so soon. She was not able to talk much about the night's events because of her constant crying. She laid on Robbie's lap and dozed off. He was close to her and she knew he was there. That's all that mattered.

Robbie scooted back so he could lean against the wall, pulling Florence back with him and keeping her head on his lap. She stirred a little, but did not wake up. He ran his fingers through her hair, pulling it away so he could see her better. As he studied the new bruises on her face, he could feel the tears coming. *You've had a rough time lately, haven't you Florence? Things will get better for you soon.*

Florence was exhausted and slept most of the time he was there, waking up only minutes before he had to leave. She thanked him for the sandwich and gave him a peck on the cheek, tears beginning to run down her cheeks again.

On his way out, Robbie peeked through the little trap doors on the other cells. Jade was in the cell farthest from Florence. She appeared to be asleep and did not see him peering through the opening. He stared for a minute. *Damn, she looks in bad shape. She is breathing, so she's not dead. I wonder what Sandra is going to do to get her to talk?*

When Robbie got back to the house, he found Sandra still asleep. He woke her gently, as she'd requested. He sat on the edge of the bed and waited as she freshened up in the bathroom.

"Follow me," she said.

They walked to the barn where Jade and Florence were held. "Wait here," Sandra told Robbie and she walked around the corner and over to Sally Beecher sitting on the bunkhouse porch. "I didn't hear them say anything," Sally said. "I peeked into the little window and Florence was sleeping on his lap."

"Okay." Sandra replied and returned to where Robbie was waiting. They went inside the barn and Sandra yelled to the guards. "Bring Jade out."

Two men escorted Jade to where Sandra waited, both Jade's arms tied in front of her. She was still scantily clad in panties and a ragged shirt. She was dirty and there were dried blood streaks on her face, arms, and legs. She was so lovely when Robbie and she had sex, but now he just barely recognized her.

Sandra began to ask questions, mostly about the other girls but a few about her plan. This went on for a half-hour and Jade said not one word. She only whimpered and moaned.

Not satisfied with the lack of answers, Sandra walked over to Jade and ripped off her shirt, revealing her full and firm breasts. Sandra pinched Jade's nipples hard, and she screamed and spit on Sandra. Sandra wiped her face with her arm and backed away. She instructed the men to tie her against the wall.

Hanging on the wall beside Jade were several whips. Sandra picked one about four feet long with multiple leather cords. She walked over to Jade and touched her back. "Such pretty skin," she said. Then she gouged the butt of the whip into her back as hard as she could, causing Jade to cry out. "That is nothing compared to what you are going to feel in a few seconds if you don't talk."

"Fuck you, fat-ass bitch!"

Sandra struck Jade as hard as she could, and red welts appeared immediately on her back. Jade screamed at the top of her lungs. Again and again Sandra slashed at her back. Jade continued to scream as loud as she could. There were more than welts now and blood began to splatter when Sandra struck the blows.

Robbie couldn't watch anymore. He put his hands over his ears and turned away, but he could not keep the screams out. He had seen more than enough. *This is cruel. This can't be happening. But it is. The woman who has been so sweet and caring to me is torturing this poor girl and seeming to like it. Damn!*

Jade suddenly went limp and hung by her arms. Her screaming stopped. Robbie put his arms down and turned back around. He stared at Jade, hanging there by her wrists, the blood trickling down her back. He couldn't hold back the tears.

Sandra hung the whip back onto its peg and turned to Robbie. "We'll see if she feels like talking tomorrow."

Robbie was in shock. He wiped the tears from his eyes.

The men untied Jade and took her back to her cell. They didn't bother to put her shirt back on.

Robbie wanted to say something to Sandra about what happened, but was afraid he might say the wrong thing. With her state of mind and pumped up on adrenalin, it might not take much to set her off. He decided it was better to keep quiet.

Sandra led him back to the house. Brenda informed Sandra that dinner would be ready in about an hour. She and Kim were busy in the kitchen. Robbie stayed with them while Sandra went into the bathroom to take a shower.

"Do you know what's going on out in the barn?" Robbie asked.

"Just another day at the Farm," Kim replied.

"And you're fine with that?"

"Sandra is tough and she may seem cruel at times, but she has a lot of responsibility," Brenda said. "Everyone has to work hard to provide food for the whole city. Most of the girls know this and are fine with it. She has her way of doing things and it works. We are safe, we eat well, and we have a lot of fun at times. It's not all work and no play. To answer your question, yes, I am fine with the way things are."

"Me too," Kim added. "You make things a lot better around here, Robbie."

"Yes, you do," Brenda said puckering and making a kissing sound at Robbie. He blushed.

"Jade and Sandra didn't get along well," Brenda added. "Jade thought the men should be doing a lot more around here. But the men who come in to help from time to time have other responsibilities. Besides, the men cause a lot of other problems. Even though the men are neuts, a lot of horny women and some good-looking men disrupt the process, neutered or not. And when there was a problem with the men, Sandra always punished the women, never the men. This especially rubbed Jade the wrong way."

"I guess I see your point, but it still seems cruel."

Robbie went to take his shower. When he finished, he noticed someone had laid out fresh clothes on the vanity. He dressed and joined the ladies for dinner.

Brenda and Kim joined Sandra and Robbie for the informal dinner at the kitchen table. What little was said during the meal was by Sandra, followed usually by "yes, ma'am."

Sandra and Robbie went to her bedroom after the meal, but it was not for sex. Sandra asked him a few questions about what he had witnessed.

"I don't understand it all, and it's sad, but I wasn't here to see what went on last night. A lot of people died. I talked to Brenda and Kim a little while you were showering. I guess you know what you're doing."

"And Jade?" she asked.

"I don't know what to say," he replied.

"Do you like her?"

"Of course. I like all the girls here, but Jade is special. I liked her from the first day. She's different—tough, smart, and headstrong; but also beautiful, tender, and caring all rolled into one. How could I not like her?"

"Well, let's get some sleep," Sandra said. "It's been a long day."

The next morning Robbie awoke in Sandra's bed, but he was alone. He got up and got dressed. Sandra was not in the house. He knew where she was though.

In the barn, Sandra had her back to him when he came in. She was interrogating Jade. Robbie walked closer so he could hear.

"You want another round of what you got yesterday, Jade?" he heard Sandra ask.

"Kill me, you stupid bitch," Jade screamed. "You're not getting a word out of me. Kill me! Kill me!"

Jade's face was bleeding again. It seemed redder than yesterday too. Robbie didn't know what Sandra or the men had done to her, but he could see she was pissed. She was going to die and she was going to make Sandra mad enough so she would put her out of her misery.

Robbie moved up beside Sandra. She looked over at him then back to Jade. When Sandra put her hand up to her face, Robbie could see blood splattered on her hands. It did not appear to be hers. It had to be Jade's. Sandra had tortured Jade again.

"That's it," Sandra said to the guards. "Take her outside."

They knew where she meant. They took her straight to the cross and tied her up just as Louise had been tied. She was blindfolded and the men retrieved their rifles. They also brought an extra rifle for Sandra.

"Last chance, Jade," she told her.

"Do it bitch!" she screamed.

Then Jade said something no one expected. "I love you, Robbie. You hear me? I love you!"

Sandra lined up alongside the men. Seconds later it was over. Jade hung limp on the ropes. She handed her rifle back to the men and walked over to Robbie who just stood behind her while she killed Jade.

"I'm going inside for breakfast." she said and headed toward the house. "Join me when you're ready."

I've really underestimated Sandra. She's been so good to me, but I haven't crossed her. I've heard the stories of Grandpa Lars all my life. How sweet and caring he was, but also how he transformed into a killing machine when it was necessary. But is what Sandra is doing necessary? Is it the same as Grandpa? I don't think so. Will she do the same to me if she catches me breaking Florence out of here? Not just me, but she'll kill Florence too. She may even go as far as to kill Sean out of spite. And what about Beka? I've got to be dead certain I can pull it off before I attempt to leave.

Robbie took a last look at Jade and followed Sandra into the house. Brenda and Kim had bacon, eggs, and toast ready and Barbara had joined them this morning as well. She was preparing fruit. They all ate another informal meal and Sandra left.

"Take good care of Robbie," she said on the way out.

Robbie didn't see Sandra again until the next morning when it was time for her to take him back to the Airport.

Chapter 25

Sean was happy to be back at the Bayfront. He worked hard and had the opportunity to have a long talk with Sonny.

"I want my own boat and learn everything I can about shrimping," he said. "I want to spend the rest of my life here and do everything you do. Will you teach me?"

"Yes," was all he said.

Sonny had work to do, so he did what he needed—he got back to it. Marcia overheard the conversation and came over to Sean and wrapped her arms around him. Marcia, who up to this time had been cold toward him, warmed up enough to hug him.

"I'll teach you about the processing part of the business," she said. "You need to know why we do what we do on the boat."

Day in and day out, Sean learned new things. There was so much to absorb—patching nets better, changing rigging, and parking the boat. Starboard or port was always confusing.

"We get priority on fuel and ice," Sonny explained. "Everyone knows how much seafood we catch and how important it is to our food supply. We all work together to find the shrimp so as not to waste fuel. And shrimp and fish need to be iced well to keep. We don't have any way to keep our catch fresh on the boat except with ice. We try not to waste it, but we get all we think we need."

Each day Sean was amazed by all the creatures of the sea—bottlenose dolphin, octopus, spider crabs and a million others, and fish with both eyes on the same side of their head . . . amazing! But what he fancied most was the shrimp. Sean absolutely loved this little crustacean. He'd never tasted shrimp before coming to Corpus Christi, and it didn't matter whether they were dried, grilled, or smoked; he loved them. The best thing about being a fisherman was they got all the shrimp they could eat. This suited Sean just fine. He wouldn't have it any other way.

The days were long and the work was hard, but Sean spent many hours virtually alone. Sonny worked hard doing everything he needed to catch shrimp; Marcia did what she needed to do to help him; and Sean did what he was told to do. They spoke when they needed, but many hours were spent in solitude. This gave Sean a lot of time to think. And think he did.

Am I doing the right thing staying here? I don't have food problems. That's always good. I hate deserting Robbie and my family, but they would want what's best for me. When can I get my own boat? When can I get my own place to live? I hope Robbie gets out of here safely.

Sonny and Sean had finished cleaning up the boat and were waiting for Marcia to return from her delivery of their catch.

"What do you think is taking her so long?" Sean asked.

"I don't know. You'll find out when I do."

"When do you think I can get a boat of my own?"

"You've learned a lot, but you don't know everything. That will take a while. Maybe next year."

"A year?"

"Yes, all good things are worth waiting for."

"That's still a long time."

Sean sat watching for Marcia's truck. "What about a place of my own?"

"What? You don't like our home?"

"Yeah, but it's not my home. If I'm going to have a family, I need my own place. Besides, it still seems like a prison to me. I know you weren't keeping me prisoner. But even though the guards are gone, it still has the feel of jail."

"I'm hurt." Sonny grimaced.

"I'm not blaming you, Sonny. I know I was forced on you. You were just doing what you were ordered to do."

"When the fishing slows down in the winter, maybe you can get started on a place of your own," Sonny said. "You can look around now when you have a little spare time to see if you can find a place you like. But don't count on having enough time to fix it up until November at least."

"That's a long time too!"

"Our priority now is catching shrimp, crabs, and fish. Other things can wait. A new house won't be nearly as nice if you're hungry."

"Good point," Sean said.

"Finally!" Sonny exclaimed as Marcia and little Lola drove up and got out of the truck. "Problem?"

"Not anymore," Marcia replied. "I ran into Sandra at the plant. They had a big problem at the Farm."

"Oh!"

"A bunch of the girls tried to kill Sandra and take over the operation. Seems they didn't like the way Sandra was running the place. Jade thought that since she was basically managing the Farm anyway, she shouldn't have to answer to Sandra anymore. On top of that, Jade seemed to have taken up a liking for Robbie. She has a bad jealous streak, and Robbie seemed to like Florence."

"What about the other girls?" Sean asked. "Was she only jealous of Florence?"

"He was just doing a job. With Florence it was different, and Jade saw this," Marcia replied. "They tried to kill Florence too."

"Wow," Sean exclaimed.

"Jade won't be a problem anymore," Marcia added.

The men knew what that meant.

"Is Robbie okay?" Sean asked.

"Yeah, he's fine."

"On a lighter side," Marcia said, "I told Sandra that you wanted to stay here. That you wanted your own boat and place to live."

"And?" Sean asked.

"She was quite pleased."

Robbie took the Cessna Skyhawk out onto the runway alone for the first time. *I think they're finally beginning to trust me.* He checked all the gauges. Everything was normal. He turned left and right, watching the wing flaps. He knew how important it was to learn every control without having to think about the consequences first. He would only get one chance to fly this thing, and he had to do it right.

On the main runway, he throttled the engine up. He could feel the wind blowing the plane around a little. *Get up enough speed and pull back gently on the steering wheel. Keep it straight down the runway. It should fly itself. But how much speed? Will I know when I get there? I know how the plane works—wing flaps, tail flaps and speed. That's it and I'm flying. Still scary though. I can do it. I just need to keep telling myself I can do it.*

Robbie throttled the plane down and turned onto the taxiway. He kept going over every detail of the takeoff procedures in his mind. After he got it into the air and home, he had to land too. He had to think about this as well. *There is no runway at home. I'll need to land on the highway. It's not nearly as wide as this runway. Can I do that? I have to.*

He pulled the plane in front of the hangar and killed the engine. He got out and checked the plane from front to rear. Then he noticed a truck pulling away from the end of the runway. He thought it strange for a truck to be out there, but with so many plans running through his head, this incident slipped away quickly.

Jorge came out to help Robbie push the plane into the hangar. Once they had it inside, they examined every single aspect of the engine. Everything checked out perfectly. He would fill the plane with fuel, and it would be ready for his escape. But he wasn't ready. He needed more time to get the entire plan down in his mind. *The toughest part will be getting Florence out and away from the Farm. Then I need to get her here without being seen. That's going to take some luck.*

Beka showed up a few days later. Robbie grabbed two sodas and they went out back and found a shady spot to talk.

"I want to go with you when you leave," she informed him.

"For sure?"

"Yes."

"Why?"

Beka leaned over and kissed him. He leaned back with a surprised look on his face.

"What's that about?"

"I like you and I want to go with you," she replied.

"I like you too, but . . ."

She leaned over and kissed him again. He didn't back away this time. He grabbed her, pulled her close, and pressed his lips to hers.

"But what?" she said.

He didn't answer. Suddenly his mind went blank. All he could think of to do was kiss her again. He pulled her tighter and put his lips to hers again, and teased the inside of her mouth with his tongue.

She pulled away this time. "When are we going to leave?" she asked with a dazed look on her face.

"I . . . I don't know yet. I've got to figure out how to get Florence out of her cell and then get her here."

"Why?" she asked.

"Why?" he said confused, not understanding the reasoning behind her question.

"Yes, why?"

"I owe her my life. I would be dead if not for her. She is alone now. I just have to get her out."

"Okay."

"She's your best friend, Beka."

"Yes, she is."

They both sat quietly staring at each other and sipping their sodas. *What have I gotten myself into now?* he thought.

He really kisses good!

Robbie paid more attention to the terrain on the trips to the Farm. He also checked the odometer on Sandra's Jeep. The distance wasn't quite as far as he had thought at six miles. *I can fast-walk that distance in about an hour, but the return trip with Florence might take a little longer. If she is weak from Sandra overworking her, if Sandra puts her to work, she might not be able to make the trip. If she doesn't get some exercise soon, her muscles may be weak and slow her down as well. I'll have to drive there in Russ's truck.*

That's all there is to it. Walking is not an option. I'll get as close as possible and go the remainder of the way on foot. Florence will have to make it back to the truck. Hopefully that won't be too much of a problem. I can carry her over my shoulder or piggyback if I need to. That won't be a problem for a short distance. I'll have to drive in the dark, retrieve Florence, and get back just as it gets daylight. First quarter or last quarter of the moon should give me enough light to see without the headlights. Full moon will make me too visible. And I'll need to cut the brake lights.

I'm definitely going to need some luck too—no one on the road between here and the Farm; no one guarding Florence in the early morning; no surprises.

Chapter 26

Back in Peaceful Valley . . .

The days and weeks dragged by. The spring flowers had all but dwindled away. The dog days of summer were here, and the heat was on in full force. The kids didn't mind so much though. They spent at least an hour or two in the river every day.

Reggie and Emily had plenty of water, but the Lindgrens' and Wimberleys' cisterns ran dry. James and Ronnie spent all morning hand-pumping water from the well and carrying it up a ladder to the top of the tank and pouring it in. The heads of the screws holding the hatch onto the top of the access hole were rusted off. It took an hour just to get the lid off so they could pour the water into the tank.

By noon, the cistern was less than a quarter full. Several days would be necessary to fill the tank. The Wimberleys' cistern was smaller and only took Lance and Zack two days to fill; however, with more family members, the tank would need filling more often. They prayed for rain every day.

The heat also aggravated tempers. John Wimberley was still intent on getting his church built, and he took his frustration out on Kathy and the kids.

"I can't have my kids growing up in a godless community," John said to Kathy who was hard at work preparing lunch. "God got us through the bad times in San Antonio, and we can't desert him now."

"We're not deserting him," Kathy replied.

"We don't pray together like we did. The neighbors are godless people, and I think their ways are rubbing off on the kids. Without God in our lives, we are all doomed."

"These people went through hell out here just to survive. Maybe they didn't have God in their daily lives, but they certainly had him on their side. Otherwise, they would not have made it," she said. "Deep down, I think they have God in their hearts. I think they've had so much to contend with over the last couple of decades, they just let him slip away. He's still there somewhere, and it will take time for them to realize it. You need to be patient."

"But our kids are going to the devil right now," he said. "We need to get them back on the path before it's too late."

"The kids will be all right," she said.

"They are out there alone. At their ages, the hormones are raging. I know; I was there once. They need a chaperone. God will keep them on the straight and narrow. But if our kids keep seeing those hoodlums without God in their hearts, something bad is going to happen."

"Quit calling them hoodlums and heathens! They are not bad people. The kids are nice and brought up well. They are polite and courteous."

"Maybe at the dinner table," he added, "but their hormones rule the day. There's trouble brewing."

"Call the kids in," she said. "And don't mention the neighbors."

"The heathens," he mumbled.

"What did you say, honey?"

"Nothing."

Charlotte, Kira, Zack, and Lance came in from their morning chores.

"Where's Brooke?" John asked.

"She went over to see Ronnie," Charlotte replied.

"What?" John said in a raised voice and his face turning red. "Dammit!"

"She'll be back before dark, Daddy," Kira said.

"I told you those heathens were going to corrupt our kids!" he added, fuming.

"Calm down, John," Kathy pleaded. "She is a grown woman—"

"And that is exactly what I'm worried about."

"And she's a smart woman," she added. "She'll be fine."

"You're damn right she's not going to get into trouble," he said, walking to the back door.

"Where are you going?"

"I'm going to get my daughter."

"Don't, John."

He didn't say a word. He grabbed his rifle on the way out.

"John! John!"

Kathy turned back to the kids as the door slammed shut. She just stood there with a befuddled look on her face, uncertain about what to say to the kids.

"Is Brooke in trouble, Mama?" Kira asked.

"Eat, kids," was all she came up with.

When John got to the clearing at the Lindgren homestead, he was hot and exhausted. His temperament had also accelerated to the point of boiling over.

"Brooke! Brooke!" he yelled.

James was coming out of the smokehouse and met him halfway to the house. "What's the matter, John?"

"Where's Brooke?" he said.

"I think she's inside with Melissa, Ronnie, and Eileen. What's up?"

"She has no business over here."

"She is welcome here anytime, as are the rest of your kids."

"But I don't want them over here."

"Why not?" James asked. "Settle down and tell me what the problem is."

"Your boy is going to get her into trouble."

"Hold on," James said. "If anyone gets in trouble, it will be a joint venture. Ronnie is a good boy, and he was brought up to respect women."

"And kids will be kids," John said. "I know their hormones are running amuck at their age. Your boy needs the fear of God—"

"Now just a damn minute," James said. "Ronnie's not going to do anything that Brooke doesn't want—"

"He's not going to do a thing one way or the other."

Brooke, Ronnie, Eileen and Melissa came outside to the porch after hearing the yelling from inside the house. "What are you fellas doing out there?" Melissa yelled.

When John saw Brooke he screamed at her. "Get over here, Brooke."

She headed in his direction, Ronnie at her side. John paused to catch his breath while he waited for her.

"Yes, Daddy?" she said when they made it to John and James.

"I don't want you over here anymore," John said harshly.

"I'm a grown woman," Brooke replied.

"You do as I say, young lady," he demanded. "As long as you live under my roof . . . now get home. I'll catch up."

She turned to Ronnie and said good-bye, tears welling up in her eyes.

"Now git!" John yelled.

Brooke took off running.

"Now you don't be coming over to see Brooke," John said to Ronnie.

"Now wait just a minute," James said.

"I mean it. You keep your boy away from my place."

"I go where I please around here," Ronnie said.

"And you'll get hurt."

"That's enough," James demanded. "I think you best be getting home now, John."

John turned to leave.

Before he had made a dozen steps, James added, "And be sure you give a proper signal when you come back over. Otherwise you could be the one who gets hurt."

John continued on without missing a step.

James turned to his son. "Come on, Ronnie, let's get back to the house."

"I like Brooke, Dad. I like her a lot."

"I know, but you best stay away from there for a while."

When they got back to the porch, Eileen had gone inside and returned with glasses and a pitcher of cool mint tea. "Something we need to talk about?" she asked.

"Looks like it," James replied.

"I'm not going to stop seeing Brooke," Ronnie said.

"You don't have to," James assured him, "but let things simmer down a bit before you go stirring up something that might get someone hurt, okay?"

"Yes, sir," he replied with a deflated look on his face.

"Maybe we need to have a meeting with the Carstons and Lins," Eileen said.

"Good idea," Melissa said. "I think Debra is taking a liking to one of the boys as well. This concerns them also."

"I think so too," Eileen agreed.

"We could have a meeting in the morning," Ronnie suggested. "I can go inform the Lins now."

"And I'll run over to see Reggie and Emily," James added.

"Then let's make it happen," Eileen said.

James and Ronnie quickly finished their drinks and headed out.

"I just knew the Wimberleys were going to be trouble," Eileen stated.

"Why is that?" Melissa asked.

"Because of their religion. Now don't get me wrong, I don't have a problem that they believe in God. You do, Melissa, but I've noticed that especially John has been growing more forceful with his faith. It's been my experience that there are always a few staunchly religious people who tend to force their religion on everyone else. I hope John is not one of them, but if he is, there may be a serious problem with the Wimberleys, and John in particular."

"I do believe in God," Melissa stated.

"But you respect my right to choose—and I choose to not believe."

"Did the way Lars died affect the way you believe?"

"If there was a God, I would hate him for taking the first man I honestly and truly loved with all my heart away from me. But I don't hate anyone or anything. It was a freak accident, and that's the way life is. You can't place blame. Should I blame the rattlesnake? No, it thought it was in danger and tried to protect itself. I would do the same thing. I have done the same thing. That's life. I know that. It hurts, but there is no one to blame."

"Well, I believe in God. I don't think I could have gotten out of Waco and made it here without the help of a higher power."

"And I'm not telling you not to believe in him. It's your life and your belief, and I'm fine with that. I'm not going to tell you not to believe in God just because I don't."

"And I'm not going to try to make you believe in him either," Melissa said.

"I know you're not, Melissa, and neither are the Wimberleys. They can look down their noses at me, but they are not going to change the way I feel and believe. They can have their religion and pray to the man in the moon, for all I care, but they will keep their religion to themselves."

"I'm just concerned for the kids," Melissa said.

"Me too. You know, when Ronnie and Debra didn't work out, I didn't know what was going to happen around here. Then when the Wimberleys showed up with five kids, there was hope."

"I think there is still hope," Melissa said.

"As do I," Eileen agreed, "but the Wimberleys must understand they cannot force their religion on anyone else, not even their kids. They can influence them, but the kids need to make up their minds for themselves. They are grown men and women, after all, or nearly so."

"We don't need another civil war around here," Melissa said.

"That's for damn sure!"

Brooke ran into the house, crying and out of breath.

"Where's your dad?" Kathy asked.

"He's coming," she said as she ran to her room and plopped down on the bed, sobbing.

"What's going on?" Charlotte asked.

"I don't know," Kathy replied. She followed Brooke into her bedroom.

"What's up?" Kathy inquired knowing all well what was the matter.

"Daddy doesn't want me to see Ronnie anymore. He made me come home."

"Your dad's upset because the neighbors don't want to help him build a church. Your dad is afraid that without a proper and regular means of worship, you kids will lose your faith in God and do something stupid. He is just concerned for you."

"No he's not," Brooke yelled. "He's only concerned for his damn church."

"Now Brooke, you know that's not true."

"No I don't. He just wants his damn church and to control us."

Brooke began to cry uncontrollably and buried her face in her pillow, so Kathy went back into the living room pulling the door to behind her.

John came in through the back as she shut the door.

"You kids will stay away from the neighbors," he announced.

"But we like them," Kira said.

"You heard me," he repeated.

"Go on outside, kids," Kathy said.

Kathy waited for the kids to leave. "You remember what I said about driving the kids away?"

"Dammit, Kathy—"

"Don't dammit me," she replied. "You are going to drive the kids away. They are going to hate you, and it will be your own fault. They are grown up now, and they need to learn things on their own."

"But—"

"No buts about it," she said. "If you want to make this bed, then sooner or later you're going to have to sleep in it."

John was quiet. Kathy walked back into the kitchen and fixed him a cool drink. He certainly needed hydrating and to calm down after the long walk home in the heat of the afternoon.

Ronnie made it back from the Lins', and Melissa and Eileen were still on the porch enjoying their conversation the best they could, considering the topic of discussion. James made it back a half-hour later.

"You should have beaten Ronnie back, James. You had the easier trip. You getting old, old man?" Melissa asked with a smile.

"Who you calling old? I see those gray hairs showing up on your head too." He laughed.

"Is the meeting a go then?" Eileen asked.

"Yep," James replied.

"The Lins will be here tomorrow too," Ronnie added. "Sam said they'd get off as soon as he finishes feeding the hogs."

"Good," James said. "How about we go in and get started on dinner? And Ronnie will help."

"Me? What did I do wrong?"

"One of these days you are going to get married, Ronnie." Eileen said. "Your wife is not going to want to cook and do dishes all the time. I know you've heard this before, but housework is man's work too, just like gardening is woman's work. A strong family works together."

"Besides," James added, "you eat more than anyone else."

James ran out to the smokehouse for meat while Ronnie followed the ladies into the house. Everyone worked side by side to prepare dinner. They then sat down and enjoyed a family meal. Afterward, they all worked to clean up the kitchen and table.

Eileen decided to read for a while before bed and Melissa crocheted, while the men took their showers. After the men got out, the ladies took their turns and adjourned for the evening.

The Lindgrens had just finished cleaning up the dishes from a late breakfast, when the first wolf howl sounded. James walked out onto the porch. He returned the howl and Reggie and Emily stepped out of the woods.

Emily went inside while Reggie joined James for a cigar on the front porch.

"Nasty habit, isn't it?" Reggie asked with a smile.

"For some," James said, returning the smile.

Shortly after they finished their cigars, they heard a wolf howl from behind the house. James and Reggie strolled around back and returned the signal. Debra came running up, while Samuel and Sally lagged behind.

"Welcome, Sam. Welcome, Sally," James said.

"Thank you," they both replied.

"You're getting around like new, Sally," Reggie said.

"Thank you for noticing," she replied. "I'm almost one hundred percent now."

Debra ran inside and Sally followed.

"Come on around to the front, Sam," James said. "I think it will be cooler there."

James grabbed a couple extra chairs while Melissa and Eileen brought drinks for everyone.

"You kids pull up chairs too," James said to Debra and Ronnie. "This concerns you as well. Probably as much, if not more, than the rest of us."

Debra and Ronnie not only joined in on the family meeting but were the focus of the discussion.

"What's up?" Reggie asked.

"John came over here yesterday afternoon and made Brooke go home," James said. "He was pissed that she was over here. I don't think he wants his kids associating with ours."

"He thinks Ronnie and Debra are going to corrupt his kids," Eileen added.

"We're not going to corrupt anyone," Debra said.

"I know," Melissa said, "but he doesn't see it that way. He thinks that because we don't have religion in our lives on a regular basis, we are going to turn his kids away from their religion."

"They're already corrupted," Ronnie blurted out.

"What do you mean?" Sally asked.

"Brooke and Charlotte don't believe in God. They said they never did, but were afraid to tell their daddy."

James got up to stretch his legs. He pulled a cigar from his pocket and held it up to Reggie. He nodded and followed James over to the edge of the porch.

"What about Kira?" Eileen asked.

"We don't know about Kira," Debra said.

"She's a baby," Ronnie added. "We don't talk to her much."

"That's not nice," Melissa noted. "She's sixteen. She's not a baby anymore."

"Well, she's a baby to us," Debra stated.

"She may not be as old as you two," Eileen said, "but she's not a baby. If we can get things worked out with the Wimberleys, you two be nicer to her. There's nothing worse than being left out and alone. Believe me, you two will be better for it."

"I was upset for a long time," Sam said, "because Ronnie hurt Debra and didn't marry her. I never said anything to Sally. It was my own fault I was upset. I blamed you, Ronnie, and I'm sorry for that, but now I understand. We cannot force kids to do things they don't want to do. Our kids are smart and can figure things out for themselves and make good decisions."

Sally agreed. "All our kids are smart because we taught them as much as we possibly could."

"Yes, we did," Eileen said.

"We've had a dilemma here in our little valley for a long time—men for women and vice versa," Emily stated. "Debra had two choices, Ronnie or Robbie. There were no available women for Sean. Now that Ronnie and Debra didn't work out . . . well, when the Wimberleys came along with five kids, there was hope some of you would get together. There is still an imbalance, but it's progress."

"But," Sam said, "if John puts his foot down and doesn't let his kids see ours, a lot of bad things can happen."

"Yes, they can," Reggie said. "No more weddings, no more grandkids, and just maybe a civil war between the families."

"Or Mr. Wimberley will not be able to stop Brooke from seeing me," Ronnie said.

"Or Zack from seeing me," Debra added.

"That's going to cause all kinds of problems for all of us," Eileen stated.

As James listened, he realized the problem was much bigger than he could have imagined. John could literally tear their valley apart. If the Wimberleys leave, Ronnie and Debra could also leave. He hated to think what might happen if they stayed and John didn't change his ways.

"I don't think Kathy is a problem," Melissa said. "I think the problem is John."

"I can fix that," Reggie said. "You know what I'd do."

"Don't talk like that," James warned. "We don't need any more accidents around here."

"I'm not talking about an accident," Reggie stated.

"Shut up, Reggie," Emily demanded. "You're bringing up some bad memories."

"Yeah, Reggie," Sam chimed in.

"Fine," Reggie said, a little disappointed.

"John is the problem," James stated. "Now what are we going to do about it?"

"I think there is only one thing to do," Eileen said. "We invite him and Kathy over here and have a direct talk with them—or more correctly, with John. We tell him how the cow chews the cabbage, and if he doesn't like it . . . well . . ."

"Well what?" James asked.

"I don't know," Eileen said. "Something, but I'm not sure what."

"I do," Reggie said with an evil look on his face.

"No!" Emily demanded.

"If John goes," Debra said, "they'll all go, and where does that leave us?"

"No Brooke and no Zack," Ronnie said. "I don't want that."

"No one does," Eileen said.

"I think we have to take that chance," Melissa said.

"I do too," Eileen added.

"Everyone agree?" Melissa asked.

The vote was unanimous. Ronnie and Debra were hesitant, but finally agreed with the rest that they didn't have a choice. A showdown was necessary.

"How about getting them over here tomorrow?" Eileen asked.

"The sooner the better," James stated.

Again, everyone agreed.

"I'll run over and invite them here tomorrow then," James said.

"Let's have lunch first," Eileen suggested. "Then you can go inform them of the meeting, James."

"Okay."

On that note, the ladies went inside to prepare the meal. Ronnie and Debra went down to the river while the men chatted on the front porch.

"Sure could use a little rain," Sam said.

"We'll get some," James replied.

"How are your hogs taking this heat?" Reggie asked Sam.

"I dug a small pond and lined it with clay and rock so it would hold water longer. Then I extended the pen around the new water hole. I carry buckets of river water to the pond most mornings."

"That's a lot of work," James said.

"I know, so I'm also trying to extend the pen down and into the river, but that's a long way. I'll get it eventually, but it will take a while."

"You need some help?"

"Thank you for asking, but the pond didn't take long to build, and the hogs are okay for now. I work on the extension to the river a little at a time."

Ronnie and Debra sat quiet on the pier and stared at the river for a long time. Both were engrossed in their thoughts. "I don't think Brooke will leave with the rest of the family if it comes to that," Ronnie finally said.

"I think Zack will stay here too," Debra stated.

"I don't know why everything has to be so hard all the time," he added.

"When has anything been easy?"

"Good point."

"Maybe we can build a house and live somewhere around here," Debra said.

"If John and Kathy leave, we can move into their place as soon as they move out," Ronnie said. "We almost lived there once before. If it comes to that, we can invite Brooke and Zack to stay with us."

"Something to think about."

Chapter 27

The Wimberleys showed up mid-morning for the meeting. The Carstons and Lins were there early. Reggie brought ice and he and James were helping the ladies prepare some cold drinks when the Wimberleys arrived. John immediately asked what the meeting was about.

"It's primarily about you," Reggie said looking at him square in the eyes.

"Me?" he asked.

"Yes," Reggie replied with a stern look on his face and not taking his eyes off John.

"Come on up and have a seat," Eileen said. "And kids, you get comfortable too. This meeting concerns all of us and you need to be part of it as well."

John and Kathy took seats and Melissa poured them all glasses of iced tea thanks to Reggie's good thinking. The kids got glasses as well and made themselves comfortable.

Eileen was the eldest Lindgren and was chosen to speak for the group.

"When I came here from San Antonio nearly twenty years ago, it was a bloody hell around here," she said. "We struggled for many years, and there was a lot of killing. We also struggled with growing food and finding replacements for other necessities. It wasn't easy."

Everyone listened intently.

"Finally, not that many years ago, things settled down. We have all been able to breathe a little easier the past few years. We thought about the growth of what we can now truthfully call Peaceful Valley. We all thought it was wonderful when you folks showed up," she said, looking directly at the Wimberleys. "We thought there would be hope for future generations to carry on long after the rest of us are dead and gone.

"We have struggled so hard the past two decades that we have not had time for religion. Some of us prefer it that way—and I'm not saying who—but when you came here and started throwing religion in our faces and practically demanded we help you build a church, some of us became angry, as did you for our refusal."

Reggie never took his eyes off John. When he opened his mouth, Reggie shushed him immediately.

Eileen smiled at Reggie. "Maybe somewhere down the road, there will be a place for a church here, but not now. I don't know what you think about the rest of us, but I've heard the rumors."

"Now . . ." John started, getting up.

This time, Reggie got up too. "I'm not going to tell you again to not interrupt. Next time I won't be as nice. Now sit down."

John sat back down in his chair and Eileen continued.

"Our kids will work and play with your kids and vice versa. They are all old enough to decide what they want, and I'm sure your kids have been brought up as good kids. We don't have a problem with our kids associating with yours. If you don't want your kids consorting with ours, then that is going to cause a dilemma around here. The main reason we have allowed you to stay here is because of your kids. Without them, the future of Peaceful Valley is less hopeful."

Eileen paused and took a drink. Again John started to speak but looked over at Reggie before uttering a word and kept quiet. Reggie's eyes were burning a hole through John's head. If looks could kill . . .

Eileen continued. "I think a couple of your kids, Brooke and Zack, have eyes for Debra and Ronnie." She looked over at the kids and all were blushing, glancing back and forth at each other. There were smiles on their faces.

"If you want to put a stop to it," she continued, "that's up to you. But I'll tell you this—if you do, you will leave."

"Damn right you'll leave," Reggie said sternly.

"John has been quiet and listening, Reggie," Eileen said, glaring at Reggie. "Now you shut up too."

"Yes, ma'am," he replied.

"I want you all to stay and get along. I want you to enjoy what we have here in Peaceful Valley, but if you refuse to do that, you will leave. And we're good at making people leave."

"Yes, we are," James said, drawing a sour look from Eileen.

"Next, I'd like to hear from the kids," Eileen stated.

Ronnie stood up first. "I like Brooke. I don't want her to leave."

"I don't want Zack to leave either," Debra said.

"I'm not going to leave," Brooke said sternly.

"Me either," both Zack and Lance said.

"We like it here, Dad," Lance added.

"I don't want to go either, Daddy," Kira said.

Everyone looked at Charlotte. She was the only one who hadn't spoken up. "While I don't share your enthusiasm, brothers and sisters, there are advantages to staying here," she finally said.

"We now have a nice home," Kathy said. "While there is still a lot of work to be done, I think I'd like to stay here and make it work. We went through hell getting here, and if we try to leave, we will be going right back into that hell. And we would likely do a lot worse than what we've found here in your valley."

All eyes turned to John. He was upset. His face was red and he was breathing heavily. But he also looked hurt, and there was a tear running down his cheek.

"Honey," Kathy said softly, looking into his eyes. "I want to stay."

John took a deep breath and looked at the Lins, the Carstons, and the Lindgrens. He then turned and looked at his kids. He wanted his church, but he knew he was beaten. He also remembered how hard it was getting here, on not only him but the entire family, especially Kathy.

"Well, John," James said, "what's it going to be?"

"We'll stay," he finally replied.

"And?" Eileen asked.

"And I'll put my dream of a church aside for now. I'll do the best I can to abide by your wishes."

"Your best better be pretty damn good, John," Reggie remarked.

John looked at Reggie but he didn't say a word. He just nodded with a deflated look on his face.

The kids jumped up and yelled. "Yay!"

Kathy leaned over and gave her husband a squeeze and kiss on the cheek. "Thank you, John. You won't regret it."

Brooke came over too and hugged her dad. "I'll be good," she whispered in his ear.

"Me too," he whispered back.

Everyone breathed a sigh of relief.

Brooke grabbed Ronnie by the arm and drug him off the porch and around back toward the river. Debra did the same with Zack.

"I'm hungry," Kira said.

"Me too," Charlotte announced.

"Lance?" Kathy asked.

"You know me, Mom. I can always eat."

"My mouth is dry," Eileen announced. "Will one of you guys fix me a nice cold glass of mint tea?"

"Yes, ma'am," Reggie replied.

"Thank you, dear, and while you guys are in there, you may as well prepare lunch too. We ladies have some stuff to catch up on."

The guys frowned and looked at each other for a second. "Why the hell not?" James said and the guys reluctantly went inside and made drinks for the ladies first and then began to work on lunch.

"You made the right choice, John," Sam said.

"I don't like it," he replied, "but I guess I'll have to live with it."

"That's right," Reggie said.

"Sometimes you have to do things you might not like," James added. "We've done a lot of things we would rather have not done, but we did them. Life is not always fair, but you do what is necessary. You may not like it, but it is the best for all concerned."

"It's not just us men," Sam added. "We have to think about the wives and kids. We work hard, we do what is necessary, and we live on."

"And when there is something important which concerns all of us," James said, "we have a meeting to discuss it and we vote on it. The vote is seldom unanimous, but majority rules."

"Next year," Reggie added, "when you've proven yourself, you will get a vote too, as will Kathy and each of your kids."

"The kids?" John asked.

"Yes, the kids," James replied. "They are grown men and women now. They may be young, but they do have minds of their own."

"That's for certain," John agreed with a half-smile.

Ronnie and Brooke walked down the riverbank a ways and found a nice shady spot to sit and talk.

"What's up with Debra?" Brooke asked.

"What do you mean?" he replied.

"She seems to have a thing for you. She stares at you a lot, but when she talks to you, she's mean at times."

"We almost got married," Ronnie divulged.

"Really?"

"I thought I loved her, and she definitely loved me, but I didn't love her the same way."

"And what way is that?"

"I do love her and will always love her, but like a sister. We grew up together, and we played like brother and sister. She loved me differently. Just before we were to be married, I realized I couldn't marry her. She didn't take it very well. I'm glad she's taken a liking to Zack."

Brooke reached over, grabbed hold of Ronnie's hand, and pulled him closer. "I like you a lot, Ronnie."

"I like you too, Brooke. Maybe we can see each other more often now without any problems."

"I would like that. Shall we go for a swim?" she asked.

"Lunch is ready," they heard from the house.

"Maybe later," he said. "I'm hungry. How about you?"

Brooke got up and gave Ronnie a hand. "Yes, let's go get a bite."

Over the next few weeks, the kids spent a lot of time playing in the woods, but when it got hot, they made their way to the river for a swim, except when it was time to eat. John was keeping to his decision and the hostilities between the families, especially between the kids and John, had virtually ceased. He may not have liked it, but he was abiding by the ultimatum laid out by Eileen.

James spent hours and hours working on Lars's old tractor. The garden would need plowing again soon in preparation for their fall planting time. *I don't know how many more years this old thing is going to last. It seems to take more and more each year to keep it going.* Frustrated, he went inside for lunch.

James expected lunch to be ready, but Melissa was sitting looking out the front window, crocheting and watching Eileen at Lars's grave.

"What are you doing, Melissa?" he asked.

"Eileen is acting a little funny lately," she replied.

"How so?"

"I don't know. She just seems different."

"Something to do with the Wimberleys?"

"I don't think so. I can't put my finger on it, but she's changed."

James walked over to Melissa and peered out of the window toward the sycamore tree. "How long has she been there?"

"A couple hours at least."

"I wouldn't worry about it."

James was getting hungry and Melissa hadn't started lunch yet. His thoughts were only focused on food. James walked back to the kitchen and fired up the stove.

"Since she started spending nights at the Carston's, she comes back and just sits there," Melissa continued. "Doesn't that seem strange to you?"

"No, not any more than coming in and no lunch fixed," he said.

"Well, it does to me," Melissa added as if she'd not heard all he'd said. "Then when she comes in, she takes a shower and is quiet for hours."

"Maybe she's just tired from the visit. She's not as young as she used to be," he replied.

"Maybe so."

Under the old sycamore tree, Eileen sat at the side of Lars's grave on the bench James had made. "I think James felt guilty, me having to sit or kneel on the ground every time I came out here to see you," Eileen said staring at the headstone. "James is so thoughtful. He is a good son, isn't he, Lars? But you already know that, don't you? I'm going to be coming to see you soon, Lars. I hope you'll still love me after what I've done."

She looked over at her headstone. *Sam will need to chisel in the final date. Sixty-*

eight . . . how did I get so old?

"Reggie filled a need that has been missing in my life since you died. Emily filled a bigger need. I don't want Reggie so much anymore, but he seems to still want me. I'm sorry, honey. Will you forgive me for what I've done?" *Why couldn't I have gone a little longer? I did just fine without for how many years? But Reggie stirred my hormones I had long thought were gone. Emily stirred them even more. It will all be over soon.*

"I'm going to see you soon darling, whether you want me or not, so get ready."

Eileen got up and slowly headed toward the house. *Ronnie won't understand. I've got to have a long talk with him. I can't until Robbie gets back. I have to talk to both of them at the same time. I can't leave without talking to Robbie first.*

Eileen went inside and took a shower. She then grabbed a book and sat where she could see Lars's portrait on the wall. She paused for a minute staring at Lars's picture. She smiled and opened her book. An hour later she dozed off in her chair.

This is damn strange, Melissa thought.

Chapter 28

Back in Corpus Christi . . .

Robbie sat on a stack of pallets waiting for Sandra to show up. He'd skipped breakfast knowing Sandra would feed him well. *I wonder who she'll introduce me to today. There seems to be an endless line of ladies somewhere waiting to have their dates with me.*

Robbie saw a cloud of dust on the far access road in the direction of the Farm. *That has to be her.* A short time later, Sandra pulled up and having no business with Russ, they headed toward the Farm.

"How's Florence?" he asked.

"You certainly are concerned about her, aren't you?" *He always asks. Does he love her? Hard to tell. At least he's taking care of his duty with the other ladies. Guess it really doesn't matter as long as he does what he's supposed to do.*

"She's been through a lot. She's not strong like you."

Sandra smiled. "I guess not."

"I'd like to see her."

"I guess that will be alright." *At least he's polite about it. Yes, he always asks, not taking anything for granted. That's good . . . maybe a little too damn good. You can't be that perfect, Robbie. No man is, not even you. Am I being naive? He certainly seems to have me wrapped around his little finger. Things don't seem quite as simple these days. But what am I going to do?*

"I think you'll notice she's doing a lot better now that she's working. Her color is better anyway."

"I'll wait for you inside," she said when they got to the Farm.

Robbie opened the Jeep door for Sandra as usual and went to the barn where Florence was kept in her cell. Sally Beecher was watching as Robbie went inside. Robbie didn't see her. After he was inside, she took her position between the oleander bush and the building, directly below the window of Florence's cell.

Robbie embraced Florence and she gave him an affectionate kiss on the lips in return. She sat down to talk, but Robbie looked out of the opening to see if the guard was nearby. He also peered out of the window to the outside. He didn't see anyone.

"When are we getting out of here?" Florence asked.

"Whisper," he said. "We can't be certain if anyone is listening. If someone finds out, we're both dead."

"In two weeks."

"Why so long?"

"It's the first quarter of the moon now. It will only get lighter outside. The last quarter will provide just enough light to see, but not so much that we'll be overly visible. That will be in two weeks."

"But that's a long time," she said with a sad face.

"At least you're getting outside now. You're getting a tan. Keeping busy, the time will seem to pass much faster. We'll be out of here before you know it."

"But the work is hard."

"Life is hard. Be patient and we'll get out of here soon. Tell me about the morning routine, Florence. When do you hear people stirring? When do they take you out? Does it sound like a lot of people around here early, or just a few? So I'm guessing you don't work on Saturdays?"

Florence patiently answered his questions. He gave her another hug.

"I've got to get going," he said. "I don't want Sandra to need to come out here and get me. I'll see you next weekend."

"Okay," she replied, the tears welling up in her eyes.

Robbie banged on the cell door and the guard let him out. He smiled over his shoulder at Florence as the door closed behind him. *She'll be okay. Yes, she will. Soon.* Robbie then hurried toward the main house, unaware that Sally lurked nearby.

Robbie ate a hearty lunch prepared by Kim and Brenda while Sandra went to the bathroom. Kim and Brenda were Sandra's most loyal followers and were now Sandra's primary cooks since Jade's death. Brenda burned the bread, but other than that, the meal was as good as any Robbie had previously eaten.

Sandra saw that Robbie was in good hands when she returned and bid them farewell. She grabbed a soda and headed to the back porch where Sally waited.

"Florence asked him when they were getting out of here, but I couldn't make out anything else. They were whispering and I couldn't understand what they were saying. I'm sorry."

"You did the best you could," Sandra said. "Now go on. I need time to think."

So they are planning to escape. Dammit, Robbie. But when? You sure have complicated things around here, you little bastard! Everything was once so easy and simple. He'll make some fine babies, but everything comes to an end sooner or later.

And what the hell is Beka doing? She is supposed to be reporting to me. Robbie is just working on the planes, she keeps saying. Nothing else! That's crap. Robbie's been planning to get out of here for a while. That's why he's so nice to me. I'll fix his little wagon. Then I'll take care of Beka. I have too many headaches these days.

Robbie soon realized Kim and Brenda were much smarter than Sandra's other girls as he got to know them better. He had been with them before, but they were primarily focused on sex. Now, they seemed more interested in real conversation.

"Most of the girls don't read much," Kim explained. "We love to. Reading is our escape from reality. Sandra has a lot of books. Would you like to see her library?"

"Yes," he replied and the girls led him to what appeared to have been a walk-in closet at one time.

"There's Dickens, Poe, Tolstoy, Whitman, and Shakespeare," Kim said, pointing to the shelves of books.

"I just love Shakespeare," Brenda said. "So romantic!"

"Speaking of romance," Kim said with a grin, "shall we go to our room?"

Both girls then grabbed Robbie's arms and dragged him out of the closet and to their boudoir.

Looks like it's going to be a long afternoon, he thought, smiling all the way to the bedroom.

Beka showed up at the Airport again during the middle of the week. She greeted Robbie with a wet kiss.

"You've gotta stop doing that," he said. "Someone is going to see us."

"And what's wrong with that?"

He couldn't think of an answer. Robbie hurried into the hangar and returned with two sodas and led her around the side of the building.

"Do you still want to get out of here?" he asked.

"Yes!"

"I realized after you left last time that you're supposed to be in love with a sailor down at the Bayfront."

"Oh yeah, him. Well, that didn't work out."

"What happened?"

"He cared more for his little boat than he did me."

"How's that?"

"He wouldn't let me drive the thing. He said girls can't drive boats. I told him that with a little practice, I could drive it as good as him. He said 'I don't think so', so I told him he could stick his little dinghy up his fat ass. Not that he has a fat ass, but you know what I mean."

Robbie chuckled.

"What?"

"Nothing. Well, if you really want to get out of here, we're leaving a week from Saturday. Early!"

"How early?"

"As soon as it gets light enough to take off, I want to be in the air. Can you be here?"

"I think so. I'll tell my mom I'm getting up early to go sailing with Charles. I think she'll buy that. I haven't told her we broke up. I'll get up early this Saturday and do a trial run to see if it works out okay."

"Don't bring too much stuff either. Bring several pairs of comfortable shoes and a heavy coat. Those are hard to come by where we're going. And plenty of underwear."

"And if I don't wear underwear?"

Robbie's mouth dropped open.

"Just kidding," she said with a smile.

"Come by next week and let me know how the trial run went."

"I will."

Chapter 29

The remainder of the week Robbie searched every square inch of the hangar for items he wanted to take with him. He pretended to be cleaning and organizing, but what he was really doing was gathering and storing useful things in a hidden but easily accessible area to quickly load into the Cessna.

All the while he was collecting items, he kept a total weight calculation. Jorge said he thought the Cessna had a maximum payload of 800 pounds. Florence, Beka, and himself would take up the bulk of that weight, so Robbie figured he could haul no more than 300 pounds of extra stuff. To be on the safe side, he decided to cut that figure in half.

This weight restriction eliminated the item he really wanted to take—the brand-new, still-in-the-crate Honda 5,000-watt generator. Without the generator, he really didn't need the extension cords either. He kept changing his mind over and over on the items to take. Finally, he got frustrated because he was messing up his head with junk when he really needed to be thinking about his escape plan. He finally decided to take a few cases of soda and nothing else. *None of this junk really matters if I screw up the escape plan or overload the plane and can't get it off the ground. Besides, I think Jorge has been watching me. Maybe he is getting a little suspicious about what I'm doing. The place is cleaner and more organized though.* He stood up straight and looked around, smiling at the neat and tidy hangar. *Yes, a few cases of soda and that's it. Settled!*

Sandra had gotten so punctual these days. *That's good. If she's keeping a firm schedule, maybe everything will go smoothly next Saturday. Don't want any surprises.*

Robbie climbed into the Jeep and Sandra seemed in an unusually jolly mood this morning.

"Brenda and Kim are pregnant," she announced, glancing over to catch his reaction.

Robbie looked over at her with big eyes.

"Surprised?" she asked.

"Yes," he replied.

"And why is that?"

"It's just something I never thought about."

"You knew you were making babies, didn't you?"

"I guess. It's just that it never occurred to me that I was actually doing it."

"You do know where babies come from don't you?"

"Yes, but I've never made any. I've never even tried."

"Well you have now. You're going to be a daddy."

"And just how does that work?"

"If you keep out of trouble and keep improving over the next year or sô, you will be assigned a wife and a kid. Since you like Florence or Beka, I might let you choose one of them for your wife. And you can choose one of your babies through the other girls."

"Why can't we have our own babies?"

"That's not normally the way it's done, but I might make an exception."

"And how's it normally done?"

Sandra paused for a second. *He can't know the truth. I'm onto you, you little bastard. I've got to be careful. I can't tell him too much.*

"Normally, all babies are conceived and born here on the Farm. That way we can monitor the birth rate and keep the population at a constant level. We keep records on who dies and match births at the same level."

"Why do you want to do that?"

"Overpopulation places too much stress on our limited resources. No one goes hungry. Everyone works hard and everyone eats well. Not like it was before—"

"Before the grid shut down?"

"Yes."

"I wasn't born yet. I don't know what it was like back then. I've been told some of the stories, but I never saw it."

"I know. I guess it's hard to know how it was when all hell broke loose without experiencing it. Many people couldn't work. Many more didn't want to, but they all expected to be taken care of, like they were owed. Here, you work or . . . well, I think you get the idea."

"What if someone gets hurt and can't?"

"They go to the hospital where they are taken care of. Everyone has thirty days of hospital time during their life. If they use up their time, they work anyway or . . ."

"I get it," he said. "Seems a little cruel."

"No one ever said life was fair." Then she got on her soapbox. "Government tried to do too much for everyone. They spent more money than they had. The people at the bottom never got what they needed in spite of this. The fat cats in political offices always got more than their share, and the ones who they were supposed to be helping still needed help.

"And the government couldn't keep their noses out of everyone's business around the world. They fought wars mostly for oil though they claimed otherwise. Others resented this, and groups and countries tried to take us down a notch or two. Terrorists, they called them. Our own government was nothing more than a bunch of terrorists in the eyes of many. It was a mess.

"Much like Jade. I guess you could say she was a terrorist. She certainly scared me when she tried to kill me and Florence. Nip it in the bud and let everyone see that you're not going to take that crap. Doesn't matter whether it's a small group like Jade's, a group from another country, or a whole country for that matter.

"Here already?" Sandra said, as they pulled up in front of the Farm house. *Time flies when you're having fun.* Robbie pondered what she had said, forgetting to open her door. Robbie snapped out of his trance when she tapped on his window.

She smiled. "Come on in. I have a surprise for you. We'll have to talk about the past some more. I enjoy reminiscing; it reminds me how much better Corpus Christi is now."

Yeah, right! For you maybe. Despite how he was feeling, Robbie held the front door for Sandra and followed her inside, but stopped in the doorway when he saw Florence all dressed up. Florence was setting the dining room table as Barbara brought in the food.

"Well, come on in, Robbie," Sandra said.

"What's going on?" he asked.

"Florence is going to join us here at the Farm as one of the girls," she announced. "I didn't tell you earlier because I didn't want to ruin the surprise."

"Is she getting out of her cell too?" he asked.

"No, not until her sentence is over, but she'll only sleep there. She'll have people watching her during the day but will be locked up at night so we don't have to worry about her. That's enough of that. You kids enjoy yourself this afternoon and evening."

Sandra headed out to the barn to check on Linda and a problem she was having with one of the combines. *Robbie will never know I'm onto him. He'll think I'd never put them together if I knew about their escape plan. When he's ready, he'll know exactly where Florence will be. That will be his demise.*

Florence and Barbara ushered Robbie to his place at the table. As they ate, Robbie had questions for Florence, but he couldn't ask them because of Barbara. *She'll tell Sandra. Maybe we'll have some time alone later.*

After lunch, Barbara led Robbie to her room with Florence tagging along behind. Barbara undressed quickly and began working on Robbie's clothes. Florence watched as Barbara undressed him, but looked away when she slipped his underwear down. She knew what was about to happen. *Can I do this? I've never done this before. Barbara looks to be a professional. How many times has she been with Robbie? She doesn't seem embarrassed at all. Will he hate me for being like the other girls? But I'm not like the other girls.*

When Barbara finished undressing Robbie, she turned to Florence. "What's the matter, Flo?"

"I've never . . ."

"I'll help you," she said and began to pull at Florence's clothes.

Robbie sat down on the edge of the bed and watched as Barbara took off Florence's dress. She slipped off her bra and dropped it to the floor. Barbara bent over and licked her breasts. This sent chills through her body and she quivered. As Barbara knelt down to remove her panties, Robbie stared at Florence's breasts, nipples pink and hard. *Her breasts are not as large as Barbara's, but very nice.*

Robbie's eyes moved downward, first to her flat stomach. His eyes followed Barbara's hands as she slid the white panties down Florence's legs, and his eyes fixed on the patch of hair, her pinkness showing through.

Barbara grabbed Florence's hand and pulled her toward Robbie. He put his arms around her and laid his head on her chest. He could feel her shaking. "It'll be all right," he whispered as he looked up and smiled. She managed a weak smile.

Barbara pushed Robbie down on the bed. "Watch, Flo. I'll show you how it's done."

A half-hour later, Barbara flopped down on the bed beside Robbie. "You crawl up on the other side of him, and we'll wait for him to recover. Then you can have your turn."

Robbie awoke early with thoughts of Florence in his head. Wonderful was the only word he could come up with to describe last night, despite Florence crying as Barbara led her out to the barn. Barbara apologized, saying those were Sandra's orders.

Robbie finished his breakfast, and since Sandra wasn't around, he went out to the barn to see Florence. She had trouble looking him in the eyes.

"I'm sorry for last night," she said.

"Why is that? You didn't do anything wrong."

"I was so embarrassed, and I messed everything up."

"You didn't mess anything up." He wrapped his arms around her and squeezed. "I was the one who messed things up," he said. "I like you a lot. I wanted our first time to be special, not something that was forced upon us."

"I wanted you," she said, "but it didn't feel like it meant anything. We were just doing it because Sandra wanted us to."

"Barbara would have told Sandra if we hadn't, and that would not have been good.

We did what we had to do," she murmured. "I want to get out of here so bad. I hate it here."

"Well, that's going to happen soon."

"When?"

"Next Saturday," he whispered in her ear.

"Really?"

"Yes."

She hugged him tighter.

"I'll be here just before daylight. I'm not exactly certain of the time, but be ready."

"I will."

"Well, I guess I better get going. Sandra will be ready soon."

"Thank you," she said giving him a kiss on the lips.

He winked and banged on the door for the guard to let him out. He smiled over his shoulder as he left the cell.

Sandra met Robbie at the Jeep. He stood at her door as she walked over.

"Thank you, sir," she said with a smile.

When Robbie got back to the hangar, he asked Jorge when the C-23 was going to make another run to Brownsville.

"Wednesday," he replied. "Why?"

"Just wondering what the workload was going to be like this week," Robbie said.

"We'll take her out on the tarmac tomorrow and crank her up. One of the pilots will be here to check out the inside. We'll check the outside and top off the fuel. The vendors will be here Tuesday with the cargo, and the pilots will go out early the next day."

"That sounds good to me," Robbie said. "But what do we do the rest of today?"

"I don't know about you," Jorge replied, "but I'm going to take a crap. Been a couple days and I'm past due."

"TMI," Robbie said and walked off.

Robbie grabbed a soda and walked around to the side of the warehouse where he and Beka had their talks. He leaned back against the building and pondered the next week.

The C-23 will be unloaded in Brownsville on Wednesday. They usually take two days to load it back up and refuel. They never get in a hurry down there. I hope they take their sweet time this time. That means they will be back here on Saturday, probably around noon. I will be home by then.

I hope I can fly the Cessna, or rather it can fly itself. I've got the controls down. If everything works like it's supposed to, I'll be fine. Then why am I so worried?

If someone with a night scope sees me going to the Farm, what do I do? What will they do if they see me driving without lights? Maybe I should leave the lights on. Maybe that will be less suspicious. It would be even less suspicious if it were daylight, but I need the cover of darkness to get Florence out. Or do I? Surely someone will be out and about at the Farm as soon as it gets light. So many details. One little mistake and I'm screwed!

Robbie finished up his soda and wandered back into the hangar. Jorge was still not to be seen. Robbie decided to go ahead and take a shower. It didn't appear there was going to be any more work today. *I need to turn in early too. I need to be sharp by Friday. Saturday is going to be a long day. I hope I don't die on Saturday.*

Chapter 30

Jorge and Robbie pulled the C-23 onto the tarmac and filled it with fuel while they waited for the fly-boys to show up.

"Pilots are never on time," Jorge remarked. "Never have any respect for a schedule around here. Not as bad as jet pilots though!"

"Damn pilots!" Robbie yelled out.

"Damn right!" Jorge yelled back.

"I think that is the first time I've seen you smile, Jorge."

"My face does that when I yell out loud," he grumbled.

"Your face does what?"

"Tightens up and makes my lips curl. Makes me look like I'm smiling, but I'm not. I don't smile!"

"Okay, Jorge," Robbie said walking around to the other side of the plane. "Could have fooled me."

"I heard that!"

Directly, the pilot showed up and went up the steps and into the cockpit without saying a word. Robbie and Jorge continued their check of the plane.

When they finished their preliminary check, Jorge walked out from under the plane in front of the cockpit so he could see the pilot and gave him a thumbs-up. "Fire in the hole," he yelled to Robbie and motioned to the pilot.

Engine one turned over and began to hum. Then engine two did the same. Jorge and Robbie watched the outside of the plane as the pilot worked the controls. Each time something moved or lit up, Jorge gave the pilot a thumbs-up.

When all systems had been checked, the pilot killed the engines. He then exited the plane and conferred with Jorge, after which he went inside and met with Russ. Thirty minutes later, he came back out, climbed into his car, and drove away.

"Why do we do this a couple days before the flight, Jorge?" Robbie asked.

"If there is a problem, we have time to fix it if we can," he replied. "The plane has been sitting for weeks. Batteries can go down or it can spring a leak. Though we check things constantly, like you said, an unused vehicle deteriorates faster. Usually not much happens, but if there is a problem, we have time to make the repair. These trips have to get off on time."

"Why is that so important?"

"The pickup was scheduled by the pilots on their last trip. Russ makes out the schedule and the pilot relays the information. There will be vendors waiting on the other end to unload the cargo and to load the plane back up with what we need on the following day. If the plane isn't there when it's supposed to be, it really messes up those Mexicans. It's happened before when we first tried to get the trade going and we missed a few shipments. If they hadn't wanted our stuff so bad, we might not have got the trade going at all."

"So when will this trip return?"

"Let me see," he said. "The plane will leave here on Wednesday and be unloaded that afternoon. The pilot and copilot usually get loaded on tequila and señoritas. By Friday morning, the pilot and copilot are sobered up, and the plane will get another going-over by them and the crew on the other end. They load it on Friday afternoon and come back on Saturday morning. At least that has been the schedule for as long as I can remember. We have our vendors scheduled to come in on Saturday, so I guess that's how it will go."

Beka showed up again early on Wednesday. The plane was pulling onto the taxiway as she drove up. She gave Robbie a smile, but stayed at her car staring at the C-23 rolling away. Robbie joined her.

"I just love to watch planes take off," she said. "They are so loud. I love it!"

Robbie looked around to see Jorge walking back into the hanger. *I guess he's seen enough planes take off and land.*

"How did the early trip to the Bayfront go?"

"Mom never said a word. I told her the night before, and I don't think I even woke her up the next morning. When I got back, all she said was, 'How was the trip?'"

"Good. Be here at daylight on Saturday and we'll get out of here. You still sure you want to do this?"

"Absolutely," she replied with a kiss.

Suddenly they heard the roar of the engines on the C-23 at the end of the runway, and they focused their attention on the plane.

They watched as the aircraft gained speed. Faster and faster. Then about three-fourths of the way down the strip, the nose raised up and it lifted off the concrete. The C-23 climbed steadily and smoothly for a while and then turned to head in the direction of Brownsville.

It looks so simple. Speed, flaps and pull the nose up slightly. I can do that.

"How about a soda?" he asked Beka.

"I'm always up for a soda," she replied.

Robbie grabbed the drinks and they walked back to their usual spot.

"I'm going to fly in my first plane ride," she said.

"Me too. I hope I don't screw up."

"You won't."

"I'll do my best."

"What's Peaceful Valley like?"

"Lots of trees and flowers most of the time. Lot of animals too."

"Are there squirrels? I think they're so cute. There are not many around here."

"Yes, they make a fine meal. Probably why there are not many here."

"You're not supposed to eat them! They're pretty to watch."

"They're still good eating."

"You know they are a rodent, don't you?"

He didn't say anything. *She can think whatever she wants now. Let her get a little hungry and she'll eat grasshoppers.* His lips curled up into a smile.

"There are a lot of cute creatures in the world, and most of them are delicious. You can enjoy their cuteness, but first and foremost, they are food. You don't just eat vegetables do you?"

"No, but—"

"We are at the top of the food chain. Upper links eat lower links. That is the way the world was created. Other animals don't think twice about eating other animals. We are animals, too."

"I guess," she said solemnly.

"You'll love the river. We swim often in the summertime. There are a few snakes and alligators, and you have to watch for them, but they usually don't bother us. Do you like fish?"

"Yes."

"And you don't have a problem killing them?"

"No."

"Well, they are animals too, you know."

She didn't say anything.

"There are birds everywhere up and down the river—woodpeckers, cardinals, kingfishers, and mockingbirds. They are always chattering in the trees. There are also turkeys, dove and quail. These are all good eating."

"Do you always think about whether they are good to eat?"

"Sure, but I like to watch them. They are all pretty in their own way. Some more than others, but all of them are nice to watch as they go about their busy days."

"I sure would like to see Sean before we leave," he said to change the subject.

"Let's go now. The boats should be getting in soon if they are not already."

"Let me ask Jorge and Russ."

Robbie came back a few minutes later. "Okay, let's go."

"Tell me more about Peaceful Valley," Beka said as they headed down to the Bayfront.

"Some creatures and plants will hurt you badly. The main thing is to always remember to watch where you're walking. There is a meadow in front of the house. Deer often come around in the late evening and early morning. We all have gardens. This is often a struggle, but we manage. We don't have any outside trade. We grow it or kill it and we eat it. We do trade with the neighbors, but no one else."

"Am I going to have to kill the animals?"

"Not at first, but you will need to learn to shoot if you don't already know how. Do you?"

"No."

"Then you'll learn. Anyway, my mom and dad live in my grandma and grandpa's house with my Grandma Eileen. My grandpa died when I was four. I have a twin brother, Ronnie. He is married to Debra, a neighbor. She's the reason Sean and I came to Corpus Christi. She chose to marry Ronnie.

"My other grandma and grandpa live two miles up the river from our house. Debra's mom and dad live a mile and a half across the river from us.

"The Westons died before I was born. Their house is two miles downstream. That's probably where Ronnie and Debra are living. That's about it. There are not many people around. We had some neighbors across the highway from us, but they died or moved away a long time ago. I don't really know what happened to them. All anyone would tell us is that they were gone.

"Sean and I ran into an old codger on the way up here, not too far from home. He lived alone and looked like he was not long for this world. He's probably dead by now. I don't think there is anyone else near. We've hunted up to a dozen miles out from the house. Just miles and miles of trees and brush. And lots of animals."

Beka pulled up at the stall where Sonny's boat was parked. Sean was cleaning on the boat after the day's trip. Robbie hopped out and yelled at him. Immediately there was a big smile on his face. Robbie ran over and Sean jumped off the boat and gave his best friend a manly hug. Beka came over and winked at Sean.

"It's good to see you guys," Sean said.

"It's good to see you too," Robbie replied.

"We're getting out of here on Saturday," Robbie whispered.

"Both of you?"

"Yes, and Florence too."

"Do you need my help?" Sean asked.

"No, I think we can handle everything. It took me a while to get it figured out, but I think I've got things covered." Robbie replied. "I wanted to see you one more time."

Sonny came to the door of the cabin. He saw Sean talking to his friends and turned and went back inside.

"You won't forget to tell Mom and Dad I'm doing okay, will you?"

"No, I won't forget."

He and Sean shook hands. Neither wanted to see the other go, but this good-bye was inevitable.

"I'm going to miss you, Sean."

"You too, Robbie."

They each had tears in their eyes by now.

"You sure you want to stay here?" Robbie asked one final time.

"Yes, I'm sure. If I ever change my mind, I can find my way home."

"Okay, buddy. I love you, Sean."

"I love you too, Rob."

They gave each other a final hug and Robbie and Beka headed back to the car. The trip back to the Airport was quiet. *I'm going to miss Sean. We haven't been apart since we were born. Sure we lived a couple miles apart, but we were never separated. We were always together. We hunted, we fished and we swam. We did everything together. All of us did . . . Debra and Ronnie too.* He tried to hold back the tears to no avail.

Robbie got out at the Airport and walked around to Beka's side. "Be here on time Saturday," he said. "If you're late, I'll leave without you. It will be too dangerous to wait around."

"I'll be here. Don't worry about that."

The hours seemed to drag by the next two days, and Robbie had a lot of trouble sleeping at night. His mind kept going over and over all the details of the escape, awake and asleep. There was not a lot of work to be done until the C-23 returned, and each hour seemed like a day. Friday was inevitable, however, and Robbie awoke late. His body must have realized that he wasn't getting enough sleep and caught up suddenly on Thursday night.

Friday morning, Robbie told Jorge it was time to take the Cessna out for another run. "I'll fill her up with fuel and check everything out, and then I'll take her out first thing in the morning."

Jorge grunted.

"I assume that is a yes?" he asked.

"Whatever."

"I'll help you when I get finished."

Robbie pulled the plane around so it was pointed at the hangar doors. He then got the fuel truck and filled the tank. He checked the tires and every minute detail he could think to check. Everything seemed fine.

He walked back to the workbench where Jorge was working on a generator. "Can I help?" he asked.

"Yeah, hand me a pair of needlenose pliers."

Robbie handed him the pliers and Jorge continued to work for a half-hour and never said another word. "I thought you needed my help?" Robbie finally asked.

"Not really."

"Okay then, I'll leave you alone."

Robbie went back over to the Cessna and gave Betty a quick once-over. He couldn't find anything else to check, so he grabbed a soda and went around to the side of the hangar.

It will be so good to see Mom and Dad again. Ronnie will be happy to see me, and will he be surprised to see Florence and Beka. Maybe I can take him flying. I bet Mom and Dad would love to fly too. Boy are they going to be surprised to see me flying a plane.

Florence could have my baby. I hadn't thought of that. If she does, I'll have to marry her. That would be the right thing to do. She said she loves me. But Beka likes me too. She may even love me. She is always kissing me.

Maybe I can have two wives. Or a wife and a mistress. There are no rules anymore. I can do whatever I want. What do Florence and Beka want? Maybe neither will want to marry me. Florence already said she wanted to. Does she really? Do I really want to marry her? Maybe they just want out of Corpus Christi. Maybe they like me because I am their ticket out of here.

The shadow made by the hangar grew until it disappeared into the trees. *How long have I been sitting here?*

Robbie got up and went back inside. Jorge was nowhere to be seen. He knocked on Russ's office door and pushed it open. There was no one inside. He ran back to Jorge's room and did the same. The hangar was empty. *What the hell is going on? Don't do this. Not this evening.*

"Hello!" he yelled.

It will be dark in a little while. "Where can they be?" he asked out loud.

He decided he needed a shower. On the way to his room he stopped by a workbench and picked up a twelve-inch screwdriver. He placed the tool under his pillow, undressed, and got into the shower. As he scrubbed, he thought about what had been done to Sean. *To have your testicles chopped off should be a crime. It is a crime. A crime against all men. I can't fail tomorrow. If I do, and if they don't kill me, I will surely have mine cut out. I'll die first.*

As he was drying off, he heard a door slam. He slipped his pants on and went out into the hangar to see Russ and Jorge walking up from the back end.

"Where have you guys been?" he asked.

"Checking the fuel level in the storage tanks out back," Jorge replied. "Where were you?"

"On the side of the hangar having a soda and watching the sun go down. Is that a problem?"

"No, we just didn't know where you were."

"Well, you didn't seem to need my help."

"I know. We need to get a truck in here next week. We're getting low on fuel for the C-23 and the light planes now that you're taking them out on a regular basis," Jorge stated.

Russ headed on to the office.

"I'm going to get my shower now," Jorge said.

Robbie went back to his room and laid down on the bed. When he woke up it was nearly midnight. *It's time!*

He opened his bedroom door and stared into the darkness. Everything was quiet. It was also very dark. *There is supposed to be some moonlight.*

After a moment his eyes adjusted somewhat and he could see enough, but not as well as he had hoped. He grabbed the screwdriver off his bed and went back into the hangar. He happened to see a claw hammer on the edge of the workbench and grabbed it. *This will make a better weapon.* He then walked very slowly toward Jorge's room.

He was quiet as a mouse as he turned the doorknob. He noticed his hand was shaking. *Careful! No mistakes.* He pushed the door in. Instinctively, he looked over his shoulder. As he made his way to the bed where Jorge lay, he could just barely make out his body. He could hear him breathing, laborious but steady. *THUMP!*

Jorge's body jumped and quivered. The hammer stuck in his forehead. Robbie wiggled it out and hit him again. He could feel the blood and brain splatter in his face. Jorge made not a sound. There was only the sound of the hammer shattering his skull. The breathing stopped. "I'm sorry," Robbie whispered.

Robbie turned and walked out, pulling the door closed behind him. He didn't know whether the moon had come from behind some clouds or what, but he could see a little better now.

There were no windows in Russ's office. Robbie made his way to the back door through which Russ had his sleeping quarters. He stood at the door for a second, turned the knob, and pushed. Russ was snoring loudly.

As quiet as possible, he made his way to Russ's bed. Russ snorted and the snoring stopped. Robbie froze. Russ grunted and groaned as he turned over in his bed. Robbie squinted to try to make out what Russ was doing. He turned over on his side facing away from Robbie and the snoring continued. Robbie raised the hammer once again. *THUMP! THUMP!*

The snoring stopped. The breathing stopped. Robbie turned and went back to his room. There he turned on the light and looked into the mirror. He needed a shower and a change of clothes. His fingers relaxed and the hammer dropped to the floor.

As he took his shower his mind was racing. He felt no remorse for what he had done. They had kidnapped him. *I did what I needed to do to get away from my enemies. I have a long way to go.*

Robbie got dressed, stuck his screwdriver back into his belt, turned out the light, and went back into the hangar. He walked over to Russ's office and reached inside to a nail in the wall where Russ always hung the keys to his truck. They were not there! Robbie turned the light on and looked on Russ's desk. No keys!

Robbie turned the light on in Russ's room. When he heard breathing, he looked at the body. *He was not breathing before! It had stopped! He was dead!* But he was breathing now. *I left the hammer in my room.* He pulled the screwdriver from his belt and walked over to Russ. *Yes, he's breathing.*

He was still facing away from Robbie. Robbie stuck the point of the screwdriver to his ribcage behind his arm. When he did, Russ rolled over onto his back and grabbed Robbie's arm and looked at him. Russ growled and Robbie jerked back but Russ held on tight.

Russ's face was covered in blood and brains, yet he was still alive. And, he had Robbie in his grip and was fighting back. His eyes, white specks in a field of red, burned into Robbie's memory.

Robbie grabbed the screwdriver from the hand Russ was holding and began hacking at his chest with the point. Each time he pulled the screwdriver out, blood oozed out of the hole. He hacked and hacked until Russ's hand slipped from his wrist and fell limp onto the bed. The breathing stopped. He lay still now but his eyes still stared at Robbie.

He dropped the tool and stepped back. He looked at Russ. *No breathing! He's dead.* Robbie just stood there for a minute, staring at the body. He then thought about Jorge. He tried to pick up the screwdriver but his hands were shaking so bad it took several attempts. He finally got it and ran to Jorge's room. He flipped the light on. Jorge was dead. Robbie could feel his heart beating inside his chest and his breathing was heavy.

Keys! Robbie went back to Russ's room and looked in the clothes lying across a chair. No keys. *Where can they be?* He ran out to the truck and looked in the ignition. *The keys!* He breathed a sigh of relief.

He went back to his room and looked into the mirror. After showering again, he dressed and stuck the screwdriver back into his belt.

Robbie went back into the hangar and grabbed two cases of soda and put them into the Cessna. Those were the only two cases left. He looked at the clock and cut out all the lights.

Robbie went out to the truck and got in. He put both hands on the steering wheel and laid his head between them. *Relax. You've got a long way to go. I hope this was the hard part. I have plenty of time.*

He just sat there with his head on the steering wheel until his breathing slowed to a normal rate. He reached for the ignition and turned the key. The truck started up and idled smoothly.

Lights or no lights? It's 3:00. If I have the lights on, anyone can see me, night scope or not.

If there are no lights, only someone with a night scope can see me, and they actually have to be looking through the scope at the time. I've thought this all out over and over again. Now I'm second guessing myself. No lights it is.

Robbie got out of the truck and pulled out his screwdriver. He broke the lens of the taillights and the bulbs. He got back into the truck and headed for the Farm.

The second-quarter moon peeked out from behind the clouds from time to time. He had no trouble seeing the road. As he drove, he looked around for lights. He could see none until he got near the Farm. There, there were only two which he assumed stayed on all the time. He parked the truck in some trees, killed the engine, and got out. He looked for what he guessed was a half-hour, listening and watching for anything unusual. There were few sounds. He could hear the gentle breeze rustling the leaves on the trees. A great horned owl hooted in the distance. He could also hear frogs croaking, but no sounds of people.

It's time to go. As he made his way alongside the road toward the Farm, he kept his eyes peeled and his ears open. It was an uneventful stroll to within a hundred yards of the barn where Florence was kept, but the adrenalin was churning and his nerves were already frazzled. He squatted next to a large tree and took another look around. *It's still very early. Take your time and don't screw this up. Do it right and we'll get out of here without a problem.*

Robbie started to get up when he noticed a flicker of light. His eyes honed in on the source. He then saw the glow. *Someone is smoking a cigarette. If he's smoking, he's not looking through a night scope if he has one. Which way is he facing?*

Robbie waited for a cloud to cover the moon, raised up, and slowly made his way around to what he thought was the man's backside. With the stealth of a bobcat sneaking up on prey, he eased toward the figure standing next to a large tree. Robbie slipped the screwdriver out of his belt and inched forward. In the blink of an eye, Robbie jammed the point of his weapon into the man's ear and deep into his skull. The man's legs buckled instantly, and he crumbled into Robbie's arms. He lowered the man to the ground with only a gentle hiss of air being forced out of his lungs.

As Robbie lay on the body, he felt something in the man's hand. It was a night scope. He grasped the scope, flicked the switch, and looked into the screen. First he saw the man's rifle leaning against the tree, but he did not want to shoot anyone. That would only wake everyone up, and he would certainly be in trouble.

Robbie had never looked into a night scope and was amazed at what he saw. He knew then how easily the men who had caught him and Sean spotted them on the roof of the building. Robbie scanned the area. He saw one more man near the barn where Florence was held. He was lucky. The man was near Florence's window. If he had gone into the barn and made the slightest noise getting Florence out of her cell, he would surely have gotten caught.

This second man, a good hundred yards away, had not heard Robbie kill the first, and he was facing the other direction looking through his night scope. Robbie moved to his left a few yards so he could see only half of the man through the scope. Should he turn around, Robbie could quickly conceal himself with the building, hopefully before the man could spot him. Again in stealth mode, Robbie worked his way toward the man. Robbie reached the barn, paused, and with night scope in one hand and his screwdriver in the other, he moved toward the target. Robbie forced the point of the screwdriver into the man's ear. Just like the previous time, this man crumbled onto the ground in a pile of quivering flesh and bone.

Robbie again scanned the area and saw no one. He headed back to the barn and pushed the door inward. The screen on the night scope showed it to be empty, and Robbie continued toward the hallway where Florence was incarcerated. He peeked around the corner. Again, he saw no guards. Robbie checked each cell, and they were empty until he reached the last door. He only saw Florence inside. She appeared to be asleep.

Robbie grabbed the key off its hook and opened the door. As quiet as possible, he walked over to Florence and put his hand over her mouth so she would be quiet if he startled her. She jumped, but didn't make a noise.

"It's me," he whispered. "It's time to go."

He shushed her and took his hand off her mouth. He helped her up.

"Not a word," he whispered.

He led her out, closing the cell door and placing the key in its proper place. Robbie scanned the area again as he peered through the doorway. Seeing no one, they made their way back to the truck without incident. He looked toward the eastern sky. It was just beginning to show a little glow. *Perfect!*

Robbie helped Florence into the truck and went around to get in. As he opened the door, he heard a gunshot from the direction of the Farm. "Shit!"

He cranked up the truck and they headed back to the Airport. Robbie could see much easier now. He parked Russ's truck in its usual spot and told Florence to remain in the vehicle while he got out and went inside the hangar. It was empty—Russ stayed dead. He was certain of this now and didn't check.

Robbie opened the hangar doors and motioned for Florence to join him. She got into Betty and Robbie walked over to the edge of the tarmac to looked for Beka's car. He didn't see anyone in sight. *She better show up soon. The sun will be up in minutes.*

Robbie crawled into the Cessna and cranked up the engine. He let it idle for a couple minutes then eased the throttle up and rolled out onto the tarmac and stopped.

"What are we waiting for?" Florence asked.

"Beka," he replied. "Sorry, didn't I tell you? Beka is coming with us. That is, if she shows up on time."

"You may have. I don't remember if you did."

He glanced to the east and back to where Beka would come from. No one. "It's time," he said and reached for the throttle.

The Cessna eased across the tarmac and down the taxiway. "Watch for Beka," he told Florence.

As he made the turn toward the end of the main runway, he took one last look down the taxiway. Still nothing. "I guess Beka is staying behind," he said.

Robbie turned the plane to the southeast, lining up with the white stripe. Then he noticed a green spot at the far end. He watched and the spot grew larger. He then recognized Beka's car.

Beka came to a screeching halt beside the Cessna and hopped out with her suitcase and purse. Robbie opened the door and grabbed her luggage. Florence moved to the rear and Beka climbed aboard into the right seat and shut the door.

"Here!" she exclaimed with a big grin on her face.

Robbie throttled the plane up and it began to move forward. More throttle. More speed. He opened the throttle to full speed. He could feel the plane reacting to the gentle wind from the south, but he held the light plane straight. Suddenly a Jeep sped by the plane.

"Sandra!" Beka screamed. The Jeep raced ahead of the plane, swerved in front of them, and began to smoke.

She's locked up the brakes, Robbie thought.

"We're going to hit her!" Florence yelled.

"We're going to die!" Beka exclaimed.

Robbie jerked back on the steering wheel and the plane jumped off the ground. He felt a bump as the plane leaped over the Jeep, but they moved forward. They didn't have enough speed to stay in the air and the plane dropped and bounced on the concrete. Robbie struggled to keep the Cessna in a straight line. On the third bounce, however, the plane cleared the runway and stayed in the air. *I hope that thump was Sandra's head.*

Robbie steadied the plane and they climbed, higher and higher, steadily climbing. When he reached the trees and brush at the end of the runway, he heard a *ping, ping, ping*. Beka screamed in pain. He looked over to see blood on her leg. *Someone is shooting at us.* Again, *ping, ping, ping.*

Robbie turned the steering wheel to the right and to the left. The plane quickly banked each time. Right and left again and the plane responded. The Cessna continued to climb and the shots stopped. He took a deep breath, looked back over to Beka, and down at her leg.

He looked at the holes in the top of the cabin. *No real damage.* He then checked the gauges. Everything seemed okay, except Beka's leg. She pulled up her dress to reveal a nasty hole oozing blood. She was crying but ripped the bottom off her dress and wrapped her leg up. Robbie noticed the tears dripping off Florence's chin as she leaned forward to get a better look at Beka's leg.

When they were almost up to the layer of puffy white clouds, Robbie eased the steering wheel forward and leveled the plane out. He turned the plane toward the Bayfront and eased off the throttle a little. It only took a couple minutes to get over the harbor, and Robbie turned the steering wheel to the left. The plane banked and he could see the parked boats. He couldn't tell which one Sean might be on. Then he noticed the fleet out in the bay. *Sean is certainly on one of those. I hope he sees us.*

Robbie continued his bank until he was pointed to the northwest. Then he straightened out and tried to find the route home.

Sean saw a flicker of light, as the sunlight reflected off one of the windshields, and he looked up into the sky. He saw the bright yellow plane and smiled. *Good luck, Robbie. Safe trip home.*

Chapter 31

As Robbie steered the Cessna back across Corpus Christi, he tried to remember where they had come into the city. *From this direction, we came in to the right of the Airport. But how far right?*

Robbie could see the Airport to his left. "Look for roads, Florence," he said. "Roads that run out of the city."

She looked out the window. Beka wiped her teary eyes and did the same.

"I see two," Florence said.

"I see one," Beka added.

Once they made it away from the buildings below, Robbie made a big circle looking at the three roads. *It all looks the same from up here. I don't know where we came into town. Think, dammit!*

He made another circle and then another.

"We can't fly around here in circles all day," Beka remarked.

"I know, but I don't know which way is home."

He made a fourth and a fifth circle. A tear formed in his eye. "If I don't find the right road, we could end up anywhere. I have to be certain. I don't know the terrain well enough to find our way once we get on the ground. I have to be certain from the air."

Then he recognized something—the building where he and Scan had spent the night and spied on the city. He made another circle. "Yes, I'm sure that's it," he said. "That's the road!"

He pointed the plane down the road and they all relaxed. He thought about his mom and dad. His main thoughts up to this point were about flying the plane. They were on their way home now. Everything was okay.

It sure will be good to get back to Peaceful Valley. Mom and Dad are going to be surprised. And Ronnie and Debra; me flying an airplane! I hope I can get this thing on the ground safely.

Robbie checked the gauges again. Everything seemed to be working perfectly. "How's your leg, Beka?" he asked.

"It hurts like hell!"

"I'm sorry," he replied. "I was so scared to fly. I didn't know if I could or not, but this thing flies really easily. It's just like driving a truck, except you can go up and down too. It's fun. I'm a pilot now!"

"I'll call you a pilot if you can get us on the ground safely," Florence said with a smile. "You can do it. I know you can."

About an hour later, he noticed a green line of trees. "See those trees?" he asked. "They have to be along the river. We must be near home."

We left home headed southwest. We got to the highway about ten miles from the house, and we hit the highway at an angle. About 45 degrees, I think. There. Home has to be in that direction.

Robbie turned the plane slightly to the right and lined out his direction toward Peaceful Valley. It didn't take long to be directly over the river. He banked the plane to the left again and began making a circle over the river, watching for houses. Nothing on the first round. Another didn't reveal any houses. The third circle, there was a house, but not the right one.

Each circle, he worked his way along the river. Around and around, and nothing but trees.

"What's that smell?" Florence asked.

Robbie sniffed as did Beka. He looked at the gauges again. They seemed fine but there was definitely an odor in the air.

Two more circles and nothing, but on the third, something looked familiar. A tower. A wind turbine tower and a house. On the next round there was another house with a large plowed garden. This was it; they were home.

Robbie pointed the nose of the plane downward as he continued his circle and made a last pass at the home with the garden. He saw someone in the garden looking upward. He couldn't tell for certain at this height, but that had to be his dad.

"Robbie, I don't want to alarm you, but there is a lot of smoke over here," Beka said.

Robbie looked over. "Yeah, I know. It's over here too. It smells like wires burning. I hope they're not important."

"We're going to die!" Florence screamed.

"No, we're not going to die," he said, "but we better get the plane on the ground."

He turned the plane toward the highway to the east. He knew this road well, and there was a long straight stretch to land the Cessna near where the old road led into the woods toward home. It only took a minute to find the road and get lined up with the pavement. He picked the spot he wanted to land and pointed the plane downward.

He passed up the landing area. He was still too high in the air. He made another circle and continued his descent.

"Hurry," Beka said. "The smoke is getting worse."

"Yes, I know," he said. "Open a window." Robbie reached over and opened the window on his side as well.

Robbie guided the plane down. He eased off on the throttle and lined up with the road.

"Hurry, Robbie," Florence said. "My eyes are burning."

"I'm doing the best I can," he replied.

Robbie's heart was pounding and his hands began to shake. The smoke was getting thick enough that his eyes were tearing badly, making it difficult to see, but he managed to line up with the road. *There is plenty of straight road ahead now. The road is steadily coming up. This seems right.* Robbie held the steering wheel steady.

Screech! Robbie cut the throttle. The plane bounced a little but then settled down onto the pavement. Robbie held the nose in a straight line.

"Fire!" Beka screamed.

Florence screamed too. "Stop!"

"I'm trying," Robbie yelled back.

Robbie pressed harder on the brakes and tried to slow the plane as quickly as he could. In spite of his efforts, it took what seemed like minutes to get the Cessna stopped. He and Beka both had their doors open long before the plane came to a complete halt.

Finally, it did stop and Beka hopped out, as did Robbie, the flames lapping at her heels. He reached for Florence who was already climbing over the front seat. Beka grabbed her suitcase and purse, and Robbie pulled Florence free of the plane.

"To the back of the plane," he yelled, and they met up there and began to run. Moments later, the Cessna exploded. The shockwave knocked them all to the pavement. Robbie rolled over on his back to see the mushroom cloud of flame and black soot rising into the air. He raised his arm up to his face to block the searing heat from the ball of fire, but this passed quickly as the flames moved up and away from them.

Robbie jumped to his feet and helped the girls up. He pulled the girls farther away from what was left of the plane in case there was another explosion. When he thought he was far enough away, he stopped and looked at the burning pile. "You okay?" he asked the girls.

"I think so," Florence replied, looking at a scrape on her leg from the pavement.

"I think my leg is bleeding again," Beka said, "and it hurts terribly."

Robbie knelt down and she lifted her torn and tattered dress. He removed and retied the temporary bandage. "That's all I can do for now."

Ronnie ran around the house and out to the garden where his dad was working. "Did you see that?" he asked.

"The airplane?"

"Yes."

"It looks like it crashed over toward the highway," James added, pointing to the dark cloud rising into the air.

"Are we going to try to help them?" Ronnie asked.

"Yes, but it's a long round-trip. We'll be overnight. We've got to prepare."

They went inside and informed Melissa and Eileen of the plane and their apparent mishap. "We'll be a few days, and we need to take some supplies," James said.

Melissa packed jerky while Eileen prepared water bottles. James and Ronnie grabbed a bedroll each and their guns. They were packed in no time and ready to leave. They kissed the ladies good-bye and headed out.

"It's got to be a fast trip," James said.

"I'm up to it. How about you, Dad?"

"Don't worry about me. You just keep up."

It was nearing dark when James stopped dead in his tracks. He squatted down and Ronnie came up beside him and did the same.

"What's up?" Ronnie whispered.

"Someone is coming up the road."

They readied their guns and waited. They could hear talking now. "Sounds like girls," Ronnie whispered.

"It does," James agreed.

James raised his rifle and looked through the scope in the direction of the voices. Directly, he saw people come into view rounding the bend in the road. He adjusted the focus and could see their faces clearly. Then he let out a loud wolf howl.

The trio stopped dead in their tracks. Robbie returned the wolf howl. The girls looked at him queerly. "Don't worry ladies, we have company—family."

James stood up and howled again and he and Ronnie headed toward Robbie and his two lady friends.

"Welcome home, son," James said.

"It's good to be home," Robbie replied.

"Who do we have here?" Ronnie asked.

"Beka and Florence, my dad, James, and my twin brother, Ronnie," Robbie said. "Beka got shot. She needs attention soon."

"Who was flying the airplane?" Ronnie asked.

"I was," Robbie said. "Long story. You'll hear all about it in time. For now, we need to get home."

"We can't do it today," James said, "but we can make it a little closer if you're up to it, Beka."

"I'll try," she said.

After a mile, Beka could go no further. Ronnie quickly made a fire. Robbie checked Beka's leg again and put on a fresh bandage, though it was not as clean as he would have liked.

"Where's Sean?" James asked as he passed around some jerky.

"He stayed behind. He's fine, but he's not coming back. Another long story."

"It's good to see you again, Mister Airplane Pilot," Ronnie said with a big smile.

"You too, brother."

"I can't believe you flew a plane."

"Me either, but it was our only way back here."

"Did you see Corpus Christi?" Ronnie asked.

"Yes, but no more questions tonight, Ronnie. I'll answer all your questions in time."

"All right," James said. "Let's get a good night's sleep, and we'll get an early start in the morning."

James and Ronnie watched the two girls snuggle up against Robbie. They looked at each other and smiled.

"Probably another long story," James whispered to Ronnie.

"Yeah, I can't wait to hear this one."

Chapter 32

Beka's leg was so stiff and sore the next morning, she could not walk any further. The boys cut up limbs while James lashed them together to make a travois to put her on. This slowed them down considerably, but not as much as if she had tried to walk. The day was hot and the travois took its toll, especially on James's muscles. Ronnie and Robbie struggled as well. By the end of the day, they realized they would be spending another night in the woods. There was plenty of time for some of Robbie's stories. Beka's leg was getting a little worse and would not get better until it could be cared for more properly when they got back to the homestead.

"Most of the men are castrated," Robbie told his dad and brother. "This gal named Sandra Hawkins and her husband took over the city after the grid shut down. They then created the type of society that she wanted. When they had successfully accomplished this, she double-crossed her husband. He thought he was going to be king, but ended up as Sandra's pawn.

"Only a few men were kept as breeders. All this was done at the Farm. The Farm is run by mostly women. Sandra was nice to me and I was spared my nuts, but Sean was not so lucky."

"Were Beka and Florence some of Sandra's girls?" Ronnie asked.

"No, Florence's dad was Sandra's ex, the one she double-crossed. He remarried and had Florence. Sandra spared him the sterilization process as well. But she used the threat of it to control him. Florence's mom and dad are dead now, and Florence was about to become one of Sandra's girls, but I rescued her. Beka is Florence's best friend. Her dad is dead too, and she didn't get along very well with her mom. That's why she came along with us."

"How did they all die?" Ronnie asked.

"I think that's enough about this subject," Robbie said.

They don't need to know everything. I can't tell them all the gory details of what happened. Those stories are for the girls to tell, not me.

"I've got to say, though, the system in Corpus Christi works," Robbie continued. "Everyone has a job, there is plenty of food, and they have a good security system. They have fuel, an ice plant, and a desalinization plant. It may seem cruel, but no one ever said life was supposed to be easy. I didn't like it, but for Sandra, most of her girls, and pretty much everyone else I saw, I guess it was okay.

"Not everyone liked Sandra though. Jade and some of her girls tried to take over, but that didn't end up well for Jade. Sandra executed her."

"Who is Jade? Or maybe *was* would be a better word," Ronnie said.

"She was one of Sandra's girls."

"And what did she want?" James asked.

"She wanted to run the city. She was Sandra's right-hand gal and was mostly taking care of the daily operation of the Farm. She thought she could do a better job without Sandra around. I think she was a little jealous of Florence and me too. Sandra caught her, tortured her first, and they tied her to a post and shot her."

"Sandra is a mean and cruel bitch," Beka said.

"She was nice to me," Robbie added.

"Yeah," Beka said, "you were her number-one stud."

Robbie blushed and couldn't look his dad or Ronnie in the eye. He looked down at the ground. "That's enough!"

"Stud?" Ronnie asked, laughing.

"Knock it off," James told Ronnie sternly.

They were quiet for a long time after that, but Ronnie kept eyeing his brother. Robbie felt his brother's eyes on him, but didn't make eye contact.

"How much farther?" Florence asked.

"Only a few more miles," James said.

"How did you learn to fly an airplane?" Ronnie finally asked.

"I told them I knew a few things about planes, and they assigned me to the Airport. I talked them into letting me drive the planes in order to maintain them better. They bought it. I got to drive the planes around on the ground, but I learned how to actually fly yesterday morning. I didn't know it, but apparently they had been keeping an eye on me from the end of the Airport. When we took off, someone shot at us. That's when Beka got shot. I guess that's what caused the fire in the plane too."

"My brother the pilot," Ronnie stated, "and the plane crasher."

"That's enough," Robbie said, giving him a serioius frown.

"Tell us more about Sean," James said.

"They put him on a shrimp boat. He hurt for a while and really resented what they did to him, but the folks he was staying with were good to him. They weren't the cause of his pain.

"Sean said there was more for him at the Bayfront and shrimping than here at home. They would give him a wife and kid if it all worked out. Sonny, the owner of the boat he worked on, was also castrated. He seemed happy with his wife, Marcia, and their kid, Lola, who was not really his kid, but that didn't seem to matter to Sonny. He enjoyed what he did and was reasonably happy. Sean saw this and thought he could be happy there as well."

"It's sad for Sam and Sally, but I'm sure they will understand," James said.

"I hope so," Robbie added. "Sean said he liked the smell of the salt water. He also liked the endless varieties of crabs, shrimp, and fish. He knew he would never be hungry. There were a lot of old houses around too. He thought he could fix one up for himself."

"How many people were there?" James asked.

"I don't know. I never got to see the whole city. There were a lot at the Farm. Maybe a few hundred. Less at the Bayfront. There were also contractors who fixed stuff and built things. They seemed to be scattered around as were the police."

"And how did you get caught?" Ronnie asked. "You were supposed to be careful."

"We were. We waited around until dark on top of a vacant building. After dark we got up and scoped out the city. Little did we know all their police on night duty had night-vision scopes. They could see us better at night than during the daytime. That was a surprise and is what got us caught."

"Finally!" Florence exclaimed when she saw the house.

They reached the old sycamore tree at mid-afternoon. No one had slept well either night, and all were dead tired when they reached the Lindgren homestead. Nevertheless, Ronnie ran ahead and alerted the family.

"Robbie's home!" he yelled. "And he brought friends."

Melissa and Eileen came to the porch and watched the others as they made their way to the house.

"We're all mighty hungry," James announced.

"We have a big pot of soup on the stove," Eileen informed him.

"And Beka has a hurt leg," Robbie stated. He then proceeded to help her off the travois and into the house.

"Put her on the sofa," Eileen instructed. "The rest of you fix a bowl, and I'll take a look at the leg."

Everyone gathered in the kitchen while Eileen retrieved a pan and went into the bathroom to run some hot water and grab some rags.

"Don't be bashful," Melissa said.

Everyone sat down at the table and dug in.

"You guys could use a shower too," Melissa pointed out.

There was a lot of chatter at the table, but Eileen concentrated on Beka's leg. She removed the bandage and cleaned all the dried blood off the area. Beka winced from time to time and let out a moan when Eileen cleaned the holes, but never complained.

Eileen ran back into the bathroom and retrieved some herbs and clean bandages. She then dressed and wrapped the leg.

"You'll limp for a while, but you'll be just fine in a couple weeks. How did you get shot?"

"Someone shot at us when we took off from the Airport. I don't know who it was," she replied. "Someone who didn't want us to escape."

"Can you sit up and eat?" Eileen asked.

"I'm starved. I'll sit up."

Eileen went to the kitchen and fixed her a bowl.

"Good soup, Mom," Robbie said between bites.

"Thank you, son. I've been worried sick about you. I'm so happy you're home."

After they all finished their soups, introductions were formally made. Melissa then showed Florence where the shower was and got her a fresh towel.

"Where's your wife, Ronnie?" Robbie asked.

"Debra and I didn't get married."

"Why not? You two were ready to get hitched when Sean and I left."

"I know. It's a long story."

"Yeah, we have some long stories too. We need to get the Lins over here and Grandma and Grandpa Carston. Some of our stories concern them too."

"Ronnie, how about you run over to the Lins' first thing in the morning, and I'll run over to the Carstons'?" James inquired.

"Sure, Dad."

"We'll go early and see if we can get them over here right away. I'm sure everyone will be eager to hear the news Robbie and his friends have to tell."

"Yeah, I want to hear some more of his stories too," Ronnie said.

"Now, what about sleeping arrangements?" Melissa said.

"Beka can sleep with me," Eileen said. "Ronnie, I'm sorry but you'll have to give the sofa up to Florence."

"Ronnie, you can make a bed on the floor in our room," Melissa added. "Robbie, you can find you a place in here."

Ronnie grumbled about his new sleeping arrangement, but Melissa insisted he give up the sofa to Florence.

James and Ronnie were up at daylight. "I'll have breakfast ready when you get back," Melissa said. "Tell them to get dressed and come on over."

Eileen and Melissa helped the kids roll up their bedding. "How was the sofa, Florence?" Melissa asked.

"It's much better than where we slept last night," she replied.

"The floor was hard," Ronnie stated.

"You'll survive," Melissa said. "You better get off to the Lins' or your dad's going to beat you back."

"Not going to happen, Mom."

"I know you slept well, Beka," Eileen said. "I didn't hear a peep out of you."

"Yes, thank you for sharing your bed."

"You're quite welcome, young lady. How's the leg?"

"It's sore but feels much better."

"We'd better get started on breakfast," Melissa said.

"I'll help," Florence added.

"Nonsense," Eileen told her. "You've had a rough ordeal. Rest. You can help around here soon enough."

Florence smiled. "Yes, ma'am."

"Robbie, be a dear and run out to the smokehouse and get a slab of bacon," Melissa said.

"Yes, ma'am."

Ronnie returned with the Lins and James with the Carstons by mid-morning. They were all smiles.

There wasn't enough room for everyone at the table, so the kids ate where they could. Some took the sofa while the others went out on the porch.

Everyone hurried through breakfast, and Eileen prepared another pitcher of mint tea.

"I'm sorry I didn't bring ice," Reggie said. "James hurried us up and I didn't think about it."

"Not a problem," Eileen said.

James and Reggie grabbed chairs, and they all joined the kids on the porch. Robbie, Beka and Florence took center stage, and the others gathered in around them.

"All right, Robbie, the floor is yours," James announced.

"Where do I start?" he asked.

The next morning, Debra showed up early and ate breakfast with the Lindgrens. Robbie decided they needed some different sleeping arrangements. "Since Ronnie and Debra didn't get married, maybe we can fix up the old Weston place and I can stay there with Beka and Florence."

"There have been a few changes around here since you left, son. A new family from San Antonio moved in. They fixed up the Weston homestead and are living there now."

"Really?"

"Yes, the Wimberleys and their five kids."

"Five?"

"Yes. Three girls and two boys, all around your age."

"Fancy that," Robbie said with a smile. "Guess we're going to have to build a new house around here somewhere."

"Looks like it," James replied. "John Wimberley has been after us to build a church, but we told him we didn't have the time or resources to build one."

"A church? What do we need a church for?"

"We don't," Eileen added, "but it does seem we have a big need for a new home. That we can spare the time and energy for."

"When do we get to meet them?"

"The kids come around often enough. You'll get to meet them soon," Melissa said.

"We don't quite see eye to eye with their parents, so we don't see them often," Eileen added.

"I guess you'll be planting soon?" Robbie asked.

"Yes," James said, "*we'll* be planting in a couple weeks."

"Of course *we will*," Robbie replied, smiling. "What will *we* be planting?"

"Potatoes, beets . . . and greens, your favorite."

Robbie smirked.

"You can give up eating," James reminded him.

"That's not going to happen."

Robbie turned to Eileen. "Grandma," he said, "I'm sorry I lost your carbine. I know it meant a lot to you, being Grandpa's and all. I couldn't help it."

"It was just a gun," she said with a smile.

"Thank you," he said and got up, wrapped his arms around her, and gave her a bear hug, which he knew she loved more than almost anything. He whispered 'I love you' in her ear.

Robbie felt bad about losing the rifle. He knew his grandmother was telling a little white lie. She never considered herself first when it came to him and Ronnie. He would make it up to her somehow.

Robbie helped Beka up. "How's your leg?" he asked.

"It hurts, but it's much better than when I got up this morning. Your grandmother gave me some herb tea. It tasted really nasty, but she assured me it was worth it."

"Can you walk a little?"

"I think so."

"Ronnie, Debra, Florence, let's go down to the river."

Florence helped Robbie with Beka. Ronnie and Debra led the way.

When they got out of earshot of the grownups, Ronnie turned and walked backward so he could face his brother and blurted out, "Well, Robbie, which one is your girlfriend?"

Robbie blushed. Then he felt both girls each squeeze an arm.

"I think we'll have to discuss that further amongst ourselves," he replied. "What about you and Debra?"

"It was my fault," he replied.

"It was *our* fault," Debra added.

Ronnie smiled and said, "Debra is more like a sister to me. I couldn't marry her."

"I like Zack Wimberley now," Debra said.

"And I like Brooke," Ronnie stated.

"She'll never love you like I did though, Ronnie dear."

Ronnie groaned and looked down his nose at her. He wasn't sure how to respond to her assertion, so he changed the subject. "I wish I could fly a plane," he said. "Was it fun?"

"Yes. Scary, but fun. At least until the damn thing caught on fire."

"But you got to fly! My brother the pilot."

"Probably my first and last flight."

Robbie helped Beka into one of the chairs on the pier.

"I like your river," Florence stated.

"Me too," Beka said. Then she yelled, pointing to a snake in the water near the pier.

"Yeah, there are a few around here," Ronnie said. He threw a stick at the reptile and it swam away.

"Remember one thing," Robbie said, "always watch where you're walking. You never know where you might find one. They're not just in the water."

"We had snakes back in Corpus," Florence said, "but we seldom saw them. I guess there weren't many."

"Well, there are plenty around here," Debra noted.

Beka sat watching the moccasin work its way down the riverbank and away from the pier. "And you go swimming in there with snakes?" Beka asked.

"They usually swim away," Ronnie said.

"When will we meet the neighbors?" Robbie asked.

"How about a swimming party tomorrow?" Ronnie suggested. "We need to celebrate your homecoming."

"Beka can't swim," Robbie noted.

"That's all right. I can watch," she said. "I think a party will be fun."

"I'll run over and get the Wimberleys first thing in the morning," Ronnie said. "Meet us over here, Debra?"

"I'll be here. Okay, I'll see you tomorrow. I better get home now. Mom worries if I get in too close to dark."

"I think I need some more of your grandmother's herbs," Beka stated.

Robbie gave Beka a hand getting up, and he and Florence helped her inside.

Chapter 33

Ronnie got an early start toward the Wimberleys'. Debra showed up at the Lindgrens' before he got back and followed Eileen to the hen house. "Our chickens aren't laying many eggs these days," Debra remarked.

"No, ours aren't either," Eileen replied. "They don't lay as much when it gets hot. I slow down a bit too because of the heat," she added.

Ronnie returned with Brooke, Charlotte, Kira, Lance, and Zack mid-morning.

"Yeeehaa!" Ronnie yelled as he swung on his rope swing and into the river.

Robbie was next in the water.

"Water's perfect," he told the girls.

Then Debra, followed by Lance, Zack, and Florence. Brooke and Charlotte chose to step off the bank, while Kira sat with Beka.

Melissa brought miniature sausage bites, toast, and egg squares to the kids for breakfast. A few bites and back into the water they went, off and on for the next hour until all the food was gone.

"Looks like everyone is getting along fine," Eileen said, peering out of the back-door window.

James came in the front door. "We may have a problem," he announced.

Melissa stopped what she was doing in the kitchen, and he got Eileen's attention as well. "What's that?" Eileen asked.

"I had a terrible dream this morning. I couldn't remember what it was after I got up, but it gave me chills. I couldn't shake the feeling and something told me to go look outside. I didn't notice the cloud at first, but just over the trees to the north, what I thought were clouds is smoke. I think Robbie's plane started a fire. And I think it's getting bigger."

"Are we in danger?" Melissa asked.

"I don't know," James replied. "That's certainly a possibility. It has been so dry around here the past month; a fire will burn quickly. At least we are on the upwind side, which will certainly help."

"What are you going to do?" Eileen asked.

"I'm going to keep an eye on it today. If it looks like it's getting closer, I'll take one of the boys with me and check it out tomorrow morning early. It's a long trip, as you well know. I think I'll run over and give Reggie a heads-up today."

"Good idea," Eileen said.

When James reached the Carstons' meadow, he let out a long wolf howl.

Reggie immediately came out onto the porch and returned the signal.

"To what do I owe the honor of this visit?" Reggie asked.

James pointed to the north. "Seems like we have a fire."

"I hadn't noticed," he replied.

"Me neither until this morning. I had a bad dream last night, and when I went outside, I noticed the smoke."

"What do we need to do?"

"Nothing for now, but I think I'll take one of the boys with me tomorrow and check it out."

"Want me to go along?"

"Nah, we can handle it. If it looks like there is going to be a problem, I'll let you know and then maybe you can make a trip with us. No sense getting worried over something that might not be a problem."

Emily came out and told James 'good morning'. "What's up?" she asked.

"Seems like we have a fire," Reggie said.

"Oh no!"

"Don't be concerned," James said. "As long as the wind stays out of the south, it probably won't be a problem."

"Probably?" she replied.

"We'll see," James said. "Don't worry for now. I'm going to check it out tomorrow and I'll let you guys know if we need be concerned."

"Thanks for letting us know," Emily said.

"I better get home now," James added.

"Thank you, James," Reggie said.

James got back home by late afternoon and walked down to the river. He was happy to see all the kids getting along so well. He was especially glad to see Beka and Florence fitting in and all the kids having fun. Young Kira sat on the pier chatting away with Beka, her arms flailing as she talked. Debra was down the riverbank near the rope swing with Zack, getting to know him better. Obviously they were making great strides in their relationship, Zack backed up against a tree and Debra leaning against him, nose to nose. Lance mingled with Florence and Robbie was lying in the grass with Charlotte.

James pulled Robbie aside. "Looks like your plane caused a fire."

"A fire?"

"Yes. I guess you left it burning when you headed home?"

"I didn't have a way to put it out. I thought it would burn itself out."

"I'm not blaming you, Robbie. It's been so dry around here the past month or so. I should have thought of a possible fire too. I knew you didn't have a way to put it out. I blame myself."

"How about we share the guilt, Dad?"

"I'm good with that," he replied with a smile.

"Now go play with the rest of the group and have fun. Tell them about the fire, and make certain John and Kathy Wimberley are told about it."

"Sure thing, Dad."

By dark, James saw no change in the smoke. Maybe it had gotten a little worse. After the sun set, however, the glow of the fire was quite apparent. When it got fully dark, the radiance was exceptionally bright. He called the rest of the family out to the porch.

"We need to check out the fire in the morning," he told them. "Ronnie, you come with me."

"I want to go too, Dad," Robbie asserted.

James nodded.

After dinner, James and Melissa went back out to the porch. James rolled a cigar and he and Melissa sat in silence, their eyes fixated on the orange horizon.

James got the boys up early and were on their way before sunup. They hurried along at a moderate pace taking only a couple short breaks.

"I guess I'm a little out of shape," Robbie stated.

"Too cushy a job will do that," Ronnie remarked.

"All right you two," James said. "You'll get back into shape by the time planting time rolls around."

By late afternoon they reached the fire. They stood amazed at the solid wall of flames. Through the fire they could see charred landscape. James estimated they were nearly two miles from the plane. There was plenty of dry grass and brush to provide fuel for combustion. The fire was spreading quickly, but thanks to the southerly breeze, the migration toward their homes was a bit slower.

They moved back from the inferno. James stepped off 200 feet, and they sat and watched. An hour went by and the flames came within fifty feet of their position. They moved back another 200 feet and again, after an hour the fire came to within fifty feet of them.

"We might as well go, boys. There is nothing we can do here."

James got up and led the way home.

"What are we going to do?" Ronnie asked.

"We wait and see what happens. We don't have the means to fight a fire like this."

In a few hours, it got too dark to see their way and they made camp. "I've estimated it will take at least eight days before the fire gets close enough to be a real concern," James said. "After that, if the progress is steady, we may have a few days more to decide what to do. If we get lucky and get some rain, it may take even longer. A heavy rain could kill the fire."

"Can we stop the fire at home?" Robbie asked.

"Maybe, if we create a firebreak along the tree line," James said. "We'll need water too, if we decide to stay and fight the fire. If we stay it will be a battle like you've never seen. And if we lose . . ."

"We won't lose," Ronnie stated.

"It may be best for all if we evacuate," James said.

"But we'll lose everything."

"But we will all be alive. Get some sleep. We'll be up early."

James and the boys arrived home at noon. They ate a quick lunch and hurried back out to inform the neighbors of a meeting the next day.

By mid-morning, everyone was at the Lindgren homestead.

"My, what a big crowd we've grown into," Eileen remarked.

"I think it's wonderful," Sally said.

"Me too," Emily agreed.

Melissa introduced Robbie, Beka, and Florence to the Wimberleys, and Eileen and Emily served drinks. The meeting started shortly thereafter.

"Robbie, Ronnie, and I went to check out the fire yesterday," James said. "The brush and grass is fairly uniform between here and there. I estimated the fire is moving this way at about 150 feet per hour. I don't think we need to be concerned for eight days, at least as long as conditions remain the same and the fire's progress remains steady. After that eight days though, if the fire is still strong and coming this way, we only have two or three days to act."

"Can we put the fire out?" John Wimberley asked.

"I don't think so," James replied.

"The fire stretches for miles and is burning unabated day and night," Robbie added. "Even with the wind blowing the heat and smoke away from us, we couldn't get within thirty feet of the flames."

"This is a dangerous fire," James said. "Even if we had two or three fire trucks, we would have trouble putting it out. If we don't get a good rain, I'm afraid that sooner or later we are going to have a problem."

"We'll pray for rain," Kathy Wimberley said with a smile.

The mood got quiet for a moment.

"It can't hurt." Eileen spoke up, despite her religious position.

"I agree," Melissa said.

"Okay," Reggie said, "what can we do if it does get near?"

"Create a firebreak around the perimeter of our homes," James said. "Outside of that? I think we will need to evacuate if the fire remains as fierce as what we saw yesterday."

"Where do we evacuate to?" Brooke asked.

"How about Corpus Christi?" Ronnie said cheerfully.

"That's not even funny!" Robbie exclaimed.

Beka and Florence shot Ronnie a sour look too.

"How's your tractor running, James?" Reggie asked.

"I've been working on it, and it'll run. I can only hope it will plow my garden. If we make a firebreak around all the homes, it may not hold up, and we may need a lot of help with our garden."

"Can the fire jump the river?" Sally Lin asked.

"There are enough embers floating around high into the air, they can fall down anywhere, even across the river," James said. "Another thing to think about is that the fire is not going to hit all our homesteads at the same time. There are a lot of bends, overhanging trees, and some places are quite narrow. I don't think the fire will even slow down. If it gets across in any one place, it's off again. It can still easily make it to your place, Sally."

"How long will it take to make the firebreaks around all four homesteads?" John asked.

"To be on the safe side," James replied, "probably four days. There are so many trees around the Lins' place that a firebreak may not do any good if the fire jumps the river."

"We need some rain," Kira stated.

"What are our chances of rain in the next week or so?" Emily asked.

"This time of year," James replied, "pretty slim, I'm afraid."

"Will the fire kill the big sycamore tree?" Eileen asked.

"Most likely," James informed her.

James knew the tree held special memories for Eileen. She wiped her eyes. The whole place could burn down and it wouldn't bother her as much as if that one tree were to die.

"We've got a week at least," James reminded everyone. "I say we watch the fire for three days, and if it's still coming, we begin to act on the fourth day. I'll work on the tractor more and hook up the disc."

"Sharpen your axes and machetes, guys," Reggie said. "We'll cut brush and saplings around the perimeter while James is discing a wide area just away from the trees."

"Sounds like the start of a plan," Melissa said.

"Anyone else have any questions?" Reggie asked.

Silence.

"Let's fix an early lunch," Eileen suggested.

The ladies went inside while the kids headed down to the river. Ronnie pulled Robbie aside. "Tell me more about the stud farm in Corpus Christi. How many girls did you fertilize? Were you hitting on Beka and Florence?"

"Gentlemen don't tell," Robbie said.

"You're no gentleman; you're my brother. I know you, remember?"

"It's none of your business then, Ronnie."

"Come on!"

"No! I've grown up a bit, okay?"

Ronnie headed toward the rest of the group. "Spoil sport," he mumbled. Ronnie turned and looked over his shoulder, frowning at Robbie, before he reached the others.

The jackass! Robbie thought.

James pulled up a chair on the porch and the other men gathered around. James offered Reggie a cigar which he readily accepted. James could see the gravity of the situation on his neighbor's faces as they stared at the cloud of smoke high in the air over the horizon.

"If there were at least a few clouds in the sky, maybe there'd be some chance for rain," James stated.

"You just never know," Reggie said.

"I really like living here on the river," James stated.

Reggie and Sam nodded.

"How are you liking the river, John?" James asked.

"It's certainly cooler than the surrounding area," he replied. "With the dog days of summer coming around, we don't have to worry about running out of water. The fish are good too."

"So you like our catfish?" Reggie asked.

"They are delicious. We didn't live near the San Antonio River while in the city, so we almost never got fresh fish. They taste so much better when you eat them the same day they're caught."

Melissa stuck her head out of the door. "Lunch is ready, James. Yell at the kids. We'll start bringing the food out to the porch."

"Let's meet up here again in three days," James suggested between mouthfuls. "I'll have another report on the fire then. And don't forget to sharpen your blades."

James lingered on the porch staring at the sky long after his neighbors went home. He knew John and Kathy would be saying a lot of prayers. When the impending disaster was over, they would then justify the result to be the will of God. They'd accept the outcome without question. James didn't believe in a higher power, but the helplessness he was feeling certainly gave him doubts.

Chapter 34

Three days passed and the meeting convened again.

"I'm sorry, but I misjudged the speed of the fire," James said. "The lighter wind the past few days has allowed it to spread this direction much faster. And it is just as strong as it was the first time we took a look at it. I estimate it will be here in three days."

"But you said it would take four days to cut the firebreaks," John reminded him.

"I know," James replied. "Everyone is going to have to help; and I mean everyone!"

"When?" Robbie asked.

"Right now!" James replied.

Charlotte and Kira began to cry. "We just got here," Kira said, wiping the tears from her eyes. "I like it here, and I don't want to move again."

Brooke tried to soothe their fears, but she began to cry as well. Likewise, Beka, Debra, and Florence joined in on the waterworks.

"We're new here too," Beka added. "I don't want to leave either."

Eileen, Melissa, Emily, Sally, and Kathy controlled their emotions better than the younger generation, but they were all sniffling.

While the men didn't cry, they were still deeply concerned.

"I'll get the tractor and start on our firebreak," James stated.

"And we'll cut brush," Reggie added.

"Okay, let's get at it," James said.

For two days, the neighbors worked, with the exception of Beka who could barely walk, side by side clearing brush, weeds, and saplings to cut a formidable firebreak around the Lindgren, Carston, and Wimberley homesteads. They started at daylight and finished at dark.

Charlotte made food and drinks to keep them fed and hydrated in the summer heat, Beka gave them moral support, while Kira delivered the nourishments.

On the third morning, the men and boys checked on the fire. It was close now and not such a long walk.

"Looks to be only a couple miles now," James said.

"I agree," Reggie and John added.

With all their hard work, they did three days' work in two, finishing all the firebreaks on their side of the river. "Let's head over to your place, Sam," James said, "and see what we can do to fireproof your home."

"Thanks, friends," Sam said.

When they finished up at Sam and Sally's, satisfied they had done all they could, everyone headed home.

James and Melissa sat on the porch for a while watching the glow to the north. "It will be here tomorrow night," James said.

"I'm scared," Melissa stated.

James stood, pulled Melissa up with him, and cuddled her in his arms. "Whatever happens, remember I love you," he whispered.

He could feel her trembling. They were all scared. He was no exception. He gave her a kiss much like the one he gave her on their wedding night.

James looked into her dazed face. "I'm going to bed. Tomorrow's going to be a rough day no matter what," he said.

Everyone took a little extra time getting to sleep. Most shed a few tears before finally dozing off.

Though he was tired and slept a restless night, James awoke well before it got light. He brushed his teeth and got dressed. It was going to be another long day regardless of whether they stayed to fight the fire or if they decided to evacuate.

He went into the living room, stretched his arms up high, and yawned. Suddenly there was a bright flash of light followed by a clap of thunder. This startled James, and he hurried to the front door. He stepped outside and a cool breeze hit him in the face. He could see the bright orange glow of the fire on the horizon. The change in wind speed and direction fanned the fire, and it was burning brightly. The fire had obviously increased in size and speed, and it was coming directly toward him. Chills ran across his skin.

Where's the rain? There is a thunderstorm, yet no rain. The storm is going to drive the fire here quickly, maybe in hours.

"Wake up!" James yelled. "Everyone get dressed."

"What's going on?" Robbie asked.

"The wind has changed and the fire is coming fast."

"How bad is it?" Ronnie asked.

"It looks bad," James replied. "Get dressed. We'll go take a look."

Everyone got up quickly and started getting dressed.

"Let's go," James told Ronnie.

"I'm going too," Robbie said.

James and the boys rushed outside and hurried past the sycamore tree and beyond. Another streak of lightning flashed across the sky.

It didn't take long for them to reach the flames. The wind fanned the fire, and it made a loud roaring sound. The smoke and heat from the flames kept the men at a distance.

Back at the house, the ladies were scurrying. When they finished dressing, Florence and Beka walked over to the front window.

"Oh my goodness! We're all going to die!" Florence exclaimed.

"We've got to get the hell out of here!" Beka shouted.

"James will tell us what we need to do when he gets back," Eileen told her as she joined them. *It's so bright now. It has to be close.*

Melissa went to the kitchen to prepare breakfast. She didn't know how long James and her sons would be, or how long it would take for the fire to get there. She only knew that whatever they needed to do would be better accomplished on a full stomach. If they had to leave, this could be their only chance to eat.

James got as close to the fire as he could. The wind blew the flames, heat, and smoke directly toward him. "The fire is less than a mile from the house," James told the boys.

Another streak of lightning flashed across the sky, immediately followed by a clap of thunder.

Where is the rain? Maybe the swirling smoke cloud is generating the lightning. Maybe there is no rain to be had.

"Get back," James yelled to the boys. "Go!" James followed the boys toward the house. At two hundred feet, James stopped and turned around. Within a minute the fire covered half that distance. "Run, boys," he yelled. "It's coming fast. It will be at the house within an hour. We've got to evacuate now! Run!"

James followed the boys as quickly as he could. Then he felt a drop of rain. Then another and another. James looked up at the sky, and more drops hit him in the face. The wind got stronger and it got cooler.

"More Rain!" he yelled.

The drops increased.

"More!" he yelled again.

Another streak of lightening and another. The claps of thunder were deafening. Suddenly, a bolt of lightning struck a nearby tree. Everyone ducked down a bit but continued to run.

The rain kept increasing, and within minutes it began to pour. The clouds opened up and drenched James and the boys, but more importantly it was dousing the flames. James stopped running, as did the boys. He walked toward the fire and the boys followed. The rain was now coming down in sheets. He walked to within feet of the rising smoke and steam. The boys walked up beside James, and they watched the flames. Finally, the flames were beaten down. The rain continued to pour and before long the flames were gone. The smoke and steam continued but they were dissipating too.

An hour went by and the rain and wind continued. The trees still smoldered a little, but for all intents and purposes, the fire was dead.

"We can go home now," James said in the calmest voice he'd used all morning.

The rain was cold and the men were soaked through to the bone, but they smiled all the way back to the house as the rain continued.

"The threat is over," James announced as he walked through the door.

"Yay!" everyone yelled.

Melissa and Eileen warmed the ham and bacon back up and started eggs. Beka and Florence set the table.

"How close did the fire get?" Florence asked.

"Too close," James replied.

After breakfast the rain began to let up, but the wind continued to blow out of the northeast. James went out to the porch and watched the rain. Little streams ran across the ground around the house and toward the river.

Melissa came out shortly and joined him. "Where did this rain come from?" she asked.

"It has to be a tropical storm. It's certainly that time of year."

Another heavy thunderstorm passed over and then subsided. There was a heavy blanket of clouds and the wind held steady. The wind was strong, but not a serious problem.

Late morning, between storms, the Carstons and Wimberleys showed up at the Lindgrens'.

"The thunder woke me up," Reggie stated. "I assume the fire is out?"

"Yes," James replied. "We went out and checked on it early this morning. When the wind changed and picked up, I thought the fire was going to get us."

"How close did it get?"

"Less than a thousand yards and it was coming fast with the wind."

"Our prayers were answered," John stated.

No one could deny that there seemed to be a higher power at work here. The rain strengthened the belief in God for some. Others passed the rain off as luck or coincidence. For all, however, it was a welcome event. No one could deny the rain saved their homes and their way of life. Peaceful Valley had survived.

"I think we have a reason to celebrate," Eileen stated.

"Yes we do," Melissa said.

"This storm should be long gone in a couple days," James said. "Let's have a celebration to top all celebrations."

"We haven't had a good party in a long time. I think we're overdue," Emily said.

The passing bands of storms got further apart, and the men decided to take a look at the remains of the fire. When they reached the charred field, they stood in awe of the destruction.

"It will grow back," Reggie stated.

James nodded his silent agreement.

Everyone showed up for the party at mid-morning. The Lins brought bacon, ham, and hominy. The Wimberleys brought fish and cornbread.

The Carstons brought plenty of ice for drinks and a big pot of Emily's famous beef stroganoff. Reggie brought several bottles of wine.

Despite the views of some, John was allowed to say blessing before the meal. No one objected.

The kids filled their plates and scattered out in the living room and onto the porch. The adults gathered around the table. The kids planned another swimming party while the adults discussed the upcoming planting season. Their thoughts and comments, however, kept reverting to the fire, the destruction, and what was in store for them in the coming months.

"When the new growth appears, there should be some good hunting over the burned area," Ronnie said

"And there are a lot of partially burned trees we can use for firewood," James added.

"I'm happy the cistern is full," Lance said from the living room.

Ronnie couldn't have agreed more.

"I'm glad we're not all going to die," Kira said.

"As we all are," Melissa replied.

They continued to eat and talk until most of the food was gone. "Kids sure can eat a lot," Eileen remarked.

Everyone laughed.

The men adjourned to the porch after the meal. James offered them each a cigar. Reggie was the only one who accepted the smoke. There was little more to discuss so they sat in silence and gazed at the tree line. There was no brush or weeds to obstruct their view. "We sure did a lot of work for nothing," James said.

"We certainly did," Reggie agreed, "but I'd do it again in a heartbeat."

"Yes, we would," John added.

After a while, the neighbors decided they should head home and get some well-deserved rest. There were many tears of relief as they parted.

The sky was clear and the wind had died down to near normal from the south. The summer heat was back on, and with the improved weather, all the kids showed up at the Lindgrens'. They decided they had to see the charred landscape left by the fire. Beka's leg slowed them down but she continued to improve. The crutch Robbie made for her helped her mobility somewhat.

Kira and Charlotte picked up charcoal for drawing pictures. The rest just stood in amazement of the blackened landscape.

"I'm glad it rained," Florence stated.

Everyone agreed.

"There's nothing else to see here," Robbie said.

Back at the house, the kids broke off into pairs—Zack and Debra, Ronnie and Brooke, Lance and Florence, Robbie and Charlotte. Beka and Kira headed up to the house and settled on the front porch.

Charlotte caught Robbie's eye, and he decided he wanted to get to know her a little better. He still thought about Florence and Beka's advances back in Corpus Christi, but Charlotte also grabbed his attention. He really didn't know what he wanted, only that he and his friends, new and old, were the future of Peaceful Valley. They were the gene pool.

Could Charlotte be the one? Could they become a couple and live the dream—happily ever after? Robbie didn't know what would happen but he was a realist and knew now was the time for them to try. They had all hoped to find love long before now. At least now they had a chance.

Ronnie and Brooke found a secluded spot and a comfortable place to lie down. They didn't need words. They looked into each other's eyes. Ronnie leaned over and kissed her gently. She wrapped her arms around him and held on.

"Come up for air, guys!" Debra said as she and Zack walked by.

Ronnie and Brooke heard her, but neither reacted. Debra and Zack continued on their way. They found their own secluded spot and got comfortable. "It's a little wet," Debra said.

"I'll wallow in the mud with you anytime, Debra."

"She smiled and planted a big kiss on his lips."

Beka and Kira knew they were the odd girls out, but they also knew many things could and would likely happen. They even discussed the possibility of a relationship between themselves. They liked men but weren't absolutely certain. They both also thought they liked women as well.

Lance backed Florence against a tree, wrapped his arms around her, and kissed her. She pushed him back and slapped him really hard. "I've had a rough time lately," she said as she began to cry. "I can't."

"I'm sorry," Lance responded. He backed off and walked toward the house. "I'm sorry," he repeated over his shoulder.

Robbie continued to talk with Charlotte, but it was mostly a one-sided conversation. Robbie listened while she went on and on about San Antonio mostly and how hard it was for her there. She then expressed how horrid the mosquitos were and how scary the snakes had been.

Robbie listened to her every ache and pain. He nodded and shook his head as needed, but said very little. When he saw Florence slap Lance only a short distance away, he got up. "Excuse me, will you, Charlotte?"

Robbie walked toward Florence leaving Charlotte with a confused look on her face. When she realized he was headed toward Florence, she got up and stomped toward the house.

"You all right, Florence?"

"Yes. Lance is a little pushy. I can't take that right now after all that has happened over the last month or so."

Robbie put his hand to her face and turned it toward him. He looked into her eyes and she looked into his. Robbie smiled and it was immediately returned. "Everything is going to be all right," he said.

"Thank you, Robbie." She leaned toward him and kissed him on the cheek.

Robbie immediately felt past feelings for Florence returning. They hit him like a freight train. Robbie returned the kiss but on the lips.

Florence relaxed. *He kisses so damn well!*

Inside the house, James brought up the need for building new homes. While he and Melissa thought it best to leave the match work to the kids to decide for themselves, they readily answered questions when asked, but tried to stay out of their arguments and discussions.

"Looks like we'll have to get a building project started soon," James said to Melissa, standing at the back door. They missed the confrontation between Lance and Florence, but caught Robbie kissing Florence down near the pier. James gave Melissa a peck on the cheek.

"Yes," she replied. "It looks like love is in the air."

Chapter 35

Planting time rolled around quickly. Everyone helped each other. The Carstons and Lindgrens provided the Wimberleys with seeds, and everyone worked hard as usual, some of the ladies working alongside the men, and the others keeping a steady supply of food and drinks going out to the workers.

By the end of the week, their hard work had paid off. Everything that was to be planted was in the ground. Eileen resumed her regular trips to the Carstons'. She was not enjoying the visits as she had a few months back. The problem was not Reggie and Emily, however; the problem was her. She made visits to Lars's grave more often. She talked to him and asked for his guidance.

Her body was not holding up to the hard work as it had when she was younger. Her arthritis bothered her more every day. Her desire to join Lars was steadily growing.

Florence thought she and Robbie were getting back together again, but Robbie turned his attention to Beka. *What the hell does he want?* Since she was out in the cold again, so to speak, she apologized to Lance for slapping him and started spending more time with him.

She didn't understand why Ronnie wanted her and Lance to join him and Brooke to a wooded location along the river between the Lindgren and Carston homesteads, but she and Lance tagged along anyway. After all, it was a beautiful day for a stroll and she hadn't been out in that direction before.

"Dad said if we were going to build a house, because of time and resources, it must be built to house two families, at least for now," Ronnie said. "I found this place. Perfect isn't it?"

"But why did you invite us?" Brooke asked.

"I like you, Brooke, a lot. And I want to marry you."

"Are you asking?"

"Yes, I am."

Brooke blushed. "I'll have to think about it for a while."

"Take all the time you need, but I'm ready."

"And why did you invite us?" Florence asked. "Lance and I aren't even close to marriage."

"You two look good together," Ronnie replied. "Robbie's taken an interest in Beka, and you guys keep hanging together. Also, we're the oldest, or at least the most mature, and could best live in the same household. Lance and I get along well. You and Brooke get along. We could be one big happy family."

"That's true," Lance said, "but Florence and I have a few problems to work out."

"I like you, Lance," Florence stated, "but I need more time." *And you've got to learn to think a little more about my feelings.*

"I can see us together, Florence, but . . ." *You talk about Robbie too much. You need to get your mind on me.*

"It'll take a while to build the house," Ronnie said. "You guys have plenty of time to smooth things out. If it works, okay; if it doesn't, well that's okay too. Well then, what do you think about this place for a house? It's close to the river, has some big trees, and it's just far enough from the other homes, yet close enough to be convenient."

Florence wasn't sure about the whole thing, but Brooke and Lance didn't seem to have a problem with Ronnie's proposition. She could see the twinkle in Brooke's eyes when she looked at him. She knew they would be married soon. Lance on the other hand . . .

"Okay, let's get the house started. We'll see who occupies it when the time comes," Ronnie said.

On the way back to the Lindgren homestead, they discussed details of the home. "We can get the wood from the burned area," Ronnie suggested. "There are a lot of straight trees, and we won't have to deal with the brush. They are going to die anyway, so we won't be wasting living trees."

"Won't the house smell burnt?" Florence asked.

"Maybe at first, but I think that will pass," Ronnie said. "All the homes here smell of wood stoves anyway. I don't think we will be able to tell the difference."

"Where are we going to get a wood stove?" Lance asked.

"There are three old homes across the highway in the burn area. They had stoves. If they survived the fire, which I think they would, then maybe we can use one of them if they're not damaged," Ronnie shared. "If not, there are more old houses around. We may need to search for a while, but I believe we can find one or two."

"When do we get started?" Brooke asked.

"How about tomorrow?" Ronnie replied.

Chapter 36

Brooke and Lance showed up early and elicited Zack's help. Their parents weren't overly optimistic, primarily due to the location of the new house. When they informed them another home would be built between their home and the Lindgren place, their tone lightened.

Robbie also agreed to help in the building process, and Debra, wanting to be near Zack also agreed to help. Charlotte and Kira offered to keep them in food and drinks while Beka offered moral support. Reggie even agreed to give them technical support since none of them had ever built a home before.

Zack, Lance, Robbie, and Brooke cleared the location while the other girls brought meals. It took two days for Ronnie and James to get the old sawmill running and delivered to the site. "The last time this old thing was used was when we built the addition for you and Robbie," James said. "I wasn't sure it would run again."

"Well, it runs good now," Ronnie said with a smile.

They cleared the location and the hard work began. One at a time, the boys manually cut and hauled good burned trees to the site of the home. The sky was clear; the air was hot, and the task was hard. By mid-afternoon each day, the boys took a two-hour break to get into the shade and hydrate. They also rested their sore muscles.

There was a lot more than a house being built. Relationships were building. Brooke worked like a man side by side with Ronnie. She even impressed him.

Brooke admired how hard Ronnie labored, and no matter how tired he was, he was always ready and willing to do a little more for her. He never got angry at her when she made a mistake or misunderstood what he was asking her to do. He never raised his voice to her, and he always had a hug and kiss for her when she needed or wanted one. By the time they had the floor finished, Ronnie proposed again and she accepted.

Lance and Florence, on the other hand, didn't get along nearly as well. Lance got a little testy when he got hot and tired. He took it out on Florence, and she didn't like it one bit. Florence was very independent and didn't take it well when Lance told her to do something. "You can ask me," she would say, "but don't tell me what to do."

Lance asked much of the time, but when afternoon rolled around, he would get more demanding and start barking orders.

"Shut up! Shut up! Shut up!" the others could hear her yelling. By the third incident, she wouldn't talk to him anymore and distanced herself from him. Lance tried not to let it bother him, though it did. He thought about his actions and tried to apologize. The third apology Florence accepted, but she still refused to work with him. She helped Ronnie and Brooke while Lance worked with Ronnie or Zack.

There was a little bickering between Debra and Zack, but for the most part, they worked out their differences and continued to work well together.

Beka's leg was nearly healed by the time the foundation and flooring was finished. She joined Lance one day and gave him a stern warning. She also told him she thought Florence had been a little hard on him. "Don't try to order me around. I like you, but I won't take it either."

Lance had a long time to think about what had happened between him and Florence. "I've learned my lesson," he promised her. "What about Robbie?"

"We're not working out" is all she said and gave him a little peck on the cheek. "You earn what you get from me."

By the time the framing was finished, Beka and Lance were getting along well. They argued a little, but were able to resolve their differences. Lance seldom told anyone to do anything anymore. He asked most of the time, but occasionally when he would slip, Beka was right there to remind him that that would get him nowhere with her. She could give him a really mean look despite her beauty, and she used it whenever she needed. It worked.

Robbie and Charlotte grew farther and farther apart. They didn't argue much, but they were just too different. They liked each other and worked well together, but her constant chatting about all the little annoyances of living in the woods also bothered him. Robbie and Beka seemed to be finished as well and he turned to Florence once again.

Charlotte and Kira always got along well as kids. They played together and enjoyed many of the same hobbies. They were content with each other. "Looks like we're the odd girls out now," Kira stated.

"Looks like it," Charlotte replied.

"Want to play lesbian?" Kira asked.

Charlotte didn't answer, but she didn't say no either.

"I'll take that as a maybe."

James and John commandeered one of the boys from time to time to help in the gardens, but for the most part, the kids worked on the house under the expert direction of Reggie Carston. Emily would join him on occasion, and Eileen stopped in regularly as well.

"The boys are doing a good job," Eileen said on several occasions.

"Of course they are," Reggie replied. "They have me showing them what to do."

"I can't believe the boys are working so hard," Emily stated.

"They are tough and persistent," Reggie added.

"Maybe more importantly though, they are highly motivated," Eileen said, looking around at some of the relationships.

"I am so happy about Ronnie and Brooke," Emily said.

"Me too," Eileen added. "I think they make a lovely couple."

As the house neared completion, the neighbors gathered for an inspection. "It still needs a few things, but it looks great," Reggie said. "The boys and gals did a great job."

"All of you should be very proud of yourselves," Eileen added.

After the inspection, Ronnie banged a couple metal pie plates together from their lunch meal to get everyone's attention. "Ladies and gentlemen, Brooke and I would like to make an announcement."

Everyone's attention turned to Ronnie.

"Some of you already know or suspected, but today I'd like to announce officially that Brooke and I are going to get married."

James and Reggie shook his hand. The ladies cried and hugged Brooke.

"This is wonderful," Eileen said. "When?"

"In three days," Ronnie said.

"Such a short time," Emily stated.

"I know, but we've been planning this for weeks. Mr. Wimberley will perform the ceremony."

"Where?"

"Right here where we're standing," Brooke said.

"Considering all the hard work we put in on this place, working side by side with friends, family, and neighbors," Ronnie added, "we thought it would be a fitting place."

"I couldn't agree with you more," Eileen said.

Over the next several days, everyone worked very hard to make the ceremony special for the kids. Numerous trips were made back and forth between the homes delivering what they needed to make the wedding a memorable event.

Kathy was a really good seamstress. Thanks to a little fabric from Emily, Kathy whipped up a beautiful wedding dress in no time. Three days later they were ready. Food was prepared and delivered and Reggie brought wine.

Everyone took their places and the ceremony started promptly at noon. Lance gave the bride away in his dad's stead. Robbie was best man, and Charlotte and Kira were bridesmaids. John delivered the ceremony in perfect form and pronounced the bride and groom as husband and wife. They kissed to seal the agreement.

As soon as they finished the main course, the ladies began to serve cake and wine. The conversations echoed in the vacant house. The only piece of furniture was the bed. No one really noticed or missed the furniture as they fixed their plates from the dishes on the kitchen counter. The party lasted for two hours, and Reggie struggled to keep everyone's glass filled for the many toasts. After everyone finished their cake, and a little more wine than they were accustomed to drinking, the groom tossed the bride's garter, caught by Robbie. Finally, Florence caught Brooke's bouquet. Of course it was rigged beforehand by Robbie and Brooke.

"It's time to let the bride and groom consummate their vows," Reggie announced. Everyone finished their wine and began to pack everything up except a bottle of wine and a couple slices of cake. A final round of hugs, congratulations, and kisses and they were alone.

Brooke and Ronnie went out to the porch and got as comfortable as they could on a couple large stumps he carried up to a shady spot. They held hands and sipped wine staring at each other with newlywed grins on their faces while they waited for sunset.

"It's still a long time before the sun goes down," Ronnie said.

"What's your point?"

"If we seal our vows now, maybe we can seal them more permanently after it gets dark."

Brooke smiled and got up. "Give me a few minutes."

Ronnie leaned back against the house, sipped his wine, and contemplated the event as long as his hormones would let him and went inside.

Chapter 37

Over the next several weeks, Eileen withdrew from the rest of the family. She spent a lot of time in the garden and at Lars's grave. The greens, potatoes, and beans were growing well. She pulled weeds and thanks to the heavy rain from the tropical storm filling the irrigation tank, she was able to keep the plants watered well.

She always carried a tablet and pencil and was constantly writing. When she was not writing, she was at the foot of Lars's grave talking to him at length, recalling all the memories she had accumulated way back to when she left San Antonio. It was a tough time for her, but now she could even laugh about the experiences.

"I was so afraid of you when I first found your place," Eileen said. "I had no idea whether you were going to rape and kill me or what. I'm so glad you turned out to be a man I could fall in love with and get along with as well as we did.

"You were so gentle and caring with me. I really needed your help to learn to survive out here. I knew nothing about how to take care of myself. I was scared of everything.

"Thank you, Lars, for teaching me how to shoot and take care of myself. And thank you for your love and patience. Thank you for not ridiculing my ignorance of all the things you knew how to do instinctively it seemed.

"It is so beautiful out here. And I love the peace and quiet. There are so many birds, squirrels, and deer. Some are so cute. Some are so tasty. Thank you for introducing me to the many foods I had never eaten before.

"I still think of Ronald and Sara Weston often. They died so brutally, and I was hurt and saddened deeply, as I know you were. I wish I could have gotten to know them and the wonderful people you have told me so many times they were.

"I really enjoyed catching more catfish than you did. I know it was luck. You were such a better fisherman than I was. You were the expert at everything. You knew how to do anything. It didn't matter what the situation, you always had the solution. You made my life more comfortable than I could have ever imagined out here in the wilderness.

"I know I aggravated you on numerous occasions. I'm sorry for each and every one. I pumped the brakes when you were towing my car back to your house. I wanted to make you mad. I wanted to show you you couldn't admonish me like you did. I was being childish I know, but you made me mad. I'm sorry if this hurt you. I wish I could take it back now, but you really did deserve it. I know you know this."

Eileen smiled and stood up to stretch her back. She laid her tablet and pencil on the bench and rubbed her butt. When she had her circulation going again, she sat back down and continued her one-sided conversation with Lars.

"Where was I?" . . . "I could see I made you mad and hurt you, but never once did you take it out on me. You took everything I handed out, maybe not with a smile, but you did take it. I love you for that.

"I loved your tender touch in bed; you made love to me in ways I couldn't have imagined. You teased every cell in my body. You made me a whole woman. Your body was so beautiful—so strong, so tough.

"The Lins and Carstons were readily accepting of me. They did not know me, but they accepted me as I was. They loved me because they loved you. They trusted your judgement.

"Do you still love me? Reggie and Emily said you wouldn't want me to hide away my desires. I thought my hormones had died along with you. In time, Reggie showed me they had not. I wouldn't have wanted you to ignore your desires if it had been me who died. I would have wanted you to find love again and to be happy. I hope you feel the same for me.

"Reggie made me feel again. I enjoy Reggie, but Emily satisfies me. Can you understand that? Reggie wants sex and I'm fine with it. Emily on the other hand needs love, the same as I do. She takes the time to give me what I need, and I do the same with her.

"I'm getting hungry. I lose track of time when I'm with you, Lars. I know James and Melissa worry about me. Melissa is always asking me if I'm getting enough to eat. I'm getting old and can't work like I did when I first moved here. I don't need as much to eat, but Melissa still asks. Sometimes I think I'm just getting in the way around here. I really don't do much anymore. I can't. I know how your arthritis bothered you. It bothers me a lot now too.

"I'm so happy Robbie is back home. He brought two wonderful ladies with him. I know he had a tough time in Corpus Christi, but the main thing is that he is home now. Peaceful Valley will grow too. With the Wimberley kids, we can grow.

"I'm really going now. My mind is slipping too. I get off on tangents all the time. I love you, Lars."

Eileen pushed off the bench with her hand and slowly straightened her back. She took a deep breath and trudged toward the house, her mind still wandering into the past. She stopped at the door and turned to take another look at the sycamore tree and Lars's grave.

"Are you all right?" Melissa asked when Eileen walked through the door.

"I'm okay. I'm hungry though."

"I'm sorry, but we ate lunch without you. We didn't want to disturb you," Melissa said.

"Thank you, Melissa."

"There are leftovers on the stove, but they're cold."

"I'll eat them as they are."

"Are you sure you're all right?"

"Yes. I'm just missing Lars a little."

"We all miss Lars every day," Melissa said.

"Yes, we do," Eileen replied with a smile. "What are the kids doing?"

"Robbie and Lance packed up and went in search of a stove for Ronnie and Brooke. They thought it would make a good wedding present. Ronnie and James are working on a wooden cistern and gutters. They don't have any water except what they carry from the river. I think a couple of the girls are helping Brooke inside the house."

"Any idea who is going to move in with them?"

"Robbie and Florence are getting tired of their living arrangement here. Florence is fine on the sofa, but she feels out of place, and Robbie doesn't like sleeping on the floor. It does seem a little crowded in here with the six of us. Robbie and Florence are not ready to get married, but they've been talking about living together."

"I think they make a good couple," Eileen said.

"They get along well. I think they will get together eventually," Melissa added.

"Me too."

"I see you're writing a lot. Something you'd like to share?"

"Not yet."

It was an easy walk across the burned area. Robbie led the way and Lance followed. Robbie knew the terrain. Lance, on the other hand, knew nothing about the area. They brought enough jerky and water for two days. Robbie wasn't certain there would be animals in the burnt area so soon after the fire, but he brought along a .22 pistol he got from Reggie. Reggie also gave him an AR-15 to replace the carbine he lost while in Corpus Christi, but he didn't think he'd need it. Lance only had a .22 bolt-action rifle, but that was perfect for small game.

Now that all the grass was burned off, it was easy to see where the original road ran. The age-old trails from vehicles were visible and easy to follow. In spite of this, it was still the next morning before they made it to the highway. Once they got to the road, they found the tire trails to the first of several houses nearby.

Robbie recalled from stories Eileen had told him, there were three families who lived along this stretch of road. Three opportunities to find a stove. The first opportunity turned up a few items, but the stove was busted into many pieces. There was little left, but some of the more durable items were easy to spot. They picked up forks, spoons, and a few knives. There were also a couple pots and a skillet—all with handles burned off by the fire. There was also some piping, but they had plenty in their own storeroom.

Robbie and Lance made their way back to the road and piled their gatherings alongside what was left of the highway. Much of the asphalt had burned away, but the gravel remained. They found a small pile of wreckage from the plane, but little was left other than the engine.

Lance and Robbie had long conversations about the girls during their trip. Robbie knew Beka better than Lance, and he had many questions for Robbie. He didn't have as many answers as Lance would have liked.

"She is independent and passionate about everything she does," Robbie told him. "You take good care of her, and she'll take good care of you. If you don't, I'll kick your ass. I like her too, you know."

Robbie didn't tell Lance, but he was glad Lance and Florence hadn't worked out. Robbie thought he loved Florence now, but his mind kept jumping back to Beka and Charlotte. He even had thoughts of Jade, Brenda, Alice, and some of the other girls. *If I love Florence, why can't I get these other girls out of my head?*

He didn't tell Lance that he thought he could have loved Beka as well as Florence, and that Beka had come on to him when they first met. Lance didn't need to know that he actually solved the dilemma of having two girlfriends, which he thought he had at one point. *Sometimes it's better to keep quiet about certain stuff. Maybe something I got from Sandra.* Robbie smiled. *Just maybe things will work out like they are supposed to work out if I give things a little time.*

The first thing the boys noticed when they found the remains of the second house was the stove. It was a large cast iron monster. It was not in perfect condition, but it appeared to be in good enough shape to be useable. It looked like an interior wall had fallen on top of it and protected it from the brunt of the fire.

When they tried to move it away from the pile of ashes, they also found out it was even heavier than they expected. At least the weeds and brush would not fight them on the trip back.

They carried the stove into the open away from the house. They cleaned and inspected it to make certain it was worth hauling all the way back home. It was. The trip would be an ordeal, but well worth the effort.

They also scrounged around for more useful items. They found more eating utensils and a couple more pots and two more skillets; no handles again, but useable. One pot was a big stainless steel one, suitable for soups and stews.

The fire had destroyed all the saplings in the area. There was nothing with which to construct a travois. They had to get the poles from the unburned area. They decided to take the pots and utensils home first and return for the stove. "Maybe we can get Zack to help," Lance said.

"Absolutely!" Robbie replied.

Halfway home, they cleaned as much of the ash off an area to sleep. "At least there will be no mosquitos or chiggers. The fire wiped them out for miles around," Robbie said.

They laid on their bedrolls and watched the stars as they talked more about the girls. It had been a long day and the boys were tired. They soon drifted off to sleep.

Lance and Robbie made the remainder of the trip easily by mid-afternoon. They stopped at the Lindgren place to get a bite to eat and all the water they could hold. They ate all their food the previous morning and had only water since yesterday afternoon. They then headed on over to the new house and delivered the utensils.

"I can clean these up, and I'm sure Ronnie can put handles on the pots," Brooke said. "Thank you so much, guys."

"We have another surprise," Lance said. "We found a stove. Robbie and I want to give it to you and Ronnie for a wedding present."

Brooke hugged her brother and Robbie. "Thank you," she said with teary eyes.

"The fire burned all the saplings and we couldn't get it back," Robbie explained. "We'll take some poles from the green area along with twine to make a travois. We still may need some help to get it here."

"We thought Zack or Ronnie could give us a hand," Lance said.

"Ronnie and James are really busy with the cistern. Maybe Zack can give you a hand."

"Do you know where he's at?"

"If he's not at the Lindgrens', my bet is the Lins'," she replied. "He and Debra are seldom away from each other."

The boys did find Zack at the Lins' and dragged him and Debra apart. Zack agreed to help with the stove. This trip, however, they took enough food and water for four days. There was no water at all in the burn area. It had been so dry for such a long time that much of the water soaked in quickly. It had rained very little since the tropical storm, and even the small creeks had dried up.

They cut saplings on the way and constructed their travois. They made it strong enough to carry the stove but used it to carry their jerky, water, rifles, and bedrolls on the trip there.

They underestimated the trip. It took five days to get the stove back, and they were all hungry and thirsty when they reached the Lindgren homestead. They hydrated then took the stove on to the new house.

Brooke was ecstatic over the stove. "Now we can cook inside. Thank you so much. Especially you, Robbie. I expect my brothers to help, but your help is so special to me."

"This is the best wedding present I could think of," Robbie said. "I'm only happy to help."

Brooke hugged Robbie and then her brothers. "Thank you."

"I've missed you," Florence said when Robbie returned to the Lindgrens'.

"I've missed you too."

"When you get cleaned up, can we talk?"

"Sure."

"You smell like charcoal . . . and dirty socks."

Robbie smiled and went into the bathroom.

After he had cleaned up, Florence approached him again. "Can we go out to the pier where we can be alone?" she asked.

Robbie grabbed their fishing poles and followed her out. Florence waited on the bench, while Robbie caught a couple crickets. He helped her bait her line and scooted up next to her.

"What do you want to talk about?" he asked.

"I've really missed you, Robbie."

"You've already said that."

"I missed you a lot."

Robbie stared at her, waiting for her to tell him why she really wanted to talk. He noticed her watery eyes and offered her his sleeve.

What's he going to think? Will he love me or hate me? I love you, Robbie Lindgren. *I'll never know how you feel until I ask.*

"I'm pregnant," she blurted out.

Robbie just stared at her.

"Did you hear me?" she asked.

"Yes."

"And?"

"I'm just trying to visualize a life with you as my wife."

"And?"

"I can see us as a family. I've had a soft place in my heart for you ever since I woke up and saw you. You saved my life. I owe you, Florence. But it's more than that. You are a beautiful woman and we've had sex together. You have a beautiful body."

Florence blushed. "But can you love me when I'm sticking out to here?" she said, indicating with her hand.

"I think so. It will just be your tummy that's big. I know I missed you the past five days. I was relieved that Lance and you didn't get along. I like being near you, and I like your company. I've never really loved anyone except my family and neighbors, so I really don't know what it's like to love someone I'm not related to. I feel close to you. When we're apart I think about you a lot. Maybe I've loved you since we first met. I've just been too stupid to realize it much of the time since."

"Well, I'm not going to push you, Robbie. If you love me, you do. And if you don't . . ."

"Let's take our time and see if it works out. We can move in with Ronnie and Brooke. Let's see if we can live together and not drive each other up the wall."

"I'm good with that," Florence replied.

"Anything else?" he asked.

"I don't think so."

"Well, let's go see if Brooke and Ronnie are okay with us moving in. If they are fine with it, we'll come back here and inform my parents, and we'll move in tomorrow."

On the way over, Robbie held out his arm to stop Florence. "Look down," he said.

"What?"

"That's a patch of poison ivy. Always watch where you're walking. This is something Grandma taught me growing up. There will always be something to hurt you. Look at it. Remember the three leaves. This plant will blister your skin, and it itches like crazy. Next time it may be thorns or a snake. Always be alert," he stressed.

She didn't say anything else and followed Robbie around the plants.

When they reached Ronnie and Brooke's, Ronnie welcomed them into their still mostly empty home. Robbie and Florence didn't waste time and laid their proposition out on the table. Brooke nodded at Ronnie and he immediately accepted their proposal.

"We won't have to do everything around here ourselves," Ronnie stated.

"Okay, brother, we're going back to gather up our stuff, and we'll be here first thing in the morning."

Chapter 38

Eileen stopped by to see Brooke and Florence on the way back from the Carstons'. "You guys are getting this place in shape fast."

"Robbie and Florence have really helped a lot," Brooke said.

"Where are the boys?"

"They're gathering firewood for the stove. The wood from the burn area burns really well. No curing time," Florence said.

"How are you and Robbie getting along?" Eileen asked Florence.

"We're doing well. Robbie works so hard. He is kind and considerate of me and my condition."

"Condition?"

"Yes. We haven't told anyone yet, not even Brooke and Ronnie. I'm pregnant."

"I'm so happy for you and Robbie. I'm going to be a great-grandma."

"We're not married yet."

"Only a technicality," Brooke replied.

"Can I tell everyone else?" Eileen asked.

"I would prefer if we wait a while, just in case my missed period is a false alarm."

"Okay, we'll wait," Eileen said. "I'll be on my way then."

"Thanks."

Eileen arrived home, but before she could make it inside, she heard screaming. It was Kira. She came running up to the house barely able to breathe.

"Calm down," Eileen said. "What's the matter?"

"Charlotte got bit by a snake."

"What kind?"

"A big one. Hurry!" she begged, beginning to cry.

"I've got to get some things," Eileen told her and hurried inside.

"Charlotte got snake bit," Eileen informed Melissa on the way to the bathroom.

"Do you need me?" Melissa asked.

"I think I can handle it," she replied.

Kira and Eileen headed to the Wimberleys'. Kira kept urging Eileen to hurry, but she was not as young as she used to be. She had to stop for a few moments several times. "I can't run like you, Kira."

Kira finally led Eileen into the house. "What kind of snake was it?" she asked Charlotte who was crying.

"Black."

"And big," Kira added.

"That's all we could get out of her," Kathy stated.

Eileen looked at the puncture wounds on her calf. "Yes, it got you bad."

Eileen pulled out a hand towel and a small knife from her tote. "Hold her," she told Kathy.

Eileen placed the towel under Charlotte's leg and cut into the already reddened holes. Charlotte screamed. Kathy struggled to hold her still. The knife was very sharp, and Eileen was swift with her cuts. It was over in seconds. The blood began to flow freely from the wounds.

Eileen pulled a small rubber hose twelve inches long and about an inch in diameter from her tote as the blood streamed down Charlotte's leg and onto the towel. She placed the end of the tube over the wounds and sucked on the other end. She did this over and over, allowing the extracted blood and poison to run down her leg.

She squeezed the area around the punctures, trying to force blood and poison toward the holes. Charlotte screamed again. She repeated the procedure with the hose.

Young Kira watched the ordeal and cried much of the time. "Is she going to die?"

"No," Kathy assured her, but she didn't know for certain and was worried about the same possibility as well.

Eileen cleaned the leg with a damp rag, and Kathy got another towel to replace the bloody one. Eileen wiped the leg but let it bleed freely, which it did for quite a while. Finally, the blood began to coagulate, and she cut a square pad to put over the wounds. Eileen pulled some herbs from her bag, placed them and the pad over the injury, and wrapped the leg up.

"Will she be okay?" Kathy asked.

"Not all black snakes are moccasins. If it was a water snake, she'll be fine in no time. If it was a cottonmouth, there will be more problems."

"When will we know?"

"Tomorrow. I'll come back over in the morning and take a look."

"Thank you for coming over so quickly," Kathy said.

"I'm sorry it had to be under these circumstances," Eileen replied. "I'll get someone to go over to Reggie's and get some ice. That will help with the swelling."

"Thank you."

"Kira, come back with me. You can bring the ice back here when someone gets to my place with it."

"I can't thank you enough," Kathy said with tears in her eyes.

"Keep her leg propped up and make her as comfortable as you can."

"I will."

On the way back home, Eileen had a long talk with Kira. "You always need to watch where you're going. There are so many things out here that can hurt you. Some of them can hurt you really badly."

"Yes, ma'am."

"My husband, Lars, died when a rattlesnake bit him in the neck."

"Is that his picture on your wall?"

"Yes, I painted that for him a long time ago."

"It's a pretty painting."

"Thank you, Kira."

"Yes, ma'am."

"Are you watching where you're going, Kira?"

"No, ma'am."

"You're distracted. When you're distracted, you're going to get hurt. Train your mind and your eyes to always be on the lookout for danger. Especially where you're walking."

"Yes, ma'am."

When they got home, James was just returning from the new house. "James, I need you to go to Reggie's for some ice. Charlotte got bitten by a snake."

James grumbled, as he had worked hard all day at the new house, but he knew it was necessary and didn't argue. He couldn't argue with Eileen anyway. When he did, she always made him the ass.

Kira and Eileen visited with Melissa until James returned. Kira took a closer look at the painting. "He looks a lot like Robbie and Ronnie."

"Yes, the boys take after their grandfather," Eileen said.

Eileen wiped the tear before anyone could notice.

James made a fast trip and Melissa had dinner ready by the time he returned. He handed the small cooler to Kira and she thanked him and left immediately.

"What's for dinner?" James asked.

"Rabbit, fresh beet greens, and spinach out of the garden, along with potatoes," she replied. "You can have pickled beets too, if you want."

"My favorite," he said. "I never turn down your beets, Eileen."

"They're my favorite too," Eileen added and smiled at the compliment.

Eileen got up early to go over to the Wimberleys' to check on Charlotte. Eileen removed the bandages and pulled the square with the herbs off the wound. Kathy handed her a wet towel, and she cleaned the blood and herbs off her leg. She felt Charlotte's forehead and then her leg. "There is still a lot of redness, but at least she doesn't feel like she has a serious fever, and there is no red streak up her leg."

"Is she going to die?" Zack asked.

"No, I don't think so," Eileen replied. "Her leg is a bit warm, but I think she'll be okay. I don't think it was a moccasin. Otherwise it would look much worse. I think it was just a water snake."

John and Kathy breathed a sigh of relief.

"I guess we're going to have to put up with you a while longer," Lance said with a smirk.

"Shut up," Charlotte scolded.

Kathy got some fresh dressings, and Eileen put more herbs on a fresh square of cloth and placed it on Charlotte's leg. She then wrapped it with the new bandages.

"Do you have any ice left?" she asked.

"No, we used it all last night," Kathy said.

"Well, keep a cool compress on the leg. If you can't keep it cool enough, send one of the kids over and we'll get some more at the Carstons'.

"Thank you," John said. "We wouldn't have known what to do."

"That's what neighbors are for," she said, smiling at him for the first time since they got here.

Chapter 39

Eileen made it a point to visit Ronnie, Brooke, Robbie, and Florence regularly. Usually she only caught Brooke and Florence there as the boys were always out working on something, hunting, or gathering wood from the burn area. They were responsible boys, worked well together, and she knew the lessons she had taught them were remembered.

Florence missed a second period and began to have morning sickness. "That's a sure sign," Eileen told her.

Eileen settled into a regular routine which kept her busy most of the day. She got up early each morning to help Melissa prepare breakfast, after which she visited Lars's grave. She continued to write in her notebook. She guarded her writings carefully. She didn't want anyone to read what she had written until she was ready for them to do so. She cleaned this and that, and even swept the floor, a task she seldom did. She had a renewed sense of joy in everything she had always considered chores.

On the way to Lars's grave, she picked flowers, never forgetting to put a fair share on Buster's grave as well. There were not many flowers this time of year, but she always managed to find enough for her needs. She often strolled around the garden looking for weeds, walked down to the river, and sat for hours just watching the water flow by.

The southerly breeze rustled the leaves and birds chirped in the trees. "I hear you, Lars. You know I heard voices after you died. I know you were trying to tell me everything was all right. Your body was dead, but you walked beside me and guided me over the years. You whispered in my ear and reminded me of stories to tell the boys as they were growing up. You kept me out of harm's way. I heard you, Lars. I still hear you. I feel your love."

A squirrel sat with a pecan in its mouth watching her talk to the wind. It scampered up a tree toward its nest or storage spot. She didn't know which, but it didn't really matter. A red-tailed hawk screeched as it sailed across the sky. There was not a sound other than the sounds of nature.

When Eileen got back inside, she cleaned her pistol, placed it back in her holster, and hung it in the proper place beside her bed. She rearranged the furniture in the bedroom and cleaned the lint from under the bed. Finally, she cleaned the bathroom and did a couple loads of laundry. Each night she was tired, but she felt a great deal of satisfaction in what she had done. She spent time with James and Melissa every chance she got. Friday night, she arranged for Beka to spend the night at the new house with the kids.

Eileen turned on the shower and adjusted the temperature. She washed her hair and every square inch of her body. After she dried off, she put her nightgown on and laid out her clothes on the dresser for the next day. She then crawled into bed and lay there thinking about tomorrow.

Saturday morning, Eileen awoke before the sun came up. It was just barely getting light. She crawled out of bed and straightened up her pillow. She placed a piece of plastic that she had gotten from the kitchen over the pillow then a folded bath towel. She grabbed her pistol and laid back down. She reached for the bundle of letters and the dish towel they were rolled up in. The letters went on her chest, the towel over her face, and the pistol into her mouth. *I love you, Lars.*

"What was that?" James said. He rolled over in bed, just barely awake, so he could see Melissa.

"What?" she replied.

"If I didn't know better, I'd say it was a gunshot."

"The kids are out hunting," she said.

"I don't think they would be hunting around here this early in the morning. Maybe thunder."

James got dressed and went into the kitchen. It was quiet. He walked out to the front porch and looked around. Nothing, so he went back inside. Melissa had finished dressing and was drawing a pot of water for coffee. James grabbed some kindling and fired up the stove.

Melissa dropped Karaicha beans into the water and let it boil for a couple minutes. She then poured them each a cup of Karaicha coffee. It wasn't real coffee, but it was as close to anything they could make from beans which grew naturally around the area.

The sun came up and James and Melissa had a second cup, saving enough for Eileen to have some as well. By the time they finished, they'd heard no noise from Eileen's room.

"She's been up every morning by now," she said.

"Maybe you should check on her."

Melissa got up and gently knocked on the door. She knocked again with the same result. She turned the knob and gently pushed the door open.

"James," she said.

James got up and walked over. He walked in and pulled back the curtain. He saw the pistol first; then the blood and the bundle of neatly tied letters on her chest. "Dammit!"

"No!" Melissa yelled.

James took the pistol and put it back in the holster which had hung on the wall for so many years. He checked her pulse. Of course, there was none.

James stood, shocked, looking at her. She'd seemed so happy the past few days. So full of life. He picked up the papers and untied the ribbon. There were letters addressed to him and Melissa, to the kids and to the neighbors. He handed them to Melissa. She looked at them and laid them on the dresser.

"What do we do now?" she asked.

"Eileen was very meticulous so we would not have a mess to clean up. Obviously she's laid out the clothes she wanted to be buried in."

"She's been planning this for a long time," Melissa stated. "I should have known something was going on. She visited Lars's grave and talked to all the kids. I thought she was so happy Robbie was back home."

"She was happy. This has been working since Dad died. She loved him more than life itself. That is why she taught the boys everything she could. She wanted them to know Lars as she did. But she knew in the end it would end up this way. This started nearly fifteen years ago. No one could have stopped it."

"What do we tell the neighbors?"

"I don't think we need to tell them anything. I think the letters will do that. I don't think she'd say she was going to commit suicide. I think she'd just say it was her time to join Lars. We'll wrap her up good and just tell everyone she died in her sleep. If the letters say differently, they'll know. Otherwise they will only know she died. Can you keep that secret?"

"I think so. I think she would want it that way. That is why she made sure Beka wasn't here, so it would only be you and me. She was very thorough."

"I think so too. Can you dress her?"

"I may cry the whole time, but I'll do my best."

"I'll get started on the grave."

James went out to the barn, grabbed a shovel, and made his way toward the sycamore tree. After a half-hour, his back needed a break and he went in to check on Melissa. She had done what she said she could. She then helped James wrap the body in the bed clothes. James ran outside to get some leather cordage and secured the sheet and spread to her body. She was ready for burial.

Melissa followed James out to the porch and took a seat, while James trudged back to the gravesite. Another half-hour went by and when Melissa saw James heading back toward the house, she went inside and drew a pitcher of water, grabbed two glasses and took them to the porch where she waited for him. He drank two glasses and took off toward the Carstons'.

James stopped by Robbie and Ronnie's and informed them. Robbie said he would go to the Lins' while Ronnie headed to the Wimberleys'. Brooke and Florence went straight to the Lindgrens' to see if they could help Melissa.

At the edge of the Carstons' meadow, James let out his wolf howl. Reggie stepped to the porch and returned the signal. Emily came to the door as well. The visit was unexpected.

"Oh no!" Emily responded with immediate tears.

Reggie had no words. He just stood with his mouth open as James explained what had happened. "I guess it was her time" was the simple explanation he gave.

Everyone met at the Lindgren place. James and Ronnie found two planks, laid them side by side, and nailed several crosspieces onto them to hold them together. The crosspieces stuck out on each side acting as handles to carry the makeshift stretcher. They took it into the house and scooted Eileen's body onto the planks.

James ran to the barn and grabbed some rope and two poles which he laid across the hole next to Lars' grave. He then returned to the house.

Lance, Zack, Ronnie, Robbie, James, and John each grabbed a handle sticking out from the planks and carried Eileen to the gravesite. They laid the stretcher on the two poles James had placed across the hole.

"I know you are probably more experienced in this type of ceremony," James said, "but I believe Eileen would prefer that Reggie performed the service."

"I understand," John replied.

The girls gathered flowers and placed them on the bundle. Everyone gathered around the body, and Reggie took his place behind the headstone.

"Some of you don't know Eileen very well, but she was the toughest and smartest lady in the valley. She was a city gal who stole Lars's heart and soul. She knew very little about the ways or the dangers of the country. But Lars was patient with her and passed on every bit of knowledge he had to her. She listened and she learned. She was funny at times and dead serious at others. Over the years she became the epitome of what a country woman should be.

"She was a protector and a lover. She loved everyone in Peaceful Valley. She laid her life on the line more than once in defense of our way of life. She could shoot the eyes out of a squirrel at a hundred yards and worked hours and hours caring for the tender plants in the garden. She was not afraid of hard work and loved every minute she spent with Ronnie and Robbie, teaching them all she knew and all that she had learned from Lars.

"Robbie and Ronnie don't remember Lars, but through Eileen, they know him better than anyone. Eileen read to the boys when they were young and insisted they read every day when they had learned to do so. They are smart boys because of her.

"Eileen loved Lars's son James like her son. And she accepted my daughter Melissa as Lars did. She probably saved Sally's life when she was burned so badly and was a best friend to Sam.

"Eileen loved Debra and Sean like they were her kids. She loved kids, period. And though she never had the chance to get to know the Westons, she was as deeply saddened by their death as Lars was, simply because they were his friends.

"Eileen learned how to make pickled beets exactly like Lars did so she could provide Emily with the treat she loved so much. I loved her at first because Lars loved her. I loved her more when I got to know her better, because she was a magnificent lady. She was a friend to all. She will be missed more than I can put into words.

"Lars, we deliver you your wife, your best friend, and the love of your life to you. May you both rest in peace and enjoy eternity together. We love you both and always will. You will never be forgotten."

Melissa grabbed the flowers from Eileen's body and the men lowered her into the hole with the ropes. The tears which began well before Reggie's first word flowed freely now.

James pulled the ropes out and everyone just stood silent for a moment staring into the abyss.

Reggie instructed everyone to grab a handful of dirt. Together, they then tossed the dirt into the hole simultaneously. Ronnie went to the shed to grab another shovel. The men all took turns filling the hole.

When the burial was finished, Melissa laid the flowers on the pile of dirt and sorted through the sealed notes Eileen had written for everyone and handed them out. "Read them at your leisure," she said. "I'm sure Eileen sealed the notes because she meant they were for your eyes only."

A couple of the girls picked more flowers they found nearby and added them to the ones Melissa had placed on the grave. They also placed a few on Lars's and Buster's graves.

Most everyone headed to the house. "I'd like to stay a while longer," Reggie told the rest.

"James, if you will take the headstone to your porch," Sam said, "I'll bring my tools over and chisel in the date."

"It will be on the porch in the morning, Sam," James replied.

Reggie sat down on the bench and waited until everyone was out of earshot.

"I hope I didn't mess up anything between you two, Lars," he said. "It was not my intention. I hope you understand. I've missed you every day, my old friend. Now I will miss the both of you equally. I love you from the bottom of my heart."

Chapter 40

When everyone had gone home, Melissa pulled out the note to her and James. She read it aloud to James.

Dear Melissa and James,

I'm sorry to leave you this way. You know how I've missed Lars for so many years. It was time for me to go. It has been such a pleasure to get to know you two, and I love you more than you can imagine. A piece of me died along with Lars. There is nothing on this earth that could have replaced him.

Teaching the boys his ways kept me alive for many years, but now they are grown and have turned into all that I or Lars could have imagined for them. I know Peaceful Valley will grow now, and I wish I could stay to be a part of that growth, but I need to be with Lars. I will check in with you from time to time. If you see an odd looking cloud or feel that something is different, it will be Lars and me telling you that we are watching.

There is no advice I can give you two. I have already done that. All I can give you is my love. I hope you will feel it for the rest of your lives, because it will be there. If you are hot and feel a little puff of wind, it will be me. If you hear footsteps and no one is there, it will be me. I am gone, but I'll never leave.

All my love,
Eileen

P.S. The exact recipe for Lars's pickled beets is in the cupboard under the recipe box. Follow the directions as I have written them, and take a jar to Emily often. She loves them so much. Tell her Lars and I sent them.

XOXOXO

When they got home, Emily fixed a pot of tea for herself and Reggie. They took their glasses to the sofa and Emily opened the note.

Dear Emily and Reggie,

I know this has to be quite a shock for you two. I'm sorry it had to end this way, but nothing lasts forever. You know that. I've felt my life slipping away for quite some time. I love you both and hope you understand how difficult living had become for me. You know how much I love Lars.

You two will be the backbone of Peaceful Valley now. Take care of everyone, as I know you will. Be patient with the Wimberleys, especially with John. He is a good man. In time he will get his church. Don't be such an ass about it, okay?

Emily, hug and kiss the grandkids and great-grandkids for me and Lars every chance you get. Reggie, you do the same. You have the most important job, Reggie. You have the means to help keep everyone safe. Make sure everybody stays armed and dangerous. Make certain all can shoot especially, but also hunt, trap, and fish. Help them learn as I have taught Robbie and Ronnie.

And finally, Emily, thank you for opening your heart and sharing your innermost feelings with me. Thank you for exploring new horizons. You satisfied a need that I hadn't known existed.

Reggie, I know I satisfied a need for you. I hope you now have a better understanding of Emily's needs and that you will grow together again. I know you can do it. I know you love her. I will be watching. I love you both and will miss you.

Love,
Eileen

XOXOXO

Reggie pulled Emily close. "I do love you, Emily."

"I love you too, Reggie."

"Shall we have something to eat? I'm hungry."

"What would you like?"

"I think I'd like some of your famous beef stroganoff."

"Stroganoff it is then. That sounds good to me too."

"And I'll help."

"Thank you, Reggie darling."

A mischievous little smile developed on his face and he patted her on the butt when she turned around.

Emily giggled.

The note Melissa gave to Kathy was for all the Wimberleys. Zack and Lance stayed with Debra and Beka for a while but promised they'd be home early. Kathy didn't feel right about reading the note until all the kids were there.

Charlotte and Kira went home with their mom and dad after the eulogy. Kira wanted to read the note immediately, but Kathy insisted she wait. Charlotte didn't care one way or the other. Her leg was beginning to hurt again, and she wanted to prop it up. It was healing, but if she walked around too much it would swell and the pain set in. She lay down on the sofa with her leg across the armrest.

The rest of the kids made it home just before dark.

"Not as early as you said," John reminded them.

"We were being careful watching for snakes," Zack replied in a smart-ass tone.

John frowned at him but said nothing.

"You boys get your showers," Kathy demanded. "When you get out I'll read the letter Eileen wrote to us. It is for all of us."

John helped Kathy prepare dinner for the first time since they'd moved in, while they waited for the boys. Reggie had given them a few packets of his pre-packaged foods, and he wasn't so sure they were real food. Kira insisted on helping as well. The meal was almost ready when the boys finished dressing. They decided to read the note after everyone had eaten. It had been a long day and they didn't eat much after the burial.

Everyone helped clean up the table and do the dishes. They gathered around Kathy as she opened the envelope.

Dear Wimberleys,

I'm sorry I didn't get to know all of you as well as I'd have liked. Charlotte's snakebite reminded me of how difficult it can be living here in the woods. I want to let you know that I was in the same position as you when I first moved here. I didn't know about the plants and animals, especially the dangerous ones, and suffered a great deal because of my ignorance. Lars taught me all I know about living out here and dealing with the dangers, from stinging nettles to alligators and everything in between. The main thing is to watch where you're walking. It took a while for Lars to train me to watch my step, but I learned. You and your kids must learn as well.

Ronnie and Robbie are a wealth of knowledge about the woods and critters. They are young, but don't let that fool you. We have taught them well, and they learned even more on their own. If you don't know something, ask them. They are always ready and willing to help others. They are good boys, as you will learn. I made certain of that.

James and Melissa are smart as well. Melissa is an excellent cook. James knows how to fix things. Lean on them when you need help. That is the way of Peaceful Valley.

The Lins are good people, and though a bit on the quiet side, are always willing to help their neighbors. And though Reggie can be a real ass at times, he knows more than you can imagine about security and explosives. Don't be afraid to ask for help. If the Carstons, Lins, or Lindgrens need something from you, they'll certainly ask.

Sincerely,
Eileen

Inside the sealed note, there were separate notes as well, one each for Charlotte and Kira. Kathy handed these notes to the girls and they went outside to read them.

My dear little Kira,

You are the youngest in the Valley. You will not always be the baby around here, but for the moment that is the way it is. But don't be a baby. You are a big girl. You are a grown woman in the eyes of many, including me. You are smart and beautiful.

You may have noticed there is a shortage of young men in Peaceful Valley. You may not need a man now, but the time may come when you will want a husband. This may not be possible. I lived for a long time without a man and got along just fine. Nature and hobbies can be very satisfying. I never had kids of my own, but enjoyed children very much. I loved Debra, Sean, Ronnie, and Robbie like they were my own and I could not have been happier. You will figure out what's best for you.

Your sister Charlotte is the other odd girl out, and I told her this same thing. You two may or may not want to talk about it. That is up to you. Two heads are better than one, and maybe between the two of you, you can figure something out. The main thing for me is that you live a happy life here. I only want the best for you and everyone else.

My love,
Eileen

The note Eileen had written to Charlotte was similar to the one to Kira. Though they did not share notes, they were in an analogous predicament—single and no available male companions. As they mature, they would need to work together to remedy this problem.

Sam tended to his hogs and then went inside to clean up. Sally and Debra prepared dinner, and when Sam finished his shower, they ate a solemn meal. The note Eileen had written lay in the middle of the table.

"I'm sure going to miss Eileen," Sally said. "She was a one-of-a-kind lady."

"Why did she have to die now?" Debra asked, tears forming in her eyes.

"We'll all die when it is our time," Sam replied. "She must have known her time was coming soon to write the notes."

Debra helped her mom clean up the table, stove, and dishes. When they finished they all went into the living room and took a seat. Sally opened the letter.

My dear friends and neighbors,

I am so sorry to leave you so suddenly, but I felt my time was growing near. I want you to know that I loved you more than you will ever know.

Sam, you kept Lars happy with your splendid bacon. For this I am forever grateful. I loved the bacon as well. Your generosity in providing anything you thought we needed or wanted was overwhelming. I just want you to know how much we always appreciated you.

Sally, you are equally generous with your time and the wonderful breads and candies you made. I love you and the friendship you showered me with so freely.

Debra, I remember you when you were only a toddler. You were the cutest baby I had ever seen. You have grown up into a beautiful woman. Any man would be lucky to have you. Zack is a smart boy, and I think you and he will make an excellent couple. I know you are a tomboy, and Zack probably likes that, but men also like ladies to be ladies. Good luck with him, and all my love.

I will be just across the river in body, but I will look in on you all from time to time.

All my love,
Eileen

Debra couldn't stop crying. "I love you too, Eileen."
"We all do," Sally said, tears in her eyes as well.

Ronnie and Brooke only stayed at his mom and dad's a short while and headed home. Ronnie didn't cry much, just like his grandpa, but he was hurting inside. He talked about Eileen all the way home and after he got out of the shower. Brooke took her shower and joined Ronnie on the porch.

"Where's the note she left for us?" Ronnie asked.

"I have it right here. Do you want me to read it?"

"Yes, I would like that."

Brooke opened the note and began to read.

My dearest Ronnie and Brooke,

When the two of you decided to get married, I was so happy you cannot imagine. I'm sorry to leave you so suddenly, but you will be okay. Ronnie, you are strong like Lars. You can take care of yourself, and you can take care of Brooke. Teach her about the dangers of the woods. Love her with all your heart, and cherish every minute you have with her. She is a wonderful lady.

Brooke, I wish we'd had time to get better acquainted. I think I know you well enough though to know you and Ronnie are made for each other. Ronnie is a smart man. He is strong and can take care of you. Listen to him. I also see the tenderness in him. Love him for the man he is but also for the boy that will always be a part of him.

I will check in on you from time to time, but also feel free to stop by the sycamore and visit me and Lars. Our place will always be open for you.

All my love,
Grandma

Robbie and Florence hung around his mom and dad's house long enough that they just barely made it to the new house before dark. Ronnie and Brooke were both tired and went to bed shortly after they arrived.

Robbie and Florence showered, went to the porch, and he read the note to Florence.

My dear Robbie and Florence,

I know you won't be able to help missing me, but remember this: I'm in a happier place now. I think you know how much I missed Lars over the years. He was my life. I see a lot of him in you, and you are strong. You will live on, and you will be happy. You were a good student and are smart. You are a survivor, and you will thrive.

As much as I wanted to stay here with you, I felt Lars pulling at me. I knew I wouldn't live much longer, and I wanted to explain some things. I am happy now. You, your brother, and new neighbors and old are the future of Peaceful Valley. Make it a strong community. Make it a happy and close-knit group.

Florence, I have not known you long, but I do love you. I love you because Robbie sees things in you that are good and wholesome. I was so happy to hear you are pregnant. You will have sons; many sons. I can feel this. Robbie will help you grow strong, and you will be as happy as I was here in Peaceful Valley. Love Robbie and learn from him. Do so and you will be as happy as I was for so many years.

You two make a beautiful couple. I hope you will one day get married, but whether you do or not makes no difference to me as long as you are together as a family.

I will check in on you guys from time to time. You may only feel a little breeze, but know I am with you always. If you have time, stop by and see us. Lars and I will always be with you under the old sycamore tree.

All my love,
Grandma

Beka showered and made her bed on the couch. Though Eileen's room was vacant, she could not sleep there tonight. She knew her memories would haunt her.

When she settled in, she opened the note from Eileen.

Dear Beka,

We have known each other for only a short time. Despite this, I feel close to you. You are smart and beautiful. Lance is a good man. He is a bit immature, but he has good intentions. I don't know where he got the idea he can order people around, maybe from his dad, but be strong and assertive. He will grow out of that with your help.

There are so many things in life that can give you joy and fulfillment. I lived without Lars for many years, and though I missed him terribly, I was as happy as possible under the circumstances.

Life is not always fair and it will never be easy around here, but you will always have the love of your neighbors and friends.

Life in the woods is very different from what you had in the city. Learn from James, Robbie, and Ronnie. They know how harsh life is here. Melissa can help you too. I don't want you to get hurt. Once you get used to the dangers around here, you will be able to see the beauty and not think twice about the many things that can hurt you.

Live long and happy. If you need to talk, you know where I will live out eternity. I will answer you if you listen with your heart.

Love and good wishes,
Eileen

Beka wiped the tears from her eyes, folded the note neatly, and placed it under her pillow. *She was such a beautiful woman. I wish she would have lived a little longer.*

She closed her eyes, and before she knew it, she wandered off to dreamland.

Chapter 41

For three days, everyone stayed home with the only exceptions being Sam to date Eileen's headstone, and Charlotte and Kira who ran an errand to the Lindgren's. Everyone was so distraught over Eileen's death they didn't feel like visiting. They did what they needed to do, but mostly they moped around, thinking of how much things would change without Eileen. She had touched everyone's heart, and they missed her. That was only natural. She had been close to everyone.

It wasn't long, however, until things were back to as near normal as they would ever be. Fall was fast approaching, and it would be winter before they knew it. There were chores to be done.

Last-minute roof repairs were made, firewood cut and stacked, and the garden which was in full swing now constantly needed attention. Some tasks needed the help of a neighbor or two, and they worked together to make certain everything that needed to be done was finished and would have earned the approval of Eileen's watchful eye.

Ronnie and Brooke grew closer with every passing day. No one doubted that Brooke would soon be pregnant. All the kids worked hard, but always made personal time for each other. Florence felt more pregnant every passing day. Her morning sickness slacked off, but never subsided. She and Robbie planned on getting married in the springtime.

Sam carved the date on Eileen's headstone, but Melissa decided there should be a formal service to place it at the head of Eileen's grave, so for the time being it laid on the porch. Everyone got busy after their short vacation to make up for lost time on their many tasks. It was two weeks later when everyone was notified there would be a ceremony to reinstall the headstone.

Sam even butchered a young pig in honor of the event. They roasted it over an open fire. Sally baked bread, and though the Wimberleys didn't have a lot to offer, one thing they did have plenty of was fruit. While the critters got much of the early fruit, a few trees were loaded, especially the pears. Kathy made a wonderful cobbler with them.

The Lindgrens never seemed to run out of pickled beets, corn, and potatoes. With the added moisture from the tropical storm early on, and the rain filling the tank supplying their watering system since, greens, carrots, turnips and radishes were plentiful.

No one knew how much wine Reggie stocked when he moved to the valley so many years ago, but even after all these years he assured everyone he would never run out. The same was true for the prepackaged survival foods he'd stored by the ton when he first moved here. He even brought some candy.

No one expected Ronnie, Brooke, Robbie, and Florence to bring anything. They just barely had a house. There were many things still needed to finish out the new place, but Ronnie and Brooke found some wild grapes. The muscadine grapes were plentiful in some areas, and they picked enough to make a dish. Brooke and Florence, with the help of a few ingredients from Emily and Reggie, made a splendid grape dip. It was perfect with the corn chips they also made.

It turned out to be a beautiful day in Peaceful Valley. The sun was bright, the wind was light, and it wasn't overly hot for that time of year. The air seemed a little drier than usual, and without the humidity, it was quite comfortable. The men had the pig roasting by mid-morning. Everyone else who had not come beforehand showed up shortly thereafter. The grownups tended to the food. The men took care of the pig along with some of Reggie's wine, while the ladies prepared the trimmings inside the house. The kids did what they always did when they were together—they swam and played. They all seemed to be getting along quite well. At least no one heard any arguments. Everyone seemed to be happy.

The pig took a little longer than the men had anticipated, but no one was concerned. It was ready shortly after midday. They had all day and no one was starving. Well, a couple of the boys claimed to be starving, but the growing boys always had ravenous appetites.

As usual there was not enough room around the dining room table with such a large gathering, and the kids spread out to the living room and porch. Everyone complimented the chefs and raved when the desserts were served. The mood was cheerful as everyone ate their fill.

Robbie told more stories about Corpus Christi, to the delight of the group. "They had rows and rows of strawberries. I wish we could grow them here. The sodas were wonderful. They had several flavors, and they fizzed in your mouth when you took a drink. They did make you burp a lot. I especially liked the strawberry and the lemon flavored drinks.

"Sean started up one of the jets they had in the hangar. It was an F-22 Raptor a fighter jet with machine guns and air-to-air rockets on the wings. You should have seen the surprise on Russ and Jorge's faces when he started the engines inside the building. They were especially annoyed when Sean shot a big hole in the side of the hangar with the machine guns. They were really loud inside the building."

Reggie laughed boisterously over the machine gun incident, and his eyes bulged with the mention of the rockets. He had more questions about the machine guns. Weapons always got his adrenalin pumping, especially powerful ones.

Beka and Florence shared a few stories as well. They were becoming accustomed to living in the valley and felt more comfortable around the others now.

"I really like baked flounder," Beka told them. "It is a funny looking fish, brown on one side and white on the other. Both of its eyes are on the brown side. The meat is so white and tender. Most saltwater fish have scales on their skin. After the scales are scraped off, we cut the skin open on the brown topside of the flounder and stuffed crab meat mixed with bread crumbs underneath and baked it to a golden brown. It is so delicious."

"Shrimp are always my favorite," Florence shared. "I don't care how they're fixed. I love them. We mostly fried them, but they are also good grilled. Sometimes we mixed them with rice, bacon, and onion, then stir-fried them in a big skillet. They're delicious that way too."

"I guess we won't ever get to have them again," Beka noted.

"I guess not," Florence said. "But we will find things around here that are equally as good."

"Yes, you will," Robbie added.

The men cleaned up the dishes and put the leftovers away. Melissa didn't give them a choice. "We cleaned up the mess at the last big get-together," she told them. "It's your turn." Reggie grumbled a little, but when he saw the sour look on Emily's face, he gave her a smile and followed James lead.

There wasn't much left except for the pig which was divided up for each family to take home according to the number of mouths that needed to be fed.

When everyone was ready, Ronnie and Lance carried the headstone to the sycamore tree and placed it near Eileen's grave. James brought a shovel and prepared the little trench for the stone. Ronnie and Lance then placed the stone and packed the dirt around the base.

Reggie opened the ceremony. A few seconds later, everyone was in tears.

"Beka, Florence, Brooke, Charlotte, and Kira," Reggie said, "if ever you might want to pattern your life after someone, this is the lady who set the example for all of us. Though she was a city girl, she absorbed every bit of country Peaceful Valley had to offer. Eileen was a crack shot, could make a meal out of practically nothing, worked like a man, and loved like a lady. There will never be another like her.

"Lars was a man among men. He patiently helped her become the woman she needed to be to survive out here, but he also let her be herself. He let her be a woman. I don't think they ever fought about anything. I think Eileen set Lars on a narrow path from the beginning.

"There is a story that has been told many times around here. I think you all should hear it again. Eileen's car was stranded down the road toward the highway. She needed her clothes out of the old Volvo, and Lars took her and the truck to retrieve the vehicle. He hooked up a towing strap to the car, and began to pull her home.

"When Lars put his hand out for her to stop so Lars could move a log across the road, she locked up the brakes jerking them to a stop. He gave her a good scolding. Eileen was steaming the remainder of the trip. So much so that every now and then she would pump the brakes, jerking on the tow strap and Lars's truck just to aggravate him. He would look in the rearview mirror, and she would be laughing her head off. Lars just shook his head and kept on driving.

"I think they both fell in love with each other by the time they finished their teas that evening as they watched the sunset from the porch.

"Eileen was book smart when she came here. She learned the ways of the city then learned the ways of the woods. In my opinion, that made her the smartest person in the valley. I know she was the happiest person here, though she did many things she was not proud of. She did what she needed for her and Lars to survive—for all of us to survive. All of us owe our lives to this little lady. A giant among women."

Everyone was speechless. Reggie had covered everything which needed covering except a prayer. John and Kathy took care of that with a brief prayer, while the girls gathered more flowers to put on Eileen's, Lars's, and Buster's graves. When that was finished, everyone slowly walked back to the house.

"I think we need to have a little meeting," Debra announced. "Zack and I have been talking to Lance and Beka about new living arrangements. I think we need to build a new house."

"What's going on?" Melissa asked.

"Zack and I want to get married," Debra replied. "I think Lance and Beka are getting there too, and we need a new place to live."

"We all get along really well together," Lance said. "I think we can build a house just like Ronnie and Robbie's and be good with that."

"And when does this need to happen?" Reggie asked.

"Next week works for me," Debra said.

"To start?"

"No, to finish."

"I don't think that's possible," James stated with a smile.

"I know," Zack said, "but we need to get going on this now."

"How about tomorrow?" Beka asked.

Everyone was quiet. James looked at Reggie. Lance looked at John. Zack looked at Robbie and Ronnie.

"Tomorrow works for me," Robbie said.

"Can you get it dried in before the weather gets nasty?" Reggie asked. "Winter will be here before you know it."

"Not five of us," Zack stated.

"I'll help," James said.

"That's six," Zack added.

"We'll all help," Brooke insisted.

Everyone agreed they would all pitch in to get the house raised. They would need to if it was to be dried in before winter set in.

"I think that about settles it," Melissa said.

"Where are we going to build it?" James asked.

"We have a spot already picked out," Debra said.

"We had a spot picked out across the river before the fire," Zack added, "but because you used so much wood from the burn area, we thought we could do the same. The river would just get in our way, so we decided to build it on this side."

"Smart kids," Reggie noted.

"There is so much partially burned wood that we can't use it all," James added. "There is plenty for another house, and we'll all have enough firewood for the winter. Building on this side of the river will make the task so much easier. Have you found a spot on this side?"

"We think so," Debra said.

"Well, I guess we had better get a good night's sleep," James said.

"We'll see you guys and gals here in the morning," Melissa added, "and we'll go take a look at your site while the boys start hauling in logs."

The neighbors headed home and James and Melissa lingered on the porch watching them disappear into the woods. James looked up at the sky, noting the building clouds.

"The weather is changing," he said.

She didn't respond and turned toward the front door.

"Eileen would be pleased," James said as he and Melissa went into the house.

Melissa looked back toward the sycamore. "Yes, she would."

Bright and early the next morning, Debra and Zack were the first to arrive at the Lindgrens' with Sam and Sally not far behind. It didn't take long for the rest of the crew to show up. James, Ronnie, and Robbie grabbed a few tools out of the shed, and everyone else had brought a shovel, post-hole digger, hoe, or rake. James brought a chainsaw, and Sam and Reggie took axes. Debra and Zack led them to the site. It was only a third of the way to the Wimberley home and near the river. The trees were big, and there was a good flat area to build on.

They cleared the area in no time and started post holes while some of the boys went after foundation logs. They all worked until the late afternoon, and everyone was bushed. They weren't hungry or thirsty; just tired.

It took a week to get the hardest part done—getting the posts in and lined up. They framed out the floor and started the floorboards. They framed out the home in three weeks and started on the roof. They got lucky and finished the roof before the heavy rains started.

The rain—or more correctly, the mud—interfered with the outside walls, but they slopped around in the slush and finished the siding. The first October cold spell blew in and cooled the workers off. They nailed plastic over the window openings until they figured out what to do about windows. The plastic was old and didn't hold up well, so they cut and nailed wood planks over the openings to keep out the weather.

"We'll have to make the windows," Reggie told them. "We have plenty of glass, just no frames."

"We can do that," Lance replied, "if you show us how to do it."

"That I can do," Reggie said with a smile.

The house was only a shell, but Debra and Zack were eager to get married. They had been talking about this moment and planning for it forever, it seemed.

They held the ceremony in the new home. Though it was only a roof and four walls, they loved it. In time, it would become much more. They were strong and energetic. They would make certain of that.

John Wimberley performed his second wedding in Peaceful Valley. It was a bare-essentials ceremony, but the kids didn't care. They wanted to move in and make it a home.

John hadn't forgotten about his church, but he was feeling more like a preacher by performing the weddings. Kathy could see the pride in his face as he performed the ceremony.

They moved the bed from Eileen's room into one bedroom and a chair and table from the Lindgren's shed into the kitchen area. Everyone shared basic utensils and a meager supply of food from their own food stocks. Zack and Debra were as happy as ducks in a pond.

Though Lance and Beka were not ready to get married, they also moved in the following week. It was more like they were camping than living in a home, but it was theirs. They were young and in love, or getting there quickly, and it didn't matter. They had their own space and could make their own decisions. Charlotte and Kira spent a lot of time at the two new homes to have a little more privacy from their parents.

It was going to get colder soon, and no one knew where there was another stove to be had. The new house needed a fireplace too. They didn't need electricity, and candles provided light. Before Lars died, he and Reggie gathered enough paraffin from some nearby oil storage tanks that they would never run out, so they didn't have to be concerned about wax for candles.

They found a few drums of mortar mix in the storeroom at the Wimberleys' which turned out to still be good. Zack and Lance gathered enough stones to make the fireplace. Another week and they finished this project, so they could at least keep warm.

Due to the weather, it wasn't always possible for Beka and Debra to cook outside on the grill the boys had fashioned out of stones and some of the mortar mix. They still needed a stove.

One day, Reggie and James brought over a stove they had made. They had hammered, bent, and riveted a makeshift stove out of scrap steel from James's shed and Reggie's bunker. It looked like shit, but they assured the new couples it would work.

Robbie and Ronnie helped Reggie and James deliver and hook up the monstrosity.

"Just don't overload it with wood," Reggie cautioned them.

Debra and Beka gave the men a queer look, but when they fired up the stove, it worked just fine.

Debra and Beka kissed and thanked Reggie and James for their effort and Ronnie and Robbie for helping deliver their new cooking device.

"It may look like hell," Beka added, "but it will sure beat trying to cook in the rain. A stove is a stove, just like a car is a car."

Everyone smiled.

The days and weeks rolled by, and Thanksgiving Day was fast approaching. It seemed like Peaceful Valley was finally living up to its name. While the Carstons would much rather have had Eileen around, they found a new love for one another. Eileen had brought them together, and they were again happy with each other.

James and Melissa didn't quite know how to act with only the two of them in the house now. Melissa had more time to read between chores and visits to the kids' homes. James was constantly fixing things for the new homes and helping the kids make a better place for themselves, but he also had a little extra time for lovemaking, which had been lacking in his and Melissa's life for quite a while.

Sam and Sally also had their home to themselves. They knew Debra was doing well, and their only concern was Sean. They missed him daily, but they hoped he was happy and could make a life for himself in Corpus Christi. They never gave up on the hope that one day he would return. It would be the happiest day of their lives.

Ronnie and Brooke thought they might be pregnant, and Florence was beginning to show a bit of tummy. She had a glow about her that could only mean she and Robbie were going to be parents in the spring. This made James and Melissa very happy. Their first grandbaby!

Zack, Debra, Lance, and Beka didn't have a lot of conveniences in their new home, but they were keeping warm when they needed to. This would become a little more difficult when the inevitable much colder weather arrived. They were, however, preparing for it. The boys sealed all the drafts around the doors and windows and fashioned a secondary wood stove out of an old barrel.

Lance and Zack worked on a cistern to get them by for the winter and gutters to fill the tank. They would need to make a larger one in the spring. There were just too many other needs now to take too long on a full-sized cistern.

They gathered firewood when they could and hunted in between. They made a smokehouse and fishing pier. Just the bare essentials for now.

The Wimberleys got along better with fewer kids in the house. Kathy made certain John was always respectful toward Charlotte and Kira. She had to constantly remind him they were adults now, despite the fact they still lived in their home. John vowed to not drive them away as he nearly did months back. His hope of a church in Peaceful Valley, now a burst bubble, made him more calm and accepting of the situation. In the back of his head, however, he vowed to get his church even if it was not much larger than an outhouse. He kept this plan to himself though. Life, values, and priorities in Peaceful Valley were different. Change is always inevitable. You cannot fight it. To do so is futile and depressing. John kept his church in the back of his mind, but outwardly he rolled with the flow.

All the households kept in constant touch with the others. They were all looking forward to Thanksgiving Day and the super feast they were preparing. There was laughter and happiness everywhere. Joy wasn't a random occurrence anymore. It was constant every day. This was completely new to Peaceful Valley. Life will always be a struggle, but at least the valley was peaceful and cheerful.

Robbie, Ronnie, and Lance, who was the best shot amongst the Wimberleys, went out turkey hunting every day. There was greenery in the burned area after a few heavy rains and the cooler weather. The turkeys liked this area and the tender vegetation, but were very hard to hunt in the wide-open expanse of charred landscape.

"Turkeys have keen eyes and are very wary of their surroundings," Robbie told Lance. Lance wasn't the best hunter, but he was a good shot. Robbie and Ronnie were the best at camouflage. Ronnie got a turkey the first day, Robbie early on the second and, with a little instruction from the others, Lance got a turkey that afternoon. There would be leftovers from their Thanksgiving feast with this much meat.

Chapter 42

Everyone was up early on Thanksgiving morning. In keeping with tradition, the party was held at James and Melissa's. It was also more convenient to have it there as the Lindgren homestead was centrally located.

Melissa and Emily each baked a turkey in their ovens, while James cut up and fried the third. Reggie and Emily were the last to arrive at the Lindgrens but came as soon as the turkey was ready.

While the portable sawmill was working well, James cut some planks to make an extension to adjoin to their existing table. He and Melissa wanted everyone to be able to eat together on this special occasion. John helped move it into position and Melissa added the tablecloth.

Melissa ordered the men out of the house as the ladies needed more room to prepare the trimmings and set the table. James offered Reggie a cigar, which he took readily.

"I'd like to try one of those," Lance said, which drew a frown then a remark from John.

"Nasty habit."

"For some, maybe," Reggie stated. He took a big puff, blew a smoke ring, and smiled.

Lance took a cigar and James helped him light it. Lance coughed a little but enjoyed the aroma. After a few puffs, he was hooked. By the time they finished their cigars, the ladies called them inside.

There wasn't a square inch of the table showing, there was so much food. Before they began, John asked if he could say a blessing. John was a changed man since their confrontation about building a church. They all knew his position hadn't changed, but he was not obnoxious and stubborn about it. He always asked to say blessing and because of this, everyone always agreed to grant his wish.

Everyone sat still while John stood and thanked God first. He then acknowledged each and every one of those seated for the wonderful bounty they were about to receive. He also thanked them for their love and friendship. He said a little prayer for Eileen, Lars, and Buster as well. Finally, he said a prayer for Sean and wished him safety and happiness. Tears ran down both Sam and Sally's cheeks.

"Thank you," Sally said.

Sam gave him a nod and a smile.

"Amen!"

John sat down and the clatter of spoons in dishes began.

"I need some potatoes," Lance said.

"Gravy over here."

"Fried turkey."

"I'd rather have dark meat."

They all froze when they heard the dog barking outside. It got so quiet you could hear a pin drop. James motioned for everyone to keep their seats while he got up and walked over to the door, grabbing his rifle from its rack.

James opened the door and stepped out to the porch. He looked around but didn't see anything. Then another bark was followed by a wolf howl, and his eyes honed in on the direction of the sounds. At the edge of the woods, he saw a small group of people and the dog.

James returned the howl and the group moved ahead in the direction of the house. James readied his rifle but did not point it at the intruders.

When they got closer, James determined there were two women, one man, and the dog. He did not recognize any of them. *How did they know about the wolf howl signal?* When they got within fifty feet, James told them to stop. James noticed both women appeared to be pregnant.

"You don't recognize me?" the man asked.

Though the voice sounded a little familiar, the face was disguised by the beard. Then the voice struck a familiar chord.

"Well, I certainly know you, James."

"Sean?"

"Yes."

James took his finger off the trigger and relaxed.

"Sam! Sally!" James yelled over his shoulder.

Lance and Ronnie were looking out the window as they walked up, but didn't recognize the strangers either. Sam came to the door with Sally on his coattails.

"I think you know him," James said.

Sam squinted as he eyed the man. "Sean?" Sam asked.

Sally recognized him immediately and yelled, "Sean! Oh my God! Sean!" She ran to him, tears flowing freely down her cheeks. "Oh my God!" she repeated over and over. She wrapped her arms around his neck and kissed him all over the face.

Sam followed Sally and wrapped them up in a group hug.

By this time everyone was out on the porch. Robbie immediately recognized the ladies. He walked out and welcomed them to the valley.

Kira went over to the dog and started petting him. The friendly canine returned the affection, licking her in the face.

"I just love dogs," she said. "What's his name?"

"He doesn't have a name," Sean replied. "I just call him Mutt."

Sean noticed her frown and said she could name him whatever she wanted.

"Good to see you, Sean," Robbie said.

"It's good to be home, buddy."

"We're just sitting down to our Thanksgiving meal," Melissa said. "Come on in."

As they all headed into the house, James put his rifle away and grabbed more chairs. Everyone squeezed in around the table while Robbie made introductions.

"Welcome Brenda and Kim," Emily said.

"How in the hell did you get here, Sean?" Reggie asked.

"It's a long story," he replied.

"There have been a lot of long stories around here lately," Robbie stated.

"I'm sure there have," Sean replied with a smile. "I've got a real whopper to tell you guys."

"Let's eat," James said, "before it gets any colder."

Everyone agreed that would be a good idea. The stories could wait.

The End?

Epilogue

Peaceful Valley grew out of disaster and turmoil. Some died and new faces arrived. Lars Lindgren, Eileen Branson Lindgren, and Buster slept peacefully beneath the old sycamore tree. Though they were dead, they were always in the hearts and minds of the residents of Peaceful Valley. Most visited their graves often, and they answered many questions and eased the troubles of some. They were good listeners, and every so often an answer would blow in on a gentle breeze.

All the members of the families who could be home were now here. Sam and Sally couldn't be happier to have both their babies near home. Sean and Robbie's adventure had come full circle. Peaceful Valley was at last peaceful and growing. Many problems had been solved, but there would be new challenges and new decisions to be made.

There were now three pregnant women in the valley. More were sure to be on the way. At one point there were too many men for the available women. Now the reverse was true. How would this affect the families? Life had always been tough here, but with so many more mouths to feed, what laid in store for the inhabitants of Peaceful Valley? What will be the next adventure and where will it take them? Who will lead the next escapade?

Into Winter is the next planned segment in the epic saga of Peaceful Valley. Look for it in the fall of 2017. Sean was all set to spend the rest of his life in Corpus Christi. You won't believe what happened after Robbie left to make Sean leave, and with Kim and Brenda.

Into Spring by Larry Landgraf (11-30-2016)

The flower has long since departed,
The plan could not be thwarted;
Siblings scattered far and wide,
Partners along for the ride.

Some will live and some will die,
You can't change the plan if you try;
Life and death go hand in hand,
This is the way throughout the land.

Snuggle down deep into the ground,
Deep enough so as not to be found;
Aided by the sun and occasional rain,
Enduring time and fighting the pain.

In for the term and counting the days,
Fighting the stress in so many ways;
Taking each day one at a time,
If I can survive it will be sublime.

Pressure is on and I've got to be tough,
Hot and dry, every day is rough;
Protected by such a thin skin,
One little flaw and I'll never win.

Months go by because that's the way,
So far I've made it through every day;
But it won't be over until winter's gone,
And it's my time to sit on the throne.

At long last my time is finally here,
I'll nudge my way out without fear;
It's time to face a new spring,
A new life such a wonderful thing.

The sun so bright aiding my fight,
Giving me strength just and right;
Juices flowing up and down,
Carrying what I need to fill my crown.

First a little yellow then some red,
Spreading wide to fill my head;
Enticing friends to join my chore,
Rewarding each from my core.

Everyone is happy with the day,
We've done it again that's the way;
Year after year always the same,
That is the way we play the game.

Into Spring is the sequel to *Into Autumn. Into Spring* was written as a stand-alone novel, but best if *Into Autumn* is read first.

Both *Into Autumn* and *Into Spring* are available on Amazon along with my second book: *How to be a Smart SOB Like Me.* This book is my autobiography republished in 2017. It has been called my rant. I call it my life survival guide.

My first book, *Dangerous Waters,* was published in 1986 and is out of print. A few limited *copies* are available. If you cannot find a copy, email me at riverrmann2@yahoo.com as I have a few copies to sell.

My next two books planned are Into Winter and Into Summer to complete my *Four Seasons* Series. I plan to write and publish them by the end of 2017 and 2018, respectively.

Thank you for reading *Into Spring,* and I hope you will enjoy my other books as well. I write short stories on my blog on my website, "Tales from the Riverside", true stories mostly about life in my swamp. I also create numerous videos which you might enjoy.

My website: http://www.intoautumn.com

My Pinterest: https://www.pinterest.com/riverrmann2/into-autumn/

Follow me on Facebook: http://www.facebook.com/intoautumn

Authors thrive or die by honest reviews. I trust you enjoyed my story and will leave a review on Amazon, Goodreads, or wherever you have access. Thank you.

THE END

About the Author

Larry Landgraf was born and raised in and around the swamp country of the Guadalupe River Delta on the Texas Gulf Coast. After four years of college, not wanting to spend the rest of his life in an office or classroom, he became a commercial fisherman. That played out in the late '80s, and he became a general contractor for another twenty-plus years. Due to a death-defying injury on the job, he turned to writing.

Trying to save his commercial fishing career, Larry wrote his first book in 1986. The career and book were a failure. He didn't write again until he published his second book, *How to be a Smart SOB Like Me,* in 2012. Then he got serious about writing and in 2015 published *Into Autumn* to launch his *Four Seasons* series. The release dates for *Into Spring* and *Into Winter* are 2017, and 2018 for *Into Summer.*

Larry divorced in 2006 when his wife of 38 years decided to walk out. This marriage produced three kids, all grown now. Larry met Ellen in January 2009 after a long search which spanned the globe. They now live together in the swamp where Larry has lived all his life. Much like Eileen Branson in *Into Autumn*, Ellen is a city gal, but loves Larry's swamp. Larry, much like Lars Lindgren in the story, wouldn't have it any other way. He teaches her the ways of the swamp, and she has plenty to teach Larry, as well.

Fresh Ink Group

Publishing
Free Memberships
Share & Read Free Stories, Essays, Articles
Free-Story Newsletter
Writing Contests

Books
E-books
Amazon Bookstore

Authors
Editors
Artists
Professionals
Publishing Services
Publisher Resources

Members' Websites
Members' Blogs
Social Media

www.FreshInkGroup.com

Email: info@FreshInkGroup.com

Twitter: @FreshInkGroup

Google+: Fresh Ink Group

Facebook.com/FreshInkGroup

LinkedIn: Fresh Ink Group

About.me/FreshInkGroup

How to Be a Smart SOB Like Me

By Larry Landgraf

Work, money, food, relationships, life in general—these are the everyday struggles for billions crowded into our challenging world. Larry Landgraf tells us his story and the many lessons he's learned for finding extraordinary happiness. *How to Be a Smart SOB Like Me* is a stark but heartfelt examination of a life well-lived. You might like him, and you might not, but you can't help but learn ways you, too, can achieve your best.

www.FreshInkGroup.com

Paper-cover ISBN-13: 978-1-936442-51-5
Hardcover ISBN-13: 978-1-936442-50-8
Ebook ISBN-13: 978-1-936442-52-2

INTO AUTUMN
A Story of Survival

By Larry Landgraf

Lars is living alone in the Texas countryside when the economy collapses and his world becomes a dystopian nightmare. Joined by outsider Eileen, he and his neighbors band together for survival in their "Peaceful Valley." They must learn to scratch out sustenance while fending off predatory invasions in an increasingly violent and lethal world. *Into Autumn* is a sweeping adventure, a thought-provoking saga that could happen to us all.

www.FreshInkGroup.com

Paper-cover ISBN-13: 978-1-936442-54-6
Hardcover ISBN-13: 978-1-936442-53-9
Ebook ISBN-13: 978-1-936442-55-3

CPSIA information can be obtained
at www.ICGtesting.com
Printed in the USA
FSOW01n1546210117
29761FS